The Tea Ladies

Amanda Hampson is a Melbourne-based author of two non-fiction books and seven novels that could not have been written without numerous cups of tea and the occasional Tim Tam.

The Tea Ladies

well did
Detective Serge
I'm the tea lady.
where the bodies
buried, it's the te
ust trying
t th

Amanda Hampson

PENGUIN

VIKING

VIKING

UK | USA | Canada | Ireland | Australia
India | New Zealand | South Africa | China

Viking is part of the Penguin Random House group of companies
whose addresses can be found at global.penguinrandomhouse.com.

Penguin
Random House
Australia

First published by Viking, 2023

Cover illustrations: dresses by CSA Images/iStock; cups by Aleksandra Novakovic/Shutterstock;
dummy by LiukasArt/Shutterstock; bullet hole by schankz/Can Stock Photo
Cover design by Debra Billson © Penguin Random House Australia Pty Ltd
Typeset in Adobe Garamond Pro by Midland Typesetters, Australia

Printed and bound in Australia by Griffin Press, an accredited
ISO AS/NZS 14001 Environmental Management Systems printer

A catalogue record for this
book is available from the
National Library of Australia

ISBN 978 1 76104 385 7

penguin.com.au

*We at Penguin Random House Australia acknowledge that Aboriginal and Torres Strait Islander
peoples are the Traditional Custodians and the first storytellers of the lands on which we live and work.
We honour Aboriginal and Torres Strait Islander peoples' continuous connection to Country, waters,
skies and communities. We celebrate Aboriginal and Torres Strait Islander stories, traditions and
living cultures; and we pay our respects to Elders past and present.*

For Jan Reggett, with love

SURRY HILLS, SYDNEY 1965

1

THE MYSTERIOUS WOMAN

From the moment she steps out into the laneway before her morning shift, Hazel Bates, tea lady at Empire Fashionwear, has the curious feeling of being watched. She glances around but sees no one. It's early, the lane is quiet and shadowed, and the air sweet with the smell of hops from the nearby brewery. Lifting her gaze to the strip of blue sky above the buildings, she's startled to see a face in an upper window of the abandoned bond store across the lane. The woman stares down at Hazel, her pale face almost ghost-like against the dim interior, and with quick urgent movements, she traces something in the dust on the window, and disappears into the gloom of the old building.

'Kovac's late again!'

Hazel turns with a start to see Irene Turnbuckle, tea lady from Silhouette Knitwear next door, standing out in the lane. She pauses to light a cigarette and walks up to join Hazel. 'Becoming a nasty habit with him, don't yer reckon?'

'I just saw someone in the old bond store,' says Hazel, pointing towards the window.

Irene glances up briefly. 'Doubt that. It's a bloody disgrace leaving that place empty all these years. That's why we've got so many rats round here.'

'I definitely saw someone . . . a woman, standing in the window.'

Irene squints through the cloud of cigarette smoke. 'Could've been a trick of the light. Or get yer eyes checked.'

'I know what I saw. She was youngish, pretty, with long, dark hair,' insists Hazel.

'Nothing wrong with yer imagination, then.'

Hazel notes the location of the window and wonders how the woman could have got in there. The two roller doors at the back of the building are padlocked, so she must have a key to the front entrance. 'It is strange. I can have a better look when I'm upstairs.'

'None of our business, anyway,' says Irene, who has firm but wildly contradictory views about who can mind whose business, especially when it comes to her own business.

'Irene dear, we're tea ladies – everything is our business,' says Hazel with a smile.

Irene gives a snort of laughter. She gets a well-worn flask from the front pocket of her apron and takes a quick swig. 'Breakfast,' she explains. 'These foreigners,' she continues, 'they're all up to some-thing. Little backhanders on the side. Shifting things around off the back of trucks onto the back of other trucks. Kovac's a cunning so-and-so, if you ask me.'

Hazel tries to see the best in Irene, making an effort to overlook her unfounded suspicions (not to mention her many unsavoury habits). In all the years Hazel has known her, she has worn the same outfit to work every day: a faded wraparound apron, shabby green-plaid house slippers and a shapeless pot-lid hat. In summer, a maroon cardigan, and an oversized black coat in the winter. She either has a cigarette glued to her lower lip or a pipe gripped between her teeth. That's Irene – everyone knows her and anyone who has crossed her in the past knows to keep their distance.

'Seems there's nothing wrong with your imagination either,' says Hazel mildly. 'But I do agree he's slipping a little. He was fifteen minutes late last week and twenty minutes the week before. It's not like him at all.'

'No flies on Hazel Bates, ladies and gents,' Irene informs an invisible audience. 'Memory like an elephant and ears to match.'

Hazel laughs. She is quietly proud of her memory and, for that matter, her ears, which are normal size but quite unique in their own way. But Irene doesn't know about that. It's one of Hazel's little secrets. Her memory has always been strong – she's good at remembering people's names, and even their children's and grandchildren's names and birthdays. She loves to match her wits with contestants on her favourite radio quiz show, 'Ask Me Anything', and there's not many folk who can say they've never had to make a shopping list. Of course, she would never brag about her abilities. There's such a thing as modesty.

When Hazel joined Empire Fashionwear as the full-time tea lady, her memory came into its own. She knows the name of every employee of the last decade, their favourite biscuit and how they like their tea or powdered coffee. Most people are 'white with one' or 'white with two', apart from the figure-conscious office girls who only eat half a grapefruit for breakfast and take their tea black without sugar, and there are always a couple of people who go the other way and insist on equal measures of tea and sugar. More importantly, she remembers whose mother is poorly, whose husband is out of work and where people spend their holidays. For her, remembering these details is as natural as breathing, not dimmed by the passing years, but honed and sharpened.

'About bloody time!' says Irene when the delivery van appears at the top of the laneway, as if they've been waiting weeks rather than minutes.

The van comes to a halt and Mr Kovac leaps out, hurrying around to open the back doors. 'Good morning, ladies!' Normally he's neatly dressed and groomed, with his dark, wavy hair slicked down and a razor-sharp side part, but today his hair is awry, his duster coat crumpled and his shoes missing their usual leathery glow.

Before Hazel can ask if everything is all right, Irene gets in. 'We've been beside ourselves here, haven't we, Mrs Bates?'

'Slight exaggeration,' corrects Hazel. 'Mildly concerned.'

Mr Kovac quickly loads boxes onto his trolley. 'I am very sorry, Mrs Bates, Mrs Turnbuckle. There was engine trouble.'

Hazel knows he's not telling the truth but assumes he has his reasons. He's a very decent sort in her view.

Irene flicks her cigarette butt down the grating. 'Yer told us that before. Get yer story straight, mister.'

'I can only apologise,' says Mr Kovac, with a deferential nod of his head.

Hazel opens the back door wide to allow his trolley through and walks ahead down the hallway to unlock the storeroom. 'Just leave them in the hall if you like, Mr Kovac. You get along and catch up on your deliveries.'

'It will only take one minute,' he insists, swiftly moving the boxes into the storeroom. 'Again, I give you my apologies.'

'It's biscuits and tea, Mr Kovac. Not fishes and loaves. No one will starve to death.'

'This is the food of industry. And let's not forget the toilet paper. We do not want to be the cause of a revolt.' He then pulls a slip of paper out of his pocket and offers it to Hazel, hovering anxiously while she glances at it. 'Mrs Bates, could you ask upstairs about my invoice? The truth is there has been a problem at the wholesalers because my account is behind. If I could pick up the cheque this afternoon that would help me very much.'

'That's very odd. We're usually so prompt. Of course, I'll take it up on my round this morning.'

'Oi!' shouts Irene from outside. 'What are yers doing in there? Apart from making me late and getting me bloody fired.'

'Thank you, Mrs Bates,' says Mr Kovac with a grateful smile. 'I will return at the end of the day with hope in my heart.'

'I'll do my very best,' Hazel assures him as he leaves. She locks the storeroom and goes into the kitchen to fill the urn and the large teapot with boiling water. She slips on her pinny and runs a comb through her hair. She checks her trolley is in order with cups and saucers, a jug of milk, a canister of sugar, teaspoons and a tin of plain biscuits and sets off along the wide hallway to the factory floor.

2

HAZEL SERVES THE EMPIRE

Hazel knows better than anyone that the role of tea lady requires a wide variety of skills. Making a good strong cup of tea and keeping the biscuits crisp are simple enough, but a truly gifted tea lady has many competencies: discretion, empathy and a healthy dose of common sense, to name just a few.

Hazel has a policy of passing on compliments but never criticisms. Wherever possible, she brings people together and brokers peace between departments. She considers it an honour to be a member of such a noble profession for there is no staff member more beloved than the tea lady. The tea lady enjoys diplomatic privilege and is welcome at all levels of the firm, from the top of the building to the ground-floor factory. The sound of Hazel's trolley, with its rattling crockery, brings a smile to every face as she moves throughout the building. (Irene, of course, does things a little differently. By her own admission, she remains employed at Silhouette Knitwear because they're afraid to sack her.)

Empire Fashionwear occupies four floors of a solid brick building in the thick of Sydney's Surry Hills garment district, each floor with its own distinct culture and character; four small empires within the one. Hazel's tea service always starts in the factory where the fifteen machinists, two pressers, a pattern cutter and the warehouse manager, Mr Butterby, all punch in at 7 am and out at 3 pm, earning themselves the first tea breaks, morning and afternoon. In Hazel's opinion, the machinists are the hardest-working employees with the worst conditions. The factory is cold and damp in winter and unbearably hot and stuffy in summer, and the noise takes some getting used to. At full pelt, the roar of the sewing machines makes the air itself tremble.

A few of the staff have been with Empire even longer than Hazel. Gloria Nuttell started as a machinist straight out of school and, over the past decade, has risen to the role of factory supervisor. In recent years, more Greek and Italian women have been applying for positions. Initially, Gloria was dead against hiring New Australians who spoke almost no English but she's been gradually won over by their hard work and sewing skills.

When Hazel walks through the door as the buzzer sounds for morning tea, the sewing machines shudder to a halt as each machinist finishes a seam or snips a thread of cotton. While they work, the radio plays the Top 40 at full blast but when the machines fall silent, Gloria turns it down and the women gather around the tea trolley to chat while Hazel serves out tea, coffee and biscuits.

As usual, Mr Butterby strides in from the warehouse to collect his tea, whistling cheerfully. 'Good morning, Mrs Bates, you're looking well today.'

In his late forties, he's a quietly handsome fellow, admired for his wide smile and efficient organisation of the warehouse. The previous storeman had become forgetful and doddery over the years and, when he retired six months ago, Butterby arrived like a refreshing southerly buster. He quickly transformed the warehouse and dispatch into a highly efficient operation.

'You're looking well yourself, Mr Butterby,' replies Hazel, handing over his tea (one sugar with a drop of milk).

Lastly, Hazel takes Gloria's coffee (black with two) to her office. It's not much of an office, just an alcove inset in the wall of the factory. On an old swivel chair with squeaky castors, Gloria propels herself along the length of a bench that is perpetually covered in layers of papers, scraps of fabric, tangles of thread collected from machines, industrial cotton reels and other paraphernalia – all dusted with ash from overflowing ashtrays. On the wall above her bench, delivery dockets and handwritten lists sprout from bulldog clips. Fabric samples and fashion pages torn from magazines are sticky-taped on top of one another.

To Hazel's eye, the alcove begs for some order but Gloria is comfortable in her nest and once confided in Hazel that she was happier at work than anywhere else in the world (which doesn't say much for her husband).

'What's happening with that new bookkeeper, Hazel?' asks Gloria, tipping back precariously on her chair to put her feet on the bench.

'Mr McCracken,' Hazel reminds her, clearing a spot to put the cup down.

'I don't know what's going on with him. I've had two calls this morning about accounts not paid.' Gloria picks up a spike packed with dockets and flicks through them. 'The buttonholers have been outstanding for over a month . . . dunno why they didn't say something earlier.'

'He seems very hardworking from what I've seen,' says Hazel, privately wondering if there's a cashflow problem. She makes it her business never to speculate aloud on these things. Before you knew it, an idle comment could be repeated as fact all over the building.

'People can look as if they're hardworking – means nothing.' Gloria sighs. 'I'll have to go upstairs and see about it, get the side eye from those snotty Queen Bees.'

'You could stop and chat to the girls in Accounts sometime, Gloria. You might be surprised. They're probably a bit intimidated by you.'

'So they should be,' says Gloria with a gravelly laugh as she lights a fresh cigarette from the glowing end of the last. 'Keep them in their places.'

When the 'back to work' buzzer sounds, Hazel is on her way to the top-floor offices of the managing directors, Mr Karp Senior and his son Frankie Karp, and their secretary, Mrs Edith Stern. This level has a plush showroom with easy chairs and a well-stocked drinks cabinet (the key carefully guarded by Edith Stern), where store buyers come to view the next season's garments. Afterwards, orders are discussed in an adjacent boardroom, also well-appointed with wall-to-wall Axminster carpet and a polished mahogany board table.

The upstairs kitchen has an oven that Hazel often uses to bake a cake or batch of scones for a meeting. The cupboards are stocked with Royal Doulton tea sets and tins of fancy biscuits such as Peppermint Slices, Iced VoVos and Montes. These are designated for management only, but Hazel has been known to surreptitiously add an 'upstairs' bikkie to the saucer of someone in need of a sweet surprise.

The two managing directors are very different characters. The elderly Mr Karp Senior (a Scotch Finger man) is always well turned out in a dark suit with his trademark red tie. He's a hard worker who built the business from a single sewing machine on his kitchen table to one with over thirty employees supplying ladies' blouses, skirts and frocks to every department store in the country.

His middle-aged son, Frankie, has a weakness for the Iced VoVos, with a habit of licking the pink fondant first before nibbling at the biscuit base. With his hair styled in a slick Brylcreemed quiff, he wears tailor-made three-piece suits designed to disguise his rotund figure. Frankie considers himself a modern man, going so far as to insist the staff address him by his first name. He also has an odd habit of referring to himself in the third person, which Hazel finds boyishly endearing. In his own mind, Frankie is someone to be emulated and admired but he is renowned for his laziness and spectacular tantrums when he doesn't get his own way.

The design side of the business is Frankie's responsibility, which is probably why Empire Fashionwear continue to manufacture much the same garments as they did a decade ago. He and his wife, Dottie, enjoy the high life and perhaps the business seems boring by comparison. Her hair always lacquered into a concrete coiffure, Dottie seems to have a limitless wardrobe of colour-coordinated suits, hats, gloves, handbags, shoes and lipsticks. She only sets foot in the building when she needs a cheque for the hairdresser, milliner or dressmaker and certainly wouldn't be seen dead in an Empire frock.

Next level down, the 2nd Floor, is devoted entirely to Accounts. The bookkeeper, Mr McCracken, is in charge of six young women (dubbed the Queen Bees by Gloria) who type up invoices, process orders and wages, accounts payable and receivable, and update garment stock sheets on clattering ledger machines. They generally come straight out of secretarial school and this department exists in a state of excitement with constant preparations for engagement parties, weddings and (inevitably) baby showers. The department's revolving door of young women keeps Hazel on her toes and her ability to read tea leaves is always in great demand on this floor.

When Hazel takes Mr McCracken's tea into his office and asks him about Mr Kovac's bill, a flicker of annoyance crosses the book-keeper's face.

'I'll see what I can do,' he says, reaching for his tea.

Not easily fobbed off, Hazel continues, 'Thank you, I wouldn't bother you normally, but Mr Kovac—'

Mr McCracken looks up and raises an eyebrow. 'It's never just tea with you, is it, Mrs Bates? Always involving yourself with things that are nothing to do with you. He could make a telephone call to accounts payable like everyone else. He doesn't need to send the tea lady.'

Hazel gives him a smile. 'It always pays to go to the top, so they say.'

'Just stick to what you know, Mrs Bates,' he says, unamused.

'He's hoping to collect a cheque today,' ventures Hazel, placing the docket firmly on the desk. 'It will be a problem if we can't get our supplies.'

Mr McCracken gives an exasperated sigh. 'After three,' he says with a little gesture of dismissal. 'And tell him to speak to me next time.'

She wants to ask why there would be a next time but thinks better of it.

Hazel's final stop is down on the 1st Floor where Misses Joan and Ivy Rosenbaum run the dressmaking department, as they have done for many years. Working directly under Frankie, they tinker with the designs each season, select the fabrics and create the final pattern for the cutter to grade the sizes. They share a talent for turning this relatively simple process into a major production – some might say an ordeal.

Solidly built, both dress entirely in black with their silver hair tortured into tight buns. They take their coffee black with a single Ginger Nut biscuit. The sisters are highly strung about most things and biscuits are no exception. Hazel has learnt from bitter experience never to run out of Ginger Nuts.

The newest member of staff, in the role of Girl Friday, is Frankie's daughter, Pixie, who is learning the business from the ground up, running errands and acting as the house model when required. Today, she stands on a low stool wearing a brown woollen dress while Miss Joan and Miss Ivy kneel on the floor, debating the length of the garment.

'It's a bit long, it could be above the knee,' suggests Pixie, reaching for her cup of milky tea. Ignored by the Rosenbaums, she turns to Hazel. 'Don't you reckon, Mrs Bates?'

'Keep still please, young lady,' says Miss Joan, without taking the pins out of her mouth. 'And we don't need to take votes on it. Leave it to the experts.' She pins the hem to mid-knee and looks to her sister with a nod of approval.

'Very elegant,' Miss Ivy agrees. 'Lovely line from the hip.'

'It's very brown,' murmurs Pixie under her breath.

Miss Ivy issues a disapproving tsk-tsk but says nothing. It's not that she's afraid to voice her opinion (quite the opposite), but Pixie is not only Frankie's daughter but Mr Karp Senior's adored granddaughter. She brings a smile to his face whenever she appears.

Out of earshot, the sisters regularly make the point that Pixie may be a perfect size 12, but she's far from a perfect house model, being gangly as a young giraffe and just as uncoordinated. They prefer the two dressmaker's dummies that never talk back.

To Hazel, who is no authority on fashion, the dress does look a little dowdy but Frankie presumably knows what he's doing. He alone understands what the department store buyers want, apparently. He has the last word on everything and no one can tell him anything he doesn't already know, including the Rosenbaums.

The Sales department is also on the 1st Floor, tucked away in a corner office. It was once occupied by three salesmen, but now just one. On the phone as usual, Doug Fysh gives Hazel a welcoming wave as she delivers his tea. He is the consummate salesman, always dressed in a grey suit, crisp white shirt and striped tie, his brogues polished to a mirror shine. Above the collar is less orderly; his chins cascading, florid cheeks expanding and his hair gradually sliding off the back of his head. Thankfully, these unfortunate developments in his appearance have not dented his buoyant self-confidence in the slightest.

Hazel hovers nearby until he finishes his call and asks, 'Doug, do you know anything about the bond store over the lane?'

'Thinking of expanding your operation, Hazel?' he asks, grinning. 'You and the other old biddies going to open a tea house? What do you call a bunch of tea ladies, eh? A clutch of tea ladies? Oh, I know, a batch of tea ladies . . . haw, haw . . .'

'It's a cosy of tea ladies, I believe,' says Hazel, patiently.

'Haw, haw . . . there you go, then.' He takes a sip of his tea. 'Why?'

'I saw someone inside the building this morning.'

'I doubt that,' he says. 'Might be a delinquent runaway or one of the street girls sleeping rough. If you're sure, better report that to someone.'

'Well, who for instance?' she asks. 'I don't know who owns it.'

'Just go down to the cop shop and tell them,' says Doug. He bites into his Monte Carlo, holding his hand under it to catch the crumbs. 'So how's that hubby of yours, anyway? Oh, I miss that life on the road, you know. The camaraderie of the travelling salesman. Out in the countryside, new town every day, different pub every night. That's the life for a man, not stuck in here behind a desk.'

'It's not ideal for me,' says Hazel. 'But I suppose I'm used to Bob being away. It's never been any different.'

'I've told you before, if you ever feel lonely, Hazel, you can find me down the Cricketers Arms more often than not. I'll shout you a shandy or two and we can have a good old yarn together. Or a Scotch if that's your poison.'

While he drinks his tea, Hazel walks over to the window on the laneway side where she can see directly into the first floor of the bond store. She tries to remember the woman's expression. It wasn't very clear but she definitely wanted Hazel to see her. The lane isn't wide, perhaps fifteen feet across, but it's difficult to see what the woman traced on the window. 'Doug, can I borrow your binoculars?' asks Hazel.

'What binoculars?' asks Doug.

'The ones you use to watch that young lady sunbaking on the roof—'

'I might have some, now I think of it,' he admits.

Hazel opens the window. With the aid of the binoculars, she can make out some letters written in the dust on the window.

'What's up? See something?' asks Doug.

'There's something written on the glass.' Hazel hands him the binoculars.

'Interesting,' he says after a moment. 'Not in English. Get me a pen and bit of paper off my desk, I'll copy it down for you.'

3

BETTY STARTS HER LIST OF CLUES

Zig Zag Lane is a grubby little alley of rear entrances and loading docks. It's always busy when the factory workers arrive and leave and when delivery drivers stand around leaning on their vans smoking. But at lunchtime it's usually quiet, and the four tea ladies who work in this part of the laneway often sit together on a low wall set back on the footpath to eat their sandwiches.

Betty Dewsnap, tea lady at Farley Frocks, considers herself to be the second most sensible of the four (after Hazel, obviously) and always brings a cushion to sit on. She's not only anxious about getting piles (on top of her many other afflictions) but has a slight flatulence problem, and so the cushion serves a practical purpose. Everyone around here knows the tea ladies and Betty finds it amusing that people get them mixed up because they couldn't be more different. For example, she always makes an effort with her appearance – lipstick and nail varnish are important. She keeps her hair nicely trimmed and puts it in rollers every night. She would describe herself as full-figured (perhaps a bit fuller than she used to be) but, despite that, has recently decided only to wear her girdle on special occasions like weddings, funerals and christenings. At a certain age, comfort is important too.

Now, Irene Turnbuckle never makes the slightest effort with her appearance. She could not care less. In fact, during a cold snap last winter, her dreadful old hat went missing and she wore a knitted tea-cosy on her head for a week.

Merl Perlman is the tea lady at Klein's Lingerie. She's twice the size of Irene (big-boned, as they say) with her iron-grey hair set in a rigid perm. She wears cats-eye spectacles with little diamantés in the corners that catch the light and sparkle when she's cross – and she gets cross quite a lot. While Irene, Hazel and Betty have been meeting here for years, Merl only joined them a year ago. She has a lot to say for herself considering she's the newcomer, although she was a schoolteacher so that might have something to do with it.

Betty settles herself on the wall beside Irene and Merl. She notices Hazel walking up the lane to join them and gives her a cheery wave, patting the space beside her invitingly.

Hazel is not the sort to stand out in a crowd; she seems to prefer going unnoticed. She's small and sturdy, and blessed with naturally wavy silver hair that frames her face like a halo and sets off her sharp grey eyes. Hazel has been Betty's dearest friend for forty years, since they worked together on the switchboard at the General Post Office in the centre of the city. They both live nearby, within walking distance of each other and, since Hazel got Betty the job at Farley's, they see each other almost every day. Hazel keeps her own counsel on most matters but, after so many years, Betty probably knows more about her than anyone. She knows about Hazel's magical ears and she knows Hazel's biggest secret but has never breathed a word to a single soul and never will.

Hazel hardly has time to say hello and sit down before Irene, puffing away on her awful pipe like an old sea captain, starts going on about her firm's secretary 'having it off' with the boss (Irene's a terrible gossip and a bit coarse sometimes).

'I haven't got hard evidence,' Irene tells them. 'But these *looks*—'

'Lingering?' interrupts Merl, making out she's an authority on this particular subject as well as everything else. 'Or smouldering? There is a difference.'

'Sort of goo-goo eyes,' says Irene. 'Say, if yer got a new couch and couldn't stop thinking how beaut it looked in yer lounge room.'

Now, Betty would be the last person to bring up the fact that Irene rents a room in a horrible old boarding house. The fact is, she doesn't have a couch, or a lounge room for that matter, so that seems a funny comment coming from her.

'I'd definitely call that lingering,' confirms Merl. 'Smouldering would be if Steve McQueen was stretched out on it.'

Betty can't help but giggle. 'Oh, you'd like that, Irene.'

'Wouldn't say no to those baby blue eyes,' Irene agrees. ''Specially if he was in the nuddy.'

Merl turns up her nose. 'Rather unhygienic on the furniture.'

'Anyway, yer wouldn't pick this girl as the type,' continues Irene. 'She's a chubby little thing.'

'Chubby people have affairs too!' Betty tugs indignantly at her own dress to rearrange the rolls around her waist. 'They're called womanly curves and also, Irene, that secretary is not chubby, she's got an hourglass figure.'

'More than an hour in her glass.' Irene bares her dentures in a fierce grin.

That's Irene, always stirring things up. Betty refuses to give her the satisfaction of an argument, apart from to say, 'You could do with putting on a pound or two yourself, Irene. You're just skin and bone.'

'You're not really chubby, Betty,' Merl reassures her. 'You've just got a small head.'

Betty frowns. 'Is that a compliment or two insults?'

'What she's saying, Betty dear, is that you are perfectly proportioned,' says Hazel, who has been silent until now. She only involves herself in these squabbles when they get too silly for words.

Irene laughs and changes the subject. 'Hazel's had a bit of excitement. Go on, tell them, Hazel. She saw a ghost in the old bond store.'

'She wasn't a ghost, she was a young woman,' corrects Hazel.

'That's strange,' says Merl. 'Did you call the police?'

'I'm not sure it's worth calling the police. There's something else, too. When I went upstairs, I could see she had traced something on the window.'

Betty feels goosebumps prickle her arms. She loves a good mystery. 'What did it say?' She takes the note from Hazel. 'Oh, I thought it was going to say HELP. What does it mean? It's not even proper writing. It's like doodling.'

'I don't know,' says Hazel. 'No idea at all. That's why I would feel a bit silly going to the police.'

Merl looks over Betty's shoulder. 'These letters are more like Chinese or Russian.'

'What did she look like?' asks Betty. 'Did she look foreign?'

'I only saw her for a moment. Actually . . .' Hazel pauses. 'I just realised something – it would be back to front.'

'I'm not sure how that helps us.' Merl holds the note at arm's length.

'She might have been kidnapped,' says Betty. 'Locked up in that place—'

'Oh, here we go, this'll be good.' Irene relights her pipe and puffs clouds of smoke over everyone's sandwiches.

Merl clucks like an old chook. 'Honestly, Irene, I don't know why you have to smoke that filthy thing. Women smoking in public is bad enough, but a pipe?'

Irene sticks her finger in her ear and wiggles it vigorously. 'Must be me hearing, did Merl just say she *didn't* know something?'

Not to be distracted, Betty continues, 'The kidnappers could be waiting for the ransom money. Let's check the papers this afternoon!'

'I say go to the police straightaway,' says Merl. 'As you know, my son-in-law is a senior police officer with the Criminal Investigations Branch—'

'Yer might have mentioned that once or three hundred times already,' says Irene.

Merl ignores her, continuing in her bossy tone. 'Write this down, Hazel – Detective Sergeant Pierce – make a note and ask for him.'

'I think I can remember that,' says Hazel politely. 'Thank you, Merl. Besides, I really don't think it warrants the CIB getting involved.'

'Anyway, if she's been kidnapped for a ransom,' says Irene, 'it's not going to be in the bloody papers, is it?'

'Language,' says Merl.

Irene continues, 'The first rule of kidnapping is to warn folk not to bring the coppers into it . . . let alone the bloody press.'

'Are you speaking from personal experience?' asks Merl, carefully flattening out her lunch wrap and folding it neatly into quarters.

Betty puts her hand up for attention. 'What I meant was, someone might be reported missing, like an heiress or minor royalty, for instance.'

'I think Betty does have a point; it's worth checking the papers,' agrees Hazel.

Betty is pleased to note that Hazel's comment shuts both Merl and Irene up. Better still, Merl gets a cake tin out of her shopping bag.

'This is just a plain old sponge with a bit of jam and cream. I had the grandkiddies over last night, mayhem as usual, so I was in a bit of a rush.'

She opens the tin to reveal four large slices of perfectly assembled sponge cake, separated by waxed paper. Merl owns a Mix Master and has a gift for cream sponges, but (in Betty's opinion) this is offset by her annoying habit of claiming a perfect sponge is not her best work.

'It's perfect, Merl,' says Hazel after her first bite, and Betty agrees.

'Not bad at all,' says Irene, wiping her mouth with the back of her hand. 'Yer know, I reckon there's something else going on upstairs at our place.'

'Apart from hanky-panky?' asks Betty.

'Yeah. Bosses' meetings. They never used to care if I was in the room. I was like part of the furniture. Now it's all hush-hush chit-chats behind closed doors.'

'That's disappointing. You're one of the family, surely,' says Betty, although it's a struggle to imagine anyone adopting Irene as part of their family.

Merl gets out her knitting and frowns at it. 'That might be a bit of a stretch.'

'And anyway, a tea lady is always the soul of discretion,' adds Hazel.

Merl snorts rudely. 'Irene's not.'

'I am so!' Irene considers this claim for a moment. 'I don't take it down the boozer, anyway.'

'I should hope not,' says Merl. 'Very inappropriate.'

'I heard some places are getting rid of tea ladies,' says Irene. 'There's a machine they put in and people get their own.'

'I can't see that happening,' scoffs Merl. 'What a waste of everyone's time! And what about the cups and saucers?'

'They use paper cups,' says Irene.

Betty laughs. 'Paper cups? That'll never catch on.'

'Mind you, I have seen tea in little bags,' says Merl. 'They're catching on too.'

'Tea in a bag!' Betty laughs. 'Well, I never. I can't see the point.'

'The bosses wouldn't be meeting about tea,' says Hazel. 'It must be something more important.'

'There's only one thing bosses meet about and that's money. Cost-cutting,' says Merl.

'"Imports" is a word I've been hearing a lot lately,' says Hazel thoughtfully. 'I heard Frankie mention Taiwan last week.'

'Is that one of those new synthetics?' asks Betty.

'Good grief, Betty, it's a place in China,' says Merl, who knows her geography. 'Crimplene. A lot of talk about Crimplene.'

'Where's that then?' asks Irene, clearly as confused as Betty.

'It's a type of fabric,' says Merl. She gives Hazel a look of disbelief, as if they are the only intelligent tea ladies in the world.

'It doesn't crush,' says Hazel. 'It's one of the drip-dry permanent-press ones you see advertised. Anyway, let's keep our ears and eyes open, see if we can scout out what's going on.'

Betty gets her notebook out of the front pocket of her pinny. 'I'll keep the notes, Hazel. We can do reconnaissance, like they did in the war.' She scribbles in her notebook and reads aloud:

'Crimplene. Taiwan. Tea bags. Hanky-panky. Imports. Mystery woman. Foreign letters.'

'Perhaps take out hanky-panky, dear,' says Hazel. 'That's not really our business.'

A van pulls up opposite, at Empire's loading dock. The driver gets out and rings the bell. A moment later, the roller door winds up with clanging chains and Mr Butterby comes out pushing a rack of frocks. Pretending he hasn't seen the four ladies perched along the wall, he takes one of the full-skirted frocks off the rack and, whistling the tune to 'I Could Have Danced All Night', waltzes the dress around the loading dock.

'Haven't got all day, mate,' says the van driver.

Ignoring him, Mr Butterby gives the tea ladies a big grin. 'Hello, girls. Got anything sweet for me today?'

'Only our smiles,' Irene calls back. 'Cheeky beggar,' she mutters under her breath.

'You don't have to flirt with him, Irene,' Merl points out.

'He's at least twenty years younger than you,' says Betty, in retaliation for Irene's nasty comments earlier. 'You probably give him the heebie-jeebies.'

'Like to keep me hand in.' Irene takes a swig from her flask. 'Is there a Mrs Butterby, do yer know?'

4

A VISIT TO THE COP SHOP

Hazel always enjoys washing up the cups and saucers. Plunging her hands into scalding water seems to sharpen the mind and gives her time to nut out problems. On her agenda today is whether she should take Doug Fysh's advice and report the incident of the mysterious woman. It wasn't even an incident, just a sighting. She wonders now if she's exaggerated the woman's expression in her own mind. Was it simply someone looking out the window who had authority to be there? In which case, it is none of her business. But then there's the message to consider . . .

On her way home, she inspects the two padlocks securing the door behind the bond store, both rusted shut. She walks around to the front of the building on the main road. The three-storey brick structure is relatively small compared to the warehouses closer to the docks; perhaps that's the reason it's been empty for so long. The two timber doors are large enough to drive a truck through and a small access hatch is inset in one of these doors. The padlocks on the large doors are bunged up with debris from years of disuse but the access door looks as though it's been unlocked recently.

As Hazel passes Surry Hills Police Station on her way home anyway, it's no bother to stop in and make a report.

The desk sergeant listens to her story with a blank expression he obviously adopts for these situations.

'What was this lady doing exactly?' he asks, pen poised over a small pad.

Hazel reiterates that the woman had been looking out the window.

'Looking *in* a window is a crime. You know, the old peeping Tom.' He wiggles his eyebrows suggestively in a way that Hazel finds a little disconcerting. 'Looking out, however . . .' He shrugs. 'Did you notice if there'd been a forced entry?'

'A small access door at the front seems to have been unlocked.'

'There you go,' he says, putting his pen down. 'Someone gained entry with a key.'

'Also, she wrote this on the window.' Hazel places the note in front of him. 'I think it's a message.'

He stares at it for a moment. 'Hieroglyphics, by the looks. She might have been a mummy ghost from ancient Egypt.' Failing to elicit a smile from Hazel, he says, 'Why don't you come back if there's any further development.'

'Is it possible for someone to just have a look?' asks Hazel.

'If we checked out every building where someone saw someone in the window . . . do you see what I'm saying?'

Hazel nods. She retrieves the note and tucks it safely into her handbag.

'Word of advice, Mrs'—he consults his little pad—'Bates. That back lane you're talking about, Zig Zag Lane, I wouldn't recommend being down there after dark. Or anywhere near the park at Frog Hollow or Lisbon Street, for that matter. Not safe for a decent lady like yourself. Or any law-abiding person.'

Hazel thanks him and hurries along the narrow streets towards home, past the boarding houses, brothels and pubs. Past the clanging, smoking foundry and small factories tucked in around the tight rows of terraced houses. Many of the houses are rundown and overcrowded; most contain several generations making do with one or two bedrooms and an outside dunny. The afternoon streets are busy with children playing and mothers gossiping on doorsteps. Men gather to talk and laugh and argue outside pubs. By closing time there will likely be at least one brawl.

Late at night, the area is a different place altogether. Inebriated couples weave their way home exchanging insults and sometimes blows, shadowy figures transact in the dark laneways and business is brisk for the working girls on Lisbon Street. Some, scantily clad, stand on street corners smoking and chatting to each other. Others, as decorous as housewives, sit on the doorsteps of tiny workers' cottages (in winter with bar heaters at their feet, in summer with a fan) while men and curious schoolboys wander up and down the narrow street checking out the wares. 'Need a girlfriend, love?' they ask. 'Come in for a cuddle, mister.' Scenes and people who are comfortingly familiar to Hazel after a lifetime living here.

Hazel stops at the butcher's to pick up a couple of chops for Bob's dinner. All her weeks have the same routine and Friday, when Bob comes home, is the high point. When he walks in the front door of 5 Glade Street at precisely 6 pm, Bob will be met by the aroma of his favourite chump chops spitting under the grill. The peas will be simmering on the stove, and the potatoes boiled, ready to mash. In the five years of their marriage, this routine has almost never varied, and Hazel still experiences a flush of excitement on Fridays and a lingering sadness on Sunday evenings when she sees him off on the train.

For twenty years, long before she met him, Bob has been the Northern Rivers sales representative for Farm & Livestock Supplies, a farming equipment company that sells everything from gumboots to tractors. Leaving Sydney on Sunday evenings, he takes the overnight sleeper to the town of Grafton, where he's based, returning overnight on Thursday to arrive Friday morning. He has a shower and breakfast at the Commercial Travellers' Association in the city and goes straight to Head Office for the weekly sales meeting. He puts in his orders and sets up appointments for the following week, then it's home to Glade Street.

Bob's in his late sixties, a little older than Hazel, and settled in his ways but he's always considerate and caring. He regularly brings her flowers or a box of Roses Chocolates and never eats her favourite Strawberry Cremes. When she met him, Hazel had been a widow for more than a decade. He'd asked her for directions in the street and, as it happened, she was walking his way. They got chatting, one thing led to another and six months later they were married. These last five years have been among the most contented of Hazel's life and she prepares for Bob's return on Fridays as if he were a royal guest. Nothing heraldic but the simple pleasures of fresh sheets and ironed pyjamas. There's a new book from the library on his bedside table (his favourites are John Le Carré and Dick Francis) and a home-baked cake in the tin.

At the sound of his key in the door, Hazel's heart gives a jolt and she hurries to his embrace and the warmth of his lips pressed on hers. She steps back to ask how he is and notices he's flushed and out of breath. 'Are you all right, dear?'

'Just a bit of heartburn.' He gives a breathless laugh. 'Might be getting too old for this lark.'

She takes his arm and leads him into the kitchen. 'What lark, Bob? Work? Or travelling?'

'I don't know.' He shakes his head as if trying to dislodge something while she slips off his jacket and loosens his tie.

'Sit down while I get you some liver salts,' she says, going to the cupboard.

He does as he's told, looking up at her with a weary smile. 'It was a long day but all the better for seeing you, my love.' He accepts a glass of fizzing liver salts and gulps it down.

Hazel sits opposite him at the kitchen table with a prickling sense of unease. 'You can retire any time, dear, you know that – and why not? We can manage. We don't need caviar and champagne.' Her thoughts race ahead to this future life with Bob home all week long. Perhaps they could get a little dog he could walk for exercise or they could take up a hobby together. He is always so tired on the weekends.

'Don't write me off just yet, my dear. There's still a few earning years in this boy. I'm feeling better already. Let's eat, why don't we?'

Hazel serves up the dinner, relieved he hasn't lost his appetite. Afterwards, they spend the evening in the front room listening to the radio and working on a jigsaw puzzle of the Taj Mahal, set up on the card table. It's the first in a series of the Seven Wonders of the World they plan to complete together. Often they have a whiskey in the evening or a glass of Hazel's homemade wine. Tonight she serves him celery wine to settle his tummy. He sips it with an expression somewhere between a smile and a grimace but gallantly insists he always enjoys her experimental concoctions.

Friday is usually an early night but when Hazel snuggles up to him in bed, Bob says, 'I am a little weary, dear. Let's save the deed till tomorrow night. Same time, same place.'

They exchange warm kisses, wishing each other a good night's sleep. It's only when she hears his first snores that Hazel realises she completely forgot to tell Bob about the business of the woman in the window. He'll certainly have some helpful advice. With that thought, she drifts off to sleep only to be woken by the jarring sound of the phone ringing in the hallway in the early hours of the morning.

5

DISASTER IN THE NIGHT

'Hazel! Is that you, Hazel?' Betty shouts down the line. 'Hazel!'

'Yes, Betty . . . it's me. I'm here.' Hazel sits down on the telephone stool. She feels around for the hall light switch, then thinks better of it – Bob needs his sleep. Now she's awake, she can hear the wail of sirens in the distance. 'What's happened?'

'The milkman just told me the bond store's on fire! What do we do, Hazel?'

It takes Hazel a split second to make a decision. 'I'm going down there now.'

'Don't go on your own, Hazel! It's not safe. What about Bob? Can he go with you?'

Hazel hesitates. 'Don't worry, I'll be fine.'

'You're not going alone. I'll meet you there,' says Betty, promptly hanging up.

Hazel slips a light coat over her nightdress and knots a headscarf under her chin.

Out in the street, the pale dawn light is tinged with orange and the faint smell of smoke hangs in the air. She hurries towards the main road, her thoughts on the mystery woman. She should have been more forceful with the desk sergeant and insisted someone inspect the place. If that young woman has perished in the fire, Hazel will never forgive herself. Then it briefly crosses her mind that the woman could have started the fire. Empty buildings don't catch fire of their own accord.

By the time she reaches the main road, there are crowds of people going in the same direction, some of them running in their eagerness to witness the spectacle. Many are wearing dressing-gowns or coats over their nightclothes as if they're all off to a huge pyjama party.

The road has been closed off by police cars with onlookers kept safely back from the burning building but still close enough to hear the crackle of fire. The brick exterior of the building is intact but black smoke pours from shattered windows on the top floor. Half-a-dozen fire engines and countless firemen with high pressure hoses send arcs of water into the heart of the fire.

At a loud cracking sound, people cry out in fear and a strange sort of exhilaration as the roof collapses inward, sending sparks and bright-red flames up into the sky. One woman lets out a scream of fright and begins to cry hysterically. A man standing beside Hazel comments grimly, 'That old place is a tinderbox.'

With the roof structure gone, the decorative facade at the top of the building begins to detach itself one brick at a time, as if being plucked by a giant hand. The bricks tumble to the ground where firemen run for cover as the debris rains down on them.

At a tug on her arm, Hazel turns to see Betty scarlet-faced and panting, a pink chiffon headscarf tied tightly over her hair rollers. 'What do we do, Hazel? We have to tell the police about the lady!' She stares at the building in dismay. 'Oh, what can we do?'

Hazel had hoped for an opportunity to speak to the police in attendance but that is clearly impossible, and probably pointless. Anyone trapped in that building will have perished for certain. Betty catches her expression and nods. She slips her arm through Hazel's and they stand together watching the firemen battle on against the blaze. There is nothing they can do but stare helplessly like everyone else. Hazel suggests they go around the block and see what's happening in Zig Zag Lane.

Trying to avoid the gathering crowds, they walk along the main road a couple of blocks and cut down a side street but still have to weave their way through people rushing to the scene. Even the young children Hazel often sees hanging around in gangs, throwing stones at people or stealing from shops, are now awake and pelting excitedly towards the fire.

Zig Zag Lane is blocked by a fire engine parked across it while the firemen drench the surrounding buildings, so they walk further up the block towards Lisbon Street and the front entrance of the Empire Fashionwear building.

'I've never seen anything like it,' says Betty tearfully. 'You forget what a fire can do when it really gets going like that. It's like being back in the war.'

Betty spent the war years in the safety and comfort of Sydney's northern suburbs, but Hazel knows exactly what she means.

The sun is coming up and the air visibly hazy with smoke. Betty begins to cough violently. Hazel takes her arm. 'Do you want to sit down for a minute, dear?'

Betty nods. 'I'm allergic to smoke . . . and my bunions are playing up. I'm sorry, Hazel. You know what I'm like . . . I'm just sensitive.'

Hazel helps her sit down on some steps. 'It was very brave of you to come out. We'll just sit quietly until you're feeling better.'

Hazel takes off her scarf and ties it over her nose and mouth. Betty does the same, careful not to disturb her curlers. She weeps quietly for a bit and then pronounces herself ready to continue, struggling to her feet.

As they turn into Lisbon Street, Hazel notices a woman near the top of the laneway. She has dark, shoulder-length hair and wears a black jacket and slacks. She crosses the street and hurries along with her head down, as if anxious not to draw attention to herself.

Hazel is almost certain it's the woman from the bond store.

A car cruises slowly along Lisbon Street and pulls up beside the woman. A man jumps out of the passenger's side and grabs her arm. They're too far away for Hazel to hear their conversation but it's clear that the woman is resisting; nevertheless she's quickly bundled into the back seat of the car. He gets in beside her, shuts the door and the car takes off. As they drive away, Hazel notices the car is a Bentley (not that common) but doesn't catch the number plate.

Betty, in the midst of a running commentary on the state of her bunions, misses the entire episode. 'I just need to put my feet up and let the fluids flow in the other direction.'

'I'm sure you're right, dear,' agrees Hazel, only half-listening. 'I want to quickly check the Empire building, then we'll get you home.'

Hazel walks up the front steps and tries the main door, surprised to find it unlocked. There are no lights on inside and she wonders aloud if perhaps the firemen have been in and left the door unlocked.

'They'd just smash down the door with their axes,' says Betty.

'I'm going to check inside,' says Hazel. 'You wait here.'

'Oh no, Hazel! What if the building catches fire? It's too dangerous.'

'What if there's someone in there? I can't just go home without making sure. I'll have a quick check around and stay on this side of the building.'

'I'm not letting you go alone,' says Betty. 'Where you go, I go, Hazel!'

'Betty, please stay here. I'll be very quick. If I'm not out in five minutes, you can get help.'

Tightening the scarf over her lower face, Hazel steps inside. She flicks the switch for the lobby light but the electricity is out. The heat in the building is suffocating and jagged black shadows flicker in the orange glow from the lane side of the building. Heart thudding, she hurries down the hall to the factory and tries the double doors – locked.

Avoiding the lift, she takes the stairs to the 1st Floor.

Betty follows her up, pausing to lean against the wall and get her breath back while Hazel takes a quick look in the sales office and the dressmakers' room.

'Hello? Anyone there?' she calls but the only sounds are the shouts and clanging of the firefighters behind the building.

'I don't like this, Hazel!' Betty cries. 'Please, let's go!'

'Wait there,' says Hazel firmly. 'I'll just check the next floor, then we'll get out.'

She pushes open the 2nd Floor door to the Accounts office and pokes her head in to scan the area. The office is neat and tidy, with all the chairs placed upside down on desks. Everything seems in order. But as her eyes adjust, Hazel notices a dark shape on the floor on the far side of the room. There's a bright flare of light outside and a loud popping sound as several windows crack with the heat.

From the hallway, Betty screams, 'Hazel! We've got to get out!'

Smoke begins to seep in through the cracked windows. Hazel knows she's right but leaving without investigation is not an option. She drops to the floor and crawls across the office on her hands and knees. As she gets closer, she can see the shape is definitely a person lying completely still.

'Betty!' she shouts over her shoulder. 'Come in here! I need help!'

'Where are you? I'm coming, Hazel,' shouts Betty through the door.

The man lies on his side. His head is slumped forward, making it difficult for Hazel to see his face. But when she kneels beside him, she knows who it is. In the dim light she can see a bleeding wound on his temple. She places her fingers at his throat and feels for a pulse. There's nothing they can do for him. He's dead.

6

A VISIT FROM THE POLICE

Hazel arrives home to find Bob waiting on the doorstep for her. Without a word, he takes her in his arms and kisses the top of her head. 'I've been worried sick about you,' he says, holding her close.

'I told you on the phone that I was all right, there was no need to worry,' says Hazel, still disoriented by the jumbled events of the morning and shaken by the whole experience.

Bob follows her inside. 'I can't believe it. I thought you were sleeping peacefully beside me, then I discover you're at the police station!'

Hazel goes into the kitchen and puts the kettle on. She gulps down a large glass of water to wash away the sour taste of smoke. She can smell it lingering in her hair and clothes and can't wait for a hot bath. While the kettle boils she leans on the bench and gazes out the window at the wonky old washhouse, lean-to bathroom and lavatory, her pots of red geraniums and the choko vine smothering the back fence. Calmed by these familiar sights, she turns to speak to Bob. 'I don't know what I was thinking, going into that building . . .'

'Neither do I,' agrees Bob.

'I just felt I had to check . . . and then when I saw someone on the floor—'

'It must have been very upsetting for you, love. Sit down, I'll fix this.'

Bob gets out the teapot, cuts a couple of slices of bread and pops them in the toaster while she explains how she had got the call from Betty. She backtracks to tell him about the woman she had seen in the window, hence her personal interest.

'But how did you end up in the Empire building? That's what I don't understand.'

'Bob, the toast's burning.' Hazel appreciates Bob waiting on her but he's hopeless at doing two things at once.

'Sorry, love!' Bob flips open the toaster, scrapes off the black bits and puts it back to toast the other side. 'Last thing you need is burnt offerings for breakfast.'

'Where was I? Oh, yes, as soon as I realised the main door was unlocked I felt something was wrong. Then I saw him just lying there, on the floor. It obviously wasn't safe to stay in the building, so Betty and I went straight down to the police station. We were there for an hour, would you believe, waiting to report a death! Then we had to go back to the Empire with the police.'

'You never liked that McCracken fellow very much as I recall.'

'To be honest, he's probably the only person I never got on with. He was always rude to me, to everyone really. Nothing personal. There was a bleeding wound on his head. Bob, do you think someone might have actually . . . murdered him?'

'I doubt it. He probably blacked out and hit his head. Smoke will do that to you. Odd that he was there in the first place. Perhaps he was cooking the books and they caught fire,' jokes Bob.

Normally Hazel finds Bob's quips amusing but the toast is burning again so she gets up from the table and takes over while Bob pours the tea. She wonders if Mr McCracken had a wife and family. She knows nothing about his personal life; he's one of the few people in the building she could say that about.

'There's one more thing,' she says, as they sit down together. 'I forgot to tell you the woman wrote something on the glass.' She shows him the note.

'That's Russian,' says Bob. 'I'm quite certain. Anyway, it's not your problem, my dear. Don't worry about it. Leave it to the professionals.' He yawns and rubs at his whiskers. 'I'm going to smarten myself up and get the papers.'

Hazel knows he'll be itching to get the racing pages and decide what to put his money on this afternoon. Still rattled by her dreadful morning, she wants to ask him not to go to the track today but instead she asks, 'Don't you need more to eat, dear?'

'Tummy's still a bit unsettled, maybe later,' he says, pushing his plate away.

Shortly after Bob goes off to the races, Detective Sergeant Pierce and a younger detective from Surry Hills Police Station, PC Dibble, arrive to interview her. While Hazel has heard about Merl's son-in-law many times, she's never met him in person. In his forties, Pierce's rugged good looks are fading, his once white nylon shirt stretched across a paunch and his brown suit pinched tight at the shoulders. He's friendly and charming and speaks warmly of Merl, which surprises Hazel. While she's fond of Merl, Hazel imagines that, with her bossy ways, she could be a difficult mother-in-law.

Hazel brings the two men cups of tea and slices of currant cake, and they all sit down in the front room. Hazel and Pierce sit opposite one another. Dibble doesn't seem to know where to put himself. He perches on the arm of a chair and takes out a notebook and pen.

Hazel and Betty had already made statements earlier in the day but Pierce asks if she could start from the beginning, so he has a complete picture. Hazel patiently goes over the details of the two reports she'd made, one about the woman, the other after finding McCracken's body.

'So, you discussed seeing the woman with your work colleagues?' asks Pierce.

Hazel nods. 'Of course and, as I mentioned, reported it to the police.'

'Mrs Bates, is there any chance it was an optical illusion, perhaps a reflection on the glass?' asks Pierce in a sympathetic tone, as if he would understand if she admitted doubt.

'No, because I saw her again early this morning. It was at some distance but it seemed she was being forced into a car – a Bentley – against her will.'

Hazel notices Pierce pause, frowning at the mention of the Bentley. 'And where was this?' he asks abruptly.

'In Lisbon Street, across the street from Zig Zag Lane.'

'Plenty of dark-haired women hanging around there at all hours of the night, as I'm sure you know,' he says.

'Not being forced into cars, one would hope,' says Hazel.

Pierce gives a dismissive shrug. 'Let's talk about Mr McCracken. How well did you know him?'

'Detective Pierce, keep in mind that I'm just the tea lady. He took his tea black with two sugars and enjoyed a Milk Arrowroot; that's all I know.'

Pierce gives her a sly smile. 'I doubt that. If anyone knows where the bodies are buried, it's the tea lady. I'm just trying to connect the dots here.'

'Perhaps you're over-estimating us. In any case, Mr McCracken wasn't the chatty sort. I don't even know where he lived.'

'Did you have any disagreements with him?' Pierce asks.

'Well, I used to give out jellybeans at morning tea on Mondays. He said people were paid to be there and didn't need to be bribed. I don't know why he picked on that. He never seemed to care about the place or the staff.'

Judging by Pierce's questions, it seems clear to Hazel that McCracken's death is suspicious and she hopes he won't consider that a motive for murder. Jellybeans sweetened Monday mornings, but it was not a tradition she would defend to the death.

'Did Mr McCracken ever ask you to pass on messages?' asks Pierce.

'What sort of messages?' she asks, puzzled.

'A note, for example. Or a message for someone? Did he ever give you anything to deliver to someone else in the company? I mean, you have a trolley—'

'Mr McCracken's business would only be with Frankie or Mr Karp Senior and he had six perfectly capable young women in his office to deliver messages. Or he could pick up the telephone. Besides, he made it clear to me on several occasions that I should not involve myself in any matters that didn't concern me.'

'What sort of matters might they be?'

'Outstanding invoices. Jellybean distribution.'

'Why do you think Mr McCracken was in the office late at night?' asks Pierce.

Hazel considers this for a moment. 'I think he may have

suffered from insomnia because the downstairs kitchen was occasionally used overnight to make tea.'

'That could be anyone in the building,' says Pierce.

'And there were sometimes dirty cups on his desk at morning tea time.'

'I see,' says Pierce, giving Dibble a nod to confirm this point is noted.

'Can I ask you a question?' asks Hazel.

Pierce raises his eyebrows in the affirmative.

'Has there been a young woman reported missing? Anyone who might fit the description I gave?'

'Not to my knowledge,' says Pierce. 'But obviously we will check that.'

To her dismay, Hazel's ears begin to tingle. Her built-in lie detectors in action. She knows he's lying and wonders why – perhaps he doesn't believe her? 'Detective Pierce, was Mr McCracken murdered?'

'That's up to the Coroner to decide. We'll have to wait for the autopsy.' Pierce stands up to leave. He pats his pockets but doesn't find what he's looking for. 'Detective Dibble will give you a number to call if you remember anything else, or if you see this mysterious woman again.'

When they have gone, Hazel carries their cups into the kitchen. She turns Pierce's upside down, draining the liquid out onto the saucer, and gazes into the cup. It's very rare that she can't divine something about a person from the tea leaves but, in this case, the leaves are scattered all around the inside of the cup. If there's meaning there, it's hidden. But Detective Dibble's tea leaves are very clear. They entwine to form several writhing snakes. Young Dibble needs to be very careful and watch his back.

When the kitchen is tidy, Hazel goes outside and sits on the back step to enjoy the last of the afternoon sun before Bob comes home from the races. She needs a few moments to turn her thoughts over. Those thoughts keep returning to Mr McCracken, wondering if there is any other information she has tucked away that could be helpful.

Mr McCracken was a very different sort to his predecessor, Mr Levy, who had been the bookkeeper at Empire for over twenty years since the firm was established in 1944. While Frankie Karp was considered a dandy, Mr Levy had been genuinely dapper. Grey hair swept back from a dignified profile, he always dressed in a tasteful suit with a colourful silk tie. Like the Karp family, he'd been a refugee who escaped the war in Europe and liked to remind people that his family had been in the *schmutter* business for generations; it was a passion for him. He ran Accounts with effortless efficiency, taking time every day to walk about the building and chat to staff. He was always interested in how things could be improved with less wastage and more profitability.

Hazel had assumed that Mr Levy, with his financial acumen, was a vital part of the business. So it had been perplexing when, for unknown reasons, Frankie practically forced Mr Levy into retirement against old Mr Karp's wishes. Hazel had overheard them arguing upstairs on several occasions but it still didn't make any sense.

According to Frankie, they needed someone younger with modern methods running the department. Hazel and her co-eaves-dropper, Edith Stern, the company secretary, both considered this very unfair. Mr Levy had managed the company's transition from handwritten ledgers to the modern ledger accounting machines that now handled all the stock control and invoicing. He was popular throughout the building (despite his passion for time and motion management) and his sudden departure came as a shock to everyone. He was almost immediately replaced by Mr McCracken, and Hazel wonders if Frankie had a quite different motive for ousting Mr Levy. But what could it possibly be?

Hazel had never seen Mr McCracken down on the other floors or chatting to the staff. He'd made no effort to get to know anyone at Empire, so perhaps he never planned to stay long. One thing is certain, he had not expected to leave the way he did.

1

BETTY SPREADS THE NEWS

Sunday morning, Betty sits at her dressing table unwinding her rollers and allowing her curls to spring free. As a child, her hair had been naturally curly and the colour of butterscotch, with freckles to match. A lot of freckles. Freckles on her freckles. She had to put up with nicknames like Carrot Top, Bluey, Ginger, Freckle Face and Fly Spot. At some point the copper gradually faded away. She didn't even realise until, in her teens, a sailor whistled at her in the street and called out, 'Give us a kiss, Goldie!'

Goldie? She'd glanced around to make quite sure he meant her, and he did!

It was true, her crowning shame had turned to glorious gold. Her freckles were now cute and there was more male attention to come. Her first boyfriend, Warren the plumber (who soon became her husband), would playfully insist on kissing every freckle on her face each time they parted. Later, the freckles also faded but, by then, Warren had lost interest anyway. They'd only been married two years when she came home from work to find a short note explaining he'd gone to live 'sum wear alse'. She was used to his appalling spelling and knew what he meant. It turned out that 'sum wear alse' was two streets away, shacked up with the wife of his boss at the plumbing firm. Betty was shocked that he would give up his marriage and his job for that awful loud-mouthed woman.

Betty and Hazel worked together at the telephone exchange at that time. There was a policy against employing married women and Hazel was the only one who knew Betty was married. When she told Hazel about the plumber's wife, Hazel suggested that perhaps Betty had already outgrown Warren and now she had been given an opportunity to start a new chapter in her life with the minimum of fuss.

When she looked at it that way, Betty could see it was probably true. With a bit of effort, she managed to forgive Warren, who was, after all, stuck with the plumber's dreadful wife, which seemed punishment enough.

The switchboard operators were all women but there were plenty of single men in other departments of the exchange and Betty threw herself into the social life on offer. But in the back of her mind was the desire to get married again as soon as possible. She liked married life. It was comfortable and she preferred it to all this swanning around being courted by this man and that.

Hazel suggested she wait until the right man caught her eye and not be so influenced by those drawn to her. So Betty invited a fellow she had long admired in the Telegrams department to a New Year's Eve party. Before long they were saying 'I do' and went on to enjoy thirty-seven years of married bliss until his death five years ago. They were never blessed with little ones, but you can't have everything you want in life, Betty knows that.

These days, Betty occupies the downstairs of a two-storey house. She has a living room with a tiny kitchen and separate bedroom, and shares a bathroom on the landing with the elderly widow who lives upstairs. It would be nice if the upstairs lady was sociable but she's not. In fact, Betty almost never sees her and often thinks it's like living with a ghost. If it wasn't for the gurgling of the plumbing she wouldn't even know the old lady was there.

Living in a small flat, Betty always likes to get outdoors on the weekends. On Saturday mornings she usually goes out and leans on the front gate to chat to neighbours passing by on their way to the shops or going down to the markets. If her knees are bad (it's hard standing up most of the day) and the day is nice, she'll put a kitchen chair out on the footpath. Sometimes she feels like the Queen, waving to this person and that, calling out good mornings to all her subjects, most of whom have also lived around here for donkey's years. She often used to visit Hazel on the weekends, but since Bob came on the scene, she leaves them to themselves. There are plenty of other folk she can drop in on and be sure of a warm welcome.

Yesterday she had spent half the day at the police station and the rest of it recovering from her ordeal. Today, on a fine Sunday morning, she sets off on her regular stroll around the block, chatting to neighbours who are out sweeping footpaths and leaning on their brooms to gossip or down on their knees giving their front steps a scrub.

By the time she returns home for lunch, several hours and numerous conversations later, the whole street has heard the dramatic and exciting tale of how she and Hazel (at great risk to themselves) heroically entered an (almost) burning building, discovered a man lying dead on the floor and had been interviewed by the police. Normally, after all that walking about and standing around, her varicose veins would be throbbing like hot coals but, today, with all the excitement and attention, she's walking on air.

8

A STRANGE MAN AT THE DOOR

Walking home from the station after seeing Bob off on Sunday evening, Hazel has an odd feeling that she's being followed. She stops to look behind her but sees nothing out of the ordinary. She buys eggs and bread at the corner shop and chats with the owner for a few minutes. When she leaves, she pauses to glance up and down the street. There's a woman dragging a small crying boy along by his arm and several children playing hopscotch but, apart from that, Glade Street is quieter than usual. She wonders if her imagination is running away with her common sense but still feels a sense of relief when she steps inside her house.

Number 5 Glade Street is the last in a row of two-storey terraces. Unlike the places opposite, which open straight onto the street, it has a wrought-iron fence with a little patch of garden squeezed in between the fence and the house. It's not much of a garden and everything Hazel has planted has died or been stolen, but it makes the place seem a little grander. The front door opens into a narrow hall with a steep staircase leading to two upstairs bedrooms. The front bedroom has a balcony and looks over the street; the smaller back bedroom has a view over the alley and neighbours' yards strung with washing. Downstairs there are just two rooms: a front lounge room and an eat-in kitchen that opens into the backyard.

In the years after Hazel's first husband died, the second bedroom had been let out to a series of boarders (some better company than others) while Hazel and her daughter, Norma, shared the larger bedroom. When Norma married a farmer and moved away to the country, Hazel had resigned herself to living with boarders for the rest of her life but then Bob came along and everything changed again. The only constant in her life has been this funny old house with all its familiar comforts and memories.

Still uneasy, Hazel walks straight through the house and out the back. She crosses the yard and opens the gate to check the alley behind. A dog starts barking furiously. Turning in its direction, she glimpses the shadow of someone hurrying around the corner. Locking the gate, she goes back into the house.

Moments later, there's a knock at the front door. Rather than open it, Hazel goes into the front room and pulls the curtain aside. She then pushes up the sash window to see a man standing at the front door holding a bunch of flowers.

He turns in surprise and gives her a friendly smile.

'Can I help you?' she asks.

'Good evening, I do apologise. I didn't mean to bother you. I was asked to deliver these flowers to you, Mrs . . .'

He holds out the bunch of flowers towards her. He seems very presentable: heavily built but fit looking and dressed casually in a smart dark sports jacket and beige trousers. His smile, more ingratiating than genuine, reveals well-tended teeth.

But that old familiar tingling tells Hazel something isn't right here. Her ears never lie. 'Are you sure you have the right house?' she asks.

'Five Glade Street? Your husband asked me to deliver these.'

'Bob?' asks Hazel in surprise, immediately regretting it.

'Let me introduce myself, Philip Sinclair,' says the man with a deferential dip of his head. 'I'm a colleague of Bob's. He's probably mentioned me.'

'I don't know who you are, or what you're after. But I do know you're not a friend of Bob's,' says Hazel. She reaches up to pull the window closed.

'You are Mrs Bateman?' calls the man.

'No,' says Hazel. 'I'm not Mrs Bateman. Bates is my name. Clearly you're at the wrong house.'

She closes the window and watches him walk off down the street. Reflecting on the conversation, she realises that Philip Sinclair wanted to confirm her name and, despite her misgivings, she gave it to him without thinking. The question is, Why did he want it and why the roundabout way of obtaining it?

Fortified by a couple of boiled eggs and a piece of toast, Hazel goes next door to the Mulligans', as she does every Sunday, to help with the kiddies' bath night. Over the years, Mrs Mulligan's increasing proportions have made getting her seven children through the bath more difficult. These days, when she kneels down, it takes several children to get her up again. To help out, Hazel and the eldest daughter, Maude, work in tandem to get all the kiddies cleaned up for the week.

When Hazel arrives through the back gate, Mrs Mulligan has the copper boiling in the washhouse and the two older boys are filling the tin bath with buckets of water.

'Come on, you kids,' calls Maude, standing at the back door. 'Hurry up!' She pushes and pulls them into line in age order, boxing them around the ears when they play up. She strips off the littlest ones in the kitchen and sends each in turn out into the yard where Hazel wields the long-handled brush and carbolic soap.

'Good evening, young Master Mulligan,' says Hazel, popping the littlest into the bath. 'My, how you've grown! We're going to need a bigger bath for you soon.'

'Don't want a bath,' he scowls and, at the first touch of the brush, lets fly with his usual high-pitched shrieks. Hazel takes no notice, talking to him gently as she scrubs him all over and inspects his scalp. When he's done, she wraps him in a threadbare towel and lifts him out. He stands and sobs quietly while she combs kerosene through his hair and wraps his head in rags (it's nit season all year round in this house), then he's dispatched upstairs to Mrs Mulligan who will put him to bed. When everyone is bathed, Maude pulls out the plug and releases the grimy water into the yard, sweeping it down with a stiff broom.

Once the younger ones are in bed, Maude does her homework in the front room while Hazel and Mrs Mulligan sit down at the kitchen table with a glass of rhubarb wine and a slice of currant cake.

Kicking off her shoes, Mrs Mulligan gives a sigh as she rests her feet on a chair. 'You don't mind, do you now, Hazel? Me feet couldn't smell worse than them kids.'

'Children always smell sweet to me,' says Hazel, avoiding the question since Mrs Mulligan's feet smell like boiled mutton and she prefers not to dwell on it.

'I hear there's been a murder at your firm, is that right? Did you know the fella at all?'

'He was our bookkeeper. I didn't know him well,' says Hazel.

'And, it was death, as far as we know. It hasn't been confirmed that he was murdered.'

'Ah, Lord knows. I hope they catch the murderer soon and he's not one of them serial killers going around killing bookkeepers all over the place. It's odd, don't you think? A professional man like that being murdered.' Mrs Mulligan laughs. 'I wish there was a fella going round murdering rent collectors. That'd suit a lot of folk round here.'

Hazel knows all about Mrs Mulligan's battles with the rent collector and feels sorry for the poor man with that unenviable job. 'I'm sure if one rent collector was disposed of another would pop up in his place,' says Hazel.

'Like nits!' says Mrs Mulligan, and they laugh together. 'So, do you have a beau calling on you while Mr Bates is away in the country, then?'

'A beau?' asks Hazel with a chuckle. 'No. That was a mistake. The flowers were not for me.'

'Is that right? Maudie said she saw the fella throw the flowers in the gutter up the street. She went and picked them up. They're in the parlour and very nice they are too. She took quite an interest, followed him down the street to his car.'

'Did she now? What made her do that?' asks Hazel.

'Buying flowers for a married lady and then throwing them away? If that's not peculiar I don't know what is.'

'You're right,' agrees Hazel. 'It is strange.'

On her way out, Hazel collects a pile of socks to be darned and looks in on Maude. Hazel's heart goes out to the girl; she's such a hard worker. She does well at school and has a real talent for drawing. Her textbooks are spread around her and the flowers in a cut-glass vase on the table. She works hard and never complains.

Mrs Mulligan takes in ironing and the front room has piles of folded washing on every surface. Hazel often wonders why they don't put some of the children to sleep in here. Upstairs, five of them sleep in one bedroom and the youngest two in with their parents. Mr Mulligan is the night watchman at the brewery and has the bed to himself during the day, so perhaps Mrs Mulligan enjoys the warmth and comfort of the little ones at night.

Maude glances up and gives Hazel a welcoming smile. 'Off now, Mrs Bates?'

'Yes, I am, dear. I hear you followed the man who came to my house this afternoon?'

'It wasn't my idea,' says Maude uncomfortably. 'Mam said to get after him and see what he was about.'

'And did you find out anything?'

Maude shrugs. 'He parked his car near the station. Flash car, too.'

'Do you remember what sort it was?'

Maude shakes her head. 'I don't know much about cars.'

'I don't suppose you remember the number plate?' asks Hazel.

'Course I do.' Maude grins. 'I wrote it down.'

9

GLORIA MAKES A SNAP DECISION

On Monday morning, Gloria Nuttell, the factory supervisor, is woken by the telephone ringing. She runs into the kitchen to answer it, surprised to hear Mrs Stern, the bosses' cranky secretary, on the line telling her that Empire will be closed for two days. 'There was a fire in the bond store and Mr McCracken was found dead in Accounts! Can you believe it? It's in the papers!' says Mrs Stern, clearly thrilled by all the excitement.

'Oh yeah?' says Gloria, half asleep and a little hungover. 'Maybe the Queen Bees stung him to death.' She attempts a laugh but her head hurts. She reaches for her smokes, cradling the phone on her shoulder while she lights up.

'It's not a joke, Mrs Nuttell. A man is dead and the entire building could have burnt to the ground – then where would we be? Anyway, you need to let your girls know that we'll be shut for two days. Mr Karp has very generously said the pays won't be docked.'

Gloria could do with having the day off but hardly any of the machinists have telephones, so she'll have to go into work anyway.

'Mrs Stern,' she says in her sweetest voice, 'I don't suppose you could be a darling and put a note on the factory door for the girls, could you? Then I can come in a bit later.'

'I'm not *your* secretary, Mrs Nuttell. Besides, I'm flat out with other things. The whole building has to be cleaned, so I have to organise that this morning.'

Mrs Stern had been happy enough to chat a moment earlier but it's not in her nature to do anyone favours. Gloria hangs up the telephone and considers the matter of McCracken. He was a pain in the bum. She'd be happy to have Levy back any day. He was an old flirt but always took his job seriously and made sure people got paid on time. But McCracken? Something odd about him, and unfriendly too.

She sticks her head around the bedroom door. Her husband, Tony, has managed to sleep through all that and she'll be glad not to have to deal with his grumpy hangover when he wakes up.

She puts on her smock, makes a cup of instant and a piece of toast and takes them to the bathroom while she does her face and hair. The hand's a bit shaky this morning and her eyeliner less than perfect – it'll just have to do. She applies pale-pink lipstick, teases her hair into a bouffant and lacquers it into place. Blowing herself a kiss in the mirror, she runs out the door to catch the early bus.

The factory always looks gloomy when the machines are silent and the chairs empty. Gloria clocks on and flicks the fluorescent light on. She can already see that every surface is covered with ash. Grit will have got into everything. It'll take days to clean this place.

Old Mr Karp comes striding out from the warehouse, accompanied by Mr Butterby. 'We'll have to dry-clean the entire warehouse stock,' says Mr Karp. 'While that's out, the warehouse itself can be cleaned. No need to have the garments pressed, our girls can do that.'

'I'll sort it out this morning,' says Mr Butterby. He gives Gloria a wink, leaving a tantalising hint of Old Spice behind as he passes.

Mr Karp, apparently not even noticing her, sweeps past and out the door. 'As for the factory—' he continues before the door swings shut behind him and Gloria is none the wiser as to his plans.

She perches on the corner of a worktable, takes a pack of cigarettes out of her smock, shakes one out and lights up. What if this place had burnt to the ground? She'd get another job somewhere but it would never be the same. There are plenty of people at Empire that she doesn't care for – one of whom has been conveniently knocked off over the weekend. Old Mr Karp and Frankie are both annoying in different ways and the Ginger Nut sisters really get her goat sometimes. The rest are not that bad. Even though she complains about them, the Queen Bees are all right and the girls in the factory are like family, better than any family she's ever had. To lose them would be the worst blow of all. And Hazel, of course, always calm and considered – that old girl doesn't miss a thing. Then there is the delightful Mr Butterby with his crooked grin and laughing eyes. Gloria wonders what it would be like to have a husband who is always cheery, not moaning about everything like Tony. Nice to dream.

When the factory door opens and a couple of machinists appear, Gloria realises she forgot to put a note on the door. If the factory closes for two days, there's going to be pressure later in the week catching up with their orders. That's not a problem for upstairs; it will be her problem. If the whole lot of them get cleaning the factory today, they'll be back in production first thing tomorrow.

Grumbling under her breath, she makes a decision and stubs out her cigarette. 'What are you waiting for?' she calls to the machinists, now standing around chatting. 'Clock on, there's work to do.' She turns on the radio and rolls up her sleeves.

10

HAZEL UNDER PRESSURE

The bond store has now been cordoned off and, despite the drizzling rain, a good-sized crowd has gathered on the main road to stare at the blackened ruin of the building. On her way to work, Hazel joins them for a few minutes, interested to have a good look at the buildings on either side.

Thanks to the heroic efforts of the firefighters, the adjoining buildings are blackened but completely intact. The building to the right is Farley Frocks, where Betty works in a similar size company to Empire. On the other side is an empty shop with two floors above it that are probably being used for some dubious enterprise, since all the windows are blacked out. But from this angle, Hazel can't see if either of the buildings was connected to the bond store.

Although Mrs Stern had rung to tell her not to come in today, Hazel decided she would anyway and is glad she did because Gloria has the factory girls washing down the walls and floors, and cleaning all the worktables and sewing machines. The company cleaners have enlisted half-a-dozen family members, all rushing up and down the stairs shouting to each other as if they are putting out a fire.

After the factory tea break, Hazel sets up a table in the lobby with the hot water urn, tea and coffee, and a box of plain biscuits. The workers can help themselves and all she needs to do is clear up occasionally. When the top-floor kitchen has been cleaned, she whips up a batch of scones and takes one to Mr Karp Senior with his tea. He gives her a thankyou wave, busy on the phone discussing an insurance claim for the dry-cleaning of hundreds of garments in the warehouse.

'I could do with a stiff drink right now,' says Edith Stern when Hazel delivers her tea. 'What a business! Someone dead right here on the premises!' She dips her Milk Coffee biscuit into her tea, deftly transferring it to her mouth before it disintegrates. 'Gives me chills to think of it. The police are coming this morning to interview Mr Karp and Frankie.'

'Where is Frankie this morning?' asks Hazel, noting it's almost eleven o'clock.

'You're asking the wrong person,' says Edith huffily. 'I'm just the secretary. Ask me where Mr Karp is at any time of the day or night, I could tell you but, as you know, Frankie is another matter altogether. Probably at the barbers, he spends more time there than at work.' Her phone rings. She picks it up and grimaces at Hazel. 'All right, we'll see you then.' She hangs up. 'Frankie's on his way.'

Hazel goes into Frankie's office and looks out the window. Grey dust hangs in the air and the window is coated with black grime. She opens it for a clearer view.

Edith joins her, looking down at the blackened shell of the bond store. 'Better not let his nibs catch you. You know how he hates people in his office when he's not here.'

'I won't be long.' Hazel leans out the window. From here, it looks as if the adjacent building and the bond store were built at the same time. Both buildings have pitched roofs and, where they once met, she can see a patch of a different material in the bricks.

'Keep an eye out for him, I'll be back in a minute,' says Hazel. She dashes downstairs and borrows Doug Fysh's binoculars, hurrying back to Frankie's office.

'What are you looking at?' asks Edith, standing at her shoulder.

'I saw a woman in the bond store the morning before the fire. Look at the building next door.' She hands Edith the binoculars. 'There's a sort of hatch that connects the two buildings through the roof space. It looks partly open.'

'What are you ladies up to in Frankie's office?' asks a voice behind them.

Edith gives a little scream and they turn to face Frankie. 'We were just inspecting the damage next door,' she says.

'I'm sure you both have better things to do.' Frankie takes off his suit jacket and places it on a hanger at the back of the door. 'How about a cup of tea, Hazel?'

'Of course,' says Hazel, with a smile.

When she brings his tea and a warm buttered scone, he gestures for her to sit down – something that has never happened before. He takes a large bite of scone and washes it down with a slurp of tea. 'It's not clear to me why you were in the building in the early hours of the morning.'

'It's very simple. A friend called me about the fire—'

'Who? Who called you? Who is this friend?'

'Betty Dewsnap, from Farley Frocks.'

'Why would this Betty Dewsnap call you? What does she do at Farley's?'

'She's the tea lady there.'

'The tea lady?' he echoes in disbelief.

'She thought I'd be interested, that's all,' explains Hazel, getting to her feet.

He motions her to sit down again. 'We haven't finished yet. Why would tea ladies be so interested in a fire? Maybe just nosy old biddies but it seems fishy to Frankie. Very fishy. Especially when our accountant is discovered dead in the building at an odd hour and by the tea lady, of all people.'

'Well, that's how it happened—'

Frankie stands up abruptly and paces up and down the office. 'What made you come into the building? How did you end up on the 2nd Floor?'

'The police seemed satisfied enough.'

'I'm just saying it's fishy. Did you know Mr McCracken?'

Hazel sighs. 'I knew how he took his tea. That's about it.'

'So you never saw him outside this building?'

'No. I've told the police all this.'

Frankie perches on the front of his desk. 'Frankie and Hazel have known each other a long time, haven't they?'

'They have,' agrees Hazel, reluctantly.

'Frankie thought they were friends. People who trusted each other.'

Hazel forces a smile at this dubious claim, not to mention his patronising tone.

'But I have a feeling you're hiding something. Being a little *secretive*. Is there something you know that you're keeping to yourself?'

Hazel is saved the bother of denial by the buzzing telephone. Frankie picks it up with an irritated sigh. 'Yes, all right. Put him through,' he says, indicating with a wave of his hand that Hazel is dismissed.

11

MEETING AT THE DELPHI MILK BAR

Hazel arrives in the downstairs kitchen to find Irene leaning against the bench, digging at the crescents of dirt under her fingernails with a toothpick while ash from her cigarette falls onto the bench. 'We're meeting at the Greek,' she says. 'The others are off round there now.'

Hazel could do with some fresh air; the whole building stinks of smoke. She pops a jacket over her pinny and follows Irene out to the laneway. They walk the couple of blocks to the Delphi Milk Bar with Irene talking all the way about the fire and the murder. The morning rain has eased and the sun emerges, brightening the day.

'It hasn't been confirmed as a murder, has it?' interrupts Hazel.

Irene taps the side of her nose with a nicotine-stained finger. 'Direct from Merl the Pearl. Coppers gunna announce it today, so her ladyship says.'

Merl and Betty are already tucked into a booth in the milk bar, and Hazel and Irene slide into the banquette opposite. They often meet here on rainy days and Mrs Angelos doesn't mind them eating their packed lunches if they order a pot or two of tea.

While Hazel explains what happened on the night of the fire, Betty's gaze is on the homemade cakes lined up on the counter but she manages to tear herself from that distraction to repeat her claim that it was just like the war.

'The war where, Betty?' asks Merl, sceptically. 'Dunkirk or Bondi?'

'Somewhere in between. You'd think a bomb had exploded,' Betty insists. 'People were screaming their heads off with terror. Weren't they, Hazel?'

'Not sure about the "heads off" part,' says Hazel, 'but it was very frightening. It made you realise how quickly the whole city could catch light if they couldn't bring a fire that size under control.'

'So,' says Merl, 'the mystery woman is clearly a suspect in the fire.'

'Or perhaps someone set fire to the building because she was in it,' suggests Hazel.

'MW – I'm calling her that for short,' Betty explains as she writes in her notebook. 'I don't have time to write Mystery Woman every five minutes. Now, suspect or victim?'

'We don't know that yet. But I can confirm that she escaped from the fire,' says Hazel. 'I saw her briefly when Betty and I were walking up to Lisbon Street. She got into a car with someone – against her will, it seemed to me.'

'Hazel, should I say "violently forced"?' asks Betty eagerly, her pen poised.

'If you don't stick to the facts, that list is going to end up like the *News of the World*,' Merl points out.

'All right,' agrees Betty. 'Do we have a model or number plate for the aforementioned vehicle, Hazel?'

'The car was a Bentley but the number plate I couldn't see.'

Hazel gives Betty a smile. 'Thank you for keeping notes, Betty dear. Very helpful.'

'We'll see,' mutters Irene, fumbling in her shopping bag with one hand as she reaches for the ashtray with the other.

'Please don't smoke in here, Irene,' says Betty. 'You know how my sinuses are.'

Irene sighs. 'I'll just roll one for later.' Deftly filling the paper with shreds of tobacco, she licks it closed and tucks it neatly behind her ear.

'Thank you. Think how much time and money you'd save if you gave up,' says Betty, not for the first time.

'You should be smoking menthols, anyway,' says Merl. 'At least they're good for your health. Not like those nasty roll-your-owns that only sailors smoke these days.'

Irene glares at them both over the top of her glasses. 'Everyone's got a bloody opinion, eh? Mind yer own beeswax, the both of yers.'

Mrs Angelos puts a tray on the table with two pots of tea, and cups and saucers.

Hazel thanks her in Greek, which always makes Mrs Angelos laugh. A few minutes later she returns with four sticky Greek pastries. 'Is special for this ladies.'

'Yer probably saying it wrong,' Irene tells Hazel when she's gone. 'That's why she always laughs.'

'No, it's correct,' confirms Merl. 'I've heard the girls in our factory say it just like that. I wouldn't go around saying it, of course, but Hazel has her own way of doing things. Anyway, let's get back to business. The bookkeeper was murdered, they say.'

Betty gives a gasp. 'Oh! Hazel, the murderer could have been hiding in the building while we were there! We could have been murdered ourselves!'

'But we weren't, so let's not concern ourselves with things that didn't happen. We've got enough on our plates as it is.' Hazel pauses for a moment to gather her thoughts. 'You know, Mr McCracken was a bit of a mystery. I was a little curious about him. I kept his cup aside several times to read, but there were no leaves left behind – not a single one.'

'Oh, that's suspicious,' says Betty. 'He didn't want you to know anything about him.'

Merl huffs dismissively. 'It's not as if he suspected Hazel might read his leaves, and disposed of them.'

Betty ignores her. 'I'm writing that down. Murdered man leaves no leaves.'

'Now, there's something else, unrelated, I think,' says Hazel. 'The other evening a man followed me home from Central Station after I saw Bob off on the train. He came to the house with some trumped-up excuse and said his name was Philip Sinclair.'

Betty looks confused. 'Do I start a new page for this, Hazel?'

'Wouldn't hurt, dear.' Hazel hands Merl the slip of paper Maude gave her. 'Do you think one of Detective Pierce's people would check this car registration?'

'I have his direct number. I'll call him personally right away,' says Merl, sliding out of the booth.

'"I have his direct number",' mimics Irene, when Merl goes off to ask Mrs Angelos if she can use the telephone. 'Big bloody deal.'

While Merl's on the phone, Hazel reiterates the conversation with Sinclair and how he'd thought her name was Bateman, adding to the confusion.

'So was he a looker, this bloke?' asks Irene.

'I really didn't notice. But if he follows me again, I'll do a full assessment.'

'You could ask if he's single too,' suggests Betty, helpfully. 'Or check his ring finger.'

Hazel laughs. 'I think that might give him the wrong idea.'

When Merl returns, they get back to discussing McCracken, and Betty wonders aloud whether she and Hazel would be considered as suspects. 'I thought he'd just fallen and hit his head.'

'Takes more than a little bump on the noggin to kill someone,' says Irene. 'Yer need something solid, like a crowbar or a hammer.'

'I suppose you'd know,' sniffs Merl.

'What do you think the murder weapon could be?' Betty's eyes fix on the ashtray. 'It could be anything nearby – like a heavy glass ashtray.'

'Because you just happened to see an ashtray?' suggests Merl. 'The police have proper scientific methods to solve crimes. Anyway, I already know. He was shot.'

'Yer kept that to yerself long enough,' says Irene, crossly.

Betty gasps. 'With a real gun?'

'Well, a pop gun wouldn't do it. Yes, a real gun,' says Merl.

Hazel gives Betty a reassuring smile. 'I agree it is shocking, dear.'

When Merl is called to the telephone, Betty slides Merl's pastry off the plate and into her mouth. Irene raises her eyebrows but says nothing.

'Registered to one Philip Sinclair,' says Merl, coming straight back.

'Oh,' says Hazel, disappointed. 'That's what he told me. I assumed it was false for some reason.'

'There's more . . .' Merl pauses dramatically. 'He's a private detective.'

12

SOMETHING ODD WITH BOB

To Hazel's relief, Bob arrives home on Friday in better shape. She's very used to him being away during the week but these last few days he seemed more distant to her, and not just geographically. His work takes him to isolated farming districts, places that are just names on a map to Hazel. She's never been that far north and has no reason to go, apart from seeing where he spends his time. It would be nice to see the places he talks about, like Glen Innes and Bingara, and also his room in the boarding house in Grafton so she could picture his weekday life, but it's a long way to go just for that.

Over dinner, she tells Bob about the visit from Philip Sinclair. As expected, he is indignant and concerned, reassuring her that he certainly did not ask a strange man to deliver flowers. 'We must report it to the police,' he says. 'The fellow's an imposter of some sort. He might have wanted to check if you were alone and be planning a break-in. That's what these people do, they see a pattern or a habit and then exploit it. He might have seen you leaving the station on a previous occasion.'

'I don't know about that, Bob, apparently he's a private detective.'

'A private detective?' he repeats. 'Are you sure?'

'Merl's son-in-law did a number-plate check.'

Bob gets up and brings the phone book back to the table. He flicks through the directory to the pink business pages and reads aloud: 'Philip Sinclair, Private Investigator. Professional. Reliable. Discreet.'

'Could it have something to do with what happened at work?' suggests Hazel. 'Mr McCracken's death, for example.'

'I doubt it. Why would a private detective come knocking on our door? It's probably just a mistake,' Bob says. 'Perhaps he's not a very good detective.'

'Possibly. But there's something else. He had my name wrong, he thought it was Bateman.'

Seemingly more interested in gnawing on his chop, Bob chokes on a bit of gristle. He coughs violently, his face turning scarlet. Hazel leaps to her feet and pats him firmly on the back. He reaches for his glass of water and gulps it down. It takes a minute or two for the normal colour to return to his cheeks. 'Oh, Bob, are you all right? You gave me a scare.'

He smiles weakly, eyes still watering. 'Something went down the wrong way. I'm fine. So, this Sinclair fellow, did he say anything else?'

'No. Just that he knew you, which is obviously not true, and you'd asked him to bring me flowers. He threw those flowers away so I don't think they were meant for anyone else. Otherwise, he would have asked if I knew where this Mrs Bateman lived.'

Hazel describes Sinclair's appearance but Bob shakes his head. 'Certainly not someone I know. If he turns up again, don't open the door to him. It worries me to think of strange men coming here bothering you when I'm away.'

'I'm all right, Bob. I can take care of myself, as I did for many years before you.'

Bob reaches over, placing his hand on hers. 'You are very precious to me, my love. That's all. I wouldn't want to lose you.'

Hazel frowns at this curious comment. 'Why would you lose me, dear?'

Bob laughs. 'Oh I'm just being silly and sentimental. Forgive me.'

While Hazel clears up, Bob wanders into the front room. She takes in a cuppa and apple cake, expecting to find him reading the evening paper or listening to the radio and working on the Taj Mahal. But he stands at the window, the curtain held aside, staring out into the night. It's difficult to tell whether he's lost in thought or watching the street. More than anything, Hazel is struck by his posture. He has an almost religious belief in the importance of good posture but here he is, shoulders slumped and looking defeated. As if he has come to the end of something that has taken a toll on him.

'Everything all right, dear?' asks Hazel.

He straightens up and turns to her, forcing a smile. 'Of course, my love. Never better.' And she has no reason to doubt him. Never once, in their time together, have her ears alerted her to Bob telling a fib. He's a supremely honest man.

13

THE DRESS THAT SHOCKS THE NATION

Gloria gets up from her desk and takes Monday's newspaper over to show Hazel while she's serving the tea. 'Look at this story about "The Shrimp", Hazel,' she says. At Hazel's blank expression she adds, 'Jean Shrimpton, the British model? She wore this little dress to the Derby Day races on the weekend – caused a real stir.'

Hazel, who obviously hasn't even heard of Jean Shrimpton, takes the paper and studies the front-page photograph. 'Very pretty,' she says, with a smile.

'Pretty? They say she's the most beautiful woman in the world.' Taking the newspaper back, Gloria studies the photograph again. Shrimpton's arms are bare. Her hair swings loose and she leans to one side, as if she's about to twirl around. She looks so girlish and free, unlike the old biddies in the background, all trussed up in their race-day ensembles with hats and handbags. A couple of them even have fur stoles slung across their shoulders. To Gloria, Jean Shrimpton looks like a breath of fresh air blowing the cobwebs out of that stuffy old world.

'What do they say about her?' asks Hazel, passing Gloria her coffee.

Gloria reads the story aloud: '"The Shrimp Shocked Them. There she was, the world's highest-paid fashion model, snubbing the iron-clad conventions of fashionable Flemington with a dress five inches above the knee, no hat, no gloves and no stockings! The shockwaves were still rumbling around fashionable Melbourne last night when Jean Shrimpton, The Shrimp, swore she hadn't realised she was setting off such an outraged upheaval at Flemington on Saturday."'

'I think she looks very pretty and natural,' says Hazel. 'What a fuss.'

'There's more,' says Gloria. '"Flemington was not amused. Fashion-conscious Derby Day racegoers were horrified. 'Insulting. A disgrace. How dare she?' If the skies had rained acid not a woman there would have given The Shrimp an umbrella."'

'Oh heavens, it makes me cross the way these newspapers set women against each other; acid rain indeed,' says Hazel.

Gloria laughs and lights up a cigarette. 'Five inches above the knee!' she marvels, squinting at the grainy picture through drifting smoke. 'Shame we're a bit old for it, eh, Hazel? If I was ten years younger I'd wear that outfit. I had terrific legs, you know. Head-turners, they were . . .' She trails off regretfully.

'Gloria dear, you have terrific legs now. You're barely thirty. I'm definitely too old but you are not.'

'Thanks, Hazel. You know, this is going to shake up the rag trade. I wonder what upstairs think about it . . .' Gloria laughs. 'The Ginger Nuts will be tearing their hair out.'

The machinists are also passing around the morning paper and it's causing quite a stir. The new girl, Alice, watches from her workbench. She often stays at her workbench during breaks. It's probably too much effort to use her sticks getting up and down.

Hazel takes morning tea over to her, and Gloria overhears Alice ask what the excitement is about. 'A photo in the paper of a young woman in a short dress,' says Hazel.

'It must be quite a dress,' says Alice.

Gloria goes over and puts the newspaper down on her work-table. 'Judge for yourself.'

Alice sighs. 'Oh, now I understand . . . Jean Shrimpton. I've seen these dresses in English magazines, they call them minis . . .'

Gloria has barely had a conversation with Alice, who always seems a bit aloof. Now seems a good opportunity but she hesitates, not knowing what else to say. Then the buzzer goes and the moment passes.

14

TROUBLE BREWING AT THE EMPIRE

By Tuesday, everyone in the Empire building is talking about The Shrimp's simple little frock. The Queen Bees barely notice Hazel's arrival with the morning tea. Several of them have stapled their skirts up above the knee, just to see how it feels. One of the ledger machine operators, who always backcombs her hair into a beehive, wears it out today. Hazel tells her how pretty it looks and gets a smacking kiss on the cheek in return. Everyone's in high spirits today. There's a sense of anticipation in the air.

Through the frosted window of Mr McCracken's office, Hazel can see someone sitting at the desk. She taps on the door and opens it.

'Mrs Bates! Delighted to see you,' says Mr Levy, looking up with a smile.

'And you too, Mr Levy. Welcome back. The usual, I presume?'

'Some things never change,' he says with a chuckle.

Parking her trolley at the door, Hazel puts two spoonfuls of coffee powder and two sugars in a cup, adds hot water from the urn and gives it a good stir. 'Is this a permanent arrangement?' she asks. 'It would be lovely to have you back.'

'It's under discussion. I would certainly like to come back.' Mr Levy takes his coffee and thanks her. 'I understand you found Mr McCracken, Hazel?'

Hazel nods. 'I did, on the night of the fire.'

'The fire, yes, we're lucky this building didn't go up in flames too. Let me ask you, what did you think of him?'

'He wasn't the friendliest of fellows but I suppose that's not essential to the job.'

'Never hurts though, does it?' Mr Levy hesitates. He then gets up and closes his door quietly, turning to Hazel. 'I'm starting to do an audit of the books.'

Hazel raises a questioning eyebrow. 'I see. There were a few problems with supplier payments recently . . .'

Mr Levy nods. 'I know you see everything that goes on around here, Hazel, so I'm always interested in your observations. Do you have any idea what McCracken's connection was with Frankie?' he asks.

'Do you mean outside work?'

'Yes. I wonder if they knew each other prior to him working here?' asks Mr Levy.

'I don't know. Why do you ask?'

'Keep this under your hat, as always, Hazel. I know you are discreet. One thing that's obvious to me is that Mr McCracken was not an experienced bookkeeper. He had his own particular methods but was not using proper procedure.'

'That is odd,' agrees Hazel. 'Frankie made him out to be the bee's knees of accounting.'

Mr Levy nods. 'First he was misrepresented, then he came to a nasty end. There is a lot more to this than meets the eye. Let me know if any new information comes your way.'

Hazel nods. 'Of course. It's good to have you back, Mr Levy.'

Mid-afternoon, Hazel is notified of a hastily called meeting in the boardroom. She duly delivers tea and biscuits to Frankie, Mr Karp Senior, Doug Fysh and Edith Stern, who is taking the minutes.

'I don't understand what Cashell's mean by "pausing" their order,' says Mr Karp Senior. 'We can't put an entire season on hold when their buyers have already committed to it.' He gives the rack of next season's samples an accusatory look, as if they have betrayed him in some way.

'That's what they're saying,' says Doug. 'I realise it's unusual—'

'Unusual?' says Frankie. 'It's outrageous.'

Mr Karp stares at Frankie for a moment. 'We need to work through this in an orderly way and be measured in our approach.'

Frankie shakes his head with annoyance. 'We'll end up with this season's stock left in the warehouse and the '66 winter and summer range redundant – when they've already committed to them.'

Mr Karp turns to Doug for confirmation.

'They're now saying the order is not finalised,' says Doug. 'As I said, it's a directive from Col Cashell himself to put orders on hold. Their buyers are meeting in the next day or so.' He pauses carefully, considering his words. 'We can't force them to take stock, even if they have committed. It would damage our relationship with them. We all know that Cashell's lead the way and the other department stores follow, so there may be more problems ahead.'

Edith's pencil flicks rapidly over her stenographer's pad. Hazel passes her a cup of tea and receives a tight smile in thanks.

Pixie appears and hovers in the doorway, apparently uncertain if she's welcome in the meeting.

'What is it?' asks Frankie, glancing up at her. 'We're busy right now.'

'Come in, my dear.' Mr Karp beckons her to take a seat at the table. 'I invited Pixie to the meeting. I want her to see how things work around here at all levels.'

Pixie slips quietly into a seat. Hazel takes her a cup of tea and a reassuring smile.

'Dad, she's eighteen. I don't know what you expect,' says Frankie. 'Distributing mail and running errands are one thing—'

'She's here to learn,' insists Mr Karp. 'Now, let's continue. I think Cashell's will come to their senses, it's just a moment of panic. Their customers are conservative, the catalogue business especially.' He picks up the newspaper and stares at it for a moment. 'Country women will never be seen in this sort of thing.'

'I'm not sure about that,' says Doug. 'By next year, this could be what women want.'

'I think it will be! We want to be more—' Pixie bursts out.

'This is Australia, not Carnaby Street,' interrupts Frankie, snatching another chocolate biscuit off the plate. 'The girl looks half-dressed, as if she's gone to the races in her slip. God help us if people think this outfit is the height of elegance.'

'What do you think, Hazel?' asks Doug. He sits back in his chair with a mischievous grin. 'Hazel knows what's what, haw haw haw . . .'

'I'm definitely not the person to ask about fashion.' Hazel senses Frankie's silent agreement but pushes on. 'But if I was twenty-two, I would love a light frock like this. Pixie is really the one to ask, she's the customer for this dress.'

All eyes turn on Pixie and for a moment it seems her courage might fail her. 'It's simple and comfortable and, I think it's . . . stylish. And Jean Shrimpton is—'

'What would Jean Shrimpton know about anything? She's a clothes horse,' says Frankie.

'What are your thoughts, Mrs Stern?' asks Mr Karp, turning to his secretary.

Edith shakes her head. 'If you want to know, I think it's disgraceful, showing her bare legs like that. No stockings or hat. Shows a disrespect for tradition. Who knows where it will lead? People will be walking around in their undergarments next.'

Frankie sighs dramatically. 'Does this help us in the slightest? I think men know what women want better than women do.'

Mr Karp nods unhappily. 'I notice this Shrimpton girl was sponsored by Orlon. We need to look more closely at these synthetics.' He picks up the newspaper again and studies it. 'It does have a nice lightness and shape in the fall. If it were any longer, it would be a sack.'

'Perhaps some of our current garments could be adapted,' suggests Doug. He gets up and goes over to the rack of samples. Selecting a couple of frocks, he holds them up. 'Just take a few inches off the hemline?'

To Hazel's surprise these dresses with their full skirts, darts and pleats, and narrow matching belts suddenly look fussy and old-fashioned. What a difference a day makes! Take a few inches off and they'll look like children's frocks.

Reading the silence in the room, Doug continues. 'The fact is, Cashell's are our biggest customer and we have no choice but to—'

'Hopefully Col Cashell comes to his senses,' interrupts Frankie.

'One dress and a couple of bony knees do not a revolution make.'

Judging by the response in the rest of the building, Hazel is almost certain he's wrong but it's hardly her place to comment, so she collects the cups and quietly slips away.

15

A BREAKTHROUGH CLUE

When Mr Kovac drops in mid-week with an extra order, Hazel shows him the note with the foreign word. 'Does this mean anything to you, Mr Kovac? My husband suggested it might be Russian.'

He takes the piece of paper from her and studies it. 'Yes, this is Russian but I cannot help you with its meaning. In Hungarian we use the Latin alphabet, so this is all Greek to me.' He smiles, pleased with his quip. 'Mrs Bates, in the building on the corner of Fort Street, there is a shoemaker named Mr Sapozhnik, on the 4th floor. He's a White Russian and not a friendly man but tell him that I sent you and he may help you with a translation.'

'Thank you, Mr Kovac, I'll do that. By the way, did you get your cheque from Mr McCracken the other day?'

'There was a cheque ready for me, thank you. It was a terrible shock to hear the man was dead. I saw it written in the newspapers that he was murdered. I don't want to show no respect to the dead but he wasn't a very good bookkeeper. There were problems with payments from the start. He might have made some enemies.'

'I doubt anyone would kill him for an overdue account,' says Hazel.

Mr Kovac looks down at the note in his hand. 'Did this Russian do this murder? Is that why you want to know all about these letters?'

Hazel shakes her head. 'The day of the fire in the bond store, I saw a young woman in the window of the building. She wrote this on the glass.'

'She wrote this for you?'

'Yes, so I feel some responsibility to find out why.'

'The shoemaker has many Russian customers, they all know each other. He is a very good shoemaker who can make the proper European shoes. Not many can do this. Make a visit with him. Don't forget to tell him my name.'

After work, Hazel walks down to Fort Street to find the shoemaker. His workshop is in a building that has been divided up into small workshops and offices, mostly related to the surrounding garment factories. Many of the doors in the dimly lit 4th-floor corridor have handwritten signs in other languages. She passes a milliner's workshop. The door is open and two women work at a table covered in fabrics and colourful netting, while they listen to the radio. In another office, an older couple sit surrounded by clothing on racks as they work on industrial overlocking machines.

The shoemaker's door is closed but she can hear the sound of tapping inside. She knocks on the door and opens it, reeling back at the powerful animal smell in the room. Leather hides are stretched out on a long table and along the back wall are shelves stacked with dozens of pairs of shoes in various stages of construction.

Mr Sapozhnik sits at a foot-shaped anvil tapping on a piece of leather.

'Yes?' he asks, scowling at her through shaggy black eyebrows.

'Hello. I'm Mrs Bates. Mr Kovac recommended I speak to you. I have some Russian I need translated.'

He taps at the leather with a tiny hammer for a full minute without speaking.

'I am not the library. This is a business here.' He pulls the leather from the anvil with a flourish, tosses it into a pile and selects another piece from the table. 'Give to me.'

Hazel puts the note in front of him. He stares at it for a second. 'Get out. Take it.' He throws the scrap of paper at her, waving her out.

Taken aback by his furious response, Hazel is not deterred. 'Is it something bad? Even so, I need to know. It's very important.'

'Is better you don't know.' Taking up his hammer, he belts at the leather. 'You look like nice lady. Now you get out!'

'I am a nice lady,' agrees Hazel. 'I need to help someone. A young woman I think might be in trouble.'

He pauses his hammering and looks at her through the thicket of his brows. 'If she is in trouble with this man, you cannot help her.'

'So it's a name?' asks Hazel. 'Surely you can tell me.'

'Is a name. Now take it and go. You see I have work to do.' He stands up from his stool and begins to rummage through a sack of offcuts, deliberately ignoring her.

'I will have to ask someone else. Mr Kovac said there are many Russians—'

He turns with a furious look. 'Don't ask no one. You understand? Throw the paper away. Forget it.'

'I can't forget it,' says Hazel firmly.

The shoemaker works on the new piece of leather but Hazel stands her ground and waits. Finally, he says, 'Borisyuk.'

'That's the name?'

'Is the name of a man you will wish you never heard. Now go.'

'Thank you,' says Hazel. She leaves his workshop with the name ringing in her head. *Borisyuk*. It's not much to go on but a lot more than she had when she arrived.

16

BETTY BAKES BUTTERFLIES

The last to arrive today, Betty settles her cushion on the wall beside the others. She gets out her packed lunch and looks up and down the lane approvingly. 'I think the laneway is much cleaner than it was before the fire.'

'*Th*ill *th*inks of *th*moke,' says Irene, puffing away on her pipe.

Merl gives her a distasteful look. 'Where are your teeth, for goodness sakes?'

'Probably fell down behind the bed, I dunno.'

'It's not that awful landlady of yours holding them hostage again?' asks Betty, who secretly loves hearing tales about Irene's horrid landlady.

Irene reflects on that possibility. 'They *dith*appeared in the night.'

'Oh she's a nasty piece of work, that one,' says Betty. 'Fancy kidnapping someone's choppers!'

'Well, if you don't own anything of value . . .' Merl purses her lips. 'I expect Irene frittered the rent money away on alcohol and greyhounds.'

'Don't worry, I'll sort you out for the rent, Irene dear,' says Hazel.

'We'll get your teeth back where they belong.'

Merl gives a disapproving huff and changes the subject. 'It seems impossible that everyone is still talking about this silly Derby Day dress.'

'Oh! Yes!' says Betty. 'Our place is in such a spin about that dress . . . if you'd call it a dress. It's more like a long top.'

Irene nods. 'My lot are worried the bottom*th* going to drop out of knitwear.'

'The twinset will never go out of style,' says Merl, with conviction. 'And cardigans . . . what would we do without cardies in winter? Even young people can't wander around in a sleeveless frock all year round. It's not practical.'

'I heard there might be some cancelled orders,' says Betty, who has made eavesdropping her top priority this week. 'Seems ridiculous over one dress.'

'It's not just one dress. I think it's a sign of something to come,' says Hazel. 'From what I can gather, this has been brewing overseas for a while. Now it's reached us, things will likely change.'

'Nonsense, a complete overreaction if you ask me,' says Merl. 'It won't affect Klein's Lingerie. Women will always want negligee and corsetry, suspenders, silk stockings . . . What is a honeymoon without a chiffon nightie?'

'That girl did not look like she was wearing corsets or stockings,' says Betty, annoyed by Merl's smug confidence.

Irene reveals her pink gums in a grin. 'Did yer *th*ee the boyfriend? The *Th*rimpton girl would be wearing her birthday *th*uit, I reckon.'

'Honestly, Irene,' says Merl. 'You've got a one-track mind.'

'Now, I have some news,' says Hazel. 'Remember the letters the woman wrote on the window?'

'MW,' confirms Betty.

'Thank you, Betty. Apparently it is a person's name: Borisyuk. I found out that he's a Russian and someone to steer clear of.'

'Oh, good work, Hazel. Let me get that down.' Betty hums happily to herself as she makes notes and reads out: 'Fire, murder, leaves no leaves, MW, PI, that's private investigator, Laxettes . . .' She frowns. 'Wrong list, sorry . . . I'm adding dangerous Russian (Borisyuk) and the missing choppers.'

Hazel nods. 'That's enough to be going on with. Not sure we need Irene's dentures on there, I expect they'll turn up when the rent's paid.'

Betty agrees, admiring Hazel's clarity of thought, and crosses that one out.

'I can't see these things being connected,' says Merl. 'Why would someone follow you? No offence, Hazel, but you are just a tea lady.'

Betty has an idea and raises her hand. 'Perhaps the PI was after a cuppa?'

'Interesting thought, Betty,' says Hazel. 'But I think it's about something quite different. I just don't know what.'

'I think we *th*ould pay the *Th*inclair character a vi*th*it.'

'Irene, I have a suggestion,' says Betty. 'Try to avoid the letter "s" – we can't understand what you're saying.'

'There's plenty of toothless people around who can speak normally, Irene. I don't know why you have to make such a meal of it,' says Merl.

'According to the phone book, Sinclair's office is in Elizabeth Bay,' says Hazel.

'Oh, that's very posh up there,' says Betty, quite impressed. 'There's moneyed people and all sorts live around there. That makes him seem more professional, don't you think?'

'I suppose so but I can't see any point going to see him,' says Hazel. 'He's not going to reveal who hired him.'

'We go when . . . he not there,' suggests Irene, navigating around the letter s.

'No, Irene. We're not going to do that,' says Hazel.

'Up to you,' says Irene. 'But if man tracking yer, better get jump on him.'

'Now you sound as if you don't speak English. I honestly wish you'd just keep your mouth closed, Irene,' says Merl. 'It's putting me off my lunch.' She folds up her lunch wrap with a sigh. 'I'm going back to work.'

'Merl! Don't go yet.' Betty has been saving her treat for last. She gets a cake tin out of her bag, taking care not to drop it on the ground (as has happened before) and opens it to reveal four butterfly cakes with fresh cream and strawberry jam tucked under their tiny wings.

Merl takes one, casts a critical eye over it, lifts off the wings and pops them in her mouth. She licks her lips and bestows the royal nod of approval in Betty's direction. And even though Betty does not need Merl's approval, her face grows warm with pride. After all, Merl not only has a Mix Master but also a proper electric stove, whereas Betty only has a little stovette, which adds an extra layer of difficulty.

'Hah! Don't even need me clacker*th* for thi*th*,' Irene says, sinking her gums into the delicate little cake.

Merl stares off in the other direction. 'I can't watch. It's too awful.'

'Delicious, Betty dear, as always,' says Hazel.

17

HAZEL PUZZLES OVER BOB

Without Bob, the house on Glade Street seems empty and lonely tonight. They had recently discussed getting a television but Hazel was resistant. She enjoys their companionable evenings and wouldn't welcome the intrusion of a television set, as well as the extra cost of the licence. But this evening she wishes there was something to distract her from the nagging worry that something strange is going on with Bob. That coughing fit wasn't caused by a piece of gristle. It was her mention of the name Bateman. Bates and Bateman, two quite different names, but one containing the other.

While he is a very honest man, like many men, Bob does enjoy getting away with things, sometimes boasting like a schoolboy who's wagged school. At one time, he used to place his bets with a local butcher who had a sideline as an illegal SP bookie. Bob found it amusing to order half a pound of mince and five bob each way on the three o'clock at Randwick. When the butcher ended up murdered in his own cold room (the newspapers gleefully report-ing his habit of keeping money inside his prosthetic leg), it gave

Bob a scare but he still dined out on the tale. He liked to dabble with risk but not danger.

There are other small things that Hazel never asks about, like the boxes of malt whiskey he buys from someone at the Commercial Travellers' Association. She's well aware that many people have no hesitation when it comes to getting something cheap or free. For example, it's a wonder that the brewery has anything left given the amount Mr Mulligan spirits away to sell at his back gate. She wouldn't ever put Bob in that category but could he be involved in something slightly dodgy and have used the name Bateman as an alias? What if he'd got himself in debt with a loan shark? Perhaps this Philip Sinclair is after him for money? The last thing Hazel would ever want to do is get Bob into trouble. Whatever is going on, he must have good reason to keep it from her.

Lost in thought, Hazel finds herself standing in the front room gazing at the framed photograph of Bob's mother, as if it might hold the answer to the mystery. A pretty young woman, she wears a high-necked blouse, her long hair caught in a graceful bun. There's a studio backdrop behind her and Hazel assumes the family must have been fairly wealthy to afford a professional photographer, although Bob has never mentioned that.

When she met Bob, he had been a widower for many years. He never talks about his first wife at all, apart from saying that they married young and had no children. Hazel has never met Bob's mother, who has been senile for years and lives in a nursing home in Grafton. But Bob still visits her every week and Hazel admires his devotion.

It suddenly occurs to Hazel that perhaps she has never known Bob to tell a lie because she's protected him from having to tell one. She never pries or cross-examines him; she's never wanted to be that sort of wife. But has she unwittingly shielded him from her radar? It had taken her years to realise exactly what was going on with her ears and understand that she possessed a unique gift. These days, she quickly picks up on the sensations that vary in intensity from a faint tingling around the rim of her ears (a little lie) to an uncomfortable throbbing (an absolute whopper). She'd never seen it as magical, simply a different form of gut instinct. She can't even say it's infallible because how can you ever know what lies people get away with? She wonders now if her love for Bob has given him immunity to her powers, and what could that mean?

18

BETTY IN DANGER

Just as she's about to get into bed, Betty hears a knock on the front door. The widow upstairs never has visitors, so it can only be for Betty or the wrong house. She puts on her brunch coat and goes out into the hallway. Keeping the safety chain on, she opens the door a crack to find a small figure in a huge black coat standing on the doorstep.

'Irene? What's happened?'

'Nothing yet. Something's gunna happen,' she says with a grin.

Betty is relieved to see Irene's teeth are back in their rightful place.

'Open the bloody door, will yer?'

'Shhh, you'll wake the old girl upstairs. I'm about to go to bed, Irene, it's after nine,' says Betty, unhooking the safety chain.

Irene steps inside and nudges the door closed behind her. 'I need yer help.'

'Oh my goodness gracious! I just know I'm not going to like this. It's going to be dangerous or illegal or both. I don't want to do it and you can't make me.'

'It's something we gotta do for Hazel,' says Irene.

Betty gathers her brunch coat tightly around her. 'You're just saying that to make me do something I don't want to do! No. What is it?'

'We're gunna pay a quick visit to that private eye.'

Betty thinks about this for a moment. 'Irene, I'm not breaking into someone's office. That's illegal. What if we get caught?'

'We won't get caught. We'll be in and out before you know it. We'll be invisible.'

Betty pushes past her and opens the front door. 'We're not invisible! And not above the law! Go home. I'm going to bed.'

'Hazel's not herself. I can see it, I'm sensitive like that.'

Betty frowns at this unlikely claim. 'That's nice, Irene, but I don't see how this is going to help her.'

'We have to find out who hired this Sinclair bloke . . . that's all I'm asking. For Hazel.'

Betty sighs. Irene knows she would do anything for Hazel. It's her weakness. She thinks of the warm bed awaiting her and turns her thoughts to Hazel, who truly hasn't been herself lately. 'Let me get my coat on,' she says finally, heaving a sigh to make sure Irene is aware of the sacrifice she's making.

The evening streets are quiet, which is fortunate because absolutely everyone turns to stare at the dreadful old motorcycle, a relic from the war that Irene has borrowed, as it clatters past. Betty, squashed in the precarious sidecar, has visions of parting ways with the motorcycle and flying off across the street. The only thing stopping her tumbling out is a metal bar and a piece of canvas clipped across the entry to the sidecar. She grips the metal bar tightly with both hands and wails every time they bump over a pothole. When they make a sharp left-hand turn, the wheel of the sidecar mounts the curb and thumps back onto the road, almost bouncing Betty out.

'I'm getting the bus back!' she screams over the roar of the engine.

'Suit yerself,' shouts Irene.

Irene manages to both smoke (ash blowing into Betty's eyes) and talk all the way to Elizabeth Bay. Distracted by the task of staying alive, Betty can only hear fragments and doesn't care what Irene has to say anyway.

The place is not difficult to find. They roar past the building in question and pull over further up the street. A woman, walking two Dalmatians, stops to stare at them as Irene helps Betty climb shakily out of the sidecar. Irene scowls furiously at the woman, muttering about nosy parkers. Betty considers this a bit rich given the woman is walking her dogs and they're planning a break-in. At that thought, Betty is appalled all over again at what she's got herself into, now on the brink of tears.

'We'll wait around the corner till the old bag goes,' says Irene.

Betty ducks her head down, hoping the woman won't be able to describe her to the police. She imagines her face on a wanted poster (Dead or Alive) outside the police station and wishes she'd taken her curlers out. 'I can't believe you talked me into this,' she says, as Irene manhandles her around the corner.

As soon as they're out of sight, Irene lights up a cigarette and leans against a wall blowing smoke rings into the still night air – as if she doesn't have a care in the world.

'I'm only doing this for Hazel, you know,' Betty reminds her crossly.

'What? I'm doing it for me own entertainment, am I?'

'Why did you have to drag me along, Irene? You could do it on your own.'

'It takes two to tango,' says Irene.

'What's that supposed to mean?' asks Betty.

'Yer need two for this game.'

'What about cat burglars? Cary Grant managed all right on his own, climbing over roofs and getting into rich ladies' jewellery boxes.'

'Do I look like a cat burglar? If yer wanna go up the drainpipe, be me guest.'

Betty has to admit that Irene, in her ratty old coat and slippers, and that dreadful crushed hat, bears no resemblance to the glamorous burglars of the movie world. And she suspects this story will not have a romantic ending.

Irene takes a flask from her pocket. She has a nip and smacks her lips. 'Want one?'

'No, I don't. I also don't think you should be drinking at a time like this.'

'No harm in a little sharpener. Come on, let's go.'

Sinclair's office is located in a two-storey building with three wide steps that lead off the street to a semi-enclosed verandah. There are windows on either side of the main door and one has 'Philip Sinclair – Private Investigator' in gold lettering on the glass.

Standing on the verandah in the shadows, they peer into the dark office. The next thing Betty knows, Irene has quietly prised one of the windows open. She shrugs off her coat and hands it to Betty. She pulls herself up over the sill and inside the building, nimble as a little monkey. A moment later she opens the front door and silently beckons Betty into the building.

Inside, Irene takes her coat back, pulls a torch out of the pocket and flashes it around the entry area. A sign for Sinclair's office points to the first floor and she hurries off up the stairs. Betty follows, her tummy aching with anxiety. 'Oops, pardon me,' she says three times in quick succession (and feels some relief!).

'Carburettor trouble, eh?' remarks Irene, examining the lock on Sinclair's office door by the light of the torch. 'Yer wanna get that seen to before yer blow a gasket.'

'It's not a joke, Irene. It's my nerves.'

Irene grunts with amusement. She inserts a thin metal rod into the lock and opens the door. 'All right, don't move nothing,' she says, when they step inside the office. 'Everything stays put.' She hands Betty a pair of white cotton gloves (the sort ladies wear to church) and flicks the torch around the office to reveal a large four-drawer filing cabinet, a bookcase filled with thick law books, several pot plants and a desk with neatly ordered files.

'Take a look at them files on the desk while I pop this open,' says Irene, training the torch on the filing cabinet.

Betty fumbles through the files on the desk with trembling hands in slippery gloves. She works in silence, her mouth too dry to speak in any case. She picks up several manila folders. In the dim light from the street lamp outside, she can see that the files have two surnames written in the top right-hand corner. She supposes that one must be the name of the client and the other the subject of investigation.

'Here yer go,' says Irene, pulling open the top drawer of the filing cabinet.

Betty looks at the row of folders, dozens of them – and that's just one drawer! Tears of despair well up. 'We'll be here all night!'

'Stop blubbing and get on with it, will yer?'

Betty gets on with it, flicking through the files as quickly as she can without missing any. 'Hold the torch higher, can you?'

'Can't yers go any faster?' asks Irene.

'I want to get out of here as much as you do!'

'Yeah? I gotta get that bike back before me neighbour gets home.'

Betty pauses to stare at her. 'I thought you said you borrowed it?'

'I did. The bloke's on night shift. He won't know. Just get on with it.'

Betty pulls off the gloves and doubles her speed, imagining her fingerprints illuminated under a blue light. At the back of the second drawer she finds a file marked Herrmann/Bateman and remembers Hazel mentioning this name that day at the Delphi Milk Bar. She takes it over to the desk. Inside are half-a-dozen black-and-white photographs: Hazel and Bob kissing goodbye at the station, Hazel walking home, coming out of the corner shop, and the house in Glade Street. There's a sheet of negatives in the file and a piece of paper with times and locations written on it.

'Just take the file,' says Irene. 'Come on, hurry up.'

'That's stealing! What if Hazel gets blamed?'

'Betty, no one will suspect Hazel. The snoop won't even know we was here.' Irene closes the drawer, gives the lock a tweak with her metal rod and tests it with a tug. 'Good as new. Let's go.'

Betty waits breathlessly on the landing while Irene locks the office door behind them.

They're halfway down the stairs when a car pulls up in front of the building. The car door opens and Betty can hear the faint static of a two-way radio. 'Irene, it's the police!' she sobs, turning back to scramble upstairs.

Behind her, Irene hurries back up. On the first-floor landing, she drops to her knees and grabs Betty's wrist. 'Get down, will yer?'

'I won't be able to get up again . . . my knees and I've got that clicky—'

Irene gives her a yank, almost pulling her off her feet. 'Shut up,' she hisses.

Betty lies on her belly, trembling and weeping silently. From this angle they can see two dark figures walking back and forth on the verandah. Torchlight flicks in through the windows.

'Did you lock that window?' whispers Betty.

'What do yer take me for?'

The front door handle rattles and the powerful beam of the police torch picks its way up the stairs, stopping barely a foot away from them. It swings back and forth across the entrance area and then snaps off, leaving the building in darkness. The silence is broken by the crackle of the radio as the car door opens and slams shut.

Betty gasps with relief as the vehicle slides away into the night. 'I hate you, Irene,' she says, staggering to her feet. 'I'm not joking. That took ten years off my life. Minimum. My blood pressure is *through the roof!*'

Irene laughs. 'At least yer know yer alive. Come on, old chook. Let's see if there's a back way out, just to be safe.'

19

A DAY OF RUFFLED FEATHERS

'Mr Kovac, I'm wondering if you actually met Mr McCracken when you picked up your cheque?' asks Hazel, as the delivery driver unloads his van on Friday morning.

'Yes. I saw him for a short period of time. He was coming out of his office when I arrived. He went back and got the cheque for me. I hear they still haven't caught the murderer,' Mr Kovac says, closing the back doors. 'Do you think it could possibly have been someone in the firm?'

'I doubt it. More likely that Mr McCracken startled an intruder.'

'He and the young Mr Karp obviously knew each other well.'

'Why do you say that?' asks Hazel.

'I hadn't met Mr McCracken before but I recognised him. I've seen the two of them in the Mermaid Club. Please let me assure you this is not a place that I visit for pleasure. I deliver goods there and take them into a cupboard off the bar area. I wouldn't set foot in that place otherwise.'

'They were together?' asks Hazel. 'Frankie Karp and Mr McCracken?'

Mr Kovac nods. 'That day the bar was almost empty, so I noticed them there, drinking together. I have also seen Mr Frankie Karp in the little park up the street a couple of times.'

He gestures towards the top of the lane. 'He was talking to a man, I think it was Mr McCracken. I noticed Mr Karp because he's a smart dresser and it is a dirty little park, so it seemed strange to me that a man of his importance would want to meet someone there.'

After he leaves, Hazel walks up to Lisbon Street. It's busy at this time of day with people going off to work. The small reserve across the road barely qualifies as a park, just a scuffed area of grass with a couple of trees where drunks sleep on newspapers at night. It seems a very unlikely place for Frankie to meet anyone, particularly McCracken when they could just as easily have talked in the office. Perhaps Mr Kovac was mistaken about that, but then he saw them together at the Mermaid Club. Based on that, it seems unlikely that Frankie doesn't know anything about McCracken's background.

'Don't worry about me, Hazel,' says Edith Stern. 'They're both out for the day. I can get my own tea, give you a break.'

Taking no notice, Hazel brings her tea and biscuits. 'You look as if you could do with a cup of tea, Edith dear.'

'Thank you. You know, Hazel, I never liked that McCracken man but the fact of a murder in this building, and one of our staff, it's rattled everyone. Then on top of that, the cancelled orders.' She nods her head in the direction of the Karps' offices. 'Right now, these two argue all day long.'

'They've always argued. You know they're just thinking out loud.'

'I wish they'd learn to think silently, like normal people,' insists Edith. 'They've gone off with Mr Fysh to meet with the department store buyers today.' She pulls a sheet of paper out of her typewriter with a sigh. 'This is a letter to the bank requesting an extension to the overdraft. All these years we've run in the black, now we're in the red. The last thing we need right now is for the firm to go bust. Who would hire us at our age, Hazel? I'll never get another job.'

'Edith, you would be a boon to any firm. I'm sure you would be snapped up.'

'I don't think so. These days they want pretty young things to brighten up the office like pot plants. What do they care about shorthand typing speeds? They use dictaphones and the girls just plonk out letters with two fingers while their nail polish is drying.'

'We'll pull through, Edith, I know we will.'

'I hope you're right, Hazel, and not just being chirpy for the sake of it.'

Hazel laughs. 'Tell me, do you know how Frankie found Mr McCracken? Was it an ad in the paper, or an employment agency?'

'It wasn't an ad or an agency. He was personally recommended by one of Frankie's business associates, as far as I know.'

'But why hire him at the expense of Mr Levy?' asks Hazel.

'Frankie has no loyalty to staff, you know that. According to him, the man was some sort of financial whiz, set to revolutionise the place. It's probably no coincidence that we're now in trouble.' Edith cranks a fresh sheet of paper into her typewriter and taps furiously at the keys. Glancing up to see Hazel still there, she adds, 'Hazel, I don't have all day to sit around gossiping, you know. I do have work to do.'

Blunt and sharp at the same time, Edith has a habit of dressing like a headmistress, her thick greying bob held in place with tortoiseshell combs, and black-framed glasses on a pale, angular face. But Hazel knows that beneath her cranky exterior, she's shrewd and observant. She lost her husband to the war and still lives with her demanding mother-in-law, a responsibility she has never managed to shake. She has known a life of loss, grief and disappointment, and Hazel is extremely fond of her.

On the 1st Floor, Pixie comes flying out of the dressmaking room, almost colliding with Hazel's trolley, and runs off down the hall. Hazel opens the door to overhear Miss Joan saying, 'You can't speak to her like that. You'll get us both into trouble.' The sisters stand at their long workbench, today covered in bolts of fabric and brown-paper patterns. At the sound of Hazel's trolley, both look up guiltily.

'She's rude and insolent,' says Miss Ivy for Hazel's benefit. 'Thinks she owns the place.'

Hazel pours their tea and adds a Ginger Nut to each saucer. 'I imagine she will one day.'

'Pffft! I hope I'm dead by then!' says Miss Ivy. 'All she had to do was collect the buttons and a sample book of fabrics we ordered from Greenfields. But the stupid girl went to a coffee shop and lost the sample book!'

'I'm sure we can get it back,' says Hazel. 'And it won't be the only one.'

'It was the new fabric samples for the summer season,' says Miss Joan. 'We had Mr Fysh, Mr Karp and Frankie all down here yesterday telling us to do something *different*. No one knows what. We are not magicians. We need time and research and direction. Not tantrums. Now this!'

Miss Ivy sips her tea and nibbles fretfully on her biscuit. 'Frankie was talking about importing goods from overseas. That will be the end of us. Twenty-two years we have been here.'

'He's thinking aloud,' says Hazel, for the second time in an hour.

Miss Joan agrees. 'We all know the import tax will make that unprofitable.'

'Perhaps Pixie has some ideas—' begins Hazel.

'Pixie is a very unreliable young person,' says Miss Joan. 'With poor taste.'

'Most of us were unreliable as young people,' ventures Hazel.

'*We* did not have the chance to be unreliable,' says Miss Ivy. 'We were orphans, living on our own in a strange country. This girl has been served her life on a silver plate.'

Difficult and demanding as they can be, Hazel has always felt sympathetic towards the sisters. When the war broke out, the two young women were put on a ship from Hamburg and sailed into the unknown. Neither had worked a day in their lives but they understood clothes and good tailoring. They learnt to sew onboard the ship and as soon as they arrived in Sydney, invested in a sewing machine. In the small room they shared in a boarding house, they began to make hand-embroidered blouses. When they had a dozen or so, they went out to show their goods. They often reminisce about those days of working through the night to fulfil orders. Somewhere along the way, Mr Karp saw their work and offered them positions as seamstresses in his new enterprise.

'But Pixie clearly admires you both,' says Hazel. 'Your design skills and talents.'

'Oh, Mrs Bates, you want to sweeten us. Your flattery will not work,' says Miss Joan.

'Pixie thinks we are two silly old women who don't know anything,' adds Miss Ivy.

Hazel offers them both another Ginger Nut. 'I can assure you that is not the case. She has nothing but respect and admiration for you.'

'And so she should,' says Miss Joan, waving the offer away. 'We expect that from her.'

'What did she say about us, precisely?' asks Miss Ivy, reaching for another biscuit.

20

CONFESSIONS AT THE DELPHI

When Mrs Angelos brings their pots of tea over to the table, Hazel forgets to say thank you at all, let alone in Greek. She's been rendered speechless. So has Merl, evidently. She gets out her knitting and attacks the tiny primrose matinee jacket with angry, stabbing needles.

Hazel looks from Betty to Irene and back again. 'I'm very grateful to you both for doing this for me, but—'

'You are a danger to yourself and others, Irene!' says Merl so loudly that a couple seated in the next booth glance around in alarm.

'Merl dear, do keep your voice down,' says Hazel, demonstrating a hushed tone.

Merl continues, 'What were you thinking, Betty? I'm shocked at the both of you. What if you'd been arrested and charged? Can you imagine the headlines?'

'What about "Tea Ladies in Hot Water"? They can have that for a small fee.' Irene cackles with laughter until it turns into a coughing fit.

Betty looks shamefaced and tearful. 'I didn't want to do it. Irene made me.'

'Did she have a gun?' asks Merl sarcastically.

'Probably,' mutters Betty. 'She keeps all sorts of things in that coat.'

Merl's still bristling with anger and Hazel knows that it's only a matter of time before she identifies some personal slight in this escapade. Sure enough, a moment later Merl continues, 'You could end up in prison and bring our whole profession into disrepute, and here am I, associating with criminals when my son-in-law's a high-ranking police detective.'

'Yer'll have more in common with him now,' says Irene, with a sly grin.

Predictably, Merl is not amused. 'I've got a good mind to report you myself.'

'I think we all understand what Merl's saying,' says Hazel, hoping to defuse the situation. 'I am very touched, but taking that risk—'

'I agree with Hazel,' says Betty. 'And Merl. We never should have done it. We could have given tea ladies everywhere a bad name. I didn't even think of that.'

Merl points a knitting needle at Irene. '*You* are turning Betty into a hardened criminal.'

Irene lights up and puffs away furiously on her cigarette. No one objects.

'Anyway, it's done now,' says Hazel. 'Was it worth all that trouble?'

'Go on, Betty, tell her,' says Irene. 'Tell her what we got.'

Betty fumbles through her shopping bag until she finds the file. 'Here it is.' She puts it on the table halfway between Merl and Hazel. 'On the front, it says Herrmann slash Bateman. The client is this Mrs Deborah Herrmann – double *r*, double *n*. It seems a bit silly having all those extra letters but she lives in Rose Bay, so she probably knows what she's doing.'

Merl glances up from her knitting. 'I hope you're not planning to break into Mrs Herrmann's place now.'

Irene shrugs thoughtfully. 'Rich pickin's up that end of town.'

Hazel glances through the file at the photographs of her and Bob and her little house on Glade Street, and a list of times and places, disturbed by what she sees. There was no sign that Sinclair had a camera and yet he was able to capture these private moments in her life.

'Another continental name,' says Betty. 'Mrs Herrmann could be MW!'

Merl shakes her head. 'Mystery Woman is Russian, this name is German.'

'She could be a Russian who married a German,' insists Betty. 'We don't know for sure that she's not this Mrs Herrmann woman – and now she's after Hazel!'

Hazel closes the file and places a calming hand on Betty's arm. 'Betty dear, you have an important role as our note keeper. We're relying on you to stick to the facts. If the file has the name Bateman, then Sinclair possibly didn't know my real name until I confirmed it.' Hazel thinks back to Bob's reaction when she mentioned the incident to him. It seems disloyal but, with the risks that Irene and Betty have taken on her behalf, it doesn't seem right to keep his response to herself. 'Bob had heard the name Bateman before, I'm quite certain of it. In fact, after I mentioned it, he was a bit peculiar the whole weekend.'

Merl pauses her knitting and peers at Hazel over the top of her glasses. 'I see.'

'What do you mean?' asks Betty.

'Preoccupied, not wanting to go out. He just wasn't himself at all.' Hazel gathers her thoughts and continues, 'I think this business is quite separate from the other business. We need to assume they are separate for the moment, otherwise we might be forcing things to fit.'

'On that note, I have new information about the McCracken case,' says Merl. 'It seems he boarded in a house in Annandale. The people in the house barely saw him so the police haven't found out any more—'

Betty sighs. 'I'm going to need a bigger notebook at this rate.'

'Can you not interrupt me please, Betty?' Merl casts off, flicking each stitch into a tight knot. 'According to Detective Pierce, they've come to a dead end.'

Betty raises her hand. 'So how did he get the job at Empire? He must have had references.'

'Frankie hired him,' says Hazel. 'There's something odd about that too.'

'Do yer always call him Detective Pierce, even when he comes around for a cup of tea?' Irene asks Merl.

'He doesn't often come around for tea,' says Merl. 'He's a very busy man.'

'He seems to have a lot of time to gossip about police business,' says Irene.

'I don't always get my information directly from him.'

'What d'yer mean?' asks Irene, determined not to let this rest.

'I get tidbits from my daughter sometimes.'

'Thought he was yer best mate,' says Irene. 'Couldn't wait to tell yers about the case. And how come he's at Surry Hills cop shop now? Was he kicked out of Criminal Investigations Branch?'

'Oh, Irene, stop stirring!' says Betty. 'We've got work to do.'

'It's really not our business,' says Merl in an icy tone. 'And, as I have said many times, in my opinion we should leave crime solving to the police and stick to our biscuits.'

'I reckon yer wrong,' says Irene. 'I reckon, right now, we know more than the coppers.'

'And we haven't even started!' cries Betty, flapping her notebook excitedly.

'Let's hear what yer got,' says Irene, giving Betty a wink.

'Must we?' sighs Merl.

Betty opens her notebook and reads: 'McCracken dead end. Herrmann double *r*, double *n* slash Sinclair. Bates slash Bateman. What's up with Bob?'

That is the biggest question Hazel has right now: What is up with Bob? It's constantly on her mind and this new information has only made it more worrying. What could Sinclair possibly want from her – and who is Mrs Herrmann?

21

RUMBLINGS DOWNSTAIRS

There was a time when Gloria Nuttell dreamt of moving upstairs to the 2nd Floor. From factory supervisor to Queen Bee was quite a leap. She imagined herself clipping about in high heels and a full-skirted frock, her manicured fingernails tapping out complex calculations on the adding machine while fending off invitations to engagement parties and whatnot. There she was, swanning about, far above the grime and roar of the factory floor.

Upstairs have a strict dress code: no pants allowed and stockings must be worn all year round. The Bees have to look well groomed, unlike in the factory where most wear smocks and anything goes. On hot afternoons, when the machinists' hands get sweaty and needles end up through fingernails, they often strip down to their slips to find some relief from the heat. No one is too fussed and Mr Butterby always pretends he hasn't even noticed they're half undressed.

Much as the idea of being a Queen Bee is appealing, Gloria knows her place is down here. This is the job she knows inside out and does well. On top of that, she and the girls are always having a laugh about something. The only really quiet one in the factory is Alice, the polio girl. She never strips down or wears rollers on Fridays, which makes sense since she can't go out dancing like the other girls. She never joins in when everyone sings along to the latest pop song on the radio, even though there's nothing holding her back in that department. Even the Greek ladies clap along or dance a few steps to get a laugh. She seems like a nice enough kid but not very friendly and a bit snooty. Probably she thinks she's too good for this place but where else would she get a job with a bung leg like that?

Today, for some reason, Hazel asks Gloria to take Alice's tea over to her worktable.

'Are they going to be laying girls off, Mrs Nuttell?' asks Alice.

'What makes you ask that?' snaps Gloria.

Alice looks startled. 'I overheard a conversation in the hall between old Mr Karp and Frankie. They were talking about cutting back because of some cancelled orders.'

'They won't cut back down here,' says Gloria, with more certainty than she feels. 'When the new designs are done, we'll be doing overtime to get the range ready. We'll need everyone here and more besides.' She glances over at Hazel, quietly collecting up the cups, and wonders if she knows more about the situation.

'My roommate works at Farley's,' continues Alice. 'She said they're going all out to do a new range.' She reaches under her worktable and pulls out some magazines.

'Have you heard of Mary Quant?' she asks. Spreading magazines out in front of Gloria, she opens one to show her. 'These frocks are very simple to make, and cheap too. There's so little finishing compared to what we do now with pleats and trimmings and double-ended darts.' She points out a photograph of a model wearing a plain black-and-white shift, the hemline well above the knee. 'Look, two darts . . . or no darts; you can have a zip or just a loop button; and the neck and sleeve trim can be bias binding with no lining.'

It's the most Gloria has ever heard the girl say. Her sad little face is all lit up as if she's now some sort of expert in the fashion world.

'In case you haven't noticed, in this place the designs come from upstairs and the Ginger Nuts are not interested in anyone else's ideas.' At Alice's puzzled expression, Gloria clarifies, 'The Rosenbaum sisters, you dope. And Mr Know-It-All Frankie, even worse. You can't tell him anything. Upstairs have the ideas. We do the work. They get the credit. We keep our jobs. That's how it goes. We don't need to waste our money on fashion magazines. Just keep our heads down.'

Alice gazes up at her. 'But if there's a problem with the current line, couldn't we at least put forward some ideas?' Her plummy way of speaking gets up Gloria's nose, as does her belief that upstairs could give a stuff about what she thinks.

'Are you a commo or something?' asks Gloria, to her own surprise.

Alice blushes crimson. 'What?'

'D'you think this is some kind of'—Gloria pauses but can't think of the word—'place where the comrades all work together?'

'No, of course not . . . I just thought . . .'

'Upstairs are upstairs. Downstairs are downstairs.' Gloria has no idea where she's going with this but is getting more annoyed by the minute, unreasonably annoyed, even by her own reckoning. She turns away to see Hazel watching her curiously.

'What?!' she asks no one in particular and stamps off back to her alcove. She plonks herself down in her wobbly chair, wishing she had an office door to slam. Everything is all topsy-turvy around here right now. People getting murdered, buildings burning down, workers rising up and having opinions. Who knows where it will end?

22

A BREAKTHROUGH WITH BOB

For the first time that Hazel can recall, Bob is late home on Friday. He's always so punctual, it's disconcerting. He arrives almost half an hour late, murmuring about a meeting at Head Office. He takes her in his arms and holds her tightly against him, breathing a heartfelt sigh.

Hazel stands on her toes and kisses him. His mouth tastes of whiskey. She slips off his jacket and hangs it up. Hand-in-hand, they walk down to the kitchen.

As Bob chats about his day over dinner, she struggles to concentrate. Her mind is on the file from Sinclair's office, locked away in the kitchen dresser, wondering how to bring the subject up. Almost without thinking, she asks, 'Bob, does the name Herrmann mean anything to you? Mrs Deborah Herrmann?'

He gazes up at the ceiling as if concentrating hard but also avoiding her eye. 'No. Means nothing to me. Why do you ask?'

Hazel's fingertips go to her ears. She wonders if she's imagining the tingling sensation. Is it possible he's never told a blatant lie before? Or has the spell he cast over her now been broken? Distracted by this thought, she hardly knows how to respond. 'Bob, be honest with me, please.'

'I am being honest, my dear. I've never heard the name before. Why do you ask?'

Her ears are alight. Lie upon lie. 'Bob, it was this Mrs Herrmann who hired that private eye to follow me.'

The colour drains from his face. 'How do you know that? Where did you get that information?'

There are three people in the world that Hazel would trust with her life: her daughter, Norma; her dear friend Betty; and Bob. Now her world is tilting on its axis and she has to tread carefully. She pauses to consider how much to tell him. 'Just take it from me, Bob. I know with absolute certainty that Mrs Herrmann hired the man. Who is she? I think you know.'

He holds his hands up in mock defence. 'I'm telling you I don't know.'

Hazel can see there's no point in continuing with this approach and the awfulness of his dishonesty is turning her stomach. 'All right,' she says, diplomatically. 'Let's drop it for the moment.'

Later, as she stands at the sink, washing the dishes, Bob comes up behind her and wraps his arms around her. 'It's been a long day. Come on, little bunny, let's have a cuddle.'

She experiences a moment of resistance but he takes her hand and she goes with him upstairs to the bedroom where they lie down on the bed together. She has no doubt that Bob loves her and, sooner or later, he will come clean and admit whatever it is he's trying to conceal. They will sort it out together.

In his loving embrace, Hazel begins to relax. All at once, he releases her and rolls away on his side, his shoulders shaking.

For a split second, she imagines he's laughing but, to her horror, he's sobbing uncontrollably. Terrible gasps tear from his throat.

She sits up and rubs his shoulder, fear gripping her heart. 'What's going on, Bob? I need to know.'

'I'm sorry, love. It's nothing to do with you . . .' he says in a choked voice.

She gets up to find a clean handkerchief in the drawer. She sits down on the side of the bed and gives it to him. He looks so unwell: cheeks scarlet and eyes bloodshot. He sits up and blows his nose noisily.

'You couldn't get me a cuppa, could you, love?'

'Of course, dear,' she says, relieved he's not asking for something stronger but perhaps he's already had one too many – it's very unlike him to be so emotional.

The kettle takes forever to boil and it feels like an age before she's back at his side.

More composed, he accepts the tea gratefully. 'Not having one?'

It hadn't occurred to her to make herself one. 'You need to tell me what's going on, Bob.'

'I'm sorry. I just have an awful lot on my mind at the moment.'

'I'm your wife. We have to talk about these things. I must know what's happening.'

He gives a sigh. 'It's my mother. I saw her on Wednesday and she wasn't at all well. I'm worried the end is near. I'm sorry, my dear, I'm going to have to go back up to Grafton tomorrow.'

Trying to ignore her tingling ears, Hazel takes his hand. 'I can come with you, if you like.'

'Thank you, but she's a difficult old thing and I don't want you to see her at her worst . . . she's my responsibility and I will bear it alone.' He presses Hazel's hand to his lips. 'I wouldn't put you through that, my dear.'

Hazel wants to weep with disappointment. None of it is true. Not one single word. Oh, Bob, dear Bob, what on earth are you up to?

23

UNEXPECTED VISITORS

Hazel wakes early on Sunday morning with an empty day stretching ahead of her. The neighbour opposite came home late last night with all the usual shouting and banging, followed by the other neighbours howling at him to shut up, followed by the dogs barking – and on it went, the familiar Saturday-night chorus of Glade Street. On top of that, someone nearby has recently acquired a rooster so the whole neighbourhood is rudely woken by its cockadoodling at dawn. This morning, she keeps her eyes closed tightly, trying to imagine the crowing is the sound of the countryside and beyond her window are rolling fields, grazing cows and kookaburras cackling high in the gum trees. But that image is quickly shattered by someone close by bellowing at the rooster.

Facing a day on her own worrying about Bob, she puts on her dressing gown and goes downstairs to make a cup of tea. While the kettle boils, she gazes out the kitchen window and considers how best to spend her day. The morning sky is already a bright enamel blue with the promise of a warm November day ahead.

Fortified by tea, she goes outside to the washhouse. Her wine-making equipment is packed up in a box on the shelf. She gets it down and checks everything she needs is there. All the jars and bottles have to be sterilised but it would be pleasant to take her shopping trolley down to the Haymarket. There are often damaged bits and pieces left from the Saturday-night market that are suitable for making into wine. Some rhubarb or honeydew melon would be nice.

Or else, she could take the Mulligan kiddies on a picnic to the park. It won't matter how dirty they get since tonight's bath night. There are sausages in the fridge she could turn into kiddie-sized sausage rolls. She has plenty of Granny Smiths and an apple cake would fill them up along with some egg-and-lettuce sandwiches. She will give the rabble a splendid day out while Mrs Mulligan enjoys Mass with her Hail Marys and confessions. In Hazel's opinion, Mrs Mulligan has nothing to confess; she's already a saint.

There's a knock on the front door and Hazel opens it to find her daughter, Norma, and twin grandsons, Barrie and Harry, on the doorstep. In a moment, her little house is full of life and warm embraces, the boys both talking at once, telling her excitedly how they had got up in the dark to drive to the city. 'It was the middle of the night, Nanna!'

'Why didn't you tell me you were coming?' asks Hazel. 'The tins are practically empty!'

'We wanted to surprise you, Mum,' says Norma, giving her another hug.

'Boys, run down to the corner shop and ask for a packet of crumpets and a tin of Milo on my account – a small tin, mind,' says Hazel.

Tripping over their own feet, the boys race out the door.

'Otherwise, perfect timing,' says Hazel. 'I'll just top up the teapot.'

Norma sits down at the kitchen table. 'Barrie has to see a specialist about his lazy eye tomorrow. So we'll stay a couple of nights, if that's all right. Where's Bob, having a lie-in?'

'You've missed him, it was a fleeting visit this week. His mother's not well. He came all the way down here on Friday and went back on Saturday.'

'Hmm, that is devoted,' says Norma, as if not entirely convinced.

The front door bursts open and the boys thunder down the hall, waving the packet of crumpets and a tin of Milo. Hazel pops two crumpets in the toaster. 'Now, what do we want on them, boys? Honey, jam or Vegemite?'

'Honeeeey,' they cry in unison.

'Settle down, boys,' says Norma. 'We're in the city now. People don't shout and run everywhere.'

'We saw a crazy man shouting at the station,' argues Harry.

'We don't want people thinking we're crazy, do we?'

'No,' agrees Barrie, the more serious of the twins. 'We definitely do not.'

'Now sit down while Nanna makes your breakfast.'

Norma is always firm with the boys and, most of the time, they obey without question. That's important on a farm, Norma always says. Children have to learn commonsense and self-control.

The four of them sit around the kitchen table eating hot-buttered crumpets dripping with honey. The boys chatter about their dog, Bessie, who has given birth to six puppies, and the tree that fell down on the implement shed. Norma catches Hazel's eye, and they exchange smiles. She leans over and plants a kiss on Hazel's cheek, saying how lovely it is to see her.

The Mulligans' picnic will have to be put off until another day –
it's not as if they knew about her plans. After breakfast, Hazel
and Norma prepare the sandwiches, apple cake and sausage rolls
for a picnic, and Hazel makes up a packet of blackcurrant jelly for
pudding this evening.

At ten o'clock they set off in Norma's car for the beach at
Nielsen Park. They spread the picnic rug on the grass under the
trees where they can look out to the pale turquoise of the shallows
and the deep blue beyond. The boys race across the white sand and
straight into the water. As their voices recede into the distance, the
two women have some quiet time to chat. Hazel had previously
mentioned the fire and McCracken's demise to Norma over the
phone, but now she explains the whole situation in detail.

'It seems strange that the police haven't found anything at all,'
muses Norma. 'They always know how fires are started, a fireman
told me that – there's always a starting point. But don't you get
involved, Mum. It all sounds very suspicious. I'm just sorry you
had to be the one to find him. What a terrible experience for
you. I don't know why you went into the building with that fire
next door.'

'Oh well, it's nothing to do with me now,' says Hazel. Keen to
change the subject, she asks, 'So what's happening on the farm,
apart from puppies and trees falling down?'

'Where do I start?' Norma laughs.

The afternoon drifts on, Hazel opens the cake tin and slices up
the apple cake, still warm from the oven, and Norma calls the boys
to come and eat. Before long it's time to pack up and go home. It's
been one of the loveliest days Hazel can remember in recent times,
and all the better for being a surprise.

24

NORMA MAKES A DISCOVERY

When they get home, Norma offers to go next door and help with the Mulligans' bath-time so that Hazel can spend more time with the twins. When she's gone, Hazel dishes out the jelly and ice-cream and mugs of hot cocoa. They sit at the kitchen table and play snakes and ladders, dominos and three rowdy games of animal snap with Harry honking like a goose and Barrie howling like a wolf, both drowning out Hazel's mild meows.

Once the boys have brushed their teeth, she takes them upstairs and sits on the bed while they take turns to read out entries from the encyclopaedia, which has become a family tradition over the years. They take up where they left off last time, after Hippocrates (whose significance was completely lost on the boys), the next entry being the Hippocratic Oath.

Barrie begins in a loud, clear voice but is soon stumbling over the difficult Greek names.

'Oh, this is so boring!' cries Harry.

'All right, let's go on to the next entry,' suggests Hazel.

Hippodrome also doesn't appeal, but Hippopotamus is more to

their liking and they laugh over the photograph of the odd, barrel-shaped creature. It seems only yesterday that Norma was working her way through this set of encyclopaedias and Hazel recalls that she also rebelled at the Hippocratic Oath. Worn out by their endeavours, the two boys are soon asleep.

Hazel goes downstairs to tidy up just as Norma returns, laughing at the antics of the Mulligan children. 'Tell me she's not pregnant again,' says Norma, sitting down at the table.

'Oh no, I don't think so – she's in her forties now. Although the last one was a surprise until her waters broke.'

'I don't know how she copes, not a moment of peace over there,' says Norma.

'She loves the family all around her. She almost never complains. Cocoa?'

Norma smiles. 'Lovely, just like old times, Mum. I'll make up the couch in a minute.'

'Just come in with me,' suggests Hazel. 'More comfy than that couch.'

'That is like old times. All those years we bunked in together. I'm glad you don't have to let the other room out any more.'

'We had some funny times with those roomers, didn't we? Remember old Miss Riley and her three-legged pug dog?'

'Hop-along,' says Norma, with a laugh. After a moment she asks, 'Mum, what's the story with Bob? He's away during the week and only here for one night?'

Hazel measures out the milk into a pot and puts it on the stove. 'This week is unusual. He'll retire one day soon and things will be different.'

'Something's bothering you, isn't it? I can tell.'

Hazel adds the cocoa, gives it a good stir and pours it out. She passes a mug over to Norma and sits down. 'Something a little odd happened the other day.'

Norma listens in silence while Hazel explains about the private eye and Mrs Herrmann.

'And what did Bob say about all this?' asks Norma.

'He said he doesn't know the woman, or this Sinclair fellow, but . . .'

Norma smiles. 'Your ears tell a different story. Nothing gets past the ears.'

'That's what's very strange; Bob has never set them off before – never! I just assumed he was very honest but now something's happened . . .'

'Well, it's not an exact science, Mum. So, does he know about your magical ears?'

'No one knows but you and Betty. It seems a little silly, so I keep it to myself.'

'What about the other thing?' asks Norma. 'Does he know about that?'

Hazel nods. 'Yes, of course.'

'That has given him some latitude, you know.'

'Norma, I don't believe Bob is doing the wrong thing by me. I think he's got himself into some other strife and is too embarrassed to admit it.'

'So now he's gone all the way back to Grafton to be with his ailing mother? You know, I've always thought it was odd that you've never met the mother, or even been up there. He must have friends who want to meet you – and no family at all?'

'He hardly spends any time in the town. He's all over the countryside meeting people and selling them gumboots and tractors, and shovels and . . . oilskins.' Hazel tries to think of a few other pieces of equipment that might account for his time. 'Rope,' she adds. 'Farmers always need rope.'

'You know what they say about men and rope, give them enough . . .' Norma smiles. 'Just kidding, Mum. I like Bob, he's a decent sort and he's made you happy. But, think about it, either his mother had him very young or she must be very old.'

'Of course she's old, Bob's sixty-six but she's a tough old bird, according to him.'

'Hang on,' says Norma. She leaves the kitchen and returns a moment later with the framed photograph of Bob's mother. 'Mum, I know you always see the best in people but sometimes we have to think suspiciously.'

'What are you suspecting the poor old lady of doing?'

'I just want to check something.' Norma turns the picture over, peels off the tape around the edge and lifts it out. She carefully removes the cardboard frame and packing paper and examines the back of the photograph, which has a date written in one corner, the ink faded.

Norma peers at it. 'Where's the magnifying glass, Mum?'

Hazel gets it out of the kitchen dresser and hands it to her. Norma moves the glass back and forth, getting the print in focus. 'Hmm . . . she certainly is ancient. If this was taken when she was twenty, she'd be'—Norma does the calculations in her head— 'a hundred and ten!'

'Are you sure?' asks Hazel.

'It's quite clear: 25th of May 1875. So, if she's twenty, she'd have been born in 1855.'

'Well, that's amazing. She really is a tough old bird. I'm surprised Bob's never mentioned it. But perhaps she's younger than twenty?' suggests Hazel, certain there's a simple explanation. It's just a matter of making the calculations work.

She takes the photograph from Norma and looks at the woman more closely. If anything, she's older – perhaps in her mid-twenties. The high-necked blouse looks old-fashioned but is hard to date. If the photograph was in colour perhaps it would reveal more than the shades of grey.

'So, I put to you, member of the jury, two possibilities: either Mrs Bates Senior is long gone. Or this is not Bob's mother,' says Norma.

'They're not the only possibilities.' Hazel hesitates. 'But I see what you're saying.'

'She could be his grandmother.' Norma finds a piece of paper and a pencil and jots down some figures. 'It's much more logical based on that date.'

'Bob has always said she's his mother. He's never mentioned his grandmother.'

'All right. Tomorrow when I'm in the city, I'm going to go to the post office and check the phone book for the Grafton area. I'll get the numbers for all the old people's homes and hospitals in the area and call them tomorrow evening. They will certainly know if there is someone of that age in the place.' She reads Hazel's expression. 'And before you bring up the cost of the trunk calls – I think it's important to find out.'

'It's not just the cost, Norma, it's really not necessary. I'll ask Bob when he comes home. I'm sure he'll have a perfectly good explanation.'

Norma raises her eyebrows sceptically. 'What about this person who hired the private detective? You haven't contacted her?'

'I can't just show up at someone's house and ask why she's having me followed.'

'I don't see why not,' says Norma. 'How dare she!'

'It's not that simple, dear,' says Hazel.

Norma reaches for her mother's hand and holds it. 'You're afraid of what you might find out. There's something not right here and I think you already know that, Mum. Let's get to the bottom of it.'

When Hazel arrives home from work on Monday afternoon, there's a list of Grafton phone numbers on the kitchen dresser in Norma's familiar hand, and once they've eaten, Norma goes into the hall to make the calls. Hazel plays catch with the boys in the backyard, torn between curiosity and guilt, still half convinced she should wait until Bob is home to make his case. Finally, Norma beckons her into the kitchen, instructing the boys to play quietly while she talks to Nanna.

Hazel gets out a bottle of her peach wine, pours them each a glass and they sit down at the table.

'I've rung all the old people's homes in the area. No Mrs Bates or Mrs Bateman. There was one place that had a Mrs Bateman but she died about twenty years ago. The woman said there had been family in Grafton but couldn't remember any names.'

Hazel takes a sip of wine, tasting the sweetness of last summer when life was simpler. 'That name again: Bateman. The mysterious Batemans.'

'Very mysterious. I wish I could stay longer, Mum. I don't like leaving you with this hanging over you.'

'Heavens, I'm quite certain there is a simple explanation.'

Norma looks at Hazel over the rim of her glass. 'I think you should call Bob's firm and check he works there.'

'I will do no such thing,' says Hazel. 'I'm not going to sneak around spying on Bob.'

'He's not being honest with you, Mum. I also think you should call this Mrs Herrmann and ask her what's going on.'

'Let me think about it, dear,' says Hazel. 'Let's not rush in.'

25

MEETING AT THE HOTEL HOLLYWOOD

Betty gives her hair a final lacquer, checks her teeth for lipstick (a nice shade of cerise to match her nail polish) and fixes a single strand of pearls around her neck. Pausing for a moment to examine her reflection, she catches a glimpse of 'pretty little Betty' (as she once heard herself described) and gives herself a smile of recognition.

Tonight she's off to an important meeting at the nearby Hotel Hollywood. It's one of very few pubs that allow unaccompanied women in the bar. Most pubs are male domains and women are not welcome unless they're tucked away in a back room out of sight, but ladies have the run of the place at the Hollywood. It's a little oasis of glamour in a suburb worn down by generations of poverty and struggle.

Betty's the first to arrive and nabs their favourite table in the corner of the cosy saloon with its polished timber tables and red plush furnishings. Hazel arrives next, wearing her second-best dress – navy with polka dots – and a white cardigan draped across her shoulders. Irene is right behind her, in the usual dreadful outfit but wearing shoes for a change – black lace-ups with a low heel, a style Betty's granny wore thirty years ago. Merl is the last to arrive, looking terrifically smart in a maroon dress and matching jacket with a diamanté brooch at her shoulder, hair freshly permed and blued. No one would ever guess they're just ordinary old tea ladies. No one needs to guess here, because almost everyone knows them.

Shirley brings them a round of shandies. 'Evening, Mrs B, Mrs P, Mrs T, Mrs D – all looking gorgeous as usual. Whose tab's this on?'

Merl volunteers and Irene (as usual) kicks off the discussion with a complaint. She wants to know why they have to waste a perfectly good outing in Detective Dibble's company. Hazel explains that she thought it would be a more relaxing place to get to know him better. Irene grumbles under her breath but eventually drops the subject.

'If you wanted someone senior to talk to,' says Merl, 'I could have asked DS Pierce to meet with us.'

'Detective Dibble has a lot of potential,' says Hazel firmly. 'He could be very helpful and is likely to be interested in what we have to say . . . oh, here he is . . .' She pauses to wave Dibble over.

He approaches their table with a wary expression on his face. When the introductions are complete, he stands there as if he doesn't know what to do next. He might have potential, thinks Betty, but he'll need help to find it. Hazel offers to buy him a drink but he elects to get his own. He goes to the bar, returning with a beer, and squashes in with them around the small table.

'So, how long have you been in the force, young man?' asks Merl in her bossy schoolteacher voice.

'Merl dear,' says Hazel, 'Detective Dibble has joined us for a chat, not an interview.'

'Yeah, next thing yer head-first in a Black Maria,' mutters Irene.

Dibble turns his solemn gaze on Irene but says nothing.

'Well, cheers!' says Hazel, raising her glass. 'Thank you for joining us, Detective.'

Dibble glances at each of them in turn. 'How can I help?'

'We might be able to help you get to the bottom of the McCracken murder,' says Hazel.

He takes a large gulp of beer. 'Okay.'

'We see and hear a lot of things. Not just us, but all sorts of other people we deal with every day: drivers, cleaners, maintenance men – people we trust,' explains Hazel.

Merl puffs out her formidable bosom. 'And there's no one more trusted and respected in the community than a tea lady.'

'Look, I'm a junior plain-clothes detective; I haven't completed my training. DS Pierce is running the murder enquiry. Just so you know.'

'Isn't that what I said? Detective Dibble is just a junior officer,' says Merl.

'Nothing wrong with our hearing, thanks very much, Merl,' says Irene.

'Everyone wants to prove themselves, obviously,' says Dibble.

Hazel leans towards him in her warm, confiding way that Betty always admires. 'But what if you could crack this case with our help? Wouldn't that be a feather in your cap?'

'I could put in a good word for you with DS Pierce, who is my son-in-law,' says Merl.

Betty notices Dibble's jaw flex at the mention of Pierce. She gets out her notebook and writes: *Dibble lockjaw.*

'I see, well, I don't want to step on his toes,' says Dibble.

Irene takes a drag on her cigarette and blows a stream of smoke out the corner of her mouth. 'There's worse things than stepping on toes,' she says. 'There's broken kneecaps.'

'Is that a threat?' asks Dibble, taking a careful look at Irene.

'Don't mind Mrs Turnbuckle, Detective,' says Hazel. 'She has an unusual sense of humour.'

'I understand you found the victim, Mrs Bates, but I don't really understand why you're so interested when you said you barely knew McCracken.'

Hazel is silent for a moment. Just another thing Betty admires about Hazel. She always gathers her thoughts; doesn't just come bursting out with them like everyone else.

'All right,' says Hazel. 'Our real interest is the missing Russian woman. I mentioned her to you at our interview but there doesn't seem to be any interest from the police in finding her.'

Dibble shrugs. 'Perhaps she's not missing?'

Ignoring this comment, Hazel continues. 'There has to be some connection between the woman, the fire and the murder, but it's the woman we're most interested in. Can I tell you what we have so far?'

'Yes, of course,' says Dibble, settling back in his chair.

'As a starting point, we've been given the name Borisyuk,' says Hazel.

If Dibble looked nervous at the mention of Pierce, he now looks thoroughly alarmed. He glances around to check that they can't be overheard. 'You don't want to bandy that name around or tangle with him. He's a very dangerous character.'

'We can be dangerous too, you know,' Betty points out. 'Scalding can be very nasty. Laxatives can be too – very nasty in large quantities.'

Irene turns to her with interest. 'Laxatives? In someone's tea?'

Kicking herself for bringing it up, Betty takes a quick sip of her drink to compose herself. 'It was just the once.'

Hazel gives her a funny look. 'Let's have a private chat about that later, dear.'

'I don't want to get mixed up with the likes of Borisyuk, that's for certain,' says Dibble. 'Don't get me wrong, I'm interested—'

'No one wants to put your life in danger,' Hazel assures him. 'Can you tell us if you have any more information about Mr McCracken – has anything new come to light?'

'He boarded at a house in Annandale but there was nothing to speak of in his room that offered more information. There's no new leads, no witnesses. So the case has sort of ground to a halt. The focus is now on the fire since you'd assume that the timing of the murder is probably not coincidental.'

'So, have you heard anything about the woman I reported?' asks Hazel.

'You're the only person who saw her in the bond store so that hasn't been verified—'

'If she turns up dead somewhere, it'll be blood on your hands,' Irene points out.

'I think that's going a bit far, Irene,' says Betty, starting to wish that Irene and Merl hadn't even come this evening, since they're being no help to Hazel.

'Could you just do one thing?' asks Hazel. 'Check the files for a missing person?'

'Of course, leave it with me,' says Dibble.

Hazel gives him a description of MW. He makes a note and, as soon as he finishes his beer, goes on his way.

When he's gone, Merl says, 'They must be desperate for recruits.'

'He's intelligent enough, he just needs more confidence,' says Hazel.

'I think you scared him, Irene,' says Betty. 'All the knee-capping and blood on your hands and whatnot.'

'Was I the one going on about laxatives?' says Irene. 'No wonder he didn't want another drink. Probably worried yer'd give him a dose of the runs.'

'You don't need laxatives,' says Merl, apparently missing the point. 'Hazel's parsnip wine will get things moving. I speak from experience.'

'You're thinking of the prune and parsnip, Merl dear,' corrects Hazel.

'Oh it was just the once,' says Betty, regretting mentioning it. 'Actually I did it twice but to the same fellow. You remember him, that factory manager who was so awful.'

'I really don't think "rough justice" fits the code of the tea lady,' says Merl in her hoity-toity tone. 'Next thing we'll be poisoning people.'

'Could be a business in that,' says Irene. 'Probably better paid.'

'I'm sure young Dibble will come around. Now, does anyone know who the tea lady at the fire station is these days?' asks Hazel.

Betty puts her hand up. 'I do. It's Effie Finch. She worked at the post office when we were there, Hazel.'

'Yes, I remember Effie Finch perfectly. Strong, forthright woman.'

Betty agrees. 'She was in the Women's Fire Auxiliary during the war, so she's quite knowledgeable in that regard.'

Hazel gives Betty a nod. 'Good. Let's make her acquaintance again.'

26

PINK SLIPS READY TO GO

Serving the factory girls, Hazel notices Gloria beckoning her over with some urgency. She takes Gloria's coffee to her alcove and clears a space on the desk for the cup. To say Gloria is untidy is an understatement. As usual, Hazel itches to put the cascading piles of paper in order, to stand the fabric sample boards in a nice strong box and empty the ashtrays piled high with butts.

Gloria leans back on her chair, her feet, in the usual canvas tennis shoes, resting on a low filing cabinet. 'What is happening upstairs, Hazel? Are they gunna panic and start laying my girls off?'

'There was some talk about Frankie going overseas—' begins Hazel.

'God help us!' Gloria drops her feet to the floor with a thump and grinds out her cigarette angrily. 'If we have to rely on Frankie the Clown to rescue us, we're really in deep trouble. This silly game has gone on too long. Why do we play along with him?'

Hazel knows exactly what she means but it's always been like this. Frankie is the prince of the empire and his subjects are forced to pretend the place couldn't run without him. They have to humour and flatter him just to get the job done.

'He'll bugger off for a month and come back with a couple of frocks for the Ginger Nuts to pick apart. We don't have time for all that nonsense right now.'

To Hazel's surprise, Gloria spreads Alice's magazines out on the desk. 'I had a look in some of the boutiques in town this week; they're already selling these sorts of frocks. I never thought I'd say this, but Alice is right. These would only take a couple of yards of fabric. Cheap to make in cotton, or polished cotton or Crimplene wash-and-wear. No lining, just facings.'

'I suspect upstairs will say these are not our style. They like to stick to what they know.'

'Dragging upstairs out of the fifties is going to be near on impossible,' says Gloria. 'And it'll cost us our jobs in the end.'

Hazel picks up a couple of magazines and looks through them. 'Next time Frankie or Mr Karp are down, why don't you show them these?'

Gloria gives a bitter laugh. She gulps down her coffee and hands Hazel the cup. 'Nice thought but also pointless.'

On the top floor, Hazel senses the sombre mood. The bosses aren't in yet but three pink slips sit on Edith Stern's desk. They are already laying people off.

'Machinists?' asks Hazel.

Edith nods. 'And one in the office. You know the drill, last on, first off.'

Hazel knows one of them will be Alice. 'What do you think, Edith? Is it really necessary just yet?'

'Ridiculous. Frankie being lazy, as usual,' she says in a low voice.

'Is there any way of delaying them?' asks Hazel.

'I don't know how. They'll go down to Accounts today and out with the pays tomorrow. I can't see anything changing before then.'

'What if they were lost, just temporarily, to buy some time?'

'Things do not get mislaid in my office,' says Edith, with a frown.

The lift door opens and Mr Karp Senior walks straight past them into his office without a word. A moment later he puts his head around the door. 'Can I trouble you for a cup of tea, please, Hazel? Do we know Frankie's plans today, Mrs Stern?'

'I haven't heard anything yet. I'll let you know if I hear from him.'

When the door is safely closed, Edith shakes her head in disgust. 'Hungover most likely,' she murmurs.

When Hazel comes back from delivering Mr Karp's tea, Edith flaps the pink slips at her. 'Hazel, could you drop these down to Mr Levy, please?' She pauses. 'Don't forget, will you? If they were accidentally mislaid I'd have to do new ones and get them signed next week.'

Hazel gives her a wink and pops the slips into the front pocket of her pinny. 'They're perfectly safe with me.'

'Any news from upstairs, Hazel?' asks Miss Joan, when Hazel arrives in the dressmakers' room. 'What's Frankie doing? Why haven't we seen him all week? Just tell us, are they letting people go?'

'Not at the moment,' says Hazel.

'We're just sitting here, waiting,' says Miss Ivy, heaving a dramatic sigh. 'This is what it must have been like before the *Titanic* went down.'

'I don't think so, dear,' says Hazel. 'It came as a surprise from what I gather. And, in any case, this ship's not going down.'

Over the years, the sisters have grown with Empire and become experts at managing Frankie's ego. Their classic designs have barely changed. Each season is a slight variation on the last: an extra gusset, some light frilling on a cuff or piping on a collar. They take pride in the fact that the buyers know what to expect each season. It's clear to Hazel that the sisters have no inkling that outside this building the world is changing. Young people are taking charge and, unless they do something, Empire could be left behind.

The door flies open and Pixie appears with a large cardboard box in her arms. 'Hello, Mrs Bates! I rushed all the way to be back in time for tea.'

'Lovely to see you, Pixie dear,' says Hazel, pouring her milky tea.

Miss Ivy takes the box and places it on the worktable. She takes out the sample cards of fabrics and lays them out side by side. 'We'll show these to Frankie when he comes down.' She gives Pixie a sidelong look. 'And where is your father today?'

Pixie gives her a blank look. 'I don't know. I'm sorry. Isn't he here?'

'Don't you live with him? Don't you drive to work with him?' asks Miss Ivy.

'I don't see that much of him, quite honestly, and I catch the bus to work.' Her voice dries to a whisper under Miss Ivy's fierce gaze. 'I don't want to be late,' she adds.

'Ladies, instead of waiting around, why don't you have Mrs Stern make an appointment for you to meet with Frankie?' suggests Hazel.

'Good idea, Hazel,' says Miss Joan.

Miss Ivy turns away to pick up the phone, and Pixie gives Hazel a quick smile.

Miss Joan continues, 'Until we get some direction from Frankie, we won't have any work for you here, Pixie. You'll have to see if one of the other departments can take you.'

Seeing Pixie's dejected expression, Hazel says quickly, 'Wonderful! A good opportunity for you to find out how things work on the ground floor. I'm sure Mrs Nuttell would be delighted to show you the ropes. After all, you'll no doubt be running the place one day.'

The sisters exchange looks but manage not to bite.

Hazel glances at her watch. 'I can take you down now and introduce you, if you like.'

She's well aware that Gloria Nuttell holds firm beliefs about the social layers of the building. She has strong opinions about everyone in the firm but hopefully not about Pixie as yet.

True to form, Gloria listens to Hazel's explanation, eyes narrowed suspiciously. 'It's noisy down here,' she says, looking Pixie up and down, ready to find fault with the girl.

'I don't mind,' says Pixie. Giving an awkward shrug, she glances around self-consciously.

'Can't be worse than having to work with the Ginger Nuts, I suppose.'

It takes a moment for a smile to dawn on Pixie's face. 'They're not that bad. Just a bit crispy sometimes.'

Gloria laughs. 'You might as well find out what goes on here, and I could do with some help. Can you go down to Greenfields and pick up ten cards of buttonholes?'

Pixie laughs. 'I'm not falling for that old chestnut.'

Gloria turns to Hazel with a grin. 'Okay, she'll do.'

27

TWO CLUES IN ONE DAY

The moment she gets home, Hazel's thoughts turn to Bob. She simply cannot imagine him doing the wrong thing by her. He's not after her money – she doesn't have enough to make that worthwhile, and he's always been generous with his own. An affair is unlikely for a man his age. How would he fit it in between his job, travelling and home? But, if being a tea lady has taught her anything, it's that human beings are strange and unpredictable creatures who regularly act against their own best interests. Nothing is ever as it appears.

She knows that Norma is right. She has to be practical and get to the bottom of this, and not let emotion cloud her vision. She goes upstairs and stands looking around the bedroom at the faded floral wallpaper, the iron bedstead, an old-fashioned wardrobe and chest of drawers that once belonged to her parents. All so familiar but are they concealing something from her? She starts with Bob's bedside cabinet, then moves on to the wardrobe, searching carefully through the pockets of each of his jackets.

He likes nice clothes and makes a point of buying quality, but it occurs to her now just how few things he owns. After they were married, he'd moved in with a single suitcase. He explained that he kept his work clothes at his digs in Grafton, and also kept several changes of clothes at the Commercial Travellers' Club. This arrangement allowed him to travel between work and home without needing to lug suitcases about. From Hazel's experience, plenty of men would leave a trail of belongings in their wake, never having the right thing in the right place. Not Bob – he ran a tight operation and she has always admired that in him.

The inside breast pocket of his navy suit jacket contains several betting slips, a pound note and a clean folded hand-kerchief. The two front pockets are empty and his other jackets yield nothing. In the pockets of his trousers she discovers a packet of spearmint chewing gum, a silver toothpick and some loose change. No mysterious telegrams or affectionate notes from strange women.

She goes carefully through the chest of drawers and finds nothing out of the ordinary. More relieved than disappointed, she takes down his favourite tweed jacket to give it a good brush and airing outside. Opening the front flap, she notices something in the lining pocket. Reaching inside, she finds something spidery and fibrous. She lifts it out carefully and lays it flat on her palm. The flowers are dry and faded but the stalks hold together to form a daisy chain.

Where would Bob come by a daisy chain? It's hardly the sort of pastime the men down at the club indulge in. Their lives revolve around betting on things like cards, horses and dogs and Bob is always at pains to place himself above his fellow salesmen as more serious-minded and honourable, but surely that didn't involve making daisy chains? Perhaps he had met a child on the train? He often recounted conversations with fellow travellers. Or perhaps the child of one of his customers? It did seem like the sort of thing lovers made for each other in the first thrall of a romance but it wasn't under his pillow, or sentimentally pressed between the pages of his journal (he doesn't keep one, as far as she knows). It was left forgotten in his pocket and probably means nothing at all. And yet she feels strangely disturbed by this tiny fragile thing.

She has sardines on toast for dinner with a glass of rhubarb wine, and listens to the six o'clock news broadcast. After she's eaten, not in the mood to be alone, she takes a finished pile of mending next door.

Mrs Mulligan sits on her front step, chatting to her neighbour on the other side as they watch the girls play hopscotch and the boys kick a ball around. The ball is flat and makes an odd thunk when it hits the asphalt but the boys don't seem to care. They shout instructions to each other and scuffle in the gutters as if the hopes of the nation rest on their bony little shoulders. It lifts Hazel's spirits to watch them play.

'Hello, Hazel,' says Mrs Mulligan. 'Caught that murderer yet?'

'I'm working on it,' says Hazel, with a smile. 'Sorry to have to tell you that Patrick's church pants are at the end of their life.'

'Ah, that's a shame. Nothing worse than having to fork out for the littlest.'

Mrs Mulligan's bulk almost fills the doorway and she moves aside to let Hazel squeeze past with the mending. In the front room, Maude sits at the table with her schoolbooks. She gets up and takes the clothes from Hazel, hugging them to her chest. 'I'll be finishing school soon. You won't need to trouble yourself with this, Mrs Bates.'

'It's no trouble at all, Maude. Do you have a job lined up?'

'Dad said he can get me a position at the brewery as a sweeper.'

Hazel tries to conceal her dismay. 'You're so good with your schoolwork and your drawing talent . . . I'm sure you could be a commercial artist if you wanted to.'

Maude shrugs modestly. 'I don't know about that.'

'As a matter of fact,' says Hazel. 'I wonder if you could help me with a little project?'

She explains what she's after and Maude agrees to give it a go.

Hazel tries to picture the Russian woman in the window as she'd seen her in that brief moment. She remembers a heart-shaped face, perhaps wider at the forehead, tapering to a narrow jaw. Definitely longish dark hair with a centre part. Beyond that, she can't be sure and Maude's drawing ends up looking like any woman with long dark hair.

'Could you read the expression on her face at all?' asks Maude.

'She looked afraid, I think, but . . . I'm not sure. I'm losing track of what I saw and what I'm imagining.'

With a few pencil strokes, Maude changes the expression in the woman's eyes but Hazel wasn't close enough to read her eyes. They go back and forth for a while but the image in Hazel's mind has begun to fade.

'It's a nice drawing all the same, dear,' she tells Maude.

Maude adds an extra line here and there. She puts down her pencil and gazes unhappily at the drawing. She looks up at Hazel, her eyes wide. 'Hang on. I just remembered something.'

She jumps up and Hazel follows her out into the backyard, where she goes straight to the outside lavatory, and comes out with a pile of newspapers, ripped roughly into squares.

'I noticed this story when I was ripping up the bog paper.' She flicks through the scraps quickly and, a few minutes later, holds a sheet aloft with a triumphant smile. 'Look! Is this her?'

It's a small article with a photograph of the Russian woman just as Hazel remembers her. 'Oh my goodness! What does it say, Maude? I don't have my glasses with me.'

Maude reads aloud: '"Soviet artiste, Natalia Ivanov, has been reported missing from The Great Moscow Circus during their first tour of Australia, which opened in Sydney this month. Madam Ivanov is a world-famous acrobat, renowned for her daring and grace, and performs as part of the 'Flying Flamingos' duo together with her husband, Ivan Ivanov. Madam Ivanov vanished three days ago and has not been heard from since. There is speculation that she may be planning to defect from behind the Iron Curtain and that Australian authorities may be concealing her whereabouts. However, this has not been confirmed by government sources at this time. The Soviet Embassy denies any knowledge of Madam Ivanov's whereabouts or intentions."'

Maude looks up from the article. 'But you said you saw her in the building that burnt down, and that was more than a week ago?'

Hazel nods, her mind whirring. All this time she's been struggling to be believed or taken seriously. Now, here it is in black and white, and with the woman's identity.

'How old is that paper, Maude?'

'Yesterday's. So she's been missing for longer than they are saying. What does it mean, Mrs Bates?'

Hazel considers this for a moment. 'I wish I knew.'

28

BOB'S SIDE OF THE STORY

'How was your week, dear?' asks Hazel, as she sets out two plates and serves up corned beef with mashed potatoes and peas.

Bob sits down at the table with a sigh. 'It was fine. As good as can be expected.'

'How's your mother? I half expected a telegram to say she'd gone.'

'The old girl bounced back. Nothing stops her. What's been happening here? No further bother with this Sinclair character? No fires or murders?' asks Bob with a chuckle. 'Never know with you, my dear.'

'I'm not committing crimes, Bob,' Hazel reminds him. 'Just an innocent bystander, but there has been a breakthrough with the Russian woman's identity.'

Hazel shows him the newspaper article and explains Maude's role in the discovery.

'Oh well, hand it over to the police, they'll deal with it. Delicious corned beef, by the way, my love.'

'Bob, the police already knew she was missing a few days before it was reported in the papers. Perhaps the desk sergeant didn't know. I suspect that Detective Dibble didn't either, but Pierce must have.'

'You may be right,' agrees Bob. He looks over her shoulder with a hopeful expression. 'Any more mustard sauce?'

'Bob, just help yourself for goodness sake.'

She is normally so accommodating, he looks a little stung at her tone but gets up and helps himself. He then eats in sulky silence, which makes Hazel less than sympathetic.

'So, she must be quite old by now?' she ventures.

'Who, dear?'

'Your mother. She must be getting on.'

Bob shrugs. 'I suppose. I forget how old she is. Just old.'

'What do you mean, you forget? You must know what year she was born.'

'I suppose so,' he says vaguely.

Hazel teeters on the brink for a moment, then plunges on. 'I had a close look at her photograph, the one in the front room, and I noticed there's a date on the back. If she was twenty when it was taken, she'd be a hundred and ten now.'

Bob laughs. 'She's old but not that old. It's on the back, you say? Probably when the studio was established.' He pauses. 'Why were you inspecting it?'

'Norma was here with the twins, she asked about your mother and . . . well, one thing led to another.'

Bob sits perfectly still, his fork poised in the air. 'Norma? It's this Sinclair fellow, isn't it? He's upset you. What are you worried about?'

'Something's not right. There's something you're not telling me, Bob, about Mrs Herrmann, and Philip Sinclair.'

'My head's spinning with all these names.'

'That's only two names and they are connected.'

Bob finishes his dinner in silence and lays his knife and fork down. 'Well, I can't shed any light on that situation but let's have a look at the photograph and see if we can sort this out.' He reaches across for her hand and gazes into her eyes. 'I can't bear for you to be upset. And now you seem to be suspicious of me . . . also an innocent bystander.' He gets up from the table. 'Pour us a dram of the hard stuff, my love.'

Hazel clears the plates away. She takes a bottle of whiskey and two cut-glass tumblers down from the cupboard and pours their drinks. Bob returns and lays the photograph on the table. The brown sticky paper comes away easily this time and he lifts the photograph out.

Without being asked, Hazel hands him the magnifying glass.

'I see what you mean,' he agrees. 'The date is very specific, to the day.' He sighs and turns the picture over, staring at it for a long moment. 'I think you might be right, I've made a mistake. This can't be my mother.'

'What do you mean?'

'This hung in my mother's bedroom for years, I remember it from when I was a boy. She was so beautiful and serene. I always thought it was her as a young woman. I never asked, and she wouldn't know any more. But, as you say, it doesn't add up. It might be her eldest sister, Auntie Agnes, or even my grandmother.' Bob picks up his glass and raises it to Hazel. 'You're quite the sleuth, my dear, well done. Mystery solved.'

To her dismay, Hazel feels the telltale tingling. She's hesitant to tell him about Norma ringing around the nursing homes; he'll be annoyed at that. 'Well, everything is not quite tidied up for me just yet, Bob.'

'Come on, let's not worry about all this. Why don't we have an early night?'

'Bob, it's barely six-thirty – just hear me out, please.' Hazel gets an envelope out of the dresser drawer and slides the daisy chain onto the table. 'Do you know what this is?'

He peers at it. 'Dried weeds?'

'It's a daisy chain I found in the inside pocket of your jacket.'

'All right, I'll confess,' he says. 'I joined a pagan cult and we dance around the fire naked with daisy chains on our heads.' He chuckles at his own joke while Hazel waits silently for a proper answer.

'There is a perfectly innocent explanation, Madam Sleuth. I found it on the train; I suppose a child left it behind. It didn't look like this, it was all fresh and pretty. I thought it was sweet and put it in my pocket thinking you would like it and then forgot about it. I really can't see the problem.'

He's right; it's not a crime to have a daisy chain in one's pocket. And the identity of the woman in the photograph could be a simple mistake. But, while Bob has perfectly reasonable explanations, he's still not telling the truth.

He gazes into her eyes. 'I think the fire and the murder have taken their toll on your nerves, my dear little bunny. Why don't you take some time off? Go and spend a week or two with Norma and the boys. That fresh country air will clear your head.'

Hazel agrees to think about it. Bob is right that her nerves are on edge but she has work to do. Apart from whatever is going on with him, she has a responsibility to Natalia Ivanov. She cannot rest until she knows that young woman is safe.

29

DRAMA UPSTAIRS

'You haven't seen Frankie anywhere in the building, have you?' asks Mr Karp, when Hazel takes his tea in on Monday morning.

'Not today.' Hazel pauses. 'In fact, not since Thursday afternoon.'

The intercom buzzes followed by Edith Stern's tinny voice: 'I'm sorry, Mr Karp, but Mrs Karp doesn't know where he is either. She hasn't seen him since last Thursday and he didn't come home over the weekend.'

'Didn't come home?' says Mr Karp faintly.

Hazel notices his voice seems weak and his skin has a pale sheen to it. 'Are you all right, Mr Karp?'

He gazes around his desk distractedly, picks up several pieces of paper and stares at them blankly. 'Why do you ask?'

'You just don't look well. Perhaps Mrs Stern should call for the doctor?'

'There's nothing wrong with me,' he says irritably. 'If we could just find Frankie. I need helping sorting out this . . . this . . .' He glares at the papers on his desk. 'Why can't I find anything?'

'Perhaps Pixie could help you—'

'Pixie?' He looks up at her in wide-eyed wonder for a second and then flops forward over his desk.

Hazel shouts for Edith to call an ambulance. Edith appears in the doorway, takes in the sight of Mr Karp and disappears again.

Hazel checks his wrist and finds a faint pulse. 'Hurry, Edith!'

'They're on their way!' Edith says, coming back into the office a moment later.

'Help me, we need to get him onto the floor.'

Edith looks aghast. 'I don't think he'll like that.'

'Come on. We'll take him by the armpits and lift together.'

Mr Karp is a small man and less of a challenge to lift than Frankie would be in these circumstances. They lay him on his side but when he stops breathing, Hazel realises they need to perform mouth-to-mouth resuscitation.

Edith covers her face with her hands. 'Can't we wait for the ambulance?'

There's no time for debate. Counting aloud, Hazel presses on Mr Karp's chest, feeling his ribs flex and crackle under the pressure. She pinches his nose and breathes several breaths into his lungs. She instructs Edith to go down and show the ambulance men up, and goes back to compressing Mr Karp's chest. The effort is enormous; perspiration trickles down her temples. It occurs to her that she might also have a heart attack. There's no time to worry about that and she works on and on, counting the compressions until she feels a firm hand on her shoulder. Two ambulance men take over. Clamping an oxygen mask on Mr Karp's face, they lift him onto a stretcher and carry him out.

Exhausted from her efforts, Hazel collapses into Mr Karp's chair.

'I expect you could do with a strong cup of tea, Hazel,' says Edith, appearing with two cups. Hazel thanks her, sighing with sweet relief at the first sip.

'I don't know what to say, Hazel. You were wonderful! Where did you learn that?'

'I do the Red Cross training every year, just in case of an emergency. It's always changing, so you have to keep up. The chest compression is the latest thing. I only hope it does the trick. Poor Mr Karp.'

'He was breathing again, so that's a good sign. Yes, poor Mr Karp. He's never had a day sick that I recall. Never.' Edith dabs at her eyes with a handkerchief. 'What if he dies, Hazel?'

Before Hazel can speculate on that possibility, Doug Fysh appears at the door, clearly taken aback at the sight of Hazel in the boss's chair. 'Ah-ha, I knew it was just a matter of time before you were running the place, Hazel.'

Hazel gets up quickly. 'It was a bit presumptuous of me to sit here.'

Edith instructs her to sit back down. 'I'll have you know that Mrs Bates just saved Mr Karp's life. She needs to rest.'

'Don't tell me, let me guess – she performed a lobotomy with nothing more than a sugar cube and a tea strainer? Haw haw haw.'

Edith bristles. 'Mr Fysh, you can be quite insufferable sometimes. It's not a laughing matter. Mr Karp is at this very moment in an ambulance on his way to hospital.'

'Oh? I had no idea. I just came up to see what happened to morning tea.'

When the situation has been explained, Doug offers a half-hearted apology and Edith points out that he should ask questions before he starts making silly jokes about things. Meanwhile Doug takes the opportunity to help himself to Mr Karp's brandy. 'And where is Frankie, anyway?' he asks.

'He's another problem,' says Edith. 'Nobody has seen him since last week. Not even his wife.'

'I see.' Doug swills his brandy around in the glass and drains it. 'Let's have a poke around in his office, see what we can find.'

'No one is allowed in his office when he's not here.'

Doug stares Edith down. 'Extraordinary circumstances, Mrs Stern.'

Edith looks over to Hazel, who gives her a nod of agreement and all three go into Frankie's office.

Frankie's desk is dominated by a large marble ashtray, a gold cigarette lighter shaped like a voluptuous woman and a gold pen stand to park his gold fountain pens in. His drawers are all locked but the key is quickly discovered under the cigarette lighter. His top drawer is dedicated to half-a-dozen boxes of cigars and accessories: lighters and various shaped cutters.

Edith holds her nose in disgust. 'What a stink, like dried cow-doo.'

Doug takes out a fat cigar and lights it with the voluptuous woman. He wanders over to Frankie's drinks cabinet, opens the mirrored doors and looks through the various bottles until he finds one that meets with his approval, and pours himself a large whiskey.

Edith gives an annoyed sigh. 'Mr Fysh, can I point out that it's barely eleven o'clock in the morning?'

'Yes you can, haw haw haw,' he says, taking in the view from the window with a cigar in one hand, drink in the other.

Edith closes the drinks cabinet, locks it and puts the key in her pocket.

'What are we looking for?' asks Hazel, in order to keep them both on track.

Doug sits down in Frankie's chair and puts his feet on the desk. 'A map of a treasure island marked with a big red X.'

'You better hope he doesn't catch you with your great clod-hoppers on his desk,' says Edith.

Doug opens the centre drawer. He gets out a handful of business cards and tosses them onto the desk. 'There's a few places to start looking for him.' He flicks through them, reading aloud: 'Lizard Bar, Piccolo Bar, Pink Pussycat, Les Girls, Mermaid Club, Leopard Room, Red Room; no shortage of questionable venues.'

'I, for one, am not setting foot in any of those places,' declares Edith.

'Well, I'm a married man and I doubt my wife would approve of me visiting topless bars. So that leaves you, Mrs Bates.'

Hazel reluctantly picks up the cards and puts them in her front pocket.

Edith sighs. 'You've done enough for today, Hazel. Give them to me, he's my responsibility.'

At the end of the day, Edith Stern marches into the downstairs kitchen in a temper. 'What I need right now is a scalding hot bath and a large block of carbolic to scrub the grime off my soul. I've been up the Cross and in and out of those dreadful striptease clubs all afternoon.' She sits down at the table and pulls off her hat.

'I've got just the thing for you,' says Hazel. She gets down the emergency flagon of cream sherry and pours Edith a small glass.

'Ah, that's better,' says Edith, taking a sip and easing her shoes off. 'I spoke to Dottie Karp. I don't think she ever knows where her husband is, so she was no help at all and not very interested either. I went to the Leopard Room and the Red Room, that awful lizard place, which is appropriately named, let me tell you – all very sordid with young girls writhing around without their singlets. There's an appalling smell in those places of . . . well, I don't want to think about it. They all know Frankie but no one's seen him in the last few days. So that was a complete waste of my time. I feel soiled by the whole experience.'

'Edith, I think it was a job well done. We had to start somewhere,' says Hazel. 'And very brave of you too. Now, will Mrs Karp notify the police?'

'I doubt it. Dottie by name, Dottie by nature. I came to ask if you would mind coming with me to the police station?'

'Of course,' agrees Hazel. 'I'll just finish up here and we can go.'

The desk sergeant that Hazel had met previously is on duty again. 'What can I do for you, young ladies?' he asks jovially.

Edith Stern explains that they want to report a missing person and gives him the basic details: address of the firm, Frankie's position there and when he was last seen. He takes down her name and asks, 'And your position with the firm?'

Edith hesitates so Hazel steps in. 'Mrs Stern is the Management and Communications . . . Manager.'

'Yes, that's right,' agrees Edith. 'Managing the managers and the communications between the managers and so on and so forth.'

The desk sergeant, apparently satisfied that Edith has the appropriate authority, takes his notebook over to the desk and feeds a form into the typewriter. He taps away, pausing to confirm the details with them as he goes. When he's finished, he whips the form out and lays it on the counter. 'We'll get this into the system and be in touch.'

'One more thing,' says Hazel. 'I came in three weeks ago and made a report about seeing a woman in the bond store before it burnt down. Do you remember?'

'Vaguely,' he says. 'This is a busy place, you know.'

Hazel puts the newspaper article about Natalia Ivanov on the counter. 'This is the woman I saw. The article states she's missing, so you must have a file on her somewhere.'

'She's a looker,' he says, studying the photograph.

'Mrs Bates did not ask for an assessment of her attractiveness,' says Edith.

'No need to get sniffy, lady. I don't know anything about it. Give me your name again and I'll pass it on to the detectives.'

'If you could give the details to Detective Dibble, please,' says Hazel. She supplies her own name and Natalia's as well but refuses to hand over the newspaper clipping in case her only evidence disappears.

As soon as they're out on the street, Edith turns to Hazel. 'I've seen that Natalia woman before – in Frankie's car.'

30

HAZEL MAKES A SHOCKING DISCOVERY

Over breakfast on Saturday morning, Bob reveals he has plans to attend an association dinner at the club that evening and, because it's bound to be a late one, will stay the night there. It seems odd to Hazel that he didn't think to mention it before now.

'I'm sorry, my sweet,' he says. 'It completely slipped my mind until I found the invitation in my briefcase. Can you forgive me?'

'You don't need my forgiveness, dear,' says Hazel. 'Right now, I'm worried about your health. You look so flushed. I want you to see the doctor in case it's blood pressure.'

'Of course I will. Anything to make you happy,' says Bob, with a smile.

When Hazel asks him why partners are never invited to these events, he says, 'You know what these blokes are like – boys will be boys. You're not missing anything, quite honestly.'

'No, Bob, I don't know what they're like. I've never met any of them, as you know, and I assume they're not boys but grown men.'

'But would you really want to be in the same room as a hundred travelling salesmen, my love? Next Saturday, you and I will go out for a slap-up meal at Grotta Capri to make up for it. I'll ring and make a booking. We'll get a taxi over there.'

'You don't need to make it up to me, Bob.'

He takes her hand tenderly. 'I don't deserve you, my love.' His tone is so genuine, she wonders if there is an element of truth in the comment.

For the rest of the morning he's distracted and restless. He makes several visits to the corner shop and is gone for fifteen minutes each time. The first time he returns empty-handed, the second with a newspaper that he flicks through and discards impatiently. It occurs to Hazel that these outings could be an excuse to go to the telephone box on the corner and make a call in private.

The club is only fifteen minutes away on the train but Bob sets off in the middle of the afternoon, behaving like a man who is running late. 'I'll be back first thing in the morning,' he says, with a brief parting kiss.

'Aren't you going to wear your good suit?' asks Hazel, surprised to see him in a grey plaid jacket and sports trousers, and not even his best shoes.

'I've got another suit at the club. I'll change there.'

She waves him off at the door, curious as to why he's in such a hurry. Does he plan to place a few bets on the way or something else entirely? Her ears have been tingling on and off all day. It's difficult to know what to believe. He seems to be piling one lie on another.

She makes a snap decision. Putting on her shoes and grabbing her handbag, she takes the shortcut down the back alley. By the time she gets to the station, he's nowhere in sight. She takes the train to Town Hall, where she gets off and walks up to Castlereagh Street.

In the years when she and Betty worked at the telephone exchange, the city centre was as familiar as her own street. They often ate their sandwiches sitting on the grass in Hyde Park or wandered about the streets window-shopping, dreaming of lovely things they couldn't afford. They'd worked there before the war and right up until the exchange was automated. After that, there was no need for switchboard girls and they were no longer girls. The city, once so familiar, is a different place today. The trams have gone, many older buildings have been pulled down and more people have cars, making the roads busier than ever.

Hazel positions herself in a doorway along from the main entry to the club, which is above the Australia Hotel. It's a warm, pleasant afternoon and she can't help but wish that she and Bob were taking a stroll in the city together. But here she is skulking in a doorway, spying on him. It feels despicable and treacherous. She doesn't even know for sure that he went to the club.

She tries to think of a plausible reason to make an enquiry at the front desk but is saved the bother when Bob comes rushing out the main doors – dressed in a tuxedo! He immediately hails a taxi and jumps in. Hazel hails the next one, instructing the driver to follow Bob's taxi.

'Who are we following, then?' asks the driver who, judging by his diminutive size and weathered profile, had a former life as a jockey. 'Husband, I'll bet. Yer can't trust any of 'em.'

Hazel checks her purse to make sure Friday's pay packet is still there for the fare. 'I do trust him, it's just—'

'Yeah, know what yer saying,' says the jockey, keeping pace with the other taxi as they head off towards the eastern suburbs. 'The ones you trust, they're the worst,' he continues, determined to educate her in the perversity of men's behaviour. 'When a man has too much trust, guaranteed he'll do the wrong thing. Too much rope, you see. Dangerous.'

Feeling rattled, Hazel doesn't really want to talk but the loneliness of the driver fills the space between them. 'You either trust someone or you don't,' she says. 'You can't trust someone a bit.'

'Take your point. One of them all-or-nothing things.' Despite her lack of encouragement, he chats amiably as they pass Double Bay and then Rose Bay, continuing on towards the last village on the peninsula.

Bob's taxi finally stops on the main road opposite an old sandstone church. He gets out and crosses over to join a well-dressed group of people gathered on the lawn at the entrance. The men wear suits and the women elaborate hats and fascinators, all gloved and bejewelled.

'Ah, silvertail wedding,' says the jockey, flicking off the meter as they pull up.

Hazel watches in bewilderment as Bob shakes all the men's hands and kisses every woman in a flurry of affection, laughing and back-slapping. He's well-known and well-loved by everyone here. There has to be a logical explanation.

'So, we're here, missus,' the jockey reminds her.

Hazel has no idea what to do next. She either has to go home or get out of this taxi. Going home is the most attractive option but she's come this far and clearly needs to see it through. 'Could you drop me on the other side of the road, please, just up the hill a little?'

The jockey makes a u-turn and stops just beyond the church. 'There yer go.'

Hazel checks the meter and hands over the cash, barely registering the cost.

'Good luck,' he says. 'Really, missus, best of luck. You seem like a nice lady.'

'Thank you; I do my best,' says Hazel. She gets out of the taxi feeling exposed and underdressed; an obvious outsider. To avoid being seen, she makes her way to a shrubby strip that runs between the church and the parking area. Concealed by bushes, she watches the crowd outside the church continue to grow.

Bob is soon joined by a woman of similar age who wears a lavender dress with a short jacket and matching handbag and shoes. She lifts her cheek for Bob's kiss, her large white hat teetering dangerously to one side. Hazel watches her inspect Bob, dust off his shoulders and straighten his tie. Not like a fussy relative, not like a sister – like a wife. Only a wife of many years treats a man like a piece of furniture that needs dusting, plumping and straightening.

Hazel is pinned to the spot as if she can't tear herself from this scene. She watches as Bob and Lavender Lady are joined by a younger couple with children. Bob playfully picks up one of the kids. He dangles the boy in the air to shrieks of laughter and two little girls lift their arms, begging for the same treatment. Lavender Lady scolds him and he puts the boy down. She takes Bob's arm and they move into the church together.

As the guests gather and file into the church, Hazel joins a small group of locals standing out on the pavement opposite the main doors, leaving the pathway free for the bridal party who soon arrive in a black Rolls Royce decorated with white bows and ribbons. A first bridal car delivers three bridesmaids in pale-pink gowns and two flower girls in simple white dresses with daisy chains encircling their little heads. The second car brings the bride, a pretty young woman in her twenties who wears an extravagant satin and lace gown with a long veil and is accompanied by an older man, also dressed in a tuxedo.

Hazel takes in every tiny detail, trying to make sense of how these people are related.

As the wedding party assembles on the porch, a middle-aged woman in a cream suit strides out of the church and takes charge. Judging by the way she fusses about rearranging the bride's veil and instructing the bridesmaids, she is the mother of the bride.

Inside the church, the organ strikes up the wedding march. With one final instruction, the woman steps aside, gesturing to the party to move forward into the church. She turns and bestows a benevolent smile on those watching from the street. Her eyes alight on Hazel. The smile vanishes. She looks so stricken that several people turn curiously to look at Hazel. The woman takes a step towards her, as if about to speak, then recovers herself, turns away and goes into the church, closing the doors behind her.

Shaken by the whole experience, Hazel leaves the church and begins to walk up the hill towards the city. She finds a bus stop and sits down to wait. Then, too agitated to sit, she gets up and begins to walk again, concentrating on staying upright and moving forward. After some time, she hears a car pull up beside her and glances around nervously, relieved to see the jockey's taxi.

He leans over and winds down the passenger-side window. 'Come on. Hop in, nice lady. I'll take yer home.'

Thanking him, Hazel collapses gratefully onto the back seat.

'Thought yer might be in trouble. Got a sense about these things. Sixth sense, yer know? This one time, took a bloke up the Gap. Said he was going for a walk. Fair enough, I think. Then I got this uneasy feeling, see? Went back and there he was about to throw his self off. I knew something was up. Felt it in me bones.'

All the way home, Hazel stares bleakly out the window as the jockey rambles on. The only thing she knows for certain is that everything she thought she knew about Bob is wrong. It's only when they stop outside 5 Glade Street that she realises the meter has been off. 'But I must pay you,' she insists.

'Don't worry about it, missus. Had to come back into town anyway. Good to have someone to chat to,' he says, turning to her with a gap-toothed grin. He hands her the card of the taxi company. 'Need a taxi, call them and ask for Bert.'

Hazel gives him a smile. 'Thank you, Bert. I'm sorry I wasn't better company.'

'We had a good chat, didn't we?' he says cheerfully.

'You didn't see who was getting married at that church, did you?'

'Nuh. But I got this morning's paper here if yer wanna have a squiz.'

'I didn't think to bring my glasses. Do you mind looking in the notices for me?'

He picks up his paper and, murmuring to himself, runs a finger down the columns.

'Ah, this'd be the one. Congratulations from Mr and Mrs Arnold Herrmann on the marriage of their daughter—'

'That's all I needed to know, thank you,' says Hazel. 'The mother of the bride was Mrs Herrmann.'

'Yeah, two *r*s and two *n*s. Can't see the point, but there yer are.'

Sitting alone in her little kitchen, Hazel imagines the newlyweds emerging from the church in a whirlwind of happiness and confetti. There's Bob, in his tuxedo, and Lavender Lady in her enormous hat.

Hazel doesn't know where they all fit in; she only knows that they do. This is Bob's other, bigger life. Bob's secret life. She realises with a jolt that it's the other way around. They are Bob's family. Hazel is his secret life.

She forces her thoughts away from that happy gathering. Now she needs to know everything. She has to find out the truth. She wonders what she knows for certain about Bob. The difficulty is where to start to unravel fact from fabrication. Where does he go during the week – home to his other wife? Where does his wife think he is from Friday to Sunday? In her mind, Hazel trawls through the past years searching for any clues that Bob has been living a fraudulent life. Nothing stands out. He has been a kind and loving husband, absent but also present. She prides herself on reading people accurately, yet has somehow been completely blind to the deception taking place right under her nose.

31

IRENE IN A SPOT OF BOTHER

Bob rings on Sunday morning to say he won't be home until after lunch. It occurs to Hazel that he's extremely considerate for someone so deceitful – he never leaves any room for doubt or speculation. There are no missing hours to wonder about, all are accounted for.

As he chats about the dinner the previous night, she realises that she's not ready to confront him. There's no point going in with accusations that he could talk his way out of. She needs time to assemble the evidence and get her thoughts in order. With what she now knows and suspects, it takes all her strength to have a normal conversation with him.

'Bob, it hardly seems worth you coming back here for a few hours,' she says, managing to adopt an even tone. 'Why don't you go to Grafton straight from the club? I've got a few errands to run this afternoon anyway.'

'Are you sure?' he asks, with obvious relief. 'Well, if you're not going to be around, my love . . . as you say, I might as well. And I've booked our dinner for next week.'

Hazel knows there will be no dinner. Her life has paused, the future unseeable. They say their goodbyes, and it seems that Bob doesn't notice the coolness in her tone.

She's barely hung up when the telephone rings again. She picks it up, expecting Bob has forgotten something, doubting she has the strength to speak to him again without bursting into tears.

'Mrs Bates? It's about Mrs Turnbuckle, I want 'er out of here. Quick smart. I had to call the doc out to her last night. Pneumonia, he reckons. I'm not a hospital. I can't have her making me boarders sick.'

It takes Hazel a moment to realise that the caller is Irene's much-loathed landlady. 'Pneumonia is not infectious,' says Hazel. 'So you have nothing to worry about on that account. Why didn't they take her to hospital if she's so ill?'

'Wouldn't go, stubborn old goat. I don't want no one dying under my roof. I want her out. She said to ring you.'

'All right, I'll come and collect her shortly.'

'Good. And I don't want her back neither,' says the landlady before hanging up.

The boarding house is a fifteen-minute walk from Hazel's, located in the most run-down street in the whole neighbourhood. Every-thing in the street is broken: windows, gates, fences, bicycles, wooden beer crates. It is as if a storm has raged through the place, smashing everything in its path. Outside the boarding house, a skinny man with a ravaged, bony face sits on a crate smoking, apparently enjoying the sight of two dogs fighting viciously in the street. A grubby child, wearing nothing but a dirty singlet, also watches the dogs. Hazel longs to pick up the poor little mite and take him home for a bath and a hot meal. But today it's Irene who needs rescuing.

In better times, the Victorian terrace must have been a grand home to a well-heeled family who would be saddened to see the iron lacework rusted and broken, the walls pitted black with soot and mould. Some of the windows are taped up and, by the look of splintered scarring on the front door, someone has tried to enter the building with an axe.

At Hazel's knock, the landlady opens the door. 'Top-o-stairs, first to yer right.' She presses herself against the wall to let Hazel past and slams the door shut behind her.

Inside, the air is thick with the smell of rancid dripping, boiled cabbage and cigarette smoke. The landlady herself has a mouldering smell, like damp washing left too long in the basket. The stairs are broken in places and creak precariously under Hazel's feet as she climbs to the first floor and knocks on Irene's door.

'Go away!' comes a croak from within. 'Go. Away. I told yer to pi*th* off and don't come back.'

'It's me, Irene dear.' Hazel slowly pushes the door open and peeks inside.

The small room is crowded with Irene's belongings in piles on the floor. Clothes spill from the old wardrobe and cover a chair. In the midst of it all, Irene is wrapped in a nest of threadbare blankets on a mattress that sags below the bedstead.

'The old bitch i*th* kicking me out,' she croaks.

'It's all right, dear. I'm going to take you over to Glade Street right now. I can ask Mr Butterby to come in the van and pick up your things this evening.'

'Not Butterby,' whispers Irene, before being overtaken by a hacking cough.

'All right. Don't worry. I'm sure Mr Mulligan will be happy to come.' Hazel helps Irene out of bed and feeds her arms into her black coat.

'Get off me. I ju*th* need me teeth.'

Hazel passes her the soupy glass of water containing her dentures. Irene gives them a shake and puts them in her pocket. 'Hat. *Thipperth.*'

With hat and slippers in place, they make their way slowly down the stairs.

The landlady stands in the hallway, blocking their exit. 'You gotta pay for the room to be fumigated. And get yer stuff out. And a week's rent for notice.'

'I'll come back this evening and pack up—' begins Hazel.

'Also, the extra week's rent for the fumigation,' interrupts the landlady.

'You're nothing but a dirty thie*th*!' croaks Irene.

'Pneumonia is an infection in the lungs, it's not the plague,' says Hazel. 'If you want to fumigate the room, that's up to you.'

'That's right, it is. Extra week's rent it'll be.'

'Fumigation is not a bad idea, in fact,' continues Hazel in a pleasant tone. 'You should really do the entire house while you're at it. There are cockroaches on the walls in Mrs Turnbuckle's room and rat droppings in the upstairs hallway. The black mould in that bedroom is very bad for the lungs.' Hazel pauses, then adopting a sympathetic tone, goes in hard. 'I imagine you're worried about the council inspector closing you down.'

The landlady flushes angrily. 'What are you talking about?'

Hazel casts her gaze over the peeling wallpaper, noticing a sea of tiny bugs on the move behind it. She stares thoughtfully at the patch of fungi growing from the cornice until the landlady's curiosity gets the better of her and she takes a look herself.

'I understand your concern,' continues Hazel. 'They might even put a demolition order on the place. It's happening a lot now with the slum clearances, they're looking for any excuse. Terrible, really.'

'Are youse calling my place a slum?'

Several tenants have gathered at the top of the stairs. The landlady casts them a venomous look, gesturing at them to move on – without success. She gives an exasperated sigh and flings the front door open. 'Go on, get out. Good riddance.'

'If you really want to be rid of us then perhaps you could call us a taxi,' says Hazel, taking Irene's arm. They step outside and the door slams behind them.

The scrapping dogs have disappeared but the craggy-faced man sits smoking as if patiently awaiting the arrival of further entertainment.

'You off, love?' he asks Irene, in a friendly tone.

'Mind yer own bloody bu*thineth*,' says Irene. 'Go away, yer bring down the tone of the neighbourhood.'

The man laughs and stays where he is, giving them a cheerful wave as they leave in the taxi. 'A friend?' asks Hazel.

'No friend of mine,' says Irene. 'Me ex-boyfriend – one of 'em, anyway.'

By the time Mr Mulligan drives Hazel back to the boarding house later in the afternoon, Irene's belongings are strewn about the pavement with several ragged-looking children poking through them. Hazel shoos them away and picks up Irene's clothes, putting them into the empty beer crates in the back of the van.

The landlady sticks her head out of the upstairs window. 'There you are, 'bout time!' She hurls Irene's maroon cardigan, a brown wig and a photograph album out the window. 'That's it, now bugger off.'

'Charming,' remarks Mr Mulligan. He picks up the photograph album, glances through it with interest and hands it to Hazel. 'She'll want this.' He tries to fit the wig on his head but it's too small. 'Oh, shame, I thought I'd look like The Beatles in that.'

'Which one?' asks Hazel, curious only because Mr Mulligan is short, bald and rotund.

'They all look the same, any one will do. Wouldn't mind having women scream at the sight of me. *Eeeeeeck!*' He waves his arms about, imitating the teenage girls that had mobbed The Beatles during their tour last year.

'Apart from Mrs Mulligan, you mean?' asks Hazel with a smile.

He laughs. 'That one's got a scream like a Stuka. Scares the life out of yer.'

He pulls a couple more crates out of the van and together they pack up Irene's bits and pieces: her old-fashioned button-up shoes, the rubber galoshes she wears over her slippers on rainy days, a few cheap knick-knacks and ornaments, a couple of packs of playing cards and a shoebox of papers tied up with string. In the end, Irene's life comes down to six crates – not much to show for six decades, thinks Hazel sadly.

Once Irene's belongings are stacked in the front room, Hazel takes hot soup and toast upstairs to her. She looks frail sitting up in bed wearing one of Hazel's floral nighties. Teeth now in place, she slurps her soup and munches on her toast, gazing around the small room approvingly. 'I'm liking this. Liking it a lot. Luxurious. But yer don't need to worry, Haze, I'll find somewhere to go . . . the People's Palace with all those other homeless folk down on their luck like me . . . or the poorhouse, I suppose.' She adds a tragic sigh.

'I don't think they have poorhouses any more, dear, so no danger of that. Let's talk about it when you're well. For the moment you're staying here. I've put all your clothes in the copper to soak and I'll get them on the line in the morning.'

'I have to get up in the morning for work.'

'I've just spoken to Merl and Betty; we're going to split your job for the next few days. No arguing. It's all in hand.'

'Yer good girls,' says Irene. 'Good mates.'

Hazel pats her hand. 'You'd do it for us.'

'To be honest, wouldn't cross me mind,' says Irene, settling back on her pillows. 'Any more soup where that came from?'

32

BETTY STEPS IN AT SILHOUETTE

Betty is hardly surprised at the state of Irene's kitchen at Silhouette Knitwear. Cups and saucers piled precariously on open shelves, and dirty dishes left in the sink over the weekend. The kitchen is barely bigger than a cupboard, with no windows and dimly lit by a single light bulb. Now Betty, Merl and Hazel are all squashed in there, bumping into each other as they try to organise everything for the day ahead.

'You're game leaving Irene home alone,' says Merl, peering suspiciously into a teapot.

'Oh Merl, that's a wicked thing to say,' says Betty. She pulls the tea trolley out into the hallway. 'She's not going to run off with Hazel's silver.'

Hazel rinses out the cups and saucers, gives them a quick dry and passes them to Betty. 'She couldn't run anywhere right now. Besides, I don't have any silver.'

'Lock up your valuables is all I'm saying,' says Merl. 'She's light-fingered, that one. I honestly don't know how she keeps this job, she's a grub.'

Betty has often wondered the same thing. Irene jokes that they are afraid to fire her, which could be true. Betty also knows that most of the staff in this factory are men who keep the automated knitting machines running. They probably think Irene is a bit of a character and don't mind her odd habits. There are a couple of women in the office and the secretary Irene's always gossiping about, but who knows what dirt Irene has on them.

'Betty, if you take this up now to the factory and office,' suggests Hazel, 'Merl can do the warehouse after her first shift this morning, then I'll do the afternoon shift.'

'You should be running the country, Hazel,' jokes Betty, hoping to cheer Hazel up.

'Tea Lady Becomes Australia's First Female Prime Minister,' says Merl, dryly.

'It's just an expression, Merl. Anyway, Hazel would do a better job than the blokes we've got in charge. She could run the country standing on her head.'

'I'm not planning on running for office or standing on my head, just getting this tea delivered today,' says Hazel.

It's clear to Betty that Hazel is not herself this morning. She's not just quiet, but positively glum, which is not like her at all. Now is not a good time but Betty makes a mental note to bring it up later, when they have a private moment together.

Betty takes the worryingly ancient cage lift up to the factory on the top floor. Knitting machines are quite a different beast to the sewing machines at her work. The balls of wool sit on vertical rods that stretch up towards high glass ceilings like the antennas of mechanical monsters. Men in grey duster coats move between the roaring machines, barely noticing when she leaves the tea and a plate of stale-looking biscuits on a bench and clearly not even slightly curious about the appearance of a new tea lady.

Back in the trembling lift, she gets out on the floor below where the two office women and the secretary also ignore her. With a few minutes to spare, she takes the trolley back to the awful little kitchen and parks it outside. She wonders again what's going on with Hazel. Having Irene staying there wouldn't bother her; she takes things like that in her stride. Betty only hopes that it's not something to do with Bob. He's made her so happy over the years, it would be terribly disappointing if he let her down now.

33

HAZEL RESORTS TO BRIBERY

'There's got to be someone here who can sign a cheque!' says Dottie Karp. She almost never sets foot in the building but now stands, hands on her hips, at Edith Stern's desk.

'Good morning, Mrs Karp, can I make you a cup of tea?' asks Hazel, delivering Edith's tea.

Dottie glances at her distractedly. 'Thank you, no.'

'You could take a cheque for Mr Karp to sign at the hospital, but none of us can sign cheques,' Edith explains.

Dottie perks up. 'Is he well enough to sign cheques?'

'They think he'll be out of hospital later this week, so if you could wait—'

'Where the hell is Frankie? That's all I want to know,' says Dottie, angry all over again.

'I expect you're worried about him,' says Edith.

'I'm not worried! I'm furious! Just typical of him to disappear like this, leaving me high and dry, without a penny.'

'Let me speak to Mr Levy, see if we can sort something out for you,' says Edith. 'I'll give you a ring later today.'

Dottie sighs impatiently. 'All right, preferably before lunch. If it's after one, call me at Rossetti's, they know me there.'

Hazel and Edith wait in silence until the lift door closes and Dottie's definitely gone.

'What an article she is,' says Edith, bitterly. 'Husband disappeared. Her father-in-law in the hospital. She probably just needs a cheque for her milliner.'

'Have the police come up with anything at all?' asks Hazel.

'They were here, asking a few questions. As we all know, Frankie gets around. They probably think he's shacked up with some dreadful tart he met at one of those cabaret clubs. They asked me if there was "another woman" in the background.'

Edith's words hit a nerve and Hazel sits down heavily in the visitor's chair, feeling breathless and dizzy.

'Are you all right, Hazel?' asks Edith.

'I'm fine. Just had a little moment.'

'Oh, Hazel, we can't have anything happen to you! Then where would we be?!'

Hazel smiles. 'You'd just have to make your own tea. Not the end of the world. Now, have you remembered anything else about Natalia Ivanov and Frankie?'

'Not really. As I told you, I saw the two of them in his car on Lisbon Street. Didn't appear to be talking. That's what seemed odd at the time. Perhaps she is the "other woman" and they are off somewhere together with no idea that people are looking for them.'

'I suppose that's possible. What if Natalia has run away from her husband and somehow ended up meeting Frankie?'

'Out of the frying pan, into the furnace,' says Edith.

'Where would she meet Frankie? He doesn't seem like a circus goer.'

'Or someone that an attractive young woman would run off with if she had any sense . . .'

'Try and remember which day you saw them together,' says Hazel.

Edith considers this for a moment. She picks up her desk calendar and flicks through the pages. 'What was the date of the fire?'

'Twenty-ninth of October, and I saw her in the bond store the morning before that.'

Edith goes to her filing cabinet, opens a drawer and looks through the files. She takes out a sheet of paper. 'It was the twenty-seventh. I typed up this letter and Mr Karp wanted it hand-delivered to the bank, so I walked it up after lunch, and that's when I saw them.'

'So, according to the papers she's been missing for a week or so, whereas it could be more like two weeks.' Hazel finds the discrepancy puzzling, as is the possible connection between Frankie, Natalia and Borisyuk.

When Hazel bumps into Pixie in the hallway, the girl seems unfazed by her father's disappearance. 'He's probably gone on a business trip,' she suggests. 'He often doesn't bother telling anyone where he's going, or when he's coming back.' She pauses and adds quietly, 'They're a bit weird, my parents, Mrs Bates. Live their own lives. They've always been like that.'

'I expect deep down we're all a bit weird,' says Hazel. 'How's your grandfather doing?'

'He's doing well, thank you. He's going to be home in a few days. Thank you for what you did. He would have died if you hadn't been there. You saved his life.'

'All part of the job, Pixie dear. By the way, how are you enjoying working downstairs?'

'I'm learning a lot from Mrs Nuttell, and Mr Butterby is very nice – he's been showing me how the dispatch section works, and all the paperwork and everything. There's a lot to it. Much more than I realised.' Pixie describes her tasks with enthusiasm, and Hazel can see how quickly she's changing. As the weeks pass, she seems more grown up and self-assured but still full of the bright optimism of youth that is sadly lacking around here right now.

There's not much optimism evident on the 1st Floor where Miss Ivy and Miss Joan sit at their long worktable playing patience with two packs of cards. The unclothed dressmaker's dummies stand sentry behind them.

'We're in the dark here,' Miss Ivy announces as soon as Hazel walks in.

'No one knows what's going on,' says Miss Joan.

'Or, if they do, they're not telling us,' adds Miss Ivy.

'I'm sure you would be the first to know,' Hazel assures them.

Doug Fysh comes out of his office to collect his tea. 'I just got off the phone with Cashell's. They've given us a deadline to present a new range.'

'I don't even want to hear it,' says Miss Joan, studying the cards in front of her.

Miss Ivy goes as far as covering her ears. 'Whatever it is, it's impossible.'

'Two weeks,' says Doug. 'We've got two weeks to come up with something. That's our last chance for the next summer range, then the buyers move on to winter.'

'Two weeks,' says Hazel, gauging the sisters' response. 'Not too bad.'

Doug grins. 'Maybe the tea ladies can brew something up for us? Haw haw.'

'Impossible,' says Miss Ivy. 'We don't even have a direction.'

Doug gives an expansive shrug. 'Everyone's in the same position; some of our competitors are already racing ahead of us.'

'We can't do anything without Frankie,' says Miss Joan, folding her arms.

Doug looks from one to the other. 'We have to come up with something. Better something than nothing, ladies.'

Hazel says, 'I think Gloria has some ideas.'

'Gloria Nuttell?' repeats Miss Ivy with a shudder. 'I dread to think.'

'I know she can be a little intimidating sometimes, but why not have a chat?'

'We have nothing to say to that woman,' says Miss Ivy.

Miss Joan agrees. 'We know she calls us the Ginger Nuts.'

'Affectionately,' says Hazel, wondering who's been stirring things up. Doug Fysh most likely.

'We'll wait until Mr Karp or Frankie come back and speak to them about all this,' says Miss Joan.

'Since we don't know when that will be, it wouldn't hurt to talk to Gloria,' says Hazel. 'Why not invite her up for a chat tomorrow morning? I'll make your favourite sour plum cake.'

'Plum cake?' says Doug. 'Count me in.'

'You know all our weaknesses,' says Miss Joan, with a sigh. 'You're absolutely heartless, Hazel.'

34

HAZEL MISSES AN IMPORTANT CALL

Arriving home from work, Hazel opens her front door to find Irene on the phone in the hallway. 'Bloody cheek! Who do yers think yer are? No, I'm not going to pa*th* on any me*th*age.' Irene slams the receiver down furiously.

'Irene? Who was that?' asks Hazel. Stepping inside, she closes the door behind her.

Irene gives a start. 'Oh, Hazel. Yer'll never gue*th*!'

'It might be easier if you just told me, dear, and try to avoid "s" if you can.'

'That Mi*thith* Herrmann woman.'

Hazel puts a hand on the wall to steady herself. 'Mrs Herrmann? Are you sure?'

'Yeah.' She stares at Hazel. 'Yer right? Come in, ol' girl. I'll make you a cuppa.'

Hazel follows her into the kitchen. She sits down and waits while Irene bashes about with the kettle, crashing cups onto saucers.

'What did she say, Irene?'

'Just wanted to *th*peak to you and I told her yer were out and *th*e gave her name and I gave her what for.'

'Irene, dear, perhaps just let the phone ring in future – people will call back later. Or, at the very least, put your teeth in and offer to take a message.'

Not bothering to let the tea steep, Irene puts an overfilled cup in front of Hazel, slopping tea into the saucer. She fishes her teeth out of her pocket and pops them in. 'So, what's her game?' she asks, sitting down opposite Hazel.

Hazel hasn't told a soul about her discovery but it seems pointless to keep it from Irene now. 'I believe that Mrs Herrmann is Bob's daughter.'

'Oh, that's nice. But I don't get it. Why have yer followed?'

Hazel sighs. 'It seems that Bob not only has a daughter but I think he has a wife as well.'

Irene closes one eye to concentrate better. 'Another wife?'

Hazel nods. She explains how she tracked Bob to the church and the wedding and Lavender Lady and the daisy chains on the flower girls.

'Mrs Herrmann was the mother of the bride. So I'm guessing, from what I saw, that the bride was Bob's granddaughter.' Hazel pauses, thinking back to that awful moment. 'When the woman saw me . . . the look on her face . . . she recognised me straight-away.' She sips her tea, reflecting on the situation. 'That's how I guessed that she was Mrs Herrmann – she'd seen the photographs of me with Bob.'

'How'd she get yer number anyways?' asks Irene.

'She knew from Mr Sinclair the name is Bates, not Bateman, and we're in the phone book.' Hazel pauses. 'It would have been helpful to find out what she wanted.'

Irene considers this for a moment. 'Ah, yeah, I see what yer saying. I mighta been a bit hasty.'

'I've obviously given the matter a lot of thought in the past couple of days. I think Mrs Herrmann suspected something was going on and hired the private detective to confirm her suspicions. Now, the question is, what does she do about it? She probably doesn't want her mother to know but she may have said something to Bob, which would account for his odd behaviour of late.'

'Bloody Bob. He's a piece of work, gunna get done for bigamy and serve him right.'

Hazel hadn't even considered him being charged. The thought of Bob going to prison is appalling. 'I'm sure his daughter wouldn't want that. And I wouldn't either.'

Irene shakes her head in despair. 'Yer too soft, Haze.'

'I'm not out to punish him, just to get to the bottom of it all.'

'Yer could blackmail him,' says Irene, brightening up. 'My old man did a bit of blackmailing between jobs. Cutting letters out of newspapers and all that. I could help yer, if yer want.'

'That's very kind of you, Irene dear. But I don't think so.'

They sit in silence for a moment, Hazel considering her options. 'I need to wait and talk to Bob when he comes home. I have to hear his side of the story.'

'Please yerself. Probably just hear a pack o' lies. He's a salesman, in't he? He knows what to tell yer. Don't believe a word of it.'

This has already crossed Hazel's mind. Bob's had years of experience telling people what they want to hear. He is the master of selected truth, it would seem.

'You seem to have recovered,' says Hazel, keen to change the subject.

'Nothing wrong with me. Good night's sleep. Box-a-birds today.'

'Perhaps the doctor was mistaken about pneumonia?'

'That quack would not know a bunion from an onion. He's a ratbag – after me money.'

'I see, well, I'm glad you're recovering.'

Irene gives a delicate cough. 'I could relapse; yer just can't tell with these things. Got anything to drink, Hazel? A tipple of something might be good for me chest.'

Hazel opens the cupboard and surveys her stock. 'I've got choko, parsnip or mulberry wine? Or a bit of plum?'

'Anythink stronger in there, on the top shelf?'

Hazel gets down Bob's good whiskey. Judging by the level, Irene has already had a tipple or two during the day. No wonder she's so chirpy.

35

GLORIA TACKLES THE GINGER NUTS

'Here she is! The delightful Mrs Nuttell!' cries Doug Fysh, coming out of his office. 'All the girls together – a well-oiled team!'

Gloria, sitting at the large dressmaker's table normally used for cutting out patterns, has endured five long minutes of awkward small talk with the Ginger Nuts so she's relieved to see Doug and, better still, Hazel with the tea and promised sour plum cake.

'You've got a plum job, Hazel, haw haw haw,' says Doug, taking his place at the table. 'You must be plum tuckered out by the end of the day.'

Hazel chuckles politely as she serves out tea and cake.

'Just a tiny piece for me,' says Miss Ivy, eyeing the cake warily.

'And me,' says Miss Joan.

Gloria's guessing that it will take more than Hazel's cake to sweeten those two sourpusses up, and accepts a generous slice just to be contrary.

'As the only male present, I suppose I'll be running the meeting,' says Doug, through a mouthful of cake.

'Mrs Bates organised the meeting. Why doesn't she run it?' says Miss Ivy, giving Hazel one of her sharp looks.

Gloria doesn't want to waste time squabbling. She lays out Alice's magazines on the table. Opening a couple up to double-page fashion spreads, she slides them across the table to the sisters. She wants to say something clever and savvy that would earn the respect of the Ginger Nuts, but nothing comes to mind.

Miss Ivy glances over the pages with an expression of distaste.

Miss Joan takes a proper look at each spread before slowly turning the page. Finally, she says, 'This is not the sort of thing we do here. They're frivolous . . . cheap looking. These styles look like children's clothes. We're known for our quality finishing and classic styles. Not our sort of thing at all.'

'Tasteless,' confirms Miss Ivy. 'And tarty.'

'You can't see what's happening right in front of you,' says Gloria through gritted teeth. 'Everything is changing – you're a couple of dinosaurs, living in the past.' She jabs her finger at the dressmaker's dummies. 'Those two are smarter than you two. And they haven't even got heads!'

'Standards of style and quality will never become extinct,' says Miss Joan frostily.

Gloria pushes back her chair and gets up. 'It's hopeless. Completely hopeless.'

'Hang on there,' says Doug. He gestures for Gloria to sit down. 'Let's not get all hasty, ladies.'

'Anyone like another slice of cake before I go?' asks Hazel, knife poised.

Miss Ivy looks longingly at the cake. 'Just a tiny piece.'

'As I said, we have two weeks to get something in front of the buyers,' says Doug.

'As we said, it's impossible,' says Miss Joan. 'Absolutely impossible. We don't have the designs, let alone the patterns and fabrics – it takes months!'

'And, if we go ahead without Frankie's approval, he'll be furious,' says Miss Ivy. 'We could lose our jobs.'

Gloria takes a deep breath to calm herself for one last attempt. 'Ladies, if we don't do something, we're all going to lose our jobs.' She points out one of the shift-style dresses. 'Look at this. It would be very quick and easy to copy. Let's say that you could get a pattern down to the cutting room tomorrow afternoon. We could then have a sample ready by Thursday arvo.'

'And who's going to explain this to Frankie?' asks Miss Ivy. 'You, Mrs Nuttell?'

'Ah, there you are!' says Hazel. 'Perfect timing.'

Everyone swivels around to see Pixie walk into the room.

'Come on in, I've saved you some cake.' Hazel places a milky cup of tea and a slice of cake on the table, and beckons the girl to sit down. 'There you go, Pixie dear. Now, more tea, anyone? I have to be getting along.'

It had occurred to Gloria earlier that it was unlike Hazel to hang around waiting on them, but as usual she had a plan, the shrewd old chook.

36

BETTY SETS UP A MEETING AT THE HOLLYWOOD

'Evening, Mrs B, Mrs T, Mrs D, Mrs P.' Shirley puts the shandies down on the table and gives Irene a cheeky grin. 'Put this round on your tab, Mrs T?'

'Still not funny,' says Irene. 'Lucky I don't have a tab, yer'd go broke.'

'Put them on mine, Shirley dear,' says Hazel.

'Shirley, please put them on my tab,' says Betty, adopting a virtuous tone. She can't believe the gall of Irene, not just imposing on Hazel at home but expecting her to pay for drinks as well!

'Of course, Mrs D, no worries. Heard you were poorly, Mrs T? Pneumonia?'

'Fighting fit now,' says Irene. 'Bit a phlegm, is all. I'm staying with Mrs B for a bit.'

Shirley gives Hazel a sympathetic look. 'We all have our cross to bear,' she says. 'Hope Puffing Billy here doesn't burn your house down, Mrs B.'

'Bloody cheek,' says Irene, taking her pipe out of her pocket.

'No, not that please,' begs Betty. 'My asthma . . .'

Irene clamps the pipe between her teeth. 'All right, keep yer hat on. I wasn't going to light the bloody thing.'

'Language,' Merl reminds her.

Worried the meeting is turning into a squabbling match, Betty gets out her notebook. 'Now, before our contact from the fire station, Effie Finch, arrives, I will just—'

'Completely confuse everyone?' interrupts Merl. 'Spare us, please.'

Irene takes her pipe out of her mouth and taps it on the table for attention. 'Never mind yer stupid list. There's something more important. Go on, Hazel, tell 'em . . . it looks like Bob's got another missus.'

Tears spring to Betty's eyes. 'Oh, Hazel! Oh no . . . that's . . . awful.'

'Thank you, Irene,' says Hazel with a sigh. 'I wasn't really planning to make an announcement this evening.'

'So this Mrs Herrmann is the other woman?' asks Merl, frowning.

Hazel forces a smile. 'I believe Mrs Herrmann is his daughter, but her mother is alive and well. So it would seem that, in fact . . . I'm the other woman.'

'Hazel, you must be . . . Bob seemed such a nice . . .' Betty trails off, dismayed. She has no idea how Hazel must feel, or how to comfort her.

'I'm not sure what to think. On one hand, you have to admire Bob for pulling it off for so long – it can't be easy having two lives. On the other hand, I'm so'—Hazel pauses to compose herself—'so angry about being lied to all these years. I can't understand how I didn't have a clue.'

'I would die of shame, if it were me,' declares Merl.

'Oh, Merl!' Betty gets out her hanky and mops her tears. 'That's a terrible thing to say to Hazel. It's not her fault.'

Irene agrees. 'Yeah, pull yer head in, Merl, what a bloody stupid thing to say!'

Hazel holds up a hand for calm. 'No one actually dies of shame, Merl; besides, I've done nothing wrong. All the shame is on Bob. I'm so disappointed in him. He's not the man I thought he was. Not by a long shot.'

'But everybody knowing . . .' argues Merl, in her usual stubborn way.

'Everyone doesn't need to know,' says Hazel. She gives each of them a pointed look (which hurts Betty's feelings a tiny bit). 'It's a private matter between me and Bob, and I'm trusting you not to gossip about it. Please keep it to yourselves, I haven't even told Norma yet.'

'Oh, Hazel, you're like a brave little ship riding the high seas, weathering every storm and soldiering on,' says Betty, brimming with admiration at Hazel's cool head.

'I know this joker who does kneecapping,' says Irene in a low voice. 'He's quite cheap. It's not his main line of work, just a sideline.'

'What's his main line of work?' asks Betty, wondering if he's in an allied business – wheelchairs, for example, or walking sticks.

'You don't wanna know,' says Irene darkly.

'Thank you for all your helpful suggestions, Irene dear, but I don't think kneecapping is really my style any more than black-mail . . . ah, here's Effie – we can talk about this later.'

'I can make a note,' says Betty, wanting to be helpful above all else.

'Leave out the kneecapping business, obviously,' says Hazel, turning her attention to their guest. 'Effie, how lovely to see you after all these years!'

'Long time, no see, Hazel ol' girl,' says Effie, settling herself at the table with a pint of beer. 'Good to see you too, Bets. Still got your dimples, I notice.'

Betty's hands stray to her cheeks; she hasn't thought about those dimples in years. By rights she should be in charge of the meeting, since she was the one who invited Effie Finch along this evening. But, as usual, power and glory are snatched from her grasp. Effie herself takes charge, introducing herself and laying on the charm for Merl and Irene.

Effie always had a swaggering self-confidence that Betty couldn't help but envy a little. She never cared at all about her appearance and famously petitioned management to allow women to wear trousers at work. She hasn't changed in that regard. Her grey hair cropped short, she wears trousers and a blue shirt with the sleeves rolled up like a man. No hat, lipstick or even a handbag!

'The name Perlman rings a bell or two,' says Effie, her full attention on Merl. 'There was a solicitor in town . . .? He had a few dazzling daughters, as I recollect.'

'That was my husband,' says Merl. 'We had four daughters; he used to call them his precious little pearls. God rest him.'

Irene inhales her shandy and Betty (who has heard all this before) takes the opportunity to pop into the Ladies and powder her nose. This proves to be a tactical mistake. When she comes back, Merl has taken over, rabbiting on about her offspring and their various careers. Anyone would think they were running the entire country the way she goes on!

As it turns out, Effie is quite capable of extricating herself. When she's heard enough, she fixes her sights on Hazel. 'Betty tells me you're interested in the bond store fire?'

'Yes, we are.' Hazel gives her a brief rundown of the story, from the sighting of Natalia to McCracken's murder and the latest development – Frankie's disappearance.

Effie nods, taking it all in. 'Well, you've come to the right place,' she says (somewhat self-importantly, in Betty's opinion). 'Arson, it was. A firebomb chucked into the building.'

Betty experiences a little shiver as she writes these explosive words in her notebook.

'I've always had a fascination for arsonists,' continues Effie. 'Ran across them during the war in the fire service. Mainly fall into a couple of camps: the crazies who want the thrill of destroying something – it's like sex to them. Then there's folk who need a building gone for some reason. Could be the building itself they want to get rid of, or they're covering up something in it – a murder or robbery, for example. In those cases, the fire is often started by someone else, someone paid to do it.'

Irene takes her pipe out of her mouth to chip in. 'There's a few round here'd chuck a burning rag into a place for ten quid.'

'I expect you're one of them,' says Merl, probably still smarting from the earlier conversation. 'Or even five quid.'

Effie looks over at Irene with some amusement. 'You fight Popeye for that pipe? I don't think I've seen a woman smoke a pipe before.'

'What's yer point?' asks Irene.

Effie laughs. 'So, where were we? The bond store. Yeah, traces of petrol and bottle glass. They've got all sorts of science these days to tell them how the fire started from the rate of burning. Fascinating stuff. Why it was burnt down is something else again. That's up to the police and insurance investigator.'

'So where did the fire start?' asks Hazel.

'You said you're in the building right behind the bond store? So, it was a Molotov cocktail – a bottle of petrol with a burning rag stuffed in it – thrown out the 2nd-floor window of your building. The lower floors of the bond store had bars on the windows, but that upper floor didn't.'

'I did notice the top windows weren't barred,' says Hazel. 'But, still, you can't throw a glass bottle through a window.'

'No, the window was broken first with a brick wrapped in a rag thrown from the same location – the cocktail goes in after. Timber floors, probably soaked with booze over the years – boom!'

'That's no ten-quid firebug,' says Irene with authority. 'Too much planning.'

'Spot on,' says Effie, giving her an approving wink.

'The arsonist had access to our building or knew someone who did,' says Hazel.

Effie agrees. 'As I said, no idea of the motive but around this area, up the Cross and Darlinghurst, firebombing is not that uncommon. It's a favourite for brothel owners who want to close down the competition. Also, getting tenants out of the slums, so they can knock them down. Then there's insurance jobs. Plenty of good reasons to firebomb a place,' she concludes cheerfully.

'You've been very helpful, Effie,' says Hazel. 'We're trying to put all the pieces together. We know that the murder victim, Mr McCracken, and my boss, Frankie Karp, were seen at the Mermaid Club together and also that the Russian woman, Natalia Ivanov, and Frankie were seen together in his car. Now we're trying to link those clues with the fire.'

'And this Frankie's also disappeared, you said?' asks Effie. 'Do you have any police connections?'

'We have an excellent connection with Detective Sergeant Pierce at Surry Hills,' says Merl.

Effie raises her eyebrows. 'Pierce? Didn't he recently get kicked out of the CIB?'

'Transferred,' says Merl coldly.

'Okay but, jeez, no smoke without fire, I dunno if I would—'

'Merl's son-in-law, Effie dear,' interrupts Hazel quickly.

'What were you about to say?' asks Merl.

'DS Pierce would be . . . an excellent contact,' says Effie.

Irene, who has been quietly packing her pipe, now lights up, enveloping them all in a cloud of smoke. 'I'll go one better. I know a fella works at the Mermaid Club.'

37

A VISIT TO THE MERMAID CLUB

Kings Cross is not the sort of place that Hazel frequents but clearly many folk find the suburb's sleazy decadence attractive. In the late afternoon, Darlinghurst Road is busy with out-of-towners and schoolboys who stare longingly at the photographs displayed outside the strip clubs and bars, keen to be shocked or titillated. Over the noise of cars cruising past can be heard the cries of spruikers outside the clubs: 'Girls! Girls! Girls! Topless girls! Biggest boobs in the Cross!'

Hazel and Irene pass a fatherly looking man in his fifties calling out, 'Dream girls! Everything you've ever dreamed of! All your dreams come true!' He glances at Irene and Hazel. 'Come on in, girls – ladies welcome.' His double-breasted suit is shiny with age and his battered fedora has seen better days. One sleeve of his suit hangs limp at his side, no doubt a legacy of the war. It's a common sight that tells at least part of the story of how he ended up earning his living this way. Hazel gives him an understanding smile and he tips his hat in acknowledgement.

Above the entrance to the Mermaid Club is an animated neon sign of a buxom hula dancer. Sparkling lights swing like tassels from her nipples. Outside the front door, a heavily built man sits on a high stool that is dwarfed by his size. He wears a short-sleeved black shirt stretched to its limits across his massive chest. He observes the passing parade with bored hostility but when his eyes alight on Irene, his expression softens. 'Hello, Mrs Turnbuckle.' He grins, revealing a gold front tooth. 'How've you been?'

'Good to see yer, Archie. This is Mrs Bates.'

Archie offers Hazel his large soft hand to shake. 'Don't see you up here much these days, Mrs Turnbuckle.'

'Just wanted to ask yer a couple of questions, Archie. Can we have a chat?' Irene gives a nod towards the club entrance. 'In private.'

Archie takes a quick look up and down the street and beckons them inside the darkened club. They follow him down a dim corridor and through a room decorated entirely in red and gold: red-and-gold flocked wallpaper and a long bar, padded in red vinyl, with gold-fringed Tiffany lights hung above it. On a semicircular stage, a young woman, wearing a gold lamé bikini and a scowl, writhes about to the sounds of Shirley Bassey lamenting 'I Who Have Nothing'. The only two men in the audience sit as far apart as possible. Hazel finds it hard to imagine anyone getting much enjoyment out of the experience.

Archie pulls back a heavy velvet curtain to reveal a door leading to a smaller room with a large red-velvet lounge against one wall and half-a-dozen gilt chairs scattered about – perhaps a private salon. 'Can I get youse a drink, ladies?' he asks, gesturing towards a bar in the corner.

'Sun's over the yard arm. I'll have a Scotch,' says Irene.

'Not for me, thank you,' says Hazel, wanting to keep her wits about her.

They sit down on the lounge while Archie gets Irene's drink.

'How's things anyway, Archie? How's yer mum doing?' asks Irene.

Bringing the Scotch over, he pulls up one of the chairs and sits down, resting his giant hands on his knees in a way that Hazel finds boyishly endearing. 'Could be better,' he says. 'She's back inside for the moment. Probably safer inside than out.'

'I reckon yer right about that,' agrees Irene. 'Yer visit her?'

'As often as I can manage,' he says, with a sad smile.

'Good boy,' says Irene. 'She's still your mum.'

Archie nods. 'What can I do for you, Mrs Turnbuckle?'

'Mrs Bates here works for Frankie Karp, do yer know him?'

Archie turns his soulful eyes on Hazel. 'Yeah. I know the fella. They call him "the Suit" round here.' He pauses and adds helpfully, 'Because of his fancy suits. What about him?'

'He's missing,' says Hazel. 'No one's seen him for more than a week.'

Archie rocks his great head from side to side as if shaking his thoughts into some sort of order. 'Dunno about missing. Between you and me, more like hiding out. Probably.'

'Does he play upstairs or down at the 457 Club?' asks Irene.

With a tilt of his head, Archie indicates down the street. 'Baccarat.'

'So he owes money?' asks Hazel.

Archie leans in and speaks softly. 'My advice to you ladies is not to ask questions about this. He'll turn up at some point when he's sorted things out. Best leave it there.'

'Won't the police be making enquiries?' asks Hazel. 'He's been reported missing.'

'Don't worry about that. It'll sort itself out. Now, you ladies better go before the boss arrives.' He stands up and takes Irene's empty glass. 'I can't tell you any more than that. I don't know where he is but probably not far away.'

As Irene and Hazel gather themselves to leave, the door opens and a man appears in the doorway. He wears a dark suit and, behind heavy black-framed glasses, has startling blue eyes. His most noticeable feature is his long hair, a shock of white, tied back in a neat ponytail. 'And you are?'

'Sorry, sir, I was just—' begins Archie nervously.

'I took a bit of a turn,' interrupts Irene. 'This nice young man helped me out.'

Hazel takes Irene's arm solicitously. 'Yes, we're very grateful for his kindness.'

The man wrinkles his nose, as if he smells something off. 'What a gentleman,' he says. 'See them out, Archie, and stay out there. I have important friends arriving.'

'Yes, sir.' Archie quickly ushers them through the bar area and out into the street. He perches back on his high stool at the door. 'Good to see you, Mrs Turnbuckle.'

'Who was that man?' Hazel asks him.

'That was the big boss. He owns the place.'

'He's not that big,' says Irene.

'Mr Borisyuk is big,' says Archie. 'Believe me.'

Although taken aback by this revelation, Hazel covers her surprise by getting the newspaper cutting about Natalia Ivanov out of her handbag. 'Before we go, do you recognise this woman?'

Archie hesitates for a second, then shakes his head slowly. 'Never seen her before.'

Hazel's ears tell a different story, but she says nothing.

Archie hands the clipping back. 'As I said, you need to steer clear of this place before you land yourselves in hot water.'

'Archie,' says Irene firmly, 'we're tea ladies. If there's one thing we can handle, it's hot water.'

He gives a grunt of amusement and glances over his shoulder into the dark entrance of the club. 'Get outta here before you get us all in real trouble.'

He gets up off his stool and, towering over the two women, raises his voice to a bellow. 'Naughty and nude! Birds and boobs! Hot to trot!'

Irene and Hazel wave their goodbyes and head towards the bus stop through the gathering crowds wandering along Victoria Street, drawn by the promise of the night.

Standing at the bus stop, Irene says, 'So he's the dangerous Russian bloke, eh? Didn't seem too bad. Dunno about the ponytail.'

Hazel shakes her head. 'He gave me the chills. I'm sure he's every bit as dangerous as they—' She stops, noticing two men walking towards them, one of them familiar. She pulls Irene into a shop doorway, silencing her protests as Detective Pierce, a cigarette dangling from his lip, wanders past. He wears the same crumpled brown suit and is accompanied by another man who, judging by his swagger, is a detective colleague. The two men stop outside the Mermaid Club where Archie greets them with handshakes, welcoming the pair into the club.

'That was Detective Pierce,' Hazel explains.

'Ha!' Irene crows. 'Merl's precious bloody son-in-law in a strip club. Wait till Her Ladyship hears about this . . .'

'Irene, she won't be finding out about it. Come on, let's get a cuppa.'

They cross the road to a coffee shop opposite the Mermaid Club and order a pot of tea.

'They could be on police business, I suppose – benefit of the doubt,' says Hazel.

'Nuh,' says Irene. 'Detectives work nine to five unless they're called out. He's on his own time. Yer can't run a baccarat school without coppers on the payroll. They're all on the take round here. This whole place'd close down overnight: the girls, brothels, gambling, sly grog shops . . . Coppers get paid to shut their eyes. Not a bad job. Wish someone'd give me a few bob to shut me eyes.'

'Seems that Pierce may be Borisyuk's "important friend" and clearly Effie knows something we don't about Merl's son-in-law. Let's wait a while, see what happens.'

'This is nice, Haze, you and me, snooping together. Mind if I smoke?'

Hazel gives her a pained look. 'If you must, dear.'

'It can wait,' says Irene, magnanimously.

Hazel looks across the street where almost every shop-top advertises massage parlours with signs propped up in blacked-out windows. The windows of one place are pushed wide open and two young women in bikini tops lean on the sill, smoking as they watch passers-by on the street below. Only in their early twenties, they look tired, as if already soured by life.

Hazel turns her attention back to Irene. 'Archie lied – he definitely recognised Natalia. So Borisyuk owns the club and Frankie and McCracken have been seen there. Now we know that Pierce frequents the place – he's obviously there for the evening. So what connects them all?'

'Easy,' says Irene, pouring herself another cup of tea. 'Money.'

38

GLORIA HATCHES A SNEAKY PLAN

'Morning, ladies,' says Gloria, putting on her jolly voice for the Ginger Nuts' benefit.

Heads together over their drawings, the sisters look up in alarm as if she's burst in with an arrest warrant. She really isn't in the mood for these two this morning. She has a nasty crick in her neck, having slept on the sofa last night after a fight with Tony.

'We're not ready yet,' says Miss Joan, gathering papers protectively.

Gloria keeps a smile pasted on her face. 'Could I just have a peek? Get an idea of where it's going?'

'They're only preliminary sketches – we need to finesse them,' says Miss Joan.

As usual, Miss Ivy chips in with one of their secret rules. 'We never show works in progress.'

'I'm worried we're running out of time. If you could just give us one design to start on . . .' says Gloria in a wheedling voice she despises.

The Ginger Nuts look at each other, pulling their old mental telepathy trick. Miss Joan pushes a couple of pages of sketches across the table.

Gloria can see that some of them are off the mark – too fussy – but at least two designs have promise. One has a Peter Pan collar and short sleeves. The other is sleeveless and completely plain with facings at the neckline: an exact replica of the Shrimpton frock that blew everyone's minds. The hems are below the knee, which makes them look sack-like. Easily fixed.

'What's wrong with these?' Gloria asks. 'They're perfect.'

'They need more styling, they're too plain,' says Miss Joan. 'Not at all elegant or feminine.'

All twitchy and tearful, the Ginger Nuts both look as if they're about to start bawling. What a bloody pair they are! Gloria manages to hold her tongue. She has to get these drawings off of them, otherwise they'll dither around for three more days making a pattern and then the whole week will be gone. She lights a ciggie to calm herself. 'Just run me through the styling,' she says in the sweetest tone she can muster.

'Both have a twenty-inch zip down the back, so she won't have to struggle out of it,' says Miss Joan. 'Generous facings on the neck and armholes, and a good hem, say four inches, to add weight to it. A bit of stiffening in this collar, so it sits nice and flat. The collar would be nice in a bright white poplin. Can you bring us up a selection of fabric samples?'

Gloria's been expecting this. 'Why not leave that to us?'

The two of them stare at her, aghast. 'We're the designers here, we don't leave something like that to the *factory*,' says Miss Ivy.

'Ladies, we have to use fabrics we already have in stock, remnants or bits we can find. Before you get your knickers in a knot, wait to see what we come up with. We've got loads of trim samples from Greenfields: rickrack braid, pompoms, woven gimp, tassel trim. We can experiment—'

'*Experiment?*' says Miss Joan in a shocked voice.

Gloria enjoys her cigarette while they cluck on about how things are done and protocol and when they finally wear themselves out, she says, 'All right, here's the deal. I'll send up some trim samples for you to look at, if I can borrow the drawings for half an hour.'

'I don't see why you need them,' says Miss Ivy, snatching the drawings up and clutching them to her bosom. 'They're no use to anyone. We'll send a pattern down when it's ready.'

Gloria wants to bang their silly heads together but manages to force a smile. 'Just to show the girls downstairs. Get them excited. I'll have them back to you by midday.'

After a long pause and more telepathy, the Ginger Nuts crumble and Miss Ivy hands over the drawings. 'Half an hour,' she says. 'Or we're coming down.'

Gloria chuckles inwardly at this idle threat. The factory famously gives these two headaches and they avoid setting foot in there.

She runs downstairs and tapes the drawings to her light box, tracing them carefully onto another piece of paper, but altering the hem length to four inches above the knee. She takes the copies across to Maria, who does all the grading of patterns into sizes. She's the best pattern-cutter they've ever had, fast and accurate.

'Size 12,' Gloria tells her, holding up the correct number of fingers, just to be sure. 'I'll find some fabrics; show you what we've got to choose from.'

Maria nods, smiling, only half understanding the last part.

In the warehouse, Gloria explains to Mr Butterby that she's after fabrics in bright colours or 'way out' patterns. 'Poplin, cotton duck or cotton twill would be perfect.'

'You won't find anything "way out" in here,' he says. 'But come and have a look.'

She follows him to the 'graveyard' at the back of the warehouse where the shelves are stacked with all the bolts of fabric that were ordered by mistake, over-ordered or sent by mills as samples. She can see from the ends of the rolls that the colours are dull greys, browns and fawns, navy checks and narrow stripes.

'Not very exciting, are they? We need something much brighter and stronger, more eye-catching. Mind-blowing,' she says.

'Mind-blowing,' murmurs Mr Butterby, glancing thoughtfully around the warehouse. 'Mrs Karp ordered some curtain fabrics. When they came, she didn't like them. I put them aside in case she changed her mind. They were pricey, too. I put them right up the top.'

He gets a stepladder and passes the boxes down from the high shelving. They're all neatly taped closed to keep the dust out, and Gloria is struck again by how organised and efficient he is, running the whole warehouse and dispatch on his own. He's been there less than a year and seems to know every nook and cranny of the place.

When Mr Butterby opens the first box, Gloria knows they've struck gold. The fabric is a good heavy cotton and the patterns, lurid for curtains, are just what she's looking for. There's bold contrasting stripes in yellow and green, giant-sized flower shapes in purple on a red background, and burnt orange with chocolate polka dots.

'Dottie must have been smoking pot when she ordered these,' says Gloria, holding a length of fabric up against her body.

Mr Butterby laughs. 'The samples they sent were very small but I certainly wouldn't want them as curtains in the bedroom – give you nightmares.'

Gloria has a sudden vision of Mr Butterby shirtless between the sheets and feels a little weak at the knees. 'Wait till you see a mini-dress in these. You won't have nightmares about that.'

'I'm sure if you're wearing it, it will look terrific,' says Mr Butterby, with a smile.

Gloria gives a hoot of laughter that startles them both. 'Don't be silly, you won't see it on me!'

Looking bemused, Mr Butterby steers the conversation back to business. 'There's three boxes and we can order more from the mill if needed. I'll get a trolley and bring them through for you.'

39

BATTLES WITH THE TAJ MAHAL

The Taj Mahal is in ruins; an untidy muddle of pieces, a love story never to be completed. The mirror image of the palace in the reflecting pool makes it all the more confusing. The minarets look very similar but Hazel's convinced that, if she can get the dome at the centre, she can work outwards to the completed edge. She is determined to finish it but her heart is not really in it. She wonders if Bob will come home tomorrow evening or call with another excuse to buy himself some time. Has Mrs Herrmann actually confronted him? Perhaps she held back until her daughter's wedding was out of the way.

Hazel thinks about the many people involved who will be hurt and angry. She thinks about Lavender Lady and the newlyweds, and those little girls with the daisy chains. Every morning, she wakes to the realisation of Bob's betrayal. Her chest hurts all the time, as if her heart is actually broken. Every morning, she weeps softly in the privacy of her room then goes out and puts on a brave face for the world.

Lost in the Taj Mahal, Hazel gradually becomes aware of

singing outside in the street. A voice, which sounds suspiciously like Irene's, belts out a tuneless rendition of 'Roll Out the Barrel'.

A moment later the front door slams (Irene has a habit of kicking doors closed behind her). 'It's only me! Yer shoulda come, we had a good ol' singsong,' she says, bringing the beery, smoky smell of the pub into the front room with her.

'Not sure I'm in the right frame of mind for a singalong,' says Hazel.

Irene picks up a piece of jigsaw. 'Dunno what yer see in this game.'

'It's usually quite relaxing. I expect you're worn out after all that singing?' suggests Hazel tactfully.

Irene parks herself on the lounge. 'Never felt more awake. How about a game of cards?'

'No, thank you, dear. I'm going up to bed myself soon.'

'I know what yer thinking, Haze. I can read yer like a book. Don't worry, I'll make meself scarce when Bob turns up tomorrow night.'

'Irene dear, there's no need . . .'

'Betty said I can kip on her lounge tomorrow night. And Saturday if needs be.'

'That's very kind of her. Kind of you both.'

'Her idea, not mine,' admits Irene. 'Yeah, am a bit stuffed, now yer mention it.'

She gets to her feet, knees crackling. They wish each other good-night. Irene coughs her way to the outhouse and back again, then she's off upstairs where the muffled sounds of her hacking cough drift down through the ceiling.

Hazel gives silent thanks for Betty's thoughtfulness.

Bob has always paid the rent and given Hazel some money for housekeeping, so that she could put her wages aside for a rainy day or a holiday. This afternoon, when she paid the rent man, she realised that without Bob she'll need to let the spare room again. Irene may be able to afford the room but getting money out of her is near impossible. So it will be back to living with a stranger in the house, not something she looks forward to.

She gives a start as the telephone rings. She hurries into the hall to answer it, expecting to hear Bob's voice. 'Mrs Bates?' the caller asks.

It occurs to Hazel that something terrible might have befallen Bob. This is how she would hear. She sinks onto the telephone stool, her voice a whisper. 'Yes, this is her.'

'My name is Deborah Herrmann.' After a pause, she asks, 'I wonder, is it possible for us to meet?'

40

CHANGE IN THE AIR

Hazel takes Doug Fysh's morning tea into his office to find him circling advertisements in the classified section of the newspaper, which can only mean one thing.

He looks up at Hazel with a worried expression. 'Honestly, those two prima donnas are going to be the death of me, and this firm,' he says, his voice below his usual hearty volume. 'You'd think they worked for Monsieur Dior himself the way they go on. It's too frustrating for words.' He turns back to his newspaper. 'Not many jobs for salesmen at the moment.'

'It hasn't come to that, surely?' asks Hazel, putting his tea in front of him.

'I'm not the captain of this enterprise. I don't have to go down with the ship. Can you ask your hubby if there's any jobs going at his firm? That'd suit me, out in the fresh air of the countryside. That's a man's world out there.'

The mention of Bob catches Hazel by surprise. She quickly changes the subject. 'I believe Mrs Nuttell has a surprise planned this morning. That might cheer you up.'

'She's a terrific lady, don't you think, Hazel? A straight shooter. I like that in a woman.'

'She is a straight shooter,' Hazel agrees. 'But I wouldn't get in her line of fire, if I was you.'

'Haw haw haw, I like to live dangerously.'

'In that case, I suggest you make yourself available in the dress-makers' room.'

'Worth the risk if Mrs Nuttell's going to be there.' He picks up his tea and follows Hazel out.

Miss Ivy and Miss Joan look up suspiciously at the sight of them. 'What are you two plotting?' asks Miss Joan.

Before they can respond, Pixie walks in wearing a short shift patterned in vivid yellow-and-blue flowers, her feet bare apart from a string of woven raffia decorated with shells.

Doug Fysh chokes on a mouthful of tea and Hazel has to slap him on the back until he recovers. 'Good God! Haw haw haw! Look at those legs!'

'Where are your shoes, girl?' asks Miss Ivy.

'Isn't that the frock we . . .?' Miss Joan falls silent as the door opens to reveal Sylvia, the most elegant of the Queen Bees. Tall and slender with a mop of red hair, she wears a bright orange dress with a pattern of chocolate polka dots and a white collar. Two more Queen Bees arrive behind her, both wearing bright, short frocks.

Doug gives a wolf whistle. 'Haw haw, more legs!'

Gloria follows them wearing her usual smock and a nervous smile. The four models stand awkwardly in the middle of the room. Now their big moment is over, they don't seem to know what to do next.

Doug begins to applaud and Hazel joins in. Miss Ivy gives them both a flinty glare.

'Our designs are not finished or approved,' says Miss Joan. 'No one asked you to make these samples. You've overstepped your role here, Mrs Nuttell.'

'We've done some calculations,' says Pixie, nervously glancing at Gloria for support. 'Using polished cotton, or gabardine, we could produce these for close to a pound which means they could retail at three to four pounds – that's half the price of our summer frocks.'

'That's because it's only half a frock,' snips Miss Ivy.

Miss Joan gives an abrupt laugh. 'The girls on Lisbon Street will snap them up. Perfect with a pair of black fishnets and a red lace brassiere.' She gets up and walks around the four models, looking them up and down. 'Where did this hideous fabric come from?'

'Mrs Karp selected it, actually,' says Gloria.

'Even if we lowered the hemline to a respectable length, the department stores won't order these,' says Miss Joan. 'You've wasted the firm's time and materials.'

'I have to agree about the department stores,' says Doug. 'Older ladies won't be seen dead in this sort of get-up. They haven't got the legs for it, for a start.'

'All the firms are redesigning their summer ranges for a younger, more modern woman. If we want to stand out, we need to be brave and get ahead of the rest,' argues Gloria. 'We can have a dozen frocks ready to show the buyers by the middle of next week.'

Doug gives a philosophical shrug. 'It will be a hard sell . . .'

Gloria continues, 'As Pixie says, these take half the fabric of our normal range and much less finishing. They're quick and cheap to make. No buttonhole or belts, just a zip down the back. Have a look at this zip, ladies.'

Gloria turns Sylvia around and points out the zip that runs from waist to neck. 'It's not metal, it's nylon. No broken needles. We can put these in ourselves. The whole garment can be made in-house.'

Intrigued despite herself, Miss Joan unzips the dress and zips it up several times. 'Nylon. What next?'

'Mr Karp will probably drop dead on the spot when he sees these,' says Miss Ivy. She glances at Pixie. 'Sorry, Pixie. That was a thoughtless comment.'

The Queen Bees have been silent throughout this discussion but now Sylvia speaks up. 'I'll be the first customer. At three quid each, I'd buy two.' The other office girls nod their enthusiastic agreement.

It's clear to everyone that a stalemate has been reached and no one is backing down. After a moment Doug ventures, 'They've got a point. We don't have anything else.'

'You're taking full responsibility are you, Mr Fysh?' asks Miss Ivy.

'No, I am,' says Pixie, blushing crimson. 'I'll take full responsibility.'

Much as Hazel admires Pixie's courage, she may be playing right into the hands of the Rosenbaum sisters and it could be costly.

41

TELEGRAM

Grafton New South Wales to Mrs Robert Bates, 5 Glade Street, Surry Hills

Urgent business keeping me here stop will make it up to you stop very sorry stop
Love Bob

42

TEA AT THE ALEXANDER

Hazel has agreed to meet Deborah Herrmann at the Alexander Tea Rooms in the city on Saturday afternoon. Before the war, the place had been a salubrious tea palace favoured by high society. These days coffee shops are popping up everywhere but the Alexander still has an olde-worlde charm about it. The front windows are dressed with swags of blue-and-white striped damask. Inside, clustered around polished mahogany tables and silver teapots, are well-dressed women. Despite wearing her good navy crepe with the pearl buttons and matching hat, Hazel feels shabby among society ladies decked out in shantung suits hung with rows of pearls. One even has a fox fur slung around her neck with the poor creature's head still attached.

A uniformed waitress directs Hazel towards a corner table. As she sits down, the door opens and the woman whom she now recognises as Mrs Herrmann stands looking around the room. Hazel gives a little wave and a polite smile.

With a brisk greeting, Mrs Herrmann sits down and beckons the waitress over to order a pot of tea for two. 'Would you like a sandwich or scone?' she asks Hazel.

'No, thank you, just tea will be fine.'

Mrs Herrmann dismisses the waitress and turns her attention to Hazel. 'You're probably wondering why I've invited you here today.'

'I presume to talk about Bob. Can I ask, does he know we're meeting?'

'No, he doesn't,' says Mrs Herrmann. Fleeting emotions cross her face. 'How did you find your way to my daughter's wedding?'

'I knew something wasn't right, so . . . I followed Bob. I really had no idea. I was as shocked as you were.'

The waitress comes back quickly with a tray and unloads the teapot and crockery. When she's gone, Mrs Herrmann says in a low voice, 'The whole thing is appalling, and when I saw you at the church . . . on our special day . . . with my mother there . . .'

'Of course, but you must understand I didn't know about you. I didn't know that Bob had . . . I still don't really know the full story. He hasn't been home.'

Mrs Herrmann visibly flinches at the word 'home' but remains silent.

Hazel pours milk into her cup and passes the jug across the table. 'I'm sorry. I promise you . . . I had no idea Bob had a family until that day at the church.'

Mrs Herrmann pours them both tea. They sit in silence for a moment and Hazel is glad of a breather.

'It seems extraordinary, but . . . what can I say? What made you follow him that day?' asks Mrs Herrmann.

Hazel wonders where to start and decides to be as honest as she can. 'I was made aware that you had hired a private investigator to find out about me.'

'How on earth did you know that?'

'I can't reveal how, only that I knew. I told Bob about it but he denied knowing the name Bateman or Herrmann. He's been very strange since that conversation and I gradually began to realise he was hiding something. He came up with the story about a dinner at the club. I knew it wasn't true, so I followed him and . . .' Hazel's eyes sting. She has a quick sip of tea and takes a couple of breaths to calm herself. 'And you? What alerted you, Mrs Herrmann?'

'These things always have a way of coming undone,' she says. 'I ran into a family friend and he let slip something about seeing Dad at Grotta Capri one evening. He obviously realised he'd been indiscreet and immediately said he might have been mistaken. So I suspected my father was having dinner with a woman, and possibly having an affair. The private eye does work for my husband's firm, gathering evidence of adultery for divorce cases. So I asked him to look into it. I have to admit I was imagining someone younger and . . . anyway, then I discovered he'd married you five years ago. I never dreamt . . .'

'No, I imagine not,' says Hazel.

After a moment of consideration, Mrs Herrmann seems to come to a decision. 'My parents have been married for forty-five years. I'm the eldest of four – my three younger brothers know nothing about this – and between us, we have nine children of various ages. My daughter was the first to be married.'

Hazel stares into her tea. The sheer scale of Bob's deception is breathtaking. Why, with such a large family, would he take on another commitment?

Mrs Herrmann gives Hazel's hand a brisk pat. 'Are you all right?'

'It's quite a lot to take in,' says Hazel, trying to steady her voice. 'I haven't confronted Bob about this because I haven't seen him since the wedding. Have you discussed it with him?'

Mrs Herrmann takes a sip of her tea and slowly puts the cup down, her hands trembling slightly. 'I can't bear the thought of it getting out . . . the humiliation . . .'

'But you have spoken to your father about it?' insists Hazel.

'The truth is, I kept it to myself for some time because I didn't want to make him choose.'

'No,' agrees Hazel. 'That wouldn't be fair to your mother.'

Mrs Herrmann gives her a tight smile. 'But when I saw you at the wedding, I knew it had gone too far and I spoke to him on the Sunday after.'

'And what did he say?' asks Hazel.

'Oh, he tried to wheedle his way out of it. I probably don't need to tell you he's a smooth talker.' She tosses her head impatiently. 'He knew he was caught but admitted nothing.'

'Should we get some legal advice as to the best course of action?' asks Hazel.

Mrs Herrmann's expression hardens. 'My husband's a solicitor. My father married you under a false name, as you know.'

'Yes, I do realise that. I expect that makes our marriage void,' says Hazel, having already considered this possibility.

'You could apply to have it annulled, but . . .' Mrs Herrmann pauses and, making an effort to soften her tone, continues, 'I want to ask you not to do that. If you care for him, please don't bring it to the attention of the authorities. I'm sure that neither of us want him charged.'

Hazel suddenly realises there is no simple way out of this mess. The last thing she wants is for Bob to go to prison, so any compromise will have to come from her. 'No, of course not.' Her tea is cold and tastes bitter. The meeting is coming to an end and, with it, her opportunity to get some straight answers. 'Can I ask exactly where Bob lives when he's away during the week? I don't know what's true any more.'

'He's the area sales rep for an agricultural supplies company based in Grafton, where he lives with my mother in our family home.'

'And where does your mother think he is from Friday to Sunday?' asks Hazel.

'He comes down to the Sydney head office on Fridays, I have established that part is true. We believed he was the secretary of the Commercial Travellers' Association with duties to perform there and that's why he stayed at the club on the weekends. It's never bothered my mother. She's president of the Country Women's Association and my brothers all live nearby in Grafton, so she has more than enough to keep her occupied while he's down here.'

'He's managed it very carefully,' says Hazel.

'On the first Saturday of the month he always joins my family lunch at Rose Bay. I often used to suggest he stay the night with us, but no. Now I know why.'

'I thought he was at the racetrack,' says Hazel. 'And what about his mother?'

Mrs Herrmann frowns. 'His mother? Grandma's been dead for years.'

'How many years?' asks Hazel.

'Let me see, probably twenty. Why do you ask?'

Hazel leaves the question unanswered. The atmosphere in the coffee shop is suddenly stifling. The clink of crockery, women's high-pitched laughter and Mrs Herrmann's curious gaze make her head throb. She thanks Mrs Herrmann. 'We probably won't meet again, but I wish your family well and, of course, I'll do as you ask.'

Mrs Herrmann nods. 'I'm terribly sorry. I feel ashamed of my father. I'm only thinking of my mother. I can see you're'—she searches for the right word—'fond of him.'

Hazel thanks her and leaves the tea shop. She walks the mile home, even though her best shoes are not at all comfortable. As soon as she gets home, she goes straight upstairs and, taking off her hat and shoes, lies down on the bed and stares at the ceiling.

It's difficult to believe that Bob knew exactly what he was doing right from the start. From their very first meeting, when he asked her for directions and they had walked together, he was carefully selecting and censoring information. It's clear now that he invented the story of his ailing mother as a precaution; an excuse to be away if he had family obligations. Everything he told her about his life was sown with seeds of truth. But why? Why create this complicated situation that must have taken so much effort to maintain all these years? Only Bob knows the true reason and, for the moment, he is avoiding that conversation.

Hazel wonders what she overlooked. What has she seen but not seen? She struggles to think of a single thing that could have given rise to suspicion. Bob knew what he was doing and, with his usual competence, managed it with ease. But, as Mrs Herrmann said, it was destined to all come tumbling down sooner or later – he surely must have realised that.

43

BETTY'S LIST GROWS LONGER

The venue for today's meeting is an old stock room at Empire Fashionwear: a dusty forgotten place used for dumping things like cardboard boxes, broken adding machines and bits of furniture that have seen better days. Betty has brought in a nice lacy tablecloth to cheer the place up for the meeting with Detective Dibble to discuss their latest findings. They're all pitching in to make the room more hospitable (apart from Irene, of course, who stands at the window smoking). Merl has baked a Victoria sponge and decorated it with tinned peach slices. Betty can hardly take her eyes off it. 'I'm only having a tiny piece,' she assures everyone. 'I think I might be getting gallstones. I can feel them gathering in my duodenum.'

'Wouldn't they be in your gallbladder, Betty dear?' asks Hazel, laying out the cups and saucers.

'If you had gallstones you'd know all about it,' says Merl. 'You'd be doubled up on the floor screaming with pain.'

'It's just a twinge right now. I obviously don't want it to get to that stage,' explains Betty.

'Well, if you're that worried, don't have any cake at all,' says Merl.

Betty gazes at the cake, the peach slices gleaming softly under the bare light globe. 'I'm sure a little bit won't hurt.'

'Who'd've thought we'd be interviewing coppers, eh? Bit of a turnaround,' remarks Irene.

'Not for us decent law-abiding folk,' says Merl.

'It's very courteous of Detective Dibble to agree to meet with us again,' says Hazel.

'And why wouldn't he meet with us?' says Betty. 'We're the ones in the know.'

Merl sighs. 'Please don't twitter on like that when he's here.'

Hazel nips out to meet Dibble in the front foyer and brings him through.

He stands in the doorway taking in the sight of Irene puffing away at the window, and Betty and Merl seated at the table with the sponge between them. 'Hello, ladies. Have I interrupted something?'

'Of course not, this is all for you. Take a seat,' says Hazel.

Dibble pulls out a chair and seats himself. 'Very nice.'

Hazel sits down at the head of the table. 'We've had a breakthrough in our investigations, so we wanted to discuss this new development.'

Betty pours the tea. 'Milk and sugar?'

Dibble nods. 'One and a bit, thanks.'

Merl pushes a large slice of cake in front of him. 'Thank you,' he says. 'This looks pretty good. My nana makes an excellent sponge.'

As usual, Merl bridles at the hint of competition. 'My sponges have won ribbons at the Royal Easter Show.'

Dibble takes a bite and gives an appreciative nod. 'All right, let's hear what you've got, ladies.'

'Earlier this week, Irene and I visited the Mermaid Club,' says

Hazel. 'We have reason to believe that our informant there has seen the missing woman, Natalia Ivanov.'

'Uh-huh,' says Dibble, his mouth full.

'He seemed to think that Frankie Karp is not "missing", but hiding to avoid a gambling debt. That may be the case but there could be something more sinister.'

'Uh-huh,' repeats Dibble.

'Then, this morning, I discussed that finding with Mr Levy, our accountant, and he revealed that just yesterday Frankie Karp ordered a bank cheque for five thousand pounds directly from the company's bank and without the knowledge of Mr Levy.'

'So he's clearly not missing if he's been to the bank,' says Dibble, discreetly wiping his fingers on Betty's tablecloth, to her slight annoyance.

Hazel continues, 'We're just getting to the interesting part. The cheque was made out to Harbin Holdings. Now, Betty has done a little investigation at the land titles office and discovered that the bond store is owned by this same company. Clearly not a coincidence.'

'I see, that is interesting,' says Dibble.

'When we were at the Mermaid Club,' continues Hazel, 'we met Mr Borisyuk, who we understand owns the club.'

'He owns quite a few clubs, not just that one. He has his fingers in a lot of pies.' Dibble sighs. 'The last time we met, I recommended that you ladies steer clear of Mr Borisyuk. You don't want to tangle with him. At this point he's probably not too concerned about a bunch of tea ladies spying on him but you don't want him taking an interest in you.'

'Well, he should be concerned,' says Betty. 'We plan to get to the bottom of this.'

'This is what I was talking about, Betty,' interrupts Merl. 'Listen to what Detective Dibble has to say without putting your two bob's worth in. Another slice, Officer?'

Dibble waves her away. 'Back to Frankie Karp. If that's the case, that he owed money and has secured that through his own firm, authorised or not . . . that's not a police matter, it's an internal matter.'

'If we can connect Frankie to Mr Borisyuk, and to Mr McCracken, and Natalia Ivanov, would you be interested in that evidence?' asks Hazel.

'Of course, I'm interested, if you could document—'

'Yer know what I reckon?' says Irene. 'The coppers haven't bothered looking for Frankie. Someone up the line already knows he's lying low and he'll turn up. And the Russian bird too. Why aren't they interested in her?'

'The police were well aware prior to the bond store fire that Mrs Ivanov was missing,' says Hazel. 'I reported seeing a woman whom I believed was in trouble, not just once but several times, and now it's in the papers. When we last met, you agreed to look for a file on her.'

'I remember, Mrs Bates. Yes, I spoke to the desk sergeant so I know you did report it but there doesn't seem to be a file. That could mean it's gone up to Criminal Investigations or, more likely, Australian Security Intelligence, because she's a foreign citizen. I haven't got to the bottom of that yet.'

'Detective Dibble, do you think she could be a spy?' asks Betty, her notebook poised.

'I don't have any theories at all,' says Dibble.

'Another thing,' says Hazel. 'We know the arsonist threw a Molotov cocktail into the bond store from the 2nd Floor of this building so it's highly likely that person also murdered McCracken.'

Dibble raises his eyebrows enquiringly. 'Where are you getting your information?'

'We have an informant,' says Betty, getting out her notebook. 'I've been keeping a list of the evidence—'

'Oh Lord, please no,' says Merl.

Not to be deterred, Betty begins to read her list aloud: 'MW, that's short for Mystery Woman; kneecapping, oh sorry, Hazel said leave that off . . .' Flustered under pressure, Betty fumbles and drops her notebook onto the floor. She leans over to pick it up, bangs her head on the corner of the table and falls silent, trying hard not to cry.

Hazel gives her a smile. 'Thank you, Betty dear, very helpful.'

'Let me ask around and see what I can find out,' says Dibble. 'In the meantime, don't talk to anyone else about all this until I get back to you.'

'You can rely on us, Detective Dibble,' says Merl, beaming at him.

When he's gone, Hazel makes more tea. Betty falls victim to a second piece of sponge cake. Irene lights her pipe, and Merl gets out her knitting.

'It's good to see he's following the rules,' says Merl.

'Cowboys, the lot of 'em,' says Irene.

'You only say that because you've been on the wrong side of them,' says Merl.

'How else yer gunna see how they operate?'

'He seems like a nice young man,' says Merl. 'Not sure he's detective material, however. He should consider a position as a bank teller, or public servant.'

'I'll make a note of that,' says Betty, feeling a little more cheerful. 'Should we polish off the rest of this cake while we're here?'

44

A SURPRISING DISCOVERY

Irene is not exactly Hazel's ideal boarder. She smokes in bed, leaves her dentures set in a macabre grin by the kitchen sink and secretly tipples on the good whiskey. At night, her hacking cough sounds like an axe splintering wood, followed by her hoicking noisily out the bedroom window.

Hazel had previously been roused by the crowing rooster; now she's woken by Irene shouting at the bird to 'put a sock in it', followed by threats to wring the creature's neck, followed by more coughing and spitting. But, Hazel reasons, everyone has their faults and Irene is the devil she knows, so marginally better than a stranger in the house.

By mid-week there has been nothing further from Bob since the telegram. Determined to push on with the Taj Mahal, Hazel sits down at the card table and starts by uncoupling the jigsaw pieces that Irene has forced into place in an effort to be helpful.

She wonders if this is how it will end and she will simply never see Bob again. Even with all she now knows, she didn't anticipate it ending so abruptly. From upstairs comes the sound of Irene coughing (or chopping wood), next door the Mulligans shout at each other, and somewhere down the street a family sings 'Happy Birthday'. Surrounded by people, Hazel feels more alone than she ever thought possible.

At eight o'clock, Norma rings and Hazel tells her the whole story of the wedding and the meeting with Mrs Herrmann.

'Oh, Mum, I don't know what to say. How could Bob put you in this terrible situation? It's criminal. Unbelievable!'

Hazel sighs. 'It's taken a while to sink in. I still can't quite believe it myself. I never thought in a million years I would be the "other woman" to come between a married couple.'

'You can't think of it like that,' says Norma. 'You couldn't possibly have known.'

'I'm kicking myself that I didn't pick up on it. I never suspected a thing.'

'Why would you? It's not as though this is commonplace, and he hid it very well. Has he taken his belongings?' asks Norma.

'No. His clothes and shoes are here. Everything's still here, as far as I know.'

'Have a good look through it all, Mum. Who knows what else he is up to.'

As she prepares for bed, Hazel thinks about Norma's comments and realises that in her earlier search she had no idea of the extent of Bob's deception. She has another good look under the bed, through the drawers and the wardrobe. Nothing but the lingering smell of shaving cream and shoe polish. She remembers noticing a briefcase on the top of the wardrobe some time ago, and wonders if it's still there. Dragging the bedside table over, she climbs onto it from the bed.

Stretching up, she feels around the top of the wardrobe until she finds the briefcase, and pulls it towards her. It's heavier than she anticipated and comes down on top of her, knocking her sideways off the bedside table and onto the floor, where she lands hard on her hip and shoulder. There's relief in the physical pain. Something solid to cry about but, before she can let loose, the bedroom door bangs open and Irene stands over her, looking like an old moth in her tatty brown chenille dressing-gown.

'Ha*th*el! Wha*th* happened!' She kneels down and helps Hazel to sit up.

'I'm all right. Just need to get my breath back. I'm fine, go back to bed.'

'Don't be ridiculo*th*!'

The briefcase lies open, papers strewn all around. Hazel picks up several pieces of paper and peers at them, nothing making any sense. The letters from one word dance across the page and join with another. 'Can you read this, Irene?'

'Wait, I'll get me teef in.' Irene gets to her feet and helps Hazel to hers.

'You do that, I'll make us a cuppa,' says Hazel. She gathers the papers together, puts them back in the briefcase and takes it downstairs to the kitchen.

Irene reappears, teeth intact, and sits down. She takes a handful of papers from the briefcase and peers at them.

Hazel pours the tea and sits down, nursing the hot mug, filled with curious dread.

Irene squints at one document for a few minutes. 'Insurance business. Life insurance by the looks. That could bring in something.'

'Please don't suggest I murder him, Irene. What else?'

'It's a letter from a solicitor about something to do with a house sale.'

Hazel has no recollection of Bob mentioning buying a property. 'Where is this property?'

'This house, 5 Glade Street. It says here.'

'Bob owns this house?' Hazel can scarcely believe her ears. 'When did he buy it? Does it say there?'

'Hmm . . . says June 1963. Couple a years ago. Get yer glasses, will yer?'

'Are you quite sure? It doesn't make any sense. So we're paying rent to Bob?'

'Ask the rent man. Probably won't tell yer anyways.'

'But Bob gives me money for the rent . . .' says Hazel, bewildered. 'So he's paying rent to himself! Why not tell me he's bought the house?'

'Dunno, but yer better hope he doesn't drop dead. The other wife will have yer out.'

'What else is in there?' asks Hazel.

'Where's yer bloody glasses, anyways?'

'To be honest, I've lost them. I have to get some new ones.'

Irene sifts through the papers, glancing at each one briefly. 'Everything in here is to do with this place. It's bills for the rates and whatnot.'

Hazel considers this for a moment. 'In other words, it was hidden up there because no one knows he owns this house.'

Irene nods. 'No one, except us.' She pulls a document out and stares at it intently for a moment. 'You're not gunna believe this, Hazel.'

45

GLORIA IN A SPIN

On Thursday morning, Mr Butterby stops by Gloria's alcove to inform her that Frankie is back at work.

'Is he now? I haven't missed him, to be honest,' says Gloria. As she leans back in her chair, it makes a loud cracking sound and tilts alarmingly.

'Oops, watch yourself . . . let me take a look at that chair for you, Mrs Nuttell.'

'Must be putting on weight,' says Gloria, with a laugh.

'I don't think so,' says Mr Butterby. 'They should get you a decent chair. Why don't you put in a requisition for a new one?'

'Yeah, suppose I could, if I had time to waste on paperwork.'

'Wait on, I'll get a couple of tools from the warehouse.'

Gloria perches on her desk and smokes a cigarette while she waits for him to return. He's never mentioned a wife or children but then he never talks about himself (unlike her husband, who never stops). She admires modesty in a man. Not for the first time, she imagines herself as Mrs Butterby, a house in the suburbs with a nice garden and a couple of kids. She always wanted kids but recently got herself on the contraceptive pill, taking care to keep the packet hidden in the bottom of her handbag. It's not that she's changed her mind; the time just doesn't feel right. Or perhaps it's the man who isn't right.

Mr Butterby returns with a handful of tools. He takes off his duster coat, flips the chair on its side, and squats down to adjust the base. As he tinkers with the mechanism, Gloria can't help but notice the strong, muscular thighs normally hidden under his coat.

'Righty-ho,' he says, flipping the chair upright. 'Try this for size, Madame.'

Gloria stubs out her cigarette and lowers herself into the chair. There is none of the usual cracking and creaking; it even spins without tipping sideways.

'Perfect,' she says. 'Thank you.'

Mr Butterby gives her a smile and a courteous bow.

'So where's bloody Frankie been anyway?' asks Gloria. 'Did he say?'

'Not to me. I only know he's back because he left his car in the loading dock to be cleaned.'

'Cheek! That's not your job, is it?'

Mr Butterby gives a shrug. 'It's quiet now the orders have slowed down.' He gestures towards the rack of frocks. 'This is the first order in a fortnight from Cashell's; normally they'd be reordering every week, as you know.'

Gloria nods. 'I'm really worried about lay-offs.'

'They wouldn't lay you off, Mrs Nuttell,' he says, with a smile. 'You're irreplaceable.'

Gloria laughs. 'I'm glad you think so, Mr Butterby.'

'Gerald,' he corrects. 'Or even Gerry, if you feel like it.'

'And I think you're the only person here who doesn't call me Gloria.'

He gives her a wink and a mock salute as he wheels the rack away. 'From today, you'll always be Gloria to me.' He walks off, whistling cheerfully.

'And you'll be Gerry to me,' she calls after him with a tinkling laugh she'd forgotten she owned.

'How lovely to hear your laughter, Gloria dear,' says Hazel, appearing out of nowhere with a cup of coffee.

Gloria hadn't even heard the tea-break buzzer go. 'Frankie's back, I hear.'

'Has he been down here already?'

'I haven't seen him but he asked Mr Butterby to clean his car.'

'Did he now?' Hazel pauses and, without another word, walks off towards the loading dock.

Gloria leans back in her chair and sips her coffee. Its silent service brings a smile to her face, which is quickly wiped off by the sight of Frankie marching into the factory. She's still deciding whether to welcome him back or pretend ignorance when she's saved the bother.

'What's going on down here?' he says, coming over. 'Why isn't anyone working?'

'Good morning,' says Gloria, wondering if he has the slightest clue how things work around here. 'We're on our morning tea break.'

'Fysh tells me there's a buyer's meeting tomorrow.' He looks around wildly. 'What have we got? We're not showing the buyers garments Frankie hasn't seen.'

Gloria wants to point out that's because Frankie disappeared for almost two weeks. 'We've got a dozen sample frocks. They're similar styles but different patterns and trimmings. They're in the pressing room now.'

'Well, let's see them.' Without waiting for a response, he strides through the factory, pushing racks of clothing aside as if he's blazing a trail through the jungle. Hurrying after him, Gloria senses this is not going to end well.

Nattering in Greek over their coffee, the pressers look up with alarm at the sight of Frankie bearing down on them. Gloria goes to a rack that has eight samples that are already pressed. She pulls the rack out and Frankie flicks through them, barely paying attention to any of the details.

'Too loud. Too short. Too tasteless.' He gives Gloria an accusing look and she wonders if he's actually referring to her. 'This is what happens when you leave women alone for five minutes. What a disaster.' He shakes his head in despair.

Gloria wonders if she's about to get fired on the spot for her part in this 'disaster'.

'Do you want to . . . what should we . . .' she begins.

Frankie brushes her concerns aside with a dismissive gesture. 'We don't have anything else, so we either cancel or show these. Either way, we make complete fools of ourselves.'

'I think we should give them a try at least,' suggests Gloria.

Frankie turns to her, flushed with annoyance. 'Do you now, Mrs Nuttell? What makes you think Frankie cares what you think?'

Gloria has witnessed Frankie's legendary rages but never had one directed solely at her. He looks so angry, she takes a step back to be out of arm's reach. It wouldn't be the first time he'd struck a member of the staff.

'Ah, there you are, Frankie,' says a voice behind them. They turn to find Hazel advancing with a cup of tea, two Iced VoVos tucked in beside it. 'I thought you might like your tea down here today.'

Poised on the brink of explosion, Frankie takes the cup from her and nibbles on his biscuit. After a moment he asks, with boyish politeness, 'Could you do a nice spread for the buyers tomorrow afternoon, Hazel, and one of your famous cakes?'

'I'd be happy to,' says Hazel. And just like that, Gloria is off the hook, for the moment.

46

SHOWTIME AT EMPIRE

From the upstairs kitchen, Hazel watches the buyers arrive in the showroom, noticing they are all men of a certain age. Not one seems to have bought a suit in the last five years, during which time men's suits have become more fitted and trim. These eight oldish men, dressed in baggy browns and greys, are about to get an eyeful of colour and flesh and it's almost impossible to predict which way it will go.

Doug Fysh, his hair slicked to a waxy shine, greets people at the door. Frankie is smartly dressed in a navy three-piece suit with a red silk handkerchief peeking out his top pocket. He laughs a little too loudly and too frequently and Hazel realises that this will be the first time he has presented a range without his father, let alone one in which he has no confidence.

She takes a tiered plate of club sandwiches to the showroom table and hands out cups of tea and coffee. The last guest to arrive is an old man with rosy cheeks and a Santa-sized belly who leans heavily on a cane. Hazel pulls out a chair at the table for him and offers a cup of tea and a sandwich. 'Save some space for my famous plum cake,' she tells him with a smile.

'I only came for the cake,' he says. 'You can bring me a large slice.'

Once Hazel has offered everyone a slice of cake, she leaves the showroom and pops into Edith Stern's office. In a fug of hair lacquer and talcum powder, Edith and Gloria are busy helping the models, two girls from the factory and four Queen Bees, into their dresses.

'The Ginger Nuts have gone home,' Gloria says bitterly. 'Do they know something we don't?'

'Never mind that,' says Pixie, brightly dressed in a red, white and blue striped shift. 'I'll go in and make the announcement. Remember, wait until you hear the music start and then just as we rehearsed it.'

The girls gather excitedly outside the showroom door while Pixie tries to get the buyers' attention. 'Excuse me! Excuse me!'

The hum of male voices continues unabated.

'Oh dear,' says Edith. 'Off to a bumpy start.'

'Attention please, everyone!' booms Doug and silence falls.

'Gentlemen,' says Pixie. 'We welcome you to the presentation of Empire's brand-new "Plum Collection" – our groovy range for the summer of 1966!' She fumbles nervously with a record player she'd set up earlier. Finally, after a painfully long pause, The Beatles' 'Hard Day's Night' fills the room.

'Off we go!' urges Gloria, pushing Sylvia through the door. The other five girls follow Sylvia in quick succession, like colourful butterflies. Dancing to the music, they hop and bop around the showroom while Gloria leans in the doorway, watching pensively.

Within a couple of minutes, Sylvia's back for the next change. Like a practised team, Edith and Hazel unzip her, whip off the frock and pull another one over her head, repeating the performance with each of the girls before they flutter back to the showroom.

Suddenly it's over and everyone's crowding back into Edith's office. The buoyant mood has gone and everyone looks deflated.

'One of them got up and walked out,' says Sylvia. 'One man said to Frankie, "Gone into the brothel business, have you? How much for two?"'

'Oh my heavens!' says Hazel, outraged. 'Who said that?'

'The old gentleman with the walking stick.'

'Oh no,' says Edith. 'That's Mr Cashell.'

Once the last buyer has been seen off into the lift, the women trail back into the showroom to find Frankie simmering with anger. 'Whose idea was this absolute debacle?' He looks at each of them in turn, from Hazel to Edith, Gloria, Pixie and even the volunteer models. Without waiting for an answer, he continues, 'That was the most humiliating experience. Not one order! Being compared to a brothel! We will never live this down. We might as well close the doors now. We are officially the laughing stock of the entire industry. Frankie should fire the lot of you for bringing the business into disrepute.'

Doug glances at his watch, looking for an excuse to leave.

'It was my idea, Dad,' says Pixie, defiance in her voice. 'Completely my idea.'

Frankie looks about to explode. 'You can come into my office, right now, young lady.' Without another word, he stalks out of the room and Pixie follows him.

'Oh dear,' says Hazel, quite shaken by the experience. 'That did end badly.'

Gloria lights a cigarette. Puffing angrily, she says, 'Frankie's wrong. They're all wrong.'

'It doesn't matter if they're wrong. They're the buyers and they didn't buy,' says Doug. 'It's over.'

47

HAZEL SUFFERS ANOTHER BLOW

When Hazel arrives home from work on Friday afternoon, she knows in an instant that Bob has been and gone. Standing in the hallway, she picks up the faint smell of his aftershave and a sense of something missing. As it turns out, not just his presence but his belongings as well. Upstairs, his clothes are gone from the wardrobe, his shoes from under the bed. His alarm clock has gone from the bedside table, but he's left his library books behind for her to return.

In the kitchen, she finds Irene sitting on the back step trimming her toenails with a penknife and swigging from a bottle of beer. 'Did you see Bob?' asks Hazel, noticing that the briefcase and papers have gone from the kitchen dresser.

Irene glances over her shoulder. 'Nup. Got back at 'bout three.'

'He must have come in the middle of the day, just to be sure,' says Hazel. 'He's taken all his things.'

Irene shrugs. 'That's that, then. Good riddance to bad rubbish. I'm going down the pub if yer want to come. Take yer time, still got me other foot to do.'

'Do you think it's wise to be using a sharp knife while you're drinking, Irene dear?'

'The drink steadies me hand and sharpens me eye.'

'Lucky you're not a surgeon,' murmurs Hazel.

'Done a bit of that. The odd bullet or two. Glass, now that's a bugger to get out; yer need good eyesight. I don't do nothing on faces, though. Leave that to the experts, I say.'

'Yes, very wise,' Hazel agrees.

She feels sick at the thought of Bob sneaking in here, going to such lengths to avoid her. The least he could do was meet face-to-face, explain himself and apologise. The very least. Until now her emotions have shifted back and forth from confusion and disbelief to grief, with some anger in between. But Bob's final act of coward-ice has made her furious. She deserves better and she deserves an explanation.

'Perhaps I will come with you, Irene,' she says. 'I'll give Betty a call, see if she'd like to come.'

Irene turns her attention back to her gnarled toes. 'We can get fish 'n' chips for tea after.'

Upstairs, the bedroom feels strangely empty, like a hotel room. As Hazel gets changed she wonders, if she could have one question answered honestly, what would it be? But regardless of the ques-tion, the answer is never going to be simple. And, in any case, Bob is not going to make himself answerable. There will be no expla-nation or apologies. It's finished and done – all that's left is the heartache to endure.

She puts on a brown-and-white check cotton frock, applies some lipstick and a little blush. Normally she'd wear either the dark blue cloche or the brown pot-lid style hat. She puts the brown on and adjusts the angle in the mirror. Gazing at her reflection, she recalls how free those young women looked this afternoon without hats and gloves and even stockings. She takes off the hat, combs her hair and goes downstairs.

'Would you like this hat, Irene?'

Irene has her head in the cupboard, taking a swig of Hazel's whiskey straight from the bottle. She wipes her mouth with the back of her hand and looks the hat over suspiciously. 'What's wrong with it?'

'Nothing at all. I just don't think I need it any more.'

'Give us a try,' Irene says. She takes off her crushed old hat and replaces it with Hazel's. She goes into the hall and looks in the mirror. 'Not bad.'

'You could retire your old one,' suggests Hazel. 'It's probably had its day.'

'Not on yer nelly,' says Irene, brushing the thing off fondly. 'Me second-best hat now.' She puts on her lipstick, not bothering with the mirror. 'I'll just have a wee,' she says, heading out the back door.

While she waits for Irene, Hazel has a curious thought and goes into the front room. As she suspected, the photograph of Bob's mother, or aunt, or perhaps a stranger's photo he picked up in a second-hand shop, has been left behind. Abandoned, just like Hazel.

The Hollywood is busy on Friday evenings. There's always a nice atmosphere with locals meeting after work. Merl couldn't make it this evening, so it's just the three of them. Shirley makes her usual jokes about putting the drinks on Irene's tab, Irene gives back the usual cheek and Hazel is grateful for these certainties in life.

'Are you all right, Hazel?' asks Betty. 'You look a bit . . . off.'

'Bob got his stuff today . . . and buggered off,' explains Irene, between gulps of shandy.

'Very delicately put,' says Hazel. 'But that's the sum of it, yes. It's probably for the best. I don't know that I could trust any explanation he might offer. I don't want to hear excuses or lies.'

'Very cowardly. I don't know anyone who's managed to pull the wool over your eyes, Hazel,' says Betty. 'Then Bob pulls something so big . . .'

Hazel sips her drink reflectively. 'It's true. I wonder if Bob believed what he was saying, believed his own lies, and somehow that got past me.'

Betty suddenly sits up, her attention fixed on a nearby table. Without warning, she leaps up with an accompanied explosion. 'Oh, beg your pardon!' Bumping the table and slopping the drinks, she rushes over to a woman who sits quietly reading the newspaper.

'She's got some rocket power there,' remarks Irene admiringly, as she mops up the spilt drinks with her sleeve. 'Enough baked beans and Betty could be the first tea lady in space.'

A moment later, Betty's back. Shaking the front page of the newspaper triumphantly, she slaps it down on the table, announcing, '"Russian High-Flyer Arson Suspect"!'

'Oh, dear!' says Hazel. 'They're trying to pin it on Natalia. Go on, Betty.'

Betty reads aloud: '"Russian national Mrs Natalia Ivanov, who has now been missing from the touring Moscow Circus for several weeks, was previously thought to be seeking asylum in this country. It has been revealed by the detective in charge of the investigation that the police want to question Mrs Ivanov in relation to the major fire incident that gutted the historic bond store in Elizabeth Street last month. Police cannot confirm if Mrs Ivanov is suspected to be part of a Russian crime syndicate known to be operating in the Kings Cross area. This is the first time the world-famous circus has toured Australia but perhaps, as a result of the diplomatic scandal now unfolding, it may be the last."'

'We have to find her,' says Hazel. 'Before something terrible happens.'

48

BETTY STARTS HER OWN INVESTIGATION

On Saturday morning, Betty stands outside her local newsagent flicking through the morning papers, disappointed to discover no further news about Natalia. She wonders if it's possible that Natalia doesn't want to be found but she has more faith in Hazel's opinion than in all the newspapers put together, and Hazel seems very sure the Russian girl is being held somewhere against her will. Betty lives three blocks away from the bond store so it makes sense to take a walk around the neighbourhood, chatting with the locals, to see if she can pick up any clues. She manages to buttonhole several people but they're in a hurry to get to the markets for their shopping.

At the end of the street, one of the oldest residents leans on his front gate smoking and watching passers-by. His wife died a couple of years ago and, since then, he hasn't bothered with the upkeep of the house and his front garden is knee-high with weeds. He gives Betty a wave. 'Did you hear I've sold up, Mrs Dewsnap?'

'Oh no! I never thought that would happen.'

He nods. 'Neither did I, frankly. My grandfather built this house, you know.'

'I do know. I thought you wanted to keep it in the family.'

'I thought that too. Always said they would carry me out in a box, but there you go.'

'What made you change your mind?' asks Betty.

'This joker has been interested, pestering me for a while. Offering me silly money. In the end, I thought, bugger it. He wants it so much, he can have it. I'm going to live with my daughter. Being on my own is no good for me, anyway. Spend half my day out here but nowadays folk are too busy to stop and chat with an old man.'

'We'll be sorry to lose you after all these years,' says Betty.

'I'll be a bit sad to go.'

'Do you know who our new neighbour will be?'

He shakes his head. 'This joker bought it on behalf of some other joker . . . a lot of different jokers involved, I have to say, all a bit cloak-and-dagger. Actually, much the same thing happened with the place over the back of me, a couple of months ago,' he says, pointing over his shoulder. 'Don't know if it's the same mob. These two are the biggest freestanding houses around here, so they might be turning them into boarding houses. Anyway, that's that. I'll be gone.'

'Well, the street won't be the same without you,' Betty tells him.

'You're right about that. My grandfather built this house,' he says wistfully.

'Yes,' says Betty. 'I remember.'

She says her goodbyes and walks around the corner to Flood Street to take a look at the house behind him, also large with a front garden and a backyard. The house is in better shape and they must be redecorating because every window has newspaper taped over it.

'Well, look who it is!'

'Hello, Violet,' says Betty, turning to greet her old friend. 'Haven't seen you for a while.'

'What are you up to?' asks Violet, sweeping litter off the pavement into the gutter.

'I heard this house had been sold recently. Have you met the new owners?'

'Never set eyes on them,' says Violet. She pauses to lean on her broom. 'There's comings and goings, but always in the dead of night.'

'What do you mean by "the dead of night"?' asks Betty, intrigued.

'Bit of a detective now, are you?' Violet grins. Her tightly permed hair, dyed a titian red, is not at all flattering and makes her look a little fast – but that's just Betty's opinion.

'I am doing a bit of detecting, actually. I'm working on something quite important at the moment, which I can't discuss, obviously, apart from to say that it involves a murder, arson and kidnapping. Don't ask me any more.' Betty mimes the zipping of her lips.

Violet laughs. 'You're a one, Betty. Always good for a laugh. Dead of night, let me think. When I get up for the lav, which is usually around eleven, I see the lights on upstairs but never seen a soul in the day.'

'Seems an odd time to be redecorating, doesn't it? In the middle of the night.'

'You're the detective, Betty, you work it out,' says Violet, going back to her sweeping. 'You still drink up at the Hollywood?'

'Most Tuesdays around five.'

'With the other detectives,' says Violet with a chuckle.

'That's right,' agrees Betty. 'If you have any pertinent information, you can find me there.'

'I s'pose there's a drink in it for me, is there?'

Betty wonders if buying Violet a drink qualifies as bribery or corruption. 'I expect so,' she says, not wanting to commit herself.

Violet stops sweeping and walks over to stand beside Betty. 'I reckon they're going to turn it into a brothel,' she says in a low voice. 'That's the last bloody thing we need in Flood Street. We'll have all sorts hanging around here at all hours. They're popping up everywhere now. Those American sailors are starting to come in, sex-starved and money to burn. If you're short of a quid, Betty, you could turn a trick yourself, they like women with big boobies and a decent sized—'

'Yes, well, nice to see you, Violet,' interrupts Betty. 'Let me know if you find out anything, please.'

Walking home, Betty stops to ask the old bloke if the paperwork has been completed on his property. 'Yep, all done,' he says.

'But you didn't see the name of the buyer?' asks Betty.

He shrugs. 'It was all very quick. The lawyer came around here and it was all over in a few minutes. What do you care, anyway?'

As she continues her walk home, Betty asks herself the same question. It's not illegal to buy a house, or even two houses. Has she become over-enthusiastic about the whole crime-fighting business? She thinks not. Quite the opposite. She has a real talent for this line of work – if only she'd known earlier in life! She doesn't have Hazel's magic ears or memory, but she's certainly nosy enough and, right now, she's curious to know who owns these houses.

49

PIXIE HAS A NEW PLAN

'Frankie's gone again!' announces Edith Stern, when Hazel brings her tea. 'He's only been back a couple of days. Couldn't get out of here fast enough. I was going home on Friday, after that awful presentation, when he told me to get the travel agent on the phone. It was well after five. He's never understood working hours. He thinks people are awaiting his instructions day and night. Anyway, he must have rung the travel agent at home because he took a flight out this morning.'

'Where's he gone?' asks Hazel.

'I have strict instructions not to tell anyone but I can tell you, Hazel. New York. He said it was urgent business, but who knows with him? Seems to me, he would have gone to Timbuktu if it meant getting out of here a bit quicker.' She pauses at the sound of the lift doors opening.

A moment later, Pixie puts her head around the office door and wishes them a good morning. She's chirpier than Hazel might have expected, given the last time they saw her, she'd been ordered into her father's office for a dressing-down.

'I was just telling Mrs Bates that your father headed off this morning,' says Edith.

Pixie nods. 'He was pretty upset on Friday, but I'm used to that. Mum always says his bark is worse than his bite. Did he say how long he was going for?'

'Not to me,' says Edith.

'Me neither,' says Pixie. 'Anyway, we got an order this morning for half-a-dozen frocks in the Plum Collection from Mark Foys, on sale or return. They want the hems lowered to two inches above the knee. We have to keep them happy, I suppose.'

'That's a good start, dear,' says Hazel encouragingly.

'It's just the beginning,' says Pixie. 'This afternoon we're going to wear the samples into the boutiques in town to see if we can get some attention that way.'

Edith looks sceptical. 'That seems a bit desperate. Why don't you invite these "boutique people" to the showroom? That's the way it's done.'

'They wouldn't come,' says Pixie, with surprising conviction. 'No one expects to see anything groovy from Empire Fashionwear. Look at our square name for a start off.'

It occurs to Hazel that Pixie is more savvy than she lets on.

Edith is not impressed. 'How can these young girls afford to buy clothes in boutiques, anyway?'

'Edith dear, if these frocks cost three pounds,' says Hazel, 'they'll be cheaper than making it yourself.'

'But how can we possibly make any money out of them? It doesn't make sense to me.'

'We have to sell a lot more garments,' says Pixie. 'But they're quicker to make, and Gloria says we can do it. We can double production straightaway.'

'Oh, it's *Gloria* now, is it?' asks Edith, crossly. 'It seems to me this building's been tipped upside down and the people at the bottom are running things now. I don't know where this is all leading to.'

'Anyway, I just came to get the samples,' says Pixie, obviously keen to avoid an argument. She walks off down the hall towards the showroom, noticeably less cheerful than when she arrived.

'It's not how things are done,' says Edith, still bridling with indignation.

'Things are changing, Edith.'

Edith feeds a sheet of paper into the typewriter and hits the carriage return unnecessarily hard. 'You can say that again.'

'Sometimes we have to trust that the next generation knows something we don't and try doing things their way.'

'I don't think young ladies should be taking over and running things, and getting uppity and just making it all up as they go along,' insists Edith.

'Why not? Because we didn't have that opportunity? Fortune favours the bold, Edith. Why not give her our blessing?'

Edith huffs in annoyance. 'As if she needs our blessing.' She begins typing and pauses. 'What happened to those pink slips you were taking downstairs?'

'Oh dear, I must have forgotten to deliver them,' says Hazel.

'Well, hang on to them for the moment. Let's see what happens.'

They hear Pixie come back down the hall wheeling the rack of dresses. Edith opens her desk drawer. 'Pixie!' she calls. 'Here, take five pounds' petty cash for expenses – you girls will need a cup of tea and a taxi. But mind, I need receipts for every penny.'

50

A VISIT FROM THE POLICE

Hazel pours tea for Merl, Betty and Irene as they wait in the stock room for Detective Dibble to arrive for another meeting. She hopes this new information will put a firecracker under the lad and wonders, not for the first time, what other factors are at play.

'Now don't be so argumentative this time,' Merl tells Irene. 'It's not as if you're under suspicion.'

'Yer don't know the things I know,' says Irene.

'My tummy's all butterflies,' says Betty.

'Trouble at the gasworks?' asks Irene with interest.

'Do you mind?' hisses Merl as the door opens and Detective Dibble and, unexpectedly, Detective Pierce enter. He glances around with obvious amusement, giving each of them a cursory nod, including his mother-in-law.

'So, what brings us back here today?' asks Dibble in a business-like way.

He's obviously nervous, which makes Hazel think it wasn't his idea to bring Pierce along. She glances across at Merl, who avoids her eye, and realises the reason Pierce is here today is that Merl is passing information along to him. Hazel files that thought for later and explains there is now new information they want to discuss.

Pierce stifles a smile, and his eyes dart towards Merl as if she might be in on the joke.

'We know there is a connection between the missing Russian woman, Natalia Ivanov, and Mr Borisyuk, who owns the Mermaid Club.'

'Says who?' asks Pierce.

'I'm sorry, we can't reveal our sources,' says Betty firmly.

'For God's sake,' murmurs Merl, without glancing up from her knitting.

'Okay, let's just stop right there,' interrupts Pierce. 'Where's this information coming from? Someone who works at the Mermaid?'

'Yer heard Mrs Dewsnap,' says Irene.

'Keep in mind that you ladies can be charged with failing to assist police in their investigations,' says Pierce, evidently no longer finding them amusing.

'Go on then,' says Irene. 'Try it. Arrest four little old ladies – see where that gets yer.'

Dibble holds up his hands. 'All right, even if she was seen at the Mermaid Club, it doesn't actually connect the woman to Mr Borisyuk who, as I explained last time, owns a number of local establishments.'

'That place is a den of vice and immorality, Ken,' says Merl, turning to Pierce. 'It's an absolute disgrace. The police should be closing these places down.'

Pierce, clearly quite used to having Merl tell him what to do, ignores her and helps himself to another biscuit.

'Let's leave that aside just for the moment,' says Hazel. 'Mrs Dewsnap has uncovered some very interesting information.'

Betty sits up straight. 'Two properties, one on my street and another directly behind it on Flood Street, were sold recently. Yesterday I went to the land titles office and discovered that both these properties were sold to the same company.'

Pierce looks at her blankly. 'There's no law against that.' He glances briefly at his watch and looks back at Betty with what he obviously imagines to be an interested expression. 'Look, unless you know where the Russian girl is, none of this is much help. People buying houses, et cetera, we don't care. Arson, murder, the missing Russian – that's what we're interested in.'

'Except that the company, Harbin Holdings Pty Limited, is the same one that owns the bond store,' says Hazel. 'So perhaps the other two properties could meet the same fate, and we think it's possible that—'

'Speculation,' says Pierce. He looks at his watch again and gives Dibble a nod.

'Before you go, Detective Sergeant,' continues Hazel, determined to get her point across. 'There's something else. One of the owners of my firm, Frankie Karp, was missing for two weeks. During that time, he drew a bank cheque for five thousand pounds in favour of Harbin Holdings. When he returned, I had a look at his car and, judging by the dust and the insects on the windscreen, it had obviously driven quite some distance in the country.'

'Ladies, going to the country for a couple of weeks is not a crime, and it's neither here nor there in this case. If you find out where the Russian is, call us.' Pierce gets to his feet.

'Not only that,' insists Hazel, refusing to give up until she's finished. She gets an envelope out of her apron pocket and opens it to reveal a tiny scrap of paper in red and gold. Everyone leans forward to peer at it. 'I found this in the boot of his car. It's the band from one of Frankie's cigars. I think it's possible that he was put in the boot of the car and this fell out of his pocket.'

Pierce shakes his head. 'There's a dozen ways it could have got in there. And, if Mr Karp was kidnapped, presumably he would make a complaint to the police himself.'

Hazel puts her final piece of evidence on the table: a strand of shredded rope. 'I also found this in the boot.'

Pierce laughs. 'That's it? Everyone has a tow rope in their boot. I do, don't you, Dibble?'

'I don't own a car, sir.'

'Exactly! Now, ladies, it's been lovely but I have criminals to catch, crime to fight.'

'Can I ask you one more question before you go?' asks Hazel.

'Sure. Just one.'

'Have you found Mr McCracken's next of kin yet?'

Pierce sighs. 'McCracken is a suspect in the arson case. Who murdered him we don't know but we can speculate they may have been trying to prevent him from destroying the bond store. McCracken may be an assumed name; there's no record of him that we can find. That's what we have. If you girls can solve it, let me know. I'll be all ears.' Full of his own importance, Pierce gives Dibble a wink, as if to say, *This is how it's done*, and they head for the door.

'Wait a minute, Ken,' says Merl, getting up from the table.

Pierce turns to find Merl advancing on him with her knitting.

'Turn around,' she says, and holds a half-finished jumper, in a complex pattern of green-and-brown diamonds, against his back for size. 'Did you say you wanted a V-neck or prefer a crew? I can do either.'

'Either's fine,' says Pierce, as he tries to shrug her off.

'Just lift your arm for me so I can check the size of the armholes,' persists Merl.

He surrenders with a groan and lifts both arms high in the air.

51

BETTY MEETS A VALUABLE CONTACT

When they arrive at the Hollywood, Hazel gets a couple of drinks from the bar while Betty watches out for Effie Finch from the fire station, who has requested a meeting with them – but only with Hazel and Betty. Much as she likes being special and included, Betty is curious as to why just the two of them. Thinking back, it was odd that Detective Pierce turned up the other day and Hazel later confided that she thought Merl was passing on information to Pierce. Not surprising, just the sort of thing Merl would do to curry favour.

Hazel arrives back with a couple of glasses of sherry, which makes a nice change. Two minutes later, Effie walks in the door and she's brought someone with her.

'Hiya, ladies,' says Effie, dropping into a chair. 'This is Mrs Li. She works at a couple of local cop shops.'

Mrs Li is in her fifties with a short black bob and a guarded expression. She sits down silently and seemingly poised to leave.

'Hello, Mrs Li,' says Hazel warmly. 'I remember you.'

Mrs Li nods. 'The Tea Ladies Guild.'

Effie laughs. 'Tea Ladies Guild? Had no idea there was such a thing.'

'Not any more,' says Hazel with a note of regret.

Betty knows exactly who Mrs Li is now. She was the reason for the collapse of the guild. It wasn't her fault, of course, but it all started with her.

'Can I get you a drink, Mrs Li?' asks Betty.

Mrs Li glances at Betty as if she's only just noticed her. 'No, thank you,' she says, and turns back to Hazel. 'How can I help you, Mrs Bates?'

Hazel tells the story for the umpteenth time, about seeing Natalia in the window, the discovery of her identity and their fears for her safety. 'We're trying to gather all the information we can to help this young woman because the police don't seem interested.'

'Which police officers are you referring to?' asks Mrs Li, leaning closer.

'Detective Sergeant Pierce is in charge of the investigation,' says Hazel.

Mrs Li's face goes completely blank. 'Anyone else?'

'Well, we do have the ear of PC Dibble, also at the Surry Hills station.'

Mrs Li looks around the bar. 'We can't talk here. Come with me.'

Hazel, Betty and Effie follow her out into the street, where Mrs Li crosses over and walks quickly up the next street and down a back alley. Betty, wondering where they could be going and already puffed out, is relieved when Mrs Li stops and opens the back gate to one of the narrow terrace houses, gesturing for them to come inside. They follow her along the path through a vegetable garden into a brightly lit kitchen where an elderly woman hovers over the stove. The woman looks up in surprise as they all file into the tiny kitchen.

Mrs Li speaks to her in Chinese and the woman gives them each a shy smile. 'My mother wants to know if you'd like some soup?' asks Mrs Li.

Betty is starving and the aroma in the kitchen has sharpened her appetite. 'Yes, please.'

Effie and Hazel also accept and the four of them sit down at the table while Mrs Li's mother ladles out soup for them. Over the delicious spicy chicken soup, Mrs Li explains that she works at two police stations, Surry Hills and Darlinghurst. It seems they have a tea lady on alternate days. When they finish eating, Mrs Li takes the bowls to the sink and makes a pot of fragrant tea. She sits down and, taking a deep breath, says, 'Mrs Bates, I wouldn't be talking to you now if we weren't already acquainted. I remember very well how you fought for me to be accepted by the guild.'

'Without success,' admits Hazel. 'I want you to know that I was not alone, a lot of us left after that – including Betty here.'

Betty nods. 'It all fell apart after that.'

'That's a shame,' says Mrs Li. 'They did a lot of good work. I can help you but you must swear not to tell anyone else about me or anything I might tell you. I could lose my job – or worse. Much worse.'

'There are two more of us working on this case,' says Betty.

Effie turns to Mrs Li. 'One of them is that scrawny little thing, smokes a corn cob pipe . . . wears holey slippers everywhere. Irene Turnbuckle.'

It's the first time that Betty has heard Irene's slippers are holy, but it explains a lot. No wonder she never takes them off. It must be a Roman Catholic thing – they have many strange and mysterious ways.

'Turnbuckle?' asks Mrs Li. 'Is she related to Fred "Tweezers" Turnbuckle, the safecracker?'

Hazel nods. 'Her husband, I believe. Divorced, I think. I'm not sure.'

'Irene hates the police more than anyone,' Betty informs her, trying to be helpful.

'All right, and the other person?' asks Mrs Li.

'The other person really is a problem,' admits Hazel. 'Merl Perlman is DS Pierce's mother-in-law.' She pauses. 'But Mrs Li, we give you our solemn promise anything you tell us will be kept in complete confidence between Betty, Effie and myself, tea ladies' honour. Irene Turnbuckle also has some very special skills to offer. The important thing is to find this young woman before something terrible befalls her.'

Mrs Li reflects on this for a moment. 'At work they think I don't speak much English.' She gives a sly smile. 'I gave that impression to protect myself and not have to talk to people. In one way it's bad because I hear them making off-colour comments and racist jokes about Chinese people.'

Betty's eyes sting with tears at the thought of Mrs Li having to listen to smut and insults. She takes out her hanky and quickly dabs them.

Mrs Li pauses to give Betty a curious look, then continues, 'But it also means that I'm treated like part of the furniture and often overhear private conversations, sometimes even interviews with suspects. I keep my ear to the ground and can tell you that the corruption and dirty dealings are on a scale most people would not believe.'

Hazel looks pained. 'Mrs Li, why do you stay there?'

Mrs Li gives a bitter laugh. 'Even if you're well-educated, it's hard enough for any woman my age to get work and even harder when you're Chinese. I need to support my mother and my son at university. To be honest, I don't know if it would be different anywhere else. At Christmas they have a whip-round for me, so there is some kindness in them, both good and bad. Detective Pierce hasn't been there long but I'm aware that he has some bad habits and friends he picked up while he was in the Criminal Investigations Branch.'

'Do you know why he was transferred to a local police station?' asks Hazel.

Mrs Li shakes her head. 'They call it a transfer but it's a demotion. The CIB are the elite detectives and I think it's usually because someone is suspected of corruption or there's been a complaint against them.'

'What about Detective Dibble?' asks Betty. 'We like him.'

'He's young and a bit green,' says Mrs Li.

'Get in the sewer and you all get covered in the same muck. After a while it doesn't even smell,' says Effie. 'They might start off with good intentions but they don't survive long, especially around here.'

Mrs Li nods her agreement. 'His biggest problem is that Pierce is his senior officer. The one person everyone respects is a man they call "the Tsar". If you've ever seen him you won't forget him. I haven't met him but I was told he has coffee at Bar Coluzzi, which I often pass. He has long white hair, black-rimmed spectacles and cold eyes like a fish.'

'Borisyuk,' says Hazel. 'I have met him briefly.'

'He's the real boss,' Mrs Li explains. 'A lot of them are involved with him one way or another. Not just turning a blind eye to his gambling parlours, brothels and protection rackets. They look after him because there are kickbacks in it. If the Tsar wanted this Natalia dead, then she would already be at the bottom of the Harbour with bricks tied to her feet.'

'It's possible,' admits Hazel. 'But I have a gut feeling they need her alive.'

'Hazel's gut is extremely accurate,' adds Betty. She recalls that it was a brick that was thrown through the bond store window, so the culprit might have access to bricks. He could be a bricklayer! She makes a quick note: *Brickie?*

'You said you saw her picked up by a car on the morning of the fire?' asks Mrs Li.

'Yes, on Lisbon Street, it was a Bentley – green, I think.'

Mrs Li nods. 'I know the Tsar has Bentleys, two or three of them, from what I hear.'

Betty sees a moment to make her mark and rushes in. 'When Merl's daughter got married to Pierce, the wedding cars were dark green Bentleys. We weren't actually invited but Merl said we could stand outside the church and watch. Hazel didn't come but I sort of felt obliged. I didn't want Merl to take offence . . .' Betty fizzles out under Mrs Li's watchful gaze. 'Anyway, I remember the bridal cars were Bentleys.'

Hazel nods. 'Very good observation, Betty dear.'

'I agree,' says Mrs Li. 'It tells us what we need to know about their relationship. So, let's assume the Russian girl is alive and they want to keep it that way for some reason. We need to pool our resources to find her, then we can worry about what to do next. I'll keep my eyes and ears open and let Effie know if I have anything to pass on to you.'

'Mrs Li, there is something else I wonder if you could possibly help with. I'm curious to know more about Mr McCracken's demise.

We know he was shot but it might be helpful to know with what sort of weapon.'

Mrs Li thinks about this for a moment. 'The filing cabinets where the briefs are kept are often left unlocked. If I got in early, I could have a look at the autopsy report.'

Hazel shakes her head in wonder. 'You're a gem, Mrs Li. I can't thank you enough.'

Mrs Li smiles for the first time. 'I am indebted to you, Mrs Bates. And I'd like to help this young woman too.'

'It is risky,' says Effie. 'Very risky.'

Mrs Li agrees. 'Let's not speak on the phone at all. Phones are bugged all the time. And we don't want to be seen together in public. If I find anything, I'll let Effie know and we can meet here.'

After thanking Mrs Li again for her help, and her mother for the soup, they part company. Effie goes her way, and Betty and Hazel walk home together.

'It's going to be tricky keeping it from Merl,' says Betty.

'It is. Mrs Li is very brave getting involved and I just don't think we can trust Merl.'

'I think we should have a code phrase,' suggests Betty. 'In case something comes up, so we can communicate secretly, like in spy films.'

'I suppose,' says Hazel. 'What do you suggest?'

'Something like . . . "the birds fly north in autumn".'

'Perhaps a sudden interest in bird migration might draw attention to itself?'

Betty agrees. 'How about . . . "they're predicting rain all week" or something like that?'

'Might be a bit depressing and also confusing if we have a fine week ahead,' says Hazel. 'Let's give it some more thought.'

Betty decides to forget about it for the moment. She's enjoying walking companionably with her dearest friend through yellow puddles of light with the bright full moon throwing dark shadows across the streets.

'The moon's very bright lately,' says Hazel, gazing up at the sky.

Of course! thinks Betty: short and simple. Hazel is so clever. They make a perfect duo: Sherlock and Watson, Batman and Robin, Hazel and Betty.

'The moon's very bright lately,' repeats Betty, to reassure Hazel she has understood.

'Yes, I just said that, Betty dear. Well, here's your street. Good night, sleep tight.'

'Don't let the bed bugs bite! See you tomorrow, Hazel.'

52

HAZEL REVEALS HER LONG-HELD SECRET

Hazel takes a sip of dandelion wine (one of her better vintages) and wonders again about the wisdom of having Irene here. The Taj Mahal had been sorted into similar textures and colours but now is completely jumbled, and Irene is the sole suspect. Then there's the dentures, the shouting and spitting, and the smell of her pipe. She smokes it in bed against Hazel's wishes, insisting that it's safe because when the smoker goes to sleep so does the pipe. The muddling of the Taj Mahal may be the last straw.

Jigsaws had been a companionable hobby Hazel shared with Bob and all the pleasure seems to have gone out of it. Betty had recently asked would it be easier if Bob had died, but Hazel would prefer to think of him settled back home with his family where he belongs.

With some effort, she turns her thoughts from Bob to Natalia Ivanov and where she could be held. Since Borisyuk owns a number of clubs and seedy dens, none of which Hazel has access to, her best hope is that Mrs Li can come up with something that points them in a direction. There are so many things they don't know about Natalia and how she might have ended up in Borisyuk's hands in the first place. Did they know each other? Apart from their nationality, the connection between them is unknown but there must be something more to it. Betty has discovered that the Great Moscow Circus – which has continued to tour the country without the 'Flying Flamingos' – will return to Sydney in a week's time, so they may be able to find out more then.

'Hello, Mrs B? You home?' Maude sings out, coming in the back door.

'I'm in the front room,' Hazel calls back.

'How's the old Taj coming along?' asks Maude, looking over the jigsaw.

'Badly. I can't seem to get moving on this one.'

'Is he not coming back, then?'

'No,' says Hazel. 'Mr Bates is not coming back, I'm sorry to say.'

'Well, I could help with it,' says Maude, sitting down. While she surveys the wreckage, Hazel goes to the kitchen. By the time she brings back tea and currant cake, the girl has almost completed the tricky top corner where shades of blue wash out to pale pink.

'I'd like to go to the Taj Mahal one day,' says Maude, taking a bite of cake. 'It's a beautiful story – we learnt about it at school.' Her sharp eyes scan the table for matching pieces. 'So there's a pattern to these different types of pieces?'

Hazel picks up a few examples. 'Edges, obviously, then there's regular and irregular, and ears and wings. We call them buggles and wuggles.'

'You're very clever to do these, Mrs B. There's a lot of concentration involved.'

'I wish I was clever, Maude. My life would have been very different.' Hazel watches the girl, her eyes alight with the pleasure of the task. 'I wonder if you could do something for me, Maude?'

'Course, anything you want.'

'A letter came today and I wonder if you could read it for me.'

Maude gives her a long, serious look.

'You're probably wondering why.'

Maude shakes her head. 'No, I'm not, Mrs B. I know why.'

Momentarily confused, Hazel says, 'It's not because I don't want to read it.'

'I know. It's because you can't. I used to think it was because of your glasses but then I realised . . . well, it's more common than you think. Dad can't read either; I have to help him all the time.'

Hazel takes a deep breath. After a lifetime of guarding her secret closely, it's strange to be discussing it openly with Maude. 'I can see the words, but the letters are all higgledy-piggledy . . . I just can't seem to . . . I've always wondered if I'd been able to stay at school longer . . . but my mother died when I was twelve and I had to help out the family, so work seemed more important than education and I left school for a job. Of course, we know differently now.'

'What sort of job did you do, if you don't mind me asking?'

'I worked in the little shop that used to be on the corner of Bourke and Fitzroy streets.' Hazel smiles at the memory. 'Working in the shop helped with my arithmetic and I started to see how much I could manage just by using my memory.'

'You have an excellent memory, Mrs B, and you're good at so many other things. None of us is perfect, are we? I'm happy to help you,' says Maude.

Hazel gives her the letter and she glances over it. 'He's got nice handwriting, that's one thing. Here we go: "Dearest Hazel, Please forgive me. I never expected this to happen. I can only tell you how sorry I am. There are obligations I must honour but I will never forget the time we had together. Yours faithfully, Bob." Bit rich ending with "Yours faithfully", don't you think?' says Maude, curling her lip.

'You're right, Maude dear, it is. Thank you for reading it. I wonder if I can ask you not to repeat this to anyone.'

'Don't worry. All your secrets are safe with me,' says Maude with sincerity. 'Now, why don't you work on the reflection in the pool and I'll do the top of the tower?' She quickly sorts the emerald-green pieces of the pool, pushing them over to Hazel's side of the card table and keeping the gold-and-blue tower on hers.

'If you ever want,' Maude says casually, 'I could help you with your learning.'

53

BETTY GETS NEWS FROM FLOOD STREET

It's only Betty and Irene at the Hollywood tonight; Irene is hardly Betty's favourite companion but she's sacrificing herself to give Hazel a break. They have barely sat down when Betty senses someone looming over her and looks up to find Violet with a pint of stout in her hand.

'Oh, Violet! You gave me a start. Come and join us. Irene, this is my friend Violet, she lives around the corner from me.'

As Violet settles herself at the table, Irene watches her with her usual suspicious look and Betty is struck by the similarities between them. Both small and wiry, Violet wears a similar squashed hat and has a couple of missing side teeth. If she dyed her hair black, like Irene, instead of red, and got herself a set of badly fitting dentures, the two could pass for sisters.

When she's finally settled, Violet announces, 'I've been doing like yer said, Betty, keeping a close eye on opposite.'

'This is the house in Flood Street I told you about,' Betty explains to Irene, feeling very important at having operatives report to her.

'From what I seen there's someone living there for sure. They never come out that I notice, but someone comes around eleven-thirty every night with a bag of something, not a suitcase, more like a shopping bag, and I also saw him with a blanket or something like that once.'

'It's definitely a man?' asks Betty, making a note.

'Yup. I borrowed some binoculars but it's still too dark to see much. Yer can't really be out in the street or yer'd be seen yerself. Be a bit strange that time of night.'

'Do they pull the curtains in the day?' asks Irene.

Violet shakes her head. 'They've got newspaper stuck all over the windows. Yer can't see nothing. Something odd there. Just thought I'd let yer know, like yer asked.'

'Well, as it happens,' begins Betty, in a confidential tone. 'As a matter of fact, we've discovered—' Irene gives her a painful nudge in the ribs with her sharp little elbow. 'Ow, Irene, watch what you're doing.'

'Wasn't an accident,' says Irene.

'Yer were saying?' asks Violet.

'Oh, I lost my train of thought,' says Betty, flustered. 'That's how we get, don't we?'

Violet holds up her pint of milk stout. 'Not me. This stuff is like a tonic. Black gold, full of iron. Have a couple every day.'

Betty pulls her cardigan down self-consciously, wondering where Violet could possibly be putting it all. If Betty downed two pints of stout a day, knowing her luck, she'd have gout within a week.

But Violet's attention is not on Betty's surplus but on Irene. 'Someone break that nose for yer?' she asks.

Brightening up, Irene grins. 'Wasn't a bloke, if that's what yer thinking. It was a bird.'

'A bird!' says Betty, taking a careful look at Irene's wonky nose. 'What type of bird?' she asks, imagining an emu or perhaps a diving magpie – they can be lethal.

'The sort that runs a brothel,' cackles Irene.

'Tell me it wasn't Molly Mullins,' says Violet. 'Up in Hotham Street.'

'The very same,' says Irene, clearly enjoying this game.

'Who won?' asks Violet. 'She was good with her fists, so I hear. No personal experience. She'd be long-dead now.'

Irene runs her fingers over the bump in her nose. 'Broke it with a broom.'

'Ow! That'd make yer eyes water,' says Violet, wincing. 'She was an ol' witch.'

'Oh Irene, what an awful thing to happen to you,' says Betty, who has never heard this story before and wonders if Irene is making it up.

'Aw, it's a long time ago. I reckon I was sixteen, thereabouts. Didn't do me looks any good. Otherwise I would have done better in the husband stakes. Could've married a bank manager instead of a bank robber.' Irene chortles at her own joke.

'Oh, yeah. I hear yer loud and clear,' agrees Violet. 'So, who's yer old man?'

'Fred "Tweezers" Turnbuckle,' says Irene.

'One of the best,' says Violet with quiet respect. 'Safecrackers are like royalty, so few good ones. Do yer remember Fat Joe Perkins?'

'Oh, yeah, rings one or two bells,' says Irene.

'He was on the Mint raid, but he did some other big jobs. Yer know, he would have worked with Tweezers on the Hilton job.'

'The security van?' asks Irene.

'Yeah. Them were the days,' sighs Violet. 'Most of the boys dead now or got life.'

'Well, that's an occupational . . . um . . . yer know . . .' Irene casts around for the right word.

'Hazard?' suggests Betty, feeling left out of the conversation.

'Risk,' Irene concludes.

'I thought me and Fatso would be retiring up to Queensland with suitcases full of money,' says Violet wistfully. 'But here's me, still stuck in a dump, working as a cleaner, paying rent, and can't even afford a bloody weekend up the coast.'

'Join the club,' agrees Irene.

Violet lights up a cigarette. 'So how'd yer get on the wrong side of Molly Mullins? If yer don't mind me asking?'

'She was me granny. Bit of a character,' says Irene. 'Another drink, Violet? My shout.'

Betty wonders if she's hearing things. Those two words have never passed Irene's lips in all the years Betty has known her; she only wishes Hazel was here to witness the historic moment.

54

GLORIA HAS A BRAINSTORM

Gloria had encouraged the excursion to the boutiques in town but had no expectation that it would work any miracles. She isn't surprised that there has only been a trickle of orders – nothing close to compensating for the department store trade. Now, they have less than a week of work ahead for the machinists.

The Ginger Nuts couldn't even pretend to be sorry when the new Collection flopped; they're quietly delighted. When Gloria was up on the 1st Floor this morning, they hid their new designs from her like schoolgirls guarding their homework. According to Doug Fysh, the sisters are now working on evening wear and cocktail frock designs. Gloria wonders how many cocktail frocks they'd need to sell to support a firm this size.

At the sound of Gerry Butterby's tuneful whistling, Gloria quickly stubs out her cigarette and flips her feet down off the desk. It's not a very ladylike habit but always helps her think.

'Morning, Gerry!' she says, swinging around in her chair with a smile.

'That chair's giving you good service now,' he says, grinning.

'I've dug up a few more bolts of fabric that might interest you. Some cotton prints, and also drip-dry samples. Pop out the back when you have a minute and I'll show you what I've got.'

Gloria laughs but it seems he's not flirting, just being helpful. She sighs inwardly at his wholesome ways and their exchange lifts her spirits for the meeting upstairs with Doug and Pixie.

Doug looks pleased to see her as usual. He's a decent enough fellow but he's starting to resemble a bloodhound. That's the trouble with drinking, muses Gloria; it stays on the inside for years, then suddenly bursts out on your face. Pixie looks so young and fresh-faced beside him. In her usual timely way, Hazel magically appears with tea and biscuits. 'Mr Levy said he'll pop up and join you,' she says.

Gloria wonders how Mr Levy knows about the meeting but, since Hazel had a hand in it, there's probably a reason. Pixie starts by explaining that she has rung around the boutiques they visited last week and invited the owners to come in and see the Collection. 'A few of them are really keen, the only problem is they're so busy, it's hard to find the time.'

'Top marks for enthusiasm, Pixie, but let's look at the facts,' says Doug. 'Let's say six turn up and order ten frocks each. Sixty garments. It's nothing. We've had a few more orders from Mark Foys but Cashell's aren't returning my calls. They're putting their orders elsewhere. I'd like to know where but it's probably not going to help us.'

'I apologise for inviting myself...' says Mr Levy, striding in and taking a seat at the table. He pauses for a moment. 'I had a meeting with the bank manager yesterday that was very concerning. As you can imagine, our cashflow has contracted severely and was not helped by a large withdrawal made against our overdraft recently.

There are also some anomalies in the accounts that I'm waiting to discuss with Mr Karp. Do we know when he'll be well enough to return to work?'

'He hopes to be back in next week,' says Pixie.

'So lay-offs are next,' says Doug in a resigned tone. 'Doubt there's any getting away from that now.'

'Lay-offs?' Mr Levy shakes his head solemnly. 'If we can't get the bank's confidence back by showing them we have forward orders, they could put us into receivership. We have to find a way to turn it around quickly, otherwise that's where we're headed. We're sailing into the unknown, a ship without a captain.'

Pixie has two bright-pink spots on her cheeks and Gloria can't help but feel sorry for her. She's ended up being responsible for the firm by default, without authority or experience. She's just a kid, after all.

Doug leans back in his chair and lights a cigarette. 'Well, what are the options? Wait to see what Frankie turns up with when he gets back? Or do Miss Ivy and Miss Joan start from scratch with a new range and try to catch up with the next season?'

'I'm not giving up on the Plum Collection,' says Pixie. 'The small shops might only take ten frocks each to start but they were excited. The customers who saw them were excited. This is what they're wearing in London now.'

'Sydney is not London, unfortunately,' says Mr Levy.

'I agree,' says Doug. 'It could take another year for this country to catch up.'

'Some girls in the shops asked if they could buy direct from us,' says Pixie.

'That's not something we can do,' says Doug. 'Bypass the stores.'

'But the stores aren't ordering from us,' argues Pixie. 'So what difference does it make?'

'The problem, young lady, is that you don't understand how things work in business,' says Doug. 'There are ways of doing things. Gentlemen's agreements. There are business courtesies, and if you don't know what that means, look it up in the dictionary.'

Gloria knows that he's right; Pixie doesn't understand the way the business works but what if she's seeing something they can't see?

'What if we did sell directly?' Gloria asks. 'Think about it. The average cost of these garments is close to a pound. Let's say one pound fifty including pressing and labelling. We can produce two dozen of these an hour or so.'

'Nine hundred and sixty garments a week,' says Mr Levy, barely pausing to think. 'More than double our normal production.'

'Haw haw haw . . . no point in producing them if we don't have any customers,' says Doug. 'We'll just end up with a warehouse full of rag material. We'd have to staff a shop – more overheads – or are you thinking about taking a stall at the markets . . . haw haw haw.'

Ignoring him, Gloria gets up and goes to the cabinet where Edith Stern lays out the morning newspapers each day. She brings one back to the table. 'What if we put an ad in the paper?' She flicks through the pages until she finds an example and shows the others. 'Something like this. We could get illustrations done of a couple of styles.'

'Mail order!' says Pixie, clapping her hands together.

'And shoot ourselves in both feet,' says Doug. 'Once the stores know we're selling directly—'

'Oh, for God's sake, Doug!' says Gloria. 'Open your bloody mind, will you? Use your imagination! We have to use a different company name and a private post office bag.'

Mr Levy nods. 'That's easily arranged, we can register a trading name.'

Doug stubs out his cigarette aggressively. 'And what if we get a hundred orders? Who's going to process all those cheques and postal notes? Who is going to package up the garments and post them? Females are fickle creatures. They'll want to exchange them for different sizes or colours. It's madness to even consider!'

'I can manage it,' says Pixie. 'I want to give it a try.'

Doug shakes his head at the stupidity of it. 'And you'll explain all this to Mr Karp, I suppose?'

Gloria realises there's something else going on here. 'Are you concerned about the idea not working, Doug? Or are you more worried it might actually be a success and you'll be out of a job?' Judging by his expression, she's hit a nerve.

'The former, obviously,' he says stiffly. 'We're all going to be out of a job if it doesn't work. I suppose it's worth a try. You could send the design to the catalogue people.' At Pixie's pained expression, he pauses. 'What now?'

'The ad needs to look "with it", that's all,' she says, turning bright red.

'With what?' asks Doug.

'Don't worry,' Gloria tells him. 'We'll come up with something.'

'And the ship sails on,' says Mr Levy. 'For the moment.'

55

A DRAMATIC NEW DEVELOPMENT

Walking up the laneway after work, Hazel hears someone call her name. Next thing, she's hustled into a dark doorway. 'It's all right, Mrs Bates, it's just me,' says Detective Dibble. 'Sorry if I frightened you, I needed to talk to you privately.'

'Well, here we are, dear. What is it? I don't mean to be rude but I need to get to the butchers before it closes.'

'Mrs Bates, you have to listen to me. Stay away from the Mermaid Club and everything to do with Mr Borisyuk. I've tried to warn you, people disappear around him and I don't want you to be one of them. You don't seem to understand that he's a powerful man with friends in high places.'

'No one is above the law, isn't that what they say?' The doorway reeks of cat pee and, concerned they might be there for a while, Hazel takes out a hanky and holds it to her nose.

'They might say that,' says Dibble. 'But if Borisyuk goes after you, no one can help you, least of all me. He has goons every-where, people he can call on to "fix" things. Before you know it, there'll be an accident or suicide that won't warrant looking into. Please – leave the murder investigation to us.'

'I'm not so concerned about Mr McCracken's murder, because he's dead. But I am worried about Natalia Ivanov, who I believe is alive but in grave danger,' says Hazel.

Dibble gives a sigh of exasperation. 'If I tell you what I know, will you drop it?'

'I might consider it, dear; tell me and I'll decide for myself.'

'She's a relative of Borisyuk – his niece, I understand,' says Dibble. 'She's a defector and he's helping her. I've been told the Arson Squad are now interested to talk to her but she's not posted as a missing person as such, and regardless of what the papers say, she's not a suspect.'

'Detective, I'm a practical person and, to me, none of that adds up. If she's supposedly defecting and he's helping her, why haven't they gone through the proper channels? I don't believe any of that story and you shouldn't either. I think she's being held against her will somewhere. I don't know why, or where, but I intend to find out.'

Dibble sticks his head out to glance up and down the laneway. 'There are KGB agents everywhere right now. They'll track her down and, when they find her, she'll be on a plane back to the USSR. That's why the police are staying out of it.'

Hazel thinks about the man she has seen a couple of times lately, once walking along the lane looking at the ruin of the bond store and another time on the main road at the front of the building. Always near the bond store. He's tall and well dressed with excellent posture. Betty also mentioned seeing him and dubbed him Mr Handsome. They had thought he might be the insurance assessor but now Hazel wonders if he is, in fact, a KGB agent.

'That information has come from DS Pierce, has it?' she asks, suspecting the story might have been concocted for some reason.

'I'm begging you to stay away from this before things turn ugly. I don't want to see you get hurt. You're a nice lady.'

'So people keep telling me,' says Hazel.

'Okay, Mrs Bates. I'm going to trust that what I'm about to tell you won't go any further.'

'Of course,' agrees Hazel. 'You have my solemn word.'

He takes another quick look outside and continues, 'I don't know exactly what's going on but I have my suspicions. One tip I'll give you is be careful what you tell Mrs Perlman. And yes, you're correct, the information is coming from my senior officer. I have to find a way to work around that but you can bring information directly to me and I'll look into it. All right?'

With Hazel's agreement, Dibble writes his home number on the back of his card and hands it to her. He ducks out of the doorway and strides off up the lane.

She waits a moment for him to get clear before she hurries off to the butchers. For the first time since Bob left, she has an appetite for lamb chops.

When the chops start to sizzle under the grill, Irene appears in the kitchen sniffing the air like a stray dog. Standing at the back door, she cleans out her pipe with a penknife, dropping the debris on the doormat. It seems to Hazel that pipe smoking involves a similar amount of work to owning a pet. There's cleaning, packing, lighting, relighting, and occasionally smoking. Presumably this is what people like about it since it's clearly popular these days, with men, not women (except Irene). She seems to enjoy chewing on the stem of the unlit pipe, and using it as a prop while she talks, like a professor giving a lecture.

Hazel drains the potatoes and adds a little butter and salt to them. 'Are you planning to smoke that now, Irene dear? I'm about to serve up.'

'Nah, getting it ready for later,' says Irene. She sits the pipe on the windowsill and seats herself at the kitchen table. 'Betty and me had an interesting conversation with her mate Violet last night, the one lives in Flood Street.'

Hazel serves them a chop each with potatoes and peas. 'Oh, yes? What did she have to say?'

'She's been watching the place opposite and this bloke comes every night at half past eleven. He brings something with him – a shopping bag – stays for quarter of an hour, then buggers off.'

'That is interesting,' says Hazel. She thinks about it for a minute or two, wondering if there is a simple explanation why he would come every night. Is there someone in that house? Someone not able to leave? If it was an elderly person, then he would come during the day, not in the middle of the night. 'Very interesting.'

'It's only me! The door was open!' calls Betty, coming down the hall. 'Oh, sorry to interrupt your tea.'

'That's all right, Betty dear, take a seat. Would you like some bread and butter?'

Betty sits down, quivering with excitement. 'Thank you, Hazel. I'm all right. I came to deliver an urgent message. It came from Effie, and she got it from . . . oh no, I can't say her name. Oh, dear . . . what is it? Something about the moon's bright . . .'

'Are you plastered?' asks Irene, holding her chop with greasy hands.

'All right, just slow down,' says Hazel. 'Don't worry who it came from, just give us the message.'

'All right. She overheard a conversation today.' Betty consults her notebook. 'Pierce and another officer were talking out the back. Pierce said "the old chooks are a bloody nuisance". The other officer said something about the Russian bird, and Pierce said "they" are going to move her, and he didn't know where and didn't want to know. He then said that it wasn't his problem and it was getting "messy".'

Hazel puts down her knife and fork. 'I know what's happened. We told Pierce that we knew that the owner of the Flood Street property was the same as the bond store.'

'Oh, of course!' says Betty. 'That makes sense. That house is only a block from the bond store – the perfect place to hide her.'

'We need to investigate Flood Street,' says Hazel. 'And we need to do it tonight.'

'Any more chops?' asks Irene, wiping her mouth with a tea towel.

56

A DANGEROUS MISSION

After some discussion, the three of them decide that Betty will go straight to Violet's place, then Irene and Hazel will meet her there, in an hour.

When Betty's gone, Irene enthusiastically discusses possible methods and tools required to break into the house, adding to Hazel's concern about the whole endeavour.

'We want to slip in and out as quietly as possible. Let's keep it simple. Are you able to get us in the front door?' asks Hazel, quickly clearing the table.

'Might be able to get me hands on a stick or two of jelly, blast it open.'

'Perhaps another time, Irene dear. Discretion is the hallmark of a good tea lady; let's stick to our code of conduct.'

'I don't reckon "break and enter" is in the code,' grumbles Irene.

'Let's think of it as an investigation,' says Hazel. 'I know locks don't present any problem for you, so if you could just work your magic, please, Irene. Quietly.'

Irene agrees with some reluctance. She goes upstairs to gather

her tools and comes back down with the pockets of her black coat bulging.

Hazel puts on a dark jacket and the black cloche she saves for funerals, imagining they might be taken for missionaries going door to door, and they set off.

In Hazel's street, there are people outside at all hours but Flood Street seems quieter, people tending to stay in their houses. Some places have cars parked outside and, judging by the blue flicker in the darkened front rooms, televisions as well.

Violet lives in a tiny rundown cottage with an attic bedroom. Her front door opens straight into a lounge room so densely packed with furniture that Hazel and Irene have to weave their way into the room. Betty has made herself comfortable with a glass of sherry among the population of china ornaments and figurines: damsels in bonnets, shepherdesses, angels cradling doves and small children embracing cats or dogs.

Violet welcomes them with biscuits and brimming glasses of sweet sherry. 'Grab something now, gals, keep yer strength up.'

Once everyone is settled, Violet tells them about what nice people the previous owners were and recounts the nightly visits of the mysterious stranger. 'He parks his car up the road a bit and strolls along, always with a bag of something. Next thing, he's on his way again.'

'He could just come to feed a cat,' suggests Betty, her flushed cheeks hinting at more than one sherry.

'Why do it in the middle of the night?' asks Violet.

'But what if he comes early tonight?' says Betty. 'What will we do?'

'Yer better stay here with Violet,' says Irene, taking charge. 'Keep a lookout. If someone comes, turn all the lights in this place on, upstairs and down.'

'Youse got any idea the cost of the electric these days?' says Violet.

Betty puts her hand up. 'We could cause a diversion. I could run out and faint, or ask him for help . . . say my cat's up a tree.'

'Don't put yourself in danger, Betty dear,' says Hazel. 'And that could also endanger Violet. But we do need a back-up plan. If Natalia's in there and they plan to move her tonight, the schedule might change.'

Irene opens her coat to reveal a police truncheon. 'I'll give him a tap with this.'

'I'm not sure about hitting anyone, Irene,' says Hazel. 'Breaking and entering is bad enough without adding assault to it.'

'There's a bit of a knack to it,' says Irene, warming to her subject. 'Just a short, sharp whack on the back of the head, not so hard as to kill 'em. The other option, a tap over the nose.'

'Well, let's hope it doesn't come to that,' says Hazel. 'Betty, if we don't come out in twenty minutes, run to the phone box on the corner and call this number.' Hazel gives her Detective Dibble's card. 'His home number is on the back.'

'Isn't this fun?' says Violet, wielding the sherry bottle. 'Another sherry, anyone?'

Hazel quickly covers her glass. 'Not for me, thank you. Too much Dutch courage can be a dangerous thing.'

'I'll have one,' says Irene. 'Just to the top, Violet.'

'Irene, it's dark enough now. I think we should go,' says Hazel, hoping to dissuade her from another drink.

Irene knocks back the glass of sherry and they slip out the front door and across the road. They walk up the short path to the house and knock on the front door. They wait a minute, and with no answer, Irene fixes the lock and the door opens. They step into the dark hallway. Irene's torchlight flicks around an empty front room. They walk further down the hall and see that the kitchen and dining room are also completely empty; clearly no one lives here.

'Let's go up,' Irene whispers. 'When I put me hand up like this . . . wait and listen.'

Hazel nods, her heart thudding as they tiptoe up the stairs. At the top is a hallway with three closed doors leading off it. Holding her breath, Hazel gently opens the first one, the bathroom. The next room is empty, and the third door is locked.

Irene hands the torch to Hazel while she selects the right tool for the job from a ring of skeleton keys. A moment later the door opens to an overwhelming stench. Hazel hears a faint mewling sound. It takes her a moment to realise it's not a cat's cry but a woman's, and the beam of the torch reveals a sight she will never forget.

The woman she saw a month ago, Natalia Ivanov, sits on a camp bed, her back against the wall and a gag tight around her mouth. One wrist is handcuffed to the bed frame. A bucket, the source of the smell, sits beside the bed.

'Jesuuus Christ,' murmurs Irene under her breath.

'It's all right,' says Hazel, approaching the woman. 'We're here to help you.'

Natalia stares into Hazel's face, her eyes widening with recognition.

'Let's get this off you, dear.'

As soon as the gag comes off, Natalia gasps and begins to talk rapidly in Russian. Irene gets to work on the handcuffs. 'Save yer breath, love,' Irene tells her. 'Can't understand a bloody word.'

Hazel notices a glass of water with a straw on a side table. She hands it to Natalia, who pours it down her throat, gasping with relief. Released from the handcuffs, she rubs her arm vigorously to get the blood flowing, talking all the while. Words spilling over each other, she gestures out the window to something beyond. Hazel puts a finger to her lips. 'We have to get out quickly,' she says, hoping Natalia understands the sentiment and the urgency.

Irene leads the way as they hurry downstairs. 'Just to be safe, let's go out the back.'

They make their way to the kitchen and through the back door into a yard piled with broken furniture, crates and tea chests overflowing with rubbish. Beyond that stands a six-foot-high fence they will have to scale.

Natalia quickly realises what's needed and the three of them work together to gather enough bits and pieces to climb over the fence into the property behind. Natalia goes first, clambering easily up the pile of debris. Holding on to the fence with one hand, she helps Hazel up, then leaps over into the neighbour's yard.

Standing at the top of the pile, Hazel can see it's quite a drop to the ground on the other side. She can't afford to sprain her ankle, or worse, break something. Natalia signals for her to wait and a minute later comes back with a metal rubbish bin. She pushes the lid down firmly and gestures for Hazel to come over.

Hazel leans her belly on the top of the fence and, with Natalia guiding her, eases her legs over. Looking back at the house on Flood Street, she realises that all the lights are now on. She checks her watch. They've only been gone ten minutes so Betty wouldn't have called for help yet.

'Get out of the road, will yer?' hisses Irene. Without bothering to wait, she scrambles up the pile of rubbish and hurls herself over the fence. Landing with a soft thump on the lawn, she's up on her feet a moment later. They walk quietly down the side path and out the front gate into the street.

'Go home. I'll let Betty and Violet know what's happened,' says Irene.

'Irene, the lights were on. There's someone in the house. I don't think you should be seen anywhere near Flood Street.'

'I'll go down the back, get in that way. Be careful.' Irene slips off into the night, almost invisible in her black coat.

Hazel takes Natalia's arm. They walk along the back lanes, Natalia talking all the way home. It's unfortunate that Hazel can't understand a single word.

57

NO PLAN IN SIGHT

As soon as they get home, Hazel runs a hot bath for Natalia. While it's filling, she goes upstairs and finds a nightdress and dressing-gown for the girl. When she comes back down, Natalia is standing in the yard gazing up at the sky with its sprinkling of stars and waning moon. She turns to Hazel, takes her in a firm grip and plants a kiss on each cheek, following up with a long embrace, and two further kisses. 'Hello. Thank you,' she says.

Hazel thanks her, hands her a towel and the clothes, and ushers her into the steamy bathroom. As she closes the door, she hears Irene calling, 'Hazel, where are yers!' and hurries inside to find Irene and Betty in the kitchen.

'Hazel, they came . . . two men in a car . . . we didn't know . . .' says Betty breathlessly.

'Betty dear, sit down and take a deep breath,' says Hazel. 'I'll put the kettle on.'

'Where is she?' asks Irene, looking around wildly.

'She's having a bath.' Hazel fills the kettle and puts it on the stove to boil.

'What if she escapes out the back way?' asks Irene.

'We're not holding her captive, we are rescuing her,' says Hazel. 'She understands that.'

'Hazel, we need something stronger than tea, and none of yer bloody celery nonsense,' says Irene. 'Let's have a tipple of the top-shelf stuff.' She glances meaningfully at the whiskey's new hiding place.

Against her better judgement (they've both had more than enough sherry), Hazel gets the last bottle of whiskey down from the shelf and pours them each a drop. Irene knocks it back and holds out her glass for another. Hazel ignores her and sits down at the table, cradling her glass. 'Now, Betty, start at the beginning.'

Betty gets out her notebook. 'Our operatives entered the property at 0800 hours—'

'I don't think that's quite right, dear. Let's just use regular time, so 8pm . . . Go on,' says Hazel.

'Then at . . .' Betty pauses. 'At a quarter past eight, a vehicle pulled up in front of the house.'

'So it didn't park up the street a bit, like before?' asks Hazel.

'No, right in front. Bold as brass. Two men got out. We couldn't see their faces but they looked like thugs.'

'Why do you say that?' asks Hazel.

'I suppose the way they walked. One of them was big and the other weedy. Violet didn't think either of them was the usual fellow. They walked straight into the house.'

'So they had a key?' asks Hazel.

'Yes. The light went on downstairs first, then upstairs, then every light in the house was on. I went outside to go and telephone Detective Dibble but the two men came running out of the house, so I ducked back inside.' Betty takes a deep breath. 'It was so scary, we didn't know what to do.'

'So the men got back in their car then?' asks Hazel.

'No, they stood for a while, looking up and down the street. We could hear them arguing, sort of quiet arguing. Then they got in the car and drove slowly up the street.'

'And you got the number plate of the car, did you, dear?'

Betty stares at her notebook with a puzzled expression.

'Here we go,' says Irene, with a sigh.

'There's no need for that, thank you.' Betty flips over a page or two. 'Ah, here it is: CTA573.' She beams at them both. 'It was a blue Holden panel van.'

'Well done, Betty,' says Hazel. 'Given that conversation our informant overheard at the police station, we know that Pierce is involved – at least indirectly. I'm quite sure that he tipped Borisyuk off.'

'I don't know where to go from here,' says Hazel. 'If only we could communicate with Natalia.'

The kitchen door opens. Natalia steps into the room. She's younger than Hazel first imagined, perhaps late twenties. It was only a glimpse at the window and it was a while ago now. In the flesh, Natalia is startlingly beautiful, petite and lithe as a ballet dancer. She looks so young and vulnerable, Hazel wonders where her mother is, and if she knows the difficulties and danger her daughter is in. The girl's trusting gaze strengthens Hazel's resolve to protect her and get her to safety somehow.

Natalia stands for a moment, staring at them, and smiles. 'Hello. Thank you. Hello. Thank you.'

'There yer go,' says Irene. 'She's got the hang of it already.'

'I'm afraid that's all she has,' says Hazel. She gives Natalia a reassuring smile. It must be unnerving to have people talk about her in another language. Especially after what she's been through these last weeks.

Encouraged, Natalia tries a variation. 'Thank you. Hello.'

'I see what yer mean,' says Irene. 'What are we going to do with her?'

'I'm not sure,' says Hazel. 'But until we work that out, we can't let anyone know she's here. Not a soul.'

'I can kip down on the sofa tonight,' offers Irene, in an unusual bout of generosity. 'She can have me bed.'

'I've got a little mattress up in the attic. She can sleep in my room. I want to keep her close by,' says Hazel.

Natalia sits down at the table with them. Her gaze falls on the bottle of whiskey. Hazel gets a glass out and pours her one.

Holding her glass high, Natalia meets the gaze of each of them in turn. She says something in Russian and they all clink glasses with some force, united in their mission.

'Now we need a plan,' says Hazel. 'Because sooner or later, someone will turn up here looking for her.'

58

IT ALL COMES APART

For the first time in her ten years at Empire, Hazel calls in sick. She and Natalia leave Glade Street just after nine in the morning. Natalia wears Irene's black coat with her hair tucked up under Irene's second-best hat. As they step out the front door she becomes Irene, plodding along in a pair of Hazel's slippers, glasses halfway down her nose, puffing on a cigarette. She's small like Irene, and at first glance, no one would pick the difference. Nevertheless, Hazel's relieved to get off the streets and step inside the dim interior of the shoemaker's building, where they take the lift to the 4th floor.

Mr Sapozhnik sits at his workbench, cutting leather with a flat-edged knife and nodding in time to a spirited orchestral piece playing on a transistor radio beside him. He looks up irritably at Hazel's cheerful greeting. 'You are back, old lady. What do you want now?' he says, continuing with his work.

'I've brought someone to meet you—' begins Hazel but Natalia interrupts her, speaking in an impassioned voice.

The shoemaker sits still for a moment, his knife held aloft. Hazel realises that Natalia has revealed her identity to him and it's clear by his expression that he already knows who she is. He rises to his feet and, alternating between Russian and English, waves them out the door. 'Out! Out! Do not return!'

The two women step back into the hallway. He slams the door behind them and pulls down the blind. Natalia looks helplessly at Hazel.

'Good heavens, how rude. Never mind, dear. We'll think of something else.'

Hazel takes her arm and they walk back down the hall. As they stand waiting for the lift, the shoemaker's door opens and Mr Sapozhnik comes rushing along the hall towards them, the knife still in his hand. Hazel instinctively places herself between him and Natalia, looking around desperately for another exit, but there is none that she can see.

'You do not go here. This way. Come! Come!' he says. 'I help.'

Hazel tightens her grip on Natalia's arm. Her tingling ears tell her that he has no intention of helping them but he holds the knife. He ushers them to the end of the hallway and into a dark stair-well. Insisting they go ahead of him, he holds the railing, hauling himself down the stairs – wielding the knife but not quite threatening them with it. Nevertheless, Hazel senses his fear and panic. A sudden move could be fatal.

As they descend, Natalia talks to Mr Sapozhnik continuously. Judging by her tone, she's trying both reason and demand. At first he ignores her, then suddenly he gives a great angry roar and Natalia falls silent.

When they reach the basement, he flicks on a light to reveal a labyrinth of service corridors with bundles of electrical wiring and plumbing overhead. He hurries them on, gesturing at each turn with grunting commands.

'Stop here.' He holds the knife at Natalia's back while he fumbles with a key in the lock of a steel door. The heavy door swings open and he gestures for them to enter. As they step into the blackness beyond, the door slams shut and they hear the key grind in the lock.

'This is not quite what I expected,' says Hazel, with a sigh. 'Not at all.'

As her eyes adjust to the darkness, it's clear that they are locked in a large underground utilities room where all the electrics and plumbing start their journey from the bowels of the building. The walls are double-storey height with one high window at the point where the basement reaches ground level.

Natalia darts around in the dark, running her hands along the walls. A moment later the fluorescent lights overhead flicker on. Now she has light, she walks around the room talking, outlining a plan in some detail. If only Hazel knew what she was saying.

Natalia stands for a few minutes examining the boiler and a furnace which has a chute for rubbish coming down from the upper levels. She lifts her gaze to the window, turning back to look again at everything in the room, calculating the possibilities.

The window is so high, Hazel is certain it would take a fireman's ladder to reach it. But it seems that Natalia has other ideas. She finds a coil of rope behind the boiler. Looping it over her shoulder, she eyes off the chute to the furnace. Hazel wonders if it operates at a particular time of day – it would be dangerously hot when the furnace started up.

Natalia takes off the hat, coat and slippers. Underneath she wears one of Norma's old dresses and she ties the skirt up in a knot to be out of the way. She climbs onto the box of the furnace and begins to shimmy up the chute, which runs at a slight angle.

With her arms wrapped around it and her bare feet gripping the sides, she slowly inches upwards until she reaches the exposed steel girders in the ceiling.

Gripping the chute between her legs, she slips the coil of rope off her shoulder and throws it over a girder. After several attempts, it lands and she's able to pull down the loose end and tie a complicated knot in it, giving it a good tug to test it.

Hazel has never been the praying type but now she murmurs something like a prayer under her breath as she watches the girl transfer her weight onto the rope. Hanging twenty feet in the air with nothing but concrete, machinery and metal below her, Natalia pauses, her eyes fixed on the window, which seems impossibly small from where Hazel stands.

Making some calculation, Natalia lowers herself down the rope for better alignment with the window and tentatively pushes herself off the chute. She swings with little momentum at first but each time she pushes off, she swings further and higher. Finally she kicks off with all her strength and, with her bare heels directly out in front of her, smashes the window, leaving a frame of jagged glass behind. She swings again and again, each time kicking out broken glass until the frame is clear and her feet are bloodied.

Hazel gives a gasp as next she watches Natalia swing with all her strength, flying through the air and out through the broken window. A second later, her face appears through the window frame and she gives Hazel a wave. At that moment, Hazel hears the key rattling in the lock. She waves her arms madly, gesturing to her to go. 'Natalia! Run! Run!'

59

DEEP TROUBLE FOR HAZEL

The door slowly opens and a giant figure fills the doorway. It's Irene's friend Archie, from the Mermaid Club. Hazel can see in his eyes that he recognises her.

'Hurry up,' says someone behind him in a plaintive nasal voice. 'We haven't got all day.'

Archie steps into the room followed by a lean, peevish-looking man in his mid-thirties. He's unremarkable apart from his left ear, which appears to have been horribly chewed, perhaps by a dog.

'Where's the Russian bird?' asks Dog Ear.

'Mate, look!' says Archie, pointing up at the broken window. 'She's gone out there. Go round the back. I'll take care of the old lady.'

Dog Ear swears furiously and charges out the door, his footsteps receding into the distance. Archie stands towering over Hazel with a sorrowful expression on his face. 'It's Mrs Bates, isn't it? What did I tell you ladies? You're in the shit now. I can't even say you escaped 'cause it's . . . well . . .'

'Unlikely?' suggests Hazel. 'I understand. Let's go.'

They walk back along the corridors, up the stairs and out into the street, where a blue panel van is parked with two wheels up on the pavement and a parking ticket on the windscreen. Archie snatches up the ticket, cursing under his breath.

He opens the door for Hazel. She slides across to the middle of the bench seat, noting that the back of the van is separated from the cab by a security grille.

Archie folds himself in beside her. 'Now, what are we going to do with you?'

'I won't let on that we know each other, if that's what you're worried about.'

'Why didn't you just leave it alone? I know you wanted to help the girl but that Russian bloke upstairs, he makes the boss's shoes. These Ruskies all know each other. He was a bad choice. Tell me where she's gone. If we can find her, there's a better chance of you getting out of here in one piece.'

'Archie dear, you seem like a lovely young man.'

'Thanks, Mrs Bates. That's nice of you to say in the circumstances. But unfortunately, part of my job is doing things to people that are definitely not nice.'

'I'd like to make things easy for you, but I honestly don't have any idea where she would go.'

Archie sighs. He winds down the window and leans his great elbow on the sill. 'The boss is not going to like it, not at all.'

'Tell me, how did you get into this business, Archie? You're obviously good with people, and kind-hearted. I could see you having your own enterprise – a coffee shop, for instance.'

Archie nods. 'You're spot on there, I need to get some money together, but not for a coffee shop. What I'd really like is a little hardware shop, selling tools and mixing paints for people. My dad used to take me to the hardware shop all the time. He was good with his hands. I got that from him. He died when I was a nipper but when I go into a hardware place, I feel . . . you know . . .'

'He's still there?' suggests Hazel.

'Yeah, it's that hardwarey smell. I still have the claw hammer he always used.'

Hazel stiffens. 'I hope you're using that responsibly, dear.'

'Oh, yeah, don't worry, I keep my fingers well clear. Dad taught me that. Uh-oh, here comes trouble.'

Dog Ear throws himself into the driver's seat and slams the door so violently that all the air rushes out of the car. He fumes silently for a moment, then turns and glares at Hazel. 'What's she doing here? Stick her in the back.'

'Mate, she's an old lady. Would you stick your nana in the back?'

Dog Ear grunts, turns on the ignition and puts his foot down.

They drive fast through the streets of Kings Cross, pulling up in a back lane where Archie escorts Hazel out of the car, taking her through a security door into the rear entrance of the Mermaid Club. They walk down a dark, grimy hallway and up three flights of stairs, before stepping into a palatial office with crystal chandeliers, gold brocade curtains and blue velvet furnishings. The centrepiece is an antique desk in a dark polished timber. On it sits a cigarette lighter identical to the one that graces Frankie's desk.

'Sit down, lady,' says Dog Ear. 'Don't move.'

'What're you going to do?' Archie asks him, politely ushering Hazel to a chair.

'Call the boss, obviously.' Dog Ear picks up the phone, then thinks better of it. 'Don't take your eyes off her,' he says, stalking out the door.

Archie squeezes himself into an armchair. He looks at her sadly. 'I'd like to help you because you're a friend of Mrs Turnbuckle's, but it's out of my hands now.'

'I'm sure you'll do what you can, Archie.'

At the sound of voices, Hazel turns to see Borisyuk walking down the hall with Dog Ear trailing behind, giving an account of what happened. As the two men enter the room, Borisyuk tells him to shut up and he instantly falls silent.

'Madam, who are you?' asks Borisyuk, standing over Hazel with a cold smile fixed on his face. 'You look familiar to me. Have we met?'

Hazel shakes her head. 'I don't believe so.' She looks down at his feet and sees that he is indeed wearing a very smart pair of leather shoes. 'Mr Sapozhnik is quite a craftsman, isn't he?' she says, directing his attention to his shoes.

Borisyuk admires his shoes briefly and turns his attention back to her. 'I'll ask you again, who are you?'

Hazel smiles. 'I'm no one special. Just a tea lady.'

'A tea lady?' He glares at Archie and Dog Ear and settles his gaze back on Hazel. 'Are you making a joke?'

'Not at all. I can demonstrate, if you like,' offers Hazel, getting up.

'Sit down please, madam. You move when I say move.'

'I wouldn't mind a cup of tea,' says Archie.

'Yeah, me too, boss,' agrees Dog Ear. 'I didn't get breakfast this morning.'

'And a biscuit wouldn't go astray,' says Archie.

'Shut up,' says Borisyuk, his penetrating gaze on Hazel. 'Where is Miss Ivanov?'

'I don't know,' says Hazel. 'I really do not know.'

Borisyuk's jaw sets in a stubborn line. 'Madam, you don't seem to realise the danger you are in. Something very nasty is going to happen if you continue to be unhelpful.'

'Um, boss,' interrupts Archie.

'What?' asks Borisyuk, without taking his eyes off Hazel.

'She's an old lady . . . like a grandma,' says Archie.

Dog Ear agrees. 'You can't kneecap a nana. My nan's already got trouble with her knees.'

Borisyuk turns to them with exaggerated patience. 'We'll get to the details in a minute.'

'She doesn't know where the girl is, boss,' says Archie. 'The Russian climbed a twenty-foot-high pipe and jumped out the window and ran away. She doesn't speak English, so I honestly don't think the old lady can tell us anything useful.'

Borisyuk looks at the two of them with a stony expression. He walks over to the window and stands staring out for several long minutes. Finally, without turning around, he says, 'Give our friend here a lift home. Search every inch of her house and don't come back until you find out where that little bitch has gone. *Capisce?*'

'Yes, boss,' says Archie.

'Yes, boss,' says Dog Ear.

Relieved, Hazel gets up to leave. 'I'm not sure what *capisce* means but I can make you boys a nice cup of tea and a bite to eat while you're having a look around.'

60

MORE RISKY BUSINESS

While Archie and Dog Ear search the front room, Hazel goes into the kitchen and puts the kettle on. A few minutes later, Archie comes in and says, 'You sit down and stay right here, Mrs Bates; don't go anywhere until we're finished.'

Hazel sits down at the table obediently, trying to appear unconcerned. Natalia is enterprising and courageous and, given the chance, quite capable of getting herself out of a fix. Hopefully she's found somewhere safe to hide and hasn't left a trail of blood behind her. The two men wander around the yard. They put their heads into the washhouse, bathroom and lavatory, look over the fence and down the side of the house. They walk back through the kitchen and thump up the stairs.

Hazel listens with trepidation as the wardrobe door bangs and the back bedroom window is opened and slammed shut. Finally their footsteps descend the stairs and Dog Ear appears in the doorway. He gives Hazel a venomous look. 'Where is she?'

'I've told you I don't know. The kettle's boiled, can I get you a cuppa? I might even have some cake in the cupboard.'

Archie joins them in the kitchen. 'Not too many places to hide here. If you think she's gone somewhere else, better to tell us now, Mrs Bates.'

'If we find out you're hiding that Russian,' says Dog Ear, 'we're gonna come back and burn this house down in the middle of the night. Barbecued chook – very tasty.' He makes a show of licking his lips.

Archie gives a helpless shrug. 'Sorry, that's how we do things, I'm afraid.'

'I understand. We all have our jobs to do,' says Hazel.

Dog Ear gives the kitchen chair a vicious kick, knocking it over, and walks off down the hall. Archie picks the chair up and sets it right. 'There you go. Nice to see you again, Mrs Bates. Give my regards to Mrs T.'

'I will, thanks, Archie, and good luck with your hardware shop.'

He gives her a wink. 'One day.'

Hovering behind the lace curtains in the front room, Hazel watches them leave. When she's quite sure they've gone, she goes out into the yard. She's almost certain that Natalia would come back here, knowing it is a safe place for her. And it's not as though she has anywhere else to go.

Hazel goes out the back gate and walks up and down the alley. Turning towards the house, she glimpses a movement, like the flap of a bird's wing, on the roof and realises it's a hand – not flapping but waving. Natalia is sitting perched up high on the steep pitched roof!

Hazel hasn't ventured into Irene's bedroom since she arrived but is not surprised to discover that it's chaotic, her belongings flung willy-nilly all over the room. She picks her way across to the window, opens it and puts her head out. Leaning out, Hazel twists herself around to see Natalia sitting on the roof, her feet resting in the gutter – which is not in good repair and far from secure.

'Natalia, come down,' calls Hazel, beckoning to her. 'It's safe to come down now.'

Hazel steps back into the room and Natalia appears at the window. Dangling from the guttering by her fingers, she places her bloodied feet on the windowsill and leaps gracefully into the bedroom, throwing her arms around Hazel in a delighted embrace. 'Hello! Thank you!'

They go downstairs where Hazel gets out the first-aid kit and cleans up Natalia's feet, treating the cuts with iodine and bandaging them. She makes them some sardines on toast. They wash up the dishes together and go into the front room.

Hazel closes the blinds, just to be sure, and sits down at the Taj Mahal, which is now taking shape, thanks to Maude. As if by invitation, Natalia sits down opposite and they work together in silence, swapping pieces and smiling at each other when a recognisable feature of the building falls into place. Finally, Hazel has an idea and goes to the telephone.

'Mr Kovac? I'm sorry to telephone you after hours.'

'This is not a problem, Mrs Bates – do you want to change your order?'

'Thank you, but, no, it's not that. Mr Sapozhnik was not as helpful as we hoped and so I'm wondering if you have any other Russian-speaking friends?'

'I apologise. He is a rude man. Hungarians are not friends with Russians. People think those from Eastern Europe are the same, but we are not. Mr Sapozhnik I might have mentioned is from the Shanghai area in China; they are known as White Russians, not Red Russians. They are the worst ones in my opinion. Not that Reds are any better, they are all Russians. Let me ask my wife. Wait one moment.' Hazel hears the muffled sounds of him talking to his wife in Hungarian and a minute later, he says, 'My wife recommends a Russian lady who was a university professor. She speaks good English and my wife said she is friendly, for a Russian. Don't have high hopes. Let me get the address. Her name is Mrs Agapov.'

'Thank you, Mr Kovac,' says Hazel. In the silence that follows, she notices there is a slight echo on the line and wonders if someone is listening in. It could be someone on an extension at Mr Kovac's house. Or it could be that one of their telephones is being tapped.

'When do you plan to go and see her, Mrs Bates? My wife could telephone and make the introduction.'

'Perhaps later in the week,' says Hazel, deliberately vague. He gives her the address, which she memorises, and she thanks him for his help. When he hangs up, there is an empty whistling sound, as though the line is still open, and then a faint click as the listener disconnects.

With a sense of urgency now, Hazel leaves Natalia working on the jigsaw and goes next door to ask Maude to look up the bus route and timetable. Aware that this is a difficult exercise for Hazel, Maude offers to come with them, but while that would be helpful, it could also be dangerous. Hazel has her write down the various stops. She can compare the letters with signage along the route.

As soon as it's dark, Hazel and Natalia slip out along the back alley and make their way to Stanmore, where Mrs Agapov lives in a quiet, tree-lined street in a large Federation-style house. Fronted by a hedge and wrought-iron fence, the house is in darkness. They knock but there is no answer. Hazel hopes the woman hasn't gone away somewhere but it's worth waiting an hour or so, at least.

She thinks about the listener on the phone and decides it's too risky to wait on the front verandah. The hedge along the front of the property is dense enough that if they sit on the lawn behind it, they'll be hidden from the street.

As they settle themselves down to wait, Natalia reaches for Hazel's hand. She holds it for a moment then brings it to her lips and kisses it. Hazel gives her a smile, grateful that her efforts are appreciated. The night is balmy and they pass the time gazing up at the sky and listening to the calls of night birds that Hazel never hears in her own suburb.

A car drives past slowly and they instinctively shrink back into the shadows. It passes again and stops further down the street. After a moment, there's the sound of a man's footsteps. He stops at the gate, so close that Hazel can smell the smoke from his cigarette. She and Natalia grasp each other's hands, afraid to even breathe.

He stands there for a good minute. Natalia squeezes Hazel's hand tightly, her face close and her eyes wide with fear. Through the hedge, Hazel sees the spark of a cigarette tossed on the pavement and ground out. The man walks back to his car and several long minutes later, drives away.

They wait in silence for another twenty minutes, then, just as Hazel is considering whether they should leave and try again tomorrow, the wrought-iron gate squeaks open. A woman walks up the path and goes inside. Lights flood the house and the woman appears briefly in the window to draw the curtains.

At Hazel's knock, the door is opened by the woman. Middle-aged, her long dark hair is streaked with grey. She stares at Hazel with a puzzled expression, then turns her gaze to Natalia and gives a gasp of recognition. 'Madame Ivanov! Come in, come in,' she says, beckoning them into a brightly lit hallway. She closes the door

behind them and takes them into a large lounge room with paint-
ings on the walls and overflowing bookshelves.

As they sit down, Natalia comes to life and Mrs Agapov listens
to her talk with a deepening frown, asking questions from time to
time. She looks over at Hazel, presumably enquiring how she fits
into the picture, and nods as Natalia explains.

'I do apologise,' Mrs Agapov says, getting to her feet. 'I haven't
even offered you a drink. What can I get you, Mrs . . .?'

'Hazel . . . Hazel Bates. Nothing for me, thank you,' says Hazel,
noting a drinks trolley packed with bottles of spirits.

Mrs Agapov pours Natalia and herself a vodka and sits back in
her armchair. 'Thank you for bringing Madame Ivanov all this way,
Mrs Bates. She has told me how brave you have been to rescue her
and get her here. Of course, I can help.'

'I'm so grateful to find someone who can,' says Hazel. 'And
who can understand what she's saying. I'm not even sure what's
happened.'

'It's a very confusing story,' says Mrs Agapov. 'A fire? Kidnapping? I'm not sure what to believe, these circus people love drama.
Anyway, she is safe now and we can return her to the circus and
to her husband. You probably know the "Flying Flamingos" are
very famous in Russia. I will now telephone a friend who I'm sure
knows someone connected to the circus. I think the tour is coming
to a close soon and so we need to move quickly. Wait here and I will
make some enquiries.'

'Does she have any idea who kidnapped her or why?' asks Hazel.

Mrs Agapov stands up to leave. 'Let me make this call and we
can discuss it further.' She goes into another room, closing the door
behind her. While she's away, Natalia smiles at Hazel from time to
time, adding, 'Hello. Thank you.'

After quite some time, Mrs Agapov returns. 'They fly back from Adelaide this evening and return to Moscow tomorrow. I can take Madame Ivanov to the hotel and meet them there. Can we drop you at your home on the way, Mrs Bates?'

'That's very kind of you, Mrs Agapov, but I would like to stay with Natalia until I see her reunited with her people. If you don't mind?'

Mrs Agapov looks a little offended. 'Of course I don't mind but you have done so much.'

'It's just that I have become very fond of her. I have a daughter and would want someone to take care of her in this situation.'

'As I said, you can entrust her to me,' says Mrs Agapov, her tone cool. 'I will take good care of her.'

Up until this moment, all has seemed well but this last comment sets off Hazel's tingling. Did something change during Mrs Agapov's telephone call? Whatever she discovered on that call seems to have rattled her. Hazel wonders if someone has warned her off. Are she and Natalia about to walk into a trap?

61

A NASTY SURPRISE AWAITS

They head towards the city in a stately manner in Mrs Agapov's Mercedes. In the back seat, Natalia keeps her head down, even though it's dark and she's unlikely to be seen.

There are so many things that Hazel wants to know but now she's not sure she can trust the answers. 'I wonder if Mrs Ivanov can describe the man who kept her captive in the house? And if she has any idea who kidnapped her? Could you ask her, please?'

'I really don't want to be involved,' says Mrs Agapov testily. Nevertheless, she asks Natalia and they speak for a few minutes.

'She says he wasn't Russian. Not young, not old. He wore a balaclava over his head, so she didn't see his face. I'm not sure if this kidnapping story is true, or exaggerated, so I would not take it all too seriously. I suspect she had a love affair and is now trying to cover it up with a story she has invented.'

Hazel doesn't argue the point but it's clear that Mrs Agapov is now trying to discredit Natalia's story when she was initially fairly receptive.

The Mercedes purrs to a halt under the portico of the Sofia Hotel in the city and a doorman appears. Natalia, wearing a headscarf, her gaze on the ground, takes Hazel's arm as they enter the foyer with its marble floors, sparkling chandeliers and furnishings in gold and royal blue. Mrs Agapov goes to the reception desk and Hazel takes the opportunity to have a good look around. The foyer has two lifts and a wide marble staircase. On one side, double glass doors lead to a restaurant and, on the other, an archway leads to a small lounge area with a few armchairs. Beyond that is a lively bar where someone plays jazz piano beneath the hum of conversation.

There are several people in the foyer: two older women, one with a small fluffy dog in her arms, and a man who sits reading a newspaper. To Hazel, he seems a little suspicious, given the lateness of the hour, but a woman soon joins him and they leave together.

Turning back towards the bar, Hazel notices a uniformed staff member walking towards them but then he mysteriously disappears in the lounge area. She takes Natalia's arm, not wanting to let go of her for a minute, and leads her into the lounge. The lighting is low but Hazel spies a service door, designed to be concealed, papered in matching blue-and-gold patterned wallpaper.

Mrs Agapov joins them, looking agitated. 'There you are. I wondered where you'd gone. They're not here yet, but we can go up and wait in the suite.'

'Why don't we have a drink at the bar instead?' suggests Hazel.

Her suggestion takes Mrs Agapov by surprise. 'We can have a drink upstairs where it's quiet. Let's go straight up now.'

'Surely we've got time for a quick one,' says Hazel. Without waiting for a reply, she pulls Natalia into the busy bar, working her way through the crowd to the far end of the room. She's now quite certain that this is a trap and she needs a moment to think.

Natalia gazes around, smiling and looking relaxed, enjoying being out in the world with no idea of the impending danger. But Hazel can see Mrs Agapov's head bobbing up and down as she frantically pushes her way through the crowd. Her desperate expression confirms Hazel's worst suspicions as she guides Natalia out of the bar into the adjoining restaurant.

The restaurant's main entry is beside the marble staircase, giving Hazel a good view of the foyer and the sight of Archie and Dog Ear, who come running down the stairs and into the bar. Natalia turns to Hazel with a look of horror – now she understands.

'Don't worry, dear. It's not over yet.' Hazel gestures for Natalia to follow her. Staying out of sight and close to the walls, they make their way back to the lounge where Hazel quickly locates the hidden door. She pushes it inwards and they step into a service corridor.

They hurry along the narrow hall until it opens out into a wider one. A waiter, leaving the kitchen with laden trolleys, glances at them curiously. They hurry on through the kitchen, where staff turn to stare and someone shouts that they're not allowed in here. Hazel gives the man a friendly wave and they keep going until they find themselves out on a loading dock that stinks of rotting vegetables. Down a couple of steps and they're out in the street, walking in the opposite direction to the main hotel entry. Natalia delivers an outraged commentary and Hazel murmurs her agreement.

Hazel sees a phone booth and they step inside. Relieved to be off the street, she takes a deep breath. Who can they trust? Detective Dibble is the first person who comes to mind but then an idea strikes. She opens her handbag and finds the card she's looking for. She puts a coin in the slot and dials the number.

Fifteen minutes later, Bert arrives in his taxi. He stops next to the phone booth, leans over and pushes open the back door. 'You in trouble again, missus?' he says, with a bark of laughter.

Hazel and Natalia scramble into the back seat. 'We are. Please just start driving, Bert,' says Hazel. 'As fast as you can away from here.'

'All right, missus. Off we go.' He pulls out and heads into the city.

Hazel thinks back to her conversation with Mrs Agapov and when the deception started. As far as she recalls, it was at the very last when Mrs Agapov said she would take good care of Natalia. Perhaps it's safe to assume that she was being honest about the circus returning to town.

'Bert, we need to find a circus,' she says. 'The Great Moscow Circus.'

'Running away to the circus, are we?' He chuckles. 'Wouldn't you be better to stick to something closer to home?' Getting no response, he adds, 'If there's a circus in town, someone will know about it.' He picks up the two-way speaker. 'Five-seven-eight. Sid, can you find out if anyone picked up circus people? Russians? Yes, I said circus. Yes, Russians. Over.'

His request is followed by crackling voices but Hazel can't make out anything at all. She tries to think of another plan. The police will be the last resort. Detective Dibble is a possibility but there is still a risk Pierce could get involved and they would be back where they started.

Finally, between calls and static, Bert manages to establish that the circus has indeed arrived and is lodging at a motel out near the airport. 'That where we're off to now, missus?'

'Yes, please,' says Hazel. 'Quick as you can.'

62

A NEW STAR AT THE CIRCUS

It's almost midnight when they reach the motel; a modest affair, nothing at all like the luxurious Sofia Hotel. It has the usual layout of a dozen rooms in two straight lines facing each other across a parking strip. Tonight there are no cars, the doors to the rooms are open and light spills across the space between them.

The guests, perhaps fifteen or twenty people, have brought chairs outside. There's music and laughter and no one notices the taxi pulling up until Natalia jumps out and calls to them. Suddenly people are on their feet, confused but moving towards her at the same time. In a moment the scene is chaotic with tears and embraces, everyone shouting at once.

Hazel and Bert stand beside the taxi watching the spectacle unfold. Natalia is being embraced by a man who lifts her clear off the ground. They kiss and speak for a few minutes then look over towards the taxi. The man releases her, leaves the group and walks towards Hazel.

In the scattered light, Hazel doesn't recognise his face at

first but notes his excellent posture. It's Mr Handsome, the mysterious man she and Betty had seen near the bond store.

'Madame, let me introduce myself – Ivan Ivanov.' He looks at
her more closely. 'We have met before?'

'Mrs Hazel Bates and no, we haven't met.'

'My wife tells me you were the one to rescue her,' he says. 'I have
been completely mad with worry. We cannot thank you enough.'

'I'm so glad to get her back to you in one piece,' says Hazel.

'Will you stay with us for a while, Mrs Hazel Bates? We leave
in the early morning but tonight we can talk. We will discover
everything.'

'Of course I can stay for a while,' says Hazel. She opens her
purse to find her emergency ten shillings but Mr Ivanov beats
her to it, handing Bert a five-pound note and thanking him for
his help.

'Gimme a call if yer need me, missus. Always something going
on with yer,' Bert chuckles, getting in his taxi.

Hazel thanks him and walks beside Mr Ivanov towards the
cluster of people gathered around Natalia. 'I'm relieved you speak
such good English,' she says. 'I thought I'd never get to the bottom
of all this.'

'I learnt as a child. It is very useful now we travel the world. Let
me introduce you to Madame Nazarova, also known as Tiger Lady.
She performs in the cage with nine tigers, very brave,' he says as they
join the group. He speaks briefly to the woman in Russian and when
he finishes, Madame Nazarova, who is stronger than she looks, grips
Hazel's shoulders and plants a firm kiss on each cheek. Mr Ivanov
moves on to introduce a tall and gangly man with a mournful face.
'This gentleman is the most important member of the entire circus,
I will say the most loved clown in all the Soviet Union.'

As the story of Hazel's endeavours spreads among the troupe, it seems everyone wants to thank and embrace her. Mr Ivanov then introduces her to a bear trainer, three handsome young acrobats, a family of highwire performers, and so it goes on until everyone is satisfied. Finally, with one arm around his wife's shoulders, he invites Hazel to come to their motel room. 'We need quiet so we can talk together. Then we call a taxi to get you home.'

Most of the floor in the room is taken up with open suitcases packed with clothes and sequinned costumes. Mr Ivanov pours them each a generous drink that Hazel assumes is vodka as she feels the tensions of the day melt away. He lights a couple of cigarettes and hands one to his wife. Outside there is singing and laughter as the celebrations go on.

In the quiet of the room, the Ivanovs catch up in short bursts of conversation, their hands clasped together, eyes fixed on each other.

Natalia settles herself on the bed, propped up on pillows. She closes her eyes, takes a sip of her drink and gives a great sigh. Mr Ivanov takes the only chair, inviting Hazel to also make herself comfortable. She eases her shoes off and sits on the bed, relieved to be still and safe.

'It is true, I have seen you before, Mrs Bates?'

'I work near the building that burnt down. That's where I first saw Mrs Ivanov before the fire, and I saw you there several times.'

'Ah, I was told by the police she was seen there. It is sad that we never talked. We could have joined together to find her.'

He chats with Natalia for a few minutes and turns to Hazel. 'Now I explain. When we arrived in Sydney, Natalia contacted her uncle. They never met before. On the telephone, he said they would discuss important family business and he would like her to come alone.'

'And that uncle is Mr Borisyuk?' asks Hazel.

'Yes. When she did not return, I didn't know how to contact him. I knew the name of the restaurant. But no one there had seen her. I had to put a call through to the family in the Soviet Union and this is not a simple matter.' He pauses to explain to Natalia, and then continues, 'Alexander Borisyuk is the brother of Natalia's mother. But when I talk with Natalia's father, he tells me this uncle is not to be trusted and I must go to the police.

'When I speak to the uncle, he tells me Natalia did not come to the restaurant. He did not meet her. By this time she has not come back for two days and nights. I went to the police near our hotel. I had to wait for one hour before a policeman came to speak to me. He talks about a building that burnt down. I didn't understand what this had to do with my wife.'

'Was the officer's name Pierce, by any chance? Detective Sergeant Pierce?' asks Hazel.

'You are correct. I was crazy with worry and fear. Later I was told she was not in the burning building.' He pauses to talk earnestly to Natalia, who leans forward and takes his hands in hers, presumably describing her ordeal. While they talk, Hazel tries to work out the timeline. It seems to her that although there was supposedly no police record, all the information Mr Ivanov was given had come from Hazel's reports.

Mr Ivanov turns back to Hazel. 'She tells me she was met at the restaurant by a friendly gentleman, a well-dressed business man—'

'Can you ask if he smoked a cigar?' asks Hazel, realising who this man could be.

Mr Ivanov confirms he did. 'This man brought her to the old building and two men, one as large as a tree and one'—he clarifies with Natalia, touching his ear—'one with a broken ear, locked her in this building with bars on the windows. This is where she saw you from the window. That night there was a fire. She climbed through the roof to another building.'

'But then she was captured again,' says Hazel. 'I saw her being pulled into a car.'

Mr Ivanov translates this for Natalia. 'Yes, by the same two men.'

'Yes, I know them. And who was the man who came to the house every night, where she was held captive?' asks Hazel.

'She says she did not see his face, he always was wearing a knitted hat for the cold that covers the mouth and nose.'

'But why? Why was she kidnapped at all?' asks Hazel.

'That is complicated and the story not complete.' He hesitates, the exhaustion evident on his face. 'Many years ago, Natalia's grandparents left Russia for China. At that time her grandfather was an engineer and worked to build the Chinese Eastern Railway in Harbin—'

'Harbin?' interrupts Hazel. 'The bond store and the house where we found Natalia are both owned by a company called Harbin Holdings.'

'I see. Natalia's mother and this uncle, Alexander, were born there, so it has a special significance. Later, the family moved to Shanghai. The grandparents were involved with the diamond business at this time and became very wealthy. Sometime later, the family made a decision to return to Russia.

'Alexander was a young man at that time. He refused to return to Russia. He left Shanghai alone with diamonds stolen from the family safe. So this is the end for his family. He writes to Natalia's mother but he has not seen her or his elderly parents for thirty years. Natalia wanted to repair this break in the family.'

He glances tenderly at his wife who has drifted off to sleep, still nursing her drink.

Hazel, on the other hand, has never felt more awake. 'So, do you think the building was set alight in an attempt to murder Natalia?'

Mr Ivanov shakes his head. 'This part I cannot understand but no, I think not. The next time I talked with her father we knew it was a kidnapping and there was a large amount to pay for her release – a very large amount. Funds that need to come from outside the Soviet Union. Alexander Borisyuk would know that the family would give everything for her return. I will soon call them with the good news.'

He smiles at Hazel. 'You are exhausted. A long story at the end of a long day. It is a miracle you came tonight because tomorrow I have to leave this country with or without my wife. I cannot stay here. We are grateful to you for everything. We will never forget what you have done. You risked your life to save Natalia.'

There's a knock on the door and Mr Ivanov gets up to answer it. He excuses himself and steps outside to talk with one of the troupe.

Hazel closes her eyes, just for a moment. When she opens them, the morning sun pours into the room. Disoriented, she sits up and looks around. The Russians and all their luggage have vanished. On the bedside table is a note and twenty pounds. She gets off the bed and makes her way to the door. Outside, a woman walks past pushing a trolley laden with towels and linen. 'They're gone, love. They must've forgotten yah.' She laughs. 'Bloody Russians.'

63

BETTY ARRIVES ON THE SCENE

Apart from a hurried telephone conversation with Hazel this morning, Betty hasn't had a chance to hear all the news. 'Knock, knock, only me!' she calls, bursting into Hazel's kitchen.

Hazel, looking wrung out, sits at the table with Irene. Without a word, Hazel stands up and she and Betty put their arms around each other. Betty cries a little – she's so relieved to have her friend home safe.

Irene ignores them, busy flattening the afternoon paper out on the table. 'Yer need to get yer glasses fixed, Hazel. I can't be doing all this reading.'

'I can read it,' offers Betty, sitting down opposite.

'I'm quite capable, thank you. Here we go: "Russian Circus Star Heads Home. Australian auth . . . auth—"'

'Authorities?' suggests Betty.

'All right . . . "authorities were relieved when Mrs Ivanov, who performs with her husband as the 'Flying Flamingos' in the Great Moscow Circus, and has been missing for some weeks, reappeared in the early hours of this morning, having missed the entire tour" – thanks to tea lady Hazel Bates.'

'Don't make things up, Irene dear,' says Hazel. 'Just stick to the facts. What else?'

Irene groans and pushes the paper across to Betty, who continues, '"The attractive brunette arrived in the nick of time to return to the USSR where she is considered a national treasure. Her disappearance was fast becoming a diplomatic nightmare with Soviet authorities accusing the Australian government of incompetence. This was the first-ever tour of Australia by the Circus and was enjoyed by thousands of people around the country. Let's hope this unfortunate incident doesn't stand in the way of the troupe returning in the future."' Betty looks up and gives Hazel a round of applause. 'Now I want to hear everything that happened after you went off to the shoemaker's. Every tiny detail!'

'I hope you're not in a hurry.' Hazel puts on the kettle and gets the cake tin down. Betty gets out cups and saucers. Irene quietly lights her pipe, obviously expecting to be waited on, as usual. They sit around the kitchen table and Hazel recounts everything that happened, from her visit to Mr Sapozhnik to Natalia scaling a rubbish chute and escaping out the window; Archie and Dog Ear searching the house and Natalia hiding on the roof (so intrepid!), then this dreadful Mrs Agapov and a trap at the Sofia Hotel, and finally a race to the airport motel and the reunion.

'Oh, so Mr Handsome was the husband all the time!' gasps Betty, who has been so absorbed in the story she completely forgot to make notes. 'If only we'd known!'

'Bloody Archie. Still, what do yer expect from a criminal,' says Irene. 'And Pierce is up to his neck, in't he? Right from the start.'

Hazel agrees. 'We can be certain now that Harbin Holdings is Borisyuk's company.'

Betty makes a note. 'I'm sure we can officially confirm it. There will be a register somewhere, I will find out.'

Hazel stares out the window thoughtfully. 'If Natalia was valuable to Borisyuk alive, it doesn't make any sense that he had the place burnt down. So we're really no closer to finding who started that fire and murdered Mr McCracken.'

'But Natalia is safe, that's what we set out to do,' says Betty. It occurs to her that much as she has enjoyed the detective work, Hazel's safety is more important. 'And, Hazel, remember we can't tell Merl any of this because it will get back.'

'Bloody traitor,' adds Irene, hacking off another slice of currant cake.

'I agree we need to keep it to ourselves,' says Hazel. 'Borisyuk will be well aware that Natalia's gone now and know that I was involved in her escape.'

Irene nods. 'Yeah, but probably not going to bother with yer now the bird's flown.'

Betty trusts that Irene (with her shrewd criminal mind) is right about this and that Hazel is not in any immediate danger. 'Perhaps we should let Detective Dibble take over?' she suggests.

But Hazel is not really listening. 'You know how sometimes you set up your trolley and you know something's missing?' she says. 'You count the cups and saucers again, check the sugar, milk, biscuits, and you just can't work it out.'

Betty puts her hand up. 'And you realise it's the teapot.'

Hazel nods. 'Yes. It's so obvious, but you can't see it.'

'What's yer bloody point?' asks Irene.

'We are missing one thing, and it's probably staring us right in the face.'

64

GLORIA DISCOVERS A BRIGHT SIDE

Gloria sits in her alcove smoking as she gazes unhappily over her reduced empire. Four workers were sacked yesterday when Old Karp returned to work. Gloria still has her job, for the moment. She'll be the last out but it may still come to that.

The buzzer goes and, right on time, Hazel comes rattling in with her trolley. She looks around at the empty worktables and the machines sitting silent, and gives Gloria such a sympathetic look, it makes her want to cry. The remaining machinists gather around the trolley, more subdued than usual. One of the Greek pressers has gone, so the other one has no one to talk to and looks very sorry for herself.

Hazel bustles over with Gloria's coffee. 'It's not over yet, dear. Don't give up. Has the postman been yet?'

Gloria nods. Now she is going to cry. 'There was nothing. Not one single order. We got it wrong. It's all my fault. The Ginger Nuts must be laughing their nutty heads off. I really believed in this, Hazel. I thought we were leading a revolution that'd save the company.' She rubs her stinging eyes. Never has she cried at work and she's not going to start now.

Hazel pops back to her trolley and returns a moment later with a crisply ironed handkerchief. Gloria takes it gratefully and dabs her eyes, leaving smudges of black mascara on it. 'Sorry, Hazel, I'll wash it out.'

'No rush, dear. I always keep a supply on hand. How's Pixie faring?'

'I haven't seen her yet. Now that Old Karp's back, I wouldn't be surprised if I get the boot,' says Gloria.

'You were doing what you thought best. I'm sure he will understand.'

When Hazel's gone, Gloria cleans up the workbenches that were hurriedly vacated. She finds a cardboard box and collects the bits left behind: parts of unfinished garments and stuff-ups, a lipstick (not her colour), half-a-dozen hair rollers, a pair of shoes and a cardigan. Under Alice's worktable she finds a box of magazine cuttings and a dozen drawings of trouser suits, miniskirts and culottes. She must have been too shy to show anyone. Gloria feels a pang of guilt, wishing she'd been a little kinder to the girl.

She takes Alice's drawings into her alcove and looks through them. It's impossible to believe that young women wouldn't love these clothes. She looks at their newspaper ad again, wondering if it wasn't quite right. The illustration shows a young woman in a short floral shift, her long hair swinging as she leaps in the air. Gloria and Pixie had worked the copy out together: *Mods & Dolly Birds jump in! Fab frocks only £3.10s including postage. Send size, cheque/postal note and return address to Mod Frock Offer, Private Bag, Surry Hills.*

They had been so excited, despite all the doubters, and couldn't have imagined it would be such a dismal failure. The whole thing is so humiliating, Gloria is embarrassed to even show her face upstairs. Her eyes fill with tears. She gets out Hazel's hanky and dabs them gently. Gerry Butterby passes by whistling 'You Are My Sunshine' but even his smile fails to cheer her up. If she's fired, she'll never see him again.

The shrill of the phone brings her back to earth. As expected, she's summoned upstairs.

In all the years she's been with Empire, she has probably been in Old Karp's office only three or four times. None of these visits were happy experiences. The Karps are not the sort of bosses who invite you upstairs to let you know you're doing a good job, only when they are pissed off about something: usually slow production, wasted materials and too many needle accidents. When you make people work faster they waste material and have accidents, but try telling them that. Anyway, this meeting isn't going to be about any of those things. The Ginger Nuts will have been in his ear, plotting against her and making sure they're in the clear. Gloria has no chance against those two. They're like family to him. On top of that, she's overstepped her role and that's something the Karps come down hard on. Everyone has their place in the Empire.

She lights another cigarette and gives herself a moment. She looks around her little alcove and thinks about all the hours she's spent in her cosy nest. She dreads having to clean it all up. On the bright side, if she's fired on the spot, she probably won't have to.

She'll miss the girls so much. In the past there had been the catty, the lazy and the thieving ones but she'd weeded them out and this is the best team she's ever had. She stubs out her cigarette, checks her make-up and calls out to no one in particular that she'll be upstairs if she's needed.

*

As Gloria comes out of the top-floor lift, Pixie is leaving her grandfather's office. She gives an embarrassed shrug and quickly detours
to take the stairs.

Mrs Stern graces Gloria with a sympathetic smile. 'Mrs Nuttell
to see you, Mr Karp,' she announces through the intercom.

To Gloria's annoyance, the Ginger Nuts are in Old Karp's
office with their evening gown designs and satin and tulle samples
covering his desk. She groans inwardly at the sight of the sample
cards of glass beading – are they making a point of selecting only
the most difficult fabrics to work with?

There are only two visitor's chairs, so Gloria has to stand. At
least she can make a quick getaway. Old Karp looks grim, nothing
new there. The lack of chairs clearly throws him off and he presses
the intercom. 'Bring an extra chair in please, Mrs Stern.'

A moment later, the door opens and Mrs Stern lugs in an extra
chair and places it between the sisters. Not in the mood for musical
chairs, Gloria is starting to wish that he'd just fire her and get it
over with.

'Now, if we're all settled,' he says, when she sits down, 'I'm trying
to work out how, in the few weeks I've been away recuperating,
everything here has gone to pieces. I'm told that you had a hand in
this, Mrs Nuttell.'

Gloria glances left and right at the sisters. She wonders where
Frankie is – shouldn't he be held to account? 'I'm not entirely
responsible,' she ventures.

'Let's hear your version, then,' says Old Karp.

Gloria struggles to remember how it all unfolded. There
were lots of ideas thrown around. They'd been so caught up in
the moment, it's hard to remember who had what idea. Anyway,
she can't dob Pixie in. 'I thought . . . well . . . a few of us thought,

that if we came up with something quickly, something cheap and easy, some groovy designs . . .'

His expression tells her this is not going down well and already she regrets the word 'groovy'. He folds his arms over his chest and leans back in his chair. 'So you took it upon yourself to undermine the firm's reputation, built over decades.'

'We tried to tell them it wouldn't work,' says Miss Ivy, in her prissy way.

Miss Joan nods. 'The whole thing went against the grain for us.'

'We were trying to save the day,' says Gloria. 'Save jobs and—'

'But instead you have embarrassed the firm in front of our most important clients. Mr Cashell himself called me to say that we're the joke of the industry. You wasted company resources and misused your position to direct staff to make garments that weren't authorised and even involved yourself in the advertising side of things, I understand.'

Gloria casts around for a defence but all she really cares about is not bursting out crying in front of the Ginger Nuts. 'We didn't have a range. I didn't want to lose my girls.'

'But we have nothing to show for all that outlay, not a single order,' he says.

'It's only been a few days; it might take a bit longer. Let's wait and see.'

'The ship has sailed, Mrs Nuttell. Fortunately Miss Ivy and Miss Joan have something on the table we can start on straightaway. Four more of your staff will go.'

'I'll go too,' says Gloria impulsively.

Old Karp nods. 'I think it's probably for the best.'

Leaving his office, Gloria takes the stairs to avoid the risk of sharing the lift with the evil sisters. Halfway down, she sits on a step and lights a cigarette. That went even worse than expected. There had been a slight chance she could talk her way out of it but nothing brilliant came to her in the moment. There will be another job for her somewhere, but Tony will hit the roof. She should have made the break from him while she had a job. Now it's too late. She doesn't know how to tell the girls that four more will get pink slips tomorrow. Her eyes sting at the thought of it.

65

BOB COMES HOME

Enjoying a quiet evening at home while Irene's at the pub, Hazel sits down with a glass of mulberry wine and looks over the Taj Mahal. Thanks to the endeavours of Maude and Natalia (and no thanks to Irene), every piece is finally in place and the temple to love is complete. It occurs to her now that the building is actually a mausoleum, and she wonders if that's significant. Her thoughts are interrupted by a knock at the door. She goes to the window and twitches the curtain to see a familiar figure standing outside. Her heart does a flip as she walks into the hall and opens the door.

'Hello, Bob,' she says quietly.

'May I come in?' he asks. 'Just for a moment?'

Hazel nods. She gestures towards the kitchen, catching a whiff of his familiar aftershave as he walks past her. In the kitchen, they stand apart in awkward silence.

'Would you like a drink, or tea?' asks Hazel.

'Hazel, I don't know what to say to you,' he says, his voice thick with emotion.

'Bob, I find that hard to believe. You've had plenty of time to think about it. You must have known you'd get caught out at some point.'

'Hazel, I love you. I want to come back.'

Hazel waits for the tingling to set in but either Bob is telling the truth or he's fooling her again. She can't trust her ears where he is concerned. 'Let's sit down,' she suggests.

They sit down opposite one another at the table and Bob continues, 'I miss you so much, my dear. I can't go on without you.' His breath catches in a sob. 'I think I'm having a nervous breakdown.'

'Bob, I have one question – why? When we met you were already married and yet, right from that first moment, you pretended otherwise. You courted me like a single man and covered your tracks like a criminal.'

He flinches at this last comment but argues, 'I was bewitched from the first.'

'Bob, don't be ridiculous, you're making it sound as if I cast a spell on you! You were old enough to know better and nothing can excuse your dishonesty. You're fortunate to have a large family, children, grandchildren—'

'I wanted someone to care just for me. Like two peas in a pod. That's how we were.'

'Can you see how selfish that is, Bob? How dishonest and childish?'

'I'm divorcing my wife. You're the one I want to spend the rest of my days with, Hazel. I bought this house for us. I bought it in your name.' He leans towards her earnestly. 'I wanted you to be secure after I'm gone. That must prove that I was always thinking of you.'

'It was a nice thought, Bob, and I appreciate it, but you did that in a devious way as well. Why didn't you discuss it with me? Why did you pretend to pay rent? I think it was because you didn't want me to know, so you could take the property back if you needed to. You were relying on the fact that I couldn't read the paperwork. Or perhaps you didn't want your name on the deed because your family would eventually find out. You always hedged your bets. So it changes nothing. You betrayed my trust; you took advantage of my good nature.'

'We were happy, Hazel. We were happy together and we can be again.'

Hazel shakes her head firmly. 'No. That time has passed and we can never go back. Now I think you better go.'

It's only on the very rare occasion that Hazel has seen Bob angry but now he seems to swell up, his face pink and puffy. 'You'll have to transfer the property back to me, in that case. You obviously can't throw me out and keep a house I paid for.'

Hazel looks him in the eye. 'I found the paperwork from the lawyers in your briefcase. Irene read the documents for me, so I already knew it was in my name. I have that deed in my possession and that's where it will remain. It will be something nice to remember you by. Thank you, Bob.'

Bob gets to his feet, his face shining with perspiration. 'That's dishonest, Hazel. I bought this place in good faith for the two of us.'

It occurs to Hazel that she needs to ask direct questions. 'Bob, has your wife thrown you out?'

'No, of course not,' he says, taken by surprise. 'She's loyal to me.'

Hazel's ears begin to tingle. 'Are you living at the club now?'

'I don't know why you'd think that,' says Bob, unconvincingly.

Hazel's ears tell the truth. 'And that's why you want my house now? So you can live here?'

Bob has the good grace to flush. 'I couldn't live here without you.'

'Bob, it takes a lot to get me angry but, right now, I feel like a volcano about to erupt. Everything you've done, every lie you've told, is smouldering inside me and I'm ready to blow sky-high. I loved you with all my heart. I trusted you. Every Friday, I had your library books and ironed handkerchief at your bedside, your chops under the grill. Every Sunday, I polished your shoes. I have shown my love every single day of our time together. You took advantage of me, and of your wife. So, to now attempt to take my home away for your own benefit – it's absolutely despicable!' Hazel takes a deep breath. She gets up, walks down the hall and opens the front door.

By the time Bob arrives at the door, Hazel has a gift for him. He accepts it in silence and walks out without a word, shoulders slumped. With mixed emotions, Hazel watches him walk down the street. He passes Irene coming the other way. She stops to stare but he plods on without speaking.

'That was bloody Bob, wasn't it?' asks Irene, coming up the path. 'He's got that photograph from the front room.'

'It was his,' says Hazel, stepping back to let her inside.

'Who was that picture of anyway?'

'I have no idea,' says Hazel. 'No idea at all.'

She walks into the front room, a great weight lifting off her shoulders. She gets out the box for the Taj Mahal and scoops the jigsaw into it. As she puts the lid on, she wonders if she might tackle the Hanging Gardens of Babylon next. Maude would enjoy that too.

66

HAZEL MEETS A STRANGER

Coming out of the lift into the foyer after morning tea, Hazel is approached by a woman who asks the way to the Accounts department. She has the weathered look of a country woman, ill at ease in her best suit and hat, and Hazel wonders what business she could have with Accounts.

'If you wait a moment, I'll pop my trolley in the kitchen and take you upstairs.'

'Thank you,' says the woman. 'That's very kind.'

Hazel wheels her trolley along to the kitchen and the woman follows, as if she's worried about being left behind. 'You're the tea lady. You must have known my husband.'

'Your husband?' asks Hazel, quickly transferring the dirty crockery into the sink.

'Sam McCracken. He worked here, in Accounts.'

Hazel turns to stare at the woman. 'You're Mrs McCracken? I'm very sorry about his passing. I didn't know your husband well but, of course, I saw him every day.' She pauses. 'I wonder, would you like a cup of tea before we go upstairs?'

'I'd love one – it's been a long trip. We're on a farm out west. It's four hours on the train . . . and all the people. So many people, I'm not used to it at all.'

Hazel beckons her to the table. 'Come in and sit down, dear. Make yourself comfy.'

Mrs McCracken sits down heavily and pulls her hat off with a sigh of relief.

Hazel closes the door. 'We won't be disturbed in here. So Mr McCracken was a farmer, you say, not a bookkeeper?'

'He did night school to learn double-entry bookkeeping many years ago but it wasn't his profession. He took this job because he thought we needed the money. That's what he said. It didn't really make any sense to me.'

Hazel passes her a cup of tea and a selection of biscuits.

'Excuse me,' says Mrs McCracken, setting on them ravenously. 'I'm starving. Anyway, he took this job and we had a bit of extra income. He telephoned once a fortnight, just a quick call. That was fine. I didn't mind him being away. Our sons work on the farm too so I'm not on my ownsome. When he didn't call, I didn't think that much of it. But then I had to call the place where he boarded to ask him something and the lady there said he died – two weeks earlier! She said someone killed him. Nobody told us. We didn't have a funeral or anything. I telephoned the police and they said they didn't know who did it. I was furious that we hadn't been notified. They said they couldn't find the next of kin. We didn't believe it. Look, between you and me, Mrs—'

'Bates, Hazel Bates.'

'Between you and me, Mrs Bates, he wasn't an easy man but he was a decent sort. Why would someone kill him? It doesn't make any sense. Firstly, he didn't know anyone here. He wasn't a man who made friends and went down the pub. He didn't really drink because it kept him awake and he had problems with insomnia his whole life. But he was a hard worker.'

Hazel gets out some more biscuits and adds them to the plate. 'It must have been difficult for him being so far from home. Tell me, dear, how did he come to get this job?'

'He was just offered it. He didn't really want it but, as I say, we needed the money.'

'But how did he come to be offered it?' asks Hazel, increasingly perplexed.

'What happened was we needed a loan to buy a new harvester – we're in the wheat business. The one we had was very old and these days there are much more efficient ones that do a better job – but it's a lot of money. It's like buying a house, it's a big investment. So we tried our local bank but the manager there doesn't cut farmers an inch of slack. So Sam decided to come to Sydney and see someone at the main branch. I don't know what happened after that. He was pretty tight-lipped about it. All I can say is that we got our loan and, next thing, he says he's got this job to help pay back the loan.'

'So you got the loan from the bank?' asks Hazel.

'No, it came from a private company. They gave him the cash.'

'Cash? Is that usual? Wouldn't it normally be a bank cheque?'

Mrs McCracken looks taken aback for a moment. 'I'm not sure. Sam said they give you the cash so you can get a discount on the equipment. But here's the silly thing – he didn't need the job, really. Now that we have the new harvester, our boys harvest all over the area and we are not so dependent on our own crop. It would have been more helpful if he had come home and helped with that instead of sitting behind a desk here. To be honest, he didn't like working here but he wouldn't be talked out of it. You know how men are, Mrs Bates.'

'I do indeed,' says Hazel, with a sympathetic smile. 'They can be very stubborn.'

'So now I've come to see what I can find out. The police don't seem to know anything. They don't even have a suspect. It's not right.'

'So – the company that gave you the loan?'

Mrs McCracken opens her handbag and gets out some papers. 'I brought the paperwork with me, just in case. Let me see.' She flicks through the documents. 'All right, Harbin Holdings Pty Ltd is the name of the company. Sam said they were a brokerage. I don't really know what that means but I suppose they get private loans for people like us that the bank won't touch.'

'At a higher interest rate?' asks Hazel.

'You'd expect that.' She pauses and looks at Hazel. 'Mrs Bates, you're the first person to take a decent interest in what happened to my husband. I tried to tell the police all this about the harvester and the job but . . . well . . . I suppose it doesn't go anywhere, really. They might have nothing to do with each other. Who can I speak to, Mrs Bates? Who can help me?'

Hazel thinks about this for a moment. 'They don't know anything in Accounts, so I don't think they will be any help to you. My advice is to walk down to the Surry Hills Police Station, it's only ten minutes. Ask to speak to Detective Dibble. If he's out, then wait or go back later. Tell him everything you told me and get him to write up a report. Tell him Hazel Bates sent you.'

Mrs McCracken makes a note, thanking her. She puts on her hat and straightens herself up. 'I'm so glad I bumped into you, Mrs Bates,' she says, as they walk into the front foyer together.

'I'm here every day. If you need help while you're in town, just pop by. Now make sure you tell Detective Dibble everything you told me – no detail is too small. Good luck, Mrs McCracken.'

67

BETTY'S CONTACTS PAY OFF

'Evening, Mrs T, Mrs B, Mrs D . . . no Mrs P tonight?' calls Shirley from behind the bar as Hazel, Betty and Irene settle at their table.

'Mrs Perlman is otherwise indisposed,' calls Betty, quite pleased with this response, even if it's a little white lie. In fact, Merl was not invited this evening. Effie had called Betty earlier suggesting they meet at the Hollywood and go down to Mrs Li's together.

While they wait for Effie, Betty explains Mrs Li's role to Irene and that she and Hazel had an earlier meeting with her. Far from being grateful she's now being included, Irene immediately starts bellyaching about being left out in the first place.

'She has to be very careful,' Betty says, regretting bringing it up.

'She was just being cautious, Irene,' explains Hazel in her special soothing voice. 'Betty and I were already acquainted with Mrs Li through the Tea Ladies Guild.'

'Oh that bunch,' grumbles Irene. 'Not much of a recom . . . recom . . .'

'Recommendation?' suggests Betty. 'Well, they wouldn't allow her to join, if that helps.'

'Oh yeah?' says Irene, brightening up. 'Why's that?'

Hazel obviously doesn't want to go into it. She simply says they were 'stuck in their ways' (putting it kindly) and leaves it at that.

When Effie joins them, Betty takes the opportunity to comment, 'We've got all the emergency services involved now – police, fire and tea.' Her little joke goes down well, even with Irene, who normally makes a point of not laughing at Betty's jokes. The only things Irene always finds amusing are her own jokes and other people's misfortune.

The four of them walk to Mrs Li's house at the appointed time and enter through the shadowy back lane. As before, the house is lit up and pleasant smells waft from the kitchen. Betty's tummy rumbles, despite having already had her dinner.

Hazel introduces Irene and Mrs Li. The two of them eye each other suspiciously. Everyone sits down around the kitchen table and, while they get settled, Mrs Li's mother serves them small cups of jasmine tea.

Mrs Li turns to Hazel. 'So, the Russian girl you were looking for, I saw in the papers she was found.' She listens, nodding silently, while Hazel recounts the story of finding Natalia and returning her safely to the circus, adding Mr Ivanov's account of the circumstances.

'I overheard Pierce and his offsider discussing this out the back yesterday,' says Mrs Li. 'He said something about "the Russian bird" getting away and the Tsar was "spewing". Pierce said that was one less thing on their plate.'

'What do you think that meant?' asks Hazel. 'That they were directly involved?'

Mrs Li considers this for a moment. 'Probably not directly, but Pierce obviously knew the Tsar was involved and there'd be a risk it could come out and make things awkward. He's already been demoted from the Criminal Investigations Branch. He'll be trying to get back in there, so needs to watch himself.'

'So when I reported seeing Natalia in the bond store, he buried that report?' says Hazel.

Mrs Li nods. 'His offsider made a joke about "no refunds" and Pierce said, "Yeah, too late, deal's done." So there must have been some money in it for them. I have to be careful not to seem as if I'm eavesdropping, so I had to leave at that point.'

'I think we can say that the case of Natalia Ivanov is resolved and there's not much more we can do,' says Hazel.

'Someone should be punished for it,' says Betty, stung by the injustice of the situation.

'If the family want to take it further that's for Interpol or ASIO to deal with but probably nothing will happen,' says Mrs Li. 'To be honest, it's hard to see how any of these people will be caught or convicted. The Tsar is like an octopus, his tentacles spread out everywhere. He has all sorts of people on the payroll.'

'I have some new information on the McCracken murder,' says Hazel. 'I met his wife yesterday and discovered they were tangled up with Borisyuk through his company Harbin Holdings, which also owned the bond store. What's puzzling is that McCracken owed them money, so it doesn't make any sense that Borisyuk would have him murdered.'

Effie speaks up. 'Pierce has been down to the fire station a couple of times talking to the chief about the fire, so who knows if that will go anywhere.'

'Do you think the chief could be involved with Borisyuk as well?' asks Hazel.

'Hard to say but it's possible. He doesn't mind a flutter,'

says Effie. 'Anyway, it's one thing proving arson but it's very difficult to find the arsonist.'

Mrs Li nods grimly. 'So that will probably quietly go away too. I managed to look at the Coroner's report. The victim was shot in the neck at close range with a .22 calibre pistol. No signs of asphyxiation, so he was dead before the fire got going.'

Irene nods. 'Small pistol. Sort of thing yer can hide in a handbag.'

'I wonder how the killer got so close to the victim,' says Mrs Li.

'So let's say the firebug gets in the building,' says Irene. 'Got a brick and a bottle of petrol in his hand. All of a sudden he runs into McCracken. He's got a bloody problem.'

Mrs Li nods. 'But if this McCracken was there in the night, he would have had the lights on, surely?'

'The door to his office was open, so perhaps he heard something and came out to investigate?' suggests Hazel. 'Or he came in after the intruder and surprised him.'

Effie asks, 'But how did the murderer get close enough to pop him in the neck?'

Mrs Li turns to Hazel. 'Was there a lot of blood when you found him?'

'Not that I could see. The power was out by then. He was wearing a coat and lying on his side. I noticed an injury on his forehead,' says Hazel.

'The bloke's carrying a pistol, he knows what he's doing,' says Irene.

Betty feels a little thrill as she notes down: *Professional assassin.* 'But how can we link him back to Borisyuk?' she asks.

'I'll tell yers something about this Tsar fellow, Borisyuk,' says Irene. 'Big-time crooks like him have one big problem. Dirty money.

He feeds it into tills at the clubs – that's fine – but this bloke's got mountains of the stuff. So let's say he buys a building and it's sort of old so he's not allowed to knock the thing down—'

'Like the bond store?' suggests Betty, helpfully.

'I'm sure you can't buy property like that with cash,' says Mrs Li.

Irene gives her a withering look. 'Just hold yer horses, I'm getting to that. He gets a big loan, buys the thing, but what he wants is the thing gone—'

'It's a perfect spot for one of these big office blocks they're building now,' says Hazel.

'Can I finish?' asks Irene crossly. 'Now he's got insurance money and can use his pile of dirty money to pay the builders with cash, buy off union bosses, give council bribes, you name it. He's got himself a big washing machine.'

'You are clever, Irene,' Betty tells her, and means it. 'I would never have thought of that.'

'Got a bit of experience in this area,' says Irene, giving Mrs Li a pointed look.

'So the connection between Borisyuk's scheme and Mr McCracken's murder is possibly just that he was in the way?' says Hazel. 'There's got to be more to it because Frankie Karp is definitely involved. He frequents the Mermaid Club and was seen with Natalia.'

'The Tsar's business is run by managers and thugs and people on contract,' says Mrs Li. 'The thugs are obvious but the managers can be anyone behind the scenes, they're hard to spot – could Frankie be one of them? Or is he running an operation himself?'

Hazel laughs at the idea. 'Frankie? No, he might be caught up in something but he's no organisational mastermind.'

A thoughtful silence settles on the room. It seems a perfect moment for Betty to bring everyone up to date with her notes (to demonstrate her organisational expertise) but then Mrs Li's mother enters the kitchen and leans over the simmering pots on the stove, and Betty's thoughts turn to soup.

68

CONFUSING CLUES

'Good morning, Mrs Bates!' calls Mr Kovac, as he gets out of his van. 'How did you get on with Mrs Agapov? Was she able to assist? There has been a lot in the news about Russians lately, I notice.'

'Oh yes, thank you—' Hazel is interrupted by someone calling her name and turns to see Mr Butterby walking up the lane from the loading dock.

'Morning, Mrs Bates. I need the key for the old stock room. I understand it's in your possession?'

'It's on the hook just inside the kitchen door,' says Hazel.

When Mr Butterby has gone, Mr Kovac asks, 'Who was that gentleman?'

'That's our storeman, Mr Butterby. He runs the warehouse and dispatch; he's relatively new.'

'Mrs Bates, I must apologise. I have given you some incorrect information. That is the man I collected the cheque from upstairs. I've never met him before but, as he was coming out of the office, I made the assumption it was the bookkeeper, Mr McCracken.'

'So he gave you the cheque – are you sure?'

'Yes. He went back in and got the cheque for me. Friendly gentleman, very pleasant.'

'But . . . the man you saw at the Mermaid Club with Frankie Karp?' asks Hazel.

Mr Kovac ponders this question. 'The light is poor in that place, I can't be sure about that now.'

'And talking in the park?' asks Hazel.

'It was at a distance, so I can't be certain. I'm very sorry if I've caused confusion.'

Hazel puzzles over this new information as she assembles the trolley for morning tea, wondering if it changes anything. The fact that Mr Butterby handed Mr Kovac a cheque is not important – he was being helpful. But now it appears that Mr McCracken and Frankie possibly didn't have a social connection. It seems that Mr Kovac is not a very reliable source of information.

69

GLORIA'S WORLD TURNS UPSIDE DOWN

On her last day of work, the mess in Gloria's nest seems overwhelming – symbolising her whole life right now. She pulls out the wastepaper basket and takes down bits of fabric and magazine clippings that have been up on the wall for years. She rolls up her 'Desiderata' poster, puts her signed photo of the Seekers in an envelope, and packs them both in a box.

'Ah, Gloria, there you are!' calls Gerry Butterby.

Gloria feels tears spring in her eyes. She turns to him, wanting nothing more than to feel his strong arms around her and to rest her head on his broad shoulder.

'I've been looking everywhere for you,' he says.

'Me too,' says Gloria, wondering what on earth she means by that. 'Why?'

He beckons her to come with him. Intrigued, she follows him out of the factory and into the old stock room. 'What should I do with these?' He points to a couple of large hessian sacks full of scraps.

'Take them to the tip, as usual,' she says, disappointed.

He looks at her with a bemused smile. 'Not scraps, mail. The post office called to say there was a new private bag address. We're supposed to collect it ourselves but no one told me about it. I wasn't sure who was handling it; the girls upstairs said to ask you.'

Gloria opens a sack and takes out an envelope addressed to Mod Frock Offer. Inside is a neatly written letter ordering three frocks in a size 12 with a postal note enclosed. She opens another and another. She can't believe it – two sacks of mail, hundreds of orders!

'There's two more sacks in the van,' says Gerry Butterby.

It takes a moment to dawn on Gloria exactly what this means and, when it does, she gives a squeal of excitement, throws her arms around his neck and plants a smacking kiss on his cheek. The gentle pressure of his hands on her hips and his warm breath on her neck sends her wobbly at the knees. He steps away first but holds her gaze. Gloria smiles, quietly marvelling at the difference a few minutes can make.

Gloria's not sure whose idea it was to tip the two sacks onto the big table in the stock room – certainly not Gerry Butterby's; he does not like mess. So it was either hers or Pixie's. They'd been jumping around like kids on candy floss, then Pixie ran upstairs with the news. Now Old Karp, the Ginger Nuts, Mrs Stern, Doug Fysh, Hazel and Mr Levy all stand looking at the great pile of letters covering the table.

Miss Ivy is silent but Miss Joan, in that snooty tone of hers, says, 'One swallow doesn't make a spring.'

Mr Levy laughs. 'We're looking at more than one swallow here, ladies!'

Pixie takes a letter off the pile and opens it. 'Most orders are for more than one garment and there's two more sacks. We could have a thousand orders already.'

'Let's get these cheques in the bank,' says Mr Levy, rubbing his hands together gleefully.

'Haw haw haw, looks like it's hit the spot,' says Doug. 'We're top of the pops!'

'And it's just the start,' says Pixie, her face glowing with excitement.

Gloria can't help but notice that Old Karp has not looked at her once. He stands staring at the pile of mail as if he doesn't know what it means. After a few minutes of silence, he gives Pixie a nod and turns to Gloria. 'Mrs Nuttell, can we get the girls we laid off back to work on Monday, please?' He gives her a smile – faint – but nevertheless a smile. 'And if you and Pixie can see me at the end of the day, we need to work out a system to process these and increase production.'

'Yes, Mr Karp. I'd be happy to,' says Gloria, as she and Pixie grin at each other across the mountain of mail.

70

BETTY STUMBLES ON A VITAL CLUE

'One minute Empire is the laughing-stock of the entire rag trade, next thing you're rolling in orders,' says Merl, joining Betty, Hazel and Irene in the laneway.

'I don't think that's fair,' says Betty, fed up to the back teeth with Merl's barbed comments and Merl generally. 'They weren't a laughing-stock. Empire took a risk and it's paying off. Good on them!'

'I agree,' says Hazel. 'It was a risk but I'm sure the department stores will come back when they realise there's a demand for these little dresses.'

'Well, I wouldn't be seen dead in something like that,' says Merl.

'Thank God for that,' says Irene, chortling wheezily.

'Anyway, we've got important business to discuss,' says Betty, and gets out her notebook.

'I see the Russian girl is back where she belongs *without* our help,' says Merl. 'I expect DS Pierce will be getting the credit. They'll probably transfer him back into the CIB with this feather in his cap.'

'Couple more feathers and he can fly back,' says Irene, with a straight face.

Betty opens her mouth to argue with Merl but thinks better of it. 'We still plan to work out who murdered Mr McCracken,' she says.

'The police will handle it,' says Merl. 'That's their job. We're tea ladies, not detectives.'

'We didn't set out to be detectives. It just happens that we're good at it,' says Hazel.

'And now I'm going to read my latest list.' Betty flips her notebook open and reads aloud: 'McCracken, Flood Street . . . I can probably cross that out now . . . two tins peaches . . . oh, that was for the sponge, forget that . . .' Realising that many items are not for Merl's ears, she begins to censor the list. 'Um . . . not sure why I wrote that . . . Maria . . .' She pauses to think. 'I'm wondering why I wrote that . . . who is Maria? Never mind . . . Octopus . . . well, that's the Tsar . . . I was quite tickled by that comparison.'

'There are so many confusing things on that list,' says Merl.

'Is that it?' asks Irene. 'We haven't got all bloody day. If that's out of the way, there's news from my place. Do yer recall the chubby secretary getting off with the boss?'

'How could we forget?' says Betty. 'And I don't know why you have to keep bringing up her figure.'

'She's about to lose it – joined the puddin' club, by the looks. Couldn't face her cuppa this morning; just wanted a dry bikkie to nibble on.'

Hazel sighs. 'We're always the first to realise, aren't we? Do you think she knows?'

'I reckon,' says Irene. 'Looked a bit down in the mouth.'

'Poor thing,' says Betty. 'I wonder what she'll do. He'll probably fire her now.'

'Brought it on herself,' says Merl. 'No sympathy whatsoever.'

'Oh, Merl, how can you be so hard-hearted!' cries Betty. 'Remember the goo-goo eyes? She's madly in love with him. She's putty in his hands.'

'She's not a bad girl,' says Irene. 'Not a nympho or nothing.'

'She may be a nice girl but next thing she'll be drinking a bottle of gin and jumping off the kitchen table to get rid of it,' argues Merl. 'Or facing a life as an unwed mother.'

'The first part sounds all right,' notes Irene. 'Wouldn't fancy the jumping, though.'

Merl gets out her knitting. 'I don't think there's any risk of you getting pregnant at this stage, Irene.'

'Let's not talk about her,' says Hazel. 'I don't think it's fair or right for us to be passing judgement on the girl, particularly when we don't even know her. She's in for a difficult time, so let's respect her privacy.'

'I agree,' says Betty stoutly.

Merl knits furiously. Finally, she weakens and gets a cake tin out of her shopping bag. She hands them each a slice in waxed paper. 'This is something new – Hummingbird cake.'

'What's all the white stuff?' asks Irene, curling her lip in disgust.

'Cream-cheese icing and coconut on the sides.' Merl holds the tin out to her. 'I can take it back if you don't want it.'

'Nah, I'll give it a go,' says Irene grudgingly. 'Not keen on cheese in a cake, though.'

'It's delicious,' says Hazel, and Betty agrees.

On her way back to work after lunch, Betty has a realisation. She turns back and hurries along the lane after Hazel.

'Hazel . . .' Betty puffs when she catches her. 'I know everyone thinks my notebook is a silly bit of nonsense. I just wanted to let you know I'm not going gaga. I just remembered why I wrote "Maria". Violet told me that one night she heard that man, who came to the house on Flood Street, whistling the song "Maria" from *West Side Story*. I know that's not important now, but I wanted to make the point that I don't just write nonsense . . .'

71

HAZEL IN DIRE STRAITS

Following the conversation with Betty, Hazel walks into the kitchen with her mind working furiously. Many men whistle. They whistle on building sites, in shops and offices. They whistle while they work and don't even realise they're doing it. Almost everyone has seen the film *West Side Story* so the choice of the song 'Maria' is not unusual. There are probably countless men across the country whistling it right now. And yet . . .

She manages the afternoon tea shift with her usual friendly efficiency but her mind is elsewhere. She bides her time until the factory knocks off for the day. Mr Butterby keeps the same hours as the factory, leaving at three. He takes the firm's van home so, with a quick check, Hazel can be quite sure he's gone.

The layout in the warehouse has changed in the last few days. Previously, frocks were pressed and hung on wheeled racks, then delivered to the stores. Now there is a long table set up to process the mail orders. The Mod Frocks are folded in colourful piles ready to be wrapped in brown paper and tied with string for the post. Hazel's destination is the workshop where Mr Butterby keeps tools for machine repairs, next to the small office where he does his paperwork. She has no idea what she's looking for. She picks up several tools and puts them down again, opens a cupboard and closes it. Everything in Mr Butterby's domain is orderly. Nothing out of place.

She wanders into the office. There's a desk against one wall, and above it is a noticeboard with orders and dockets clipped neatly to it. She opens the drawers of the desk. Each contains neat stacks of docket books and order pads. She reaches into the back of the drawers but finds nothing, not even a stray paperclip.

The ground floor is normally the busiest and noisiest part of the building, but with everyone gone home for the day, it is oppressively quiet. The only sounds are distant traffic and the ticking of the clock on Mr Butterby's desk. Then she notices another sound: a door closing, footsteps coming in her direction. The last thing she wants is to be caught snooping. She considers the two options: either brazen it out or hide, and decides on the latter.

Getting on her knees, she crawls under the desk. It has solid sides, so, sitting with her back against the wall and her feet tucked up, she's well hidden. The person goes into the workshop and rattles around. Minutes later, the footsteps recede into the distance.

Hazel waits a few moments to be sure. She shifts a little to avoid something hard sticking into her back. Rearranging herself to see what it is, she realises it's a small knob. It's too dark to see any detail but, running her fingers around the area, she finds the edge of a cupboard door concealed in the wall. She pulls at the knob but it doesn't budge. Below it, she can feel a lock inset.

She crawls out from under the desk and takes a good look at the wall. In the light from the only window it's difficult to be sure but it seems to Hazel that a false wall has been added at a later time to create a hidden void. If you weren't looking for it, you would never know it was there.

She takes another look through the desk for the key. It may be that Mr Butterby keeps it on him but the cupboard itself is so well hidden, he probably doesn't need to be too careful. She works meticulously through the drawers, and checks behind the account books on the shelves. Then she has an idea. She crawls back under the desk and runs her hand behind the drawers, and there it is, hanging from a nail.

Wishing she had a torch, she puts the key in the lock and opens the door. It's so dark inside, it's impossible to tell how big the space is or see its contents. Mr Butterby is not a smoker, so he won't have a cigarette lighter or matches – but Gloria will.

She slips out through the warehouse into the factory, and quickly finds a lighter on Gloria's desk. Back under Mr Butterby's desk, she reaches through the cupboard door and flicks the lighter on. The flame illuminates a cupboard containing half-a-dozen of the boxes the industrial-size cotton reels come in. She opens one and looks inside to find a black balaclava and two sets of hand-cuffs. If that wasn't enough, the next box takes her breath away. It contains four handguns, two of them small pistols. Other boxes are packed with different types of ammunition; one of them contains boxes of .22 calibre bullets. Lastly, on the floor of the cupboard is a half-gallon can of petrol and a metal funnel.

She quickly neatens up the boxes, her hands trembling now. She knows that Mr Butterby, with his eye for order, will notice even the slightest variation. She locks the cupboard and returns the key to its hiding place. Leaving the office, she hurries through the ware-house, stopping to return Gloria's cigarette lighter on the way.

'Hello, Mrs Bates. To what do we owe the pleasure?'

'Oh, Mr Butterby! I was just . . . ah . . . looking around to see if there were any cups and saucers left behind. People forget to return them to the trolley sometimes.'

'You won't find any stray crockery in my area,' he says. 'I'm sure you know that.'

'It pays to look everywhere. Mr Karp gets very annoyed when we have to buy new crockery.'

'Does he now?' he says, humouring her. 'We can't have that.'

'No, we can't . . . well, I must be getting home.'

'Have a good evening, Mrs Bates.'

Hazel walks back to the kitchen and closes the door behind her. Who is Mr Butterby? What does he know about her? She desperately wants to leave the building immediately but there's no one on this floor right now and if he's waiting for her . . . She pushes down her fear and tries to think clearly. She picks up the phone and calls the Surry Hills Police Station. The switchboard operator answers the call.

'I need to speak to Detective Dibble urgently.'

'PC Dibble is not at his desk. Can I take a message?'

'This is Mrs Bates, Hazel Bates,' says Hazel. 'Ask him to come—'

Hazel feels a heavy hand on her shoulder. The receiver is lifted out of her hand.

'Cancel that message,' Mr Butterby tells the operator. 'My mother's senile. Sorry you were bothered.' He hangs the phone up and pushes the door closed behind him. He points a pistol straight at her head. 'What are we going to do with you, Mrs Bates? You're out of your depth and now you're a problem. Who do you work for?'

'I work here, Mr Butterby. I'm just an ordinary tea lady.'

'I find that hard to believe. In any case, I'm sorry to say that your tea-lady days are over, which is a shame because you do make a decent cup of tea. If only you had stuck to that and not stuck your nose into other people's business. Now you're a nuisance. So, what we're going to do is wait here until the building is completely empty.'

'And then?' asks Hazel, with growing dread.

Butterby ponders this question. 'I don't like killing old ladies; makes me feel a little icky, so I'm annoyed at being put in this position.'

Hazel notes that killing old ladies seems to be something he does regularly. 'But you did kill Mr McCracken . . .'

'Ah, the wheat farmer,' he sighs, lowering the pistol. 'Unfortunately he got in the way of a job I had to do. Caught me by surprise. Who would expect the bookkeeper to turn up for work at half-past four in the morning?'

'That job was firebombing the bond store, I presume?' asks Hazel.

'Correct. So you see what I'm saying, Mrs Bates? If everyone just stuck to their own job we would not be in this pickle now.'

Hazel murmurs her agreement, desperately searching for another angle. 'So you and Mr McCracken knew each other outside of work?'

'Why do you ask?' Butterby sounds genuinely curious.

'You both joined the firm around the same time, I suppose.'

'Life's not that simple, Mrs Bates. Let's just say, I knew why he was here but he knew nothing about me.' Mr Butterby continues, 'So, back to business. The least messy end, from my point of view, is this: Once everyone's gone for the day, you and I will take a trip up to the roof. All right, there'll be a few unpleasant seconds on the way down but, falling from a building this height, you'll die instantly. People will be shocked that you ended your life thus but who knows what goes on in a tea lady's tortured mind?'

They stare at each other for a moment. She wants to believe he's bluffing but her ears tell her that he's completely serious. This is how her life will end. She thinks about Norma and the boys; Betty and Irene; and even Merl. Maude next door and the Mulligan children. She thinks about Bob. She imagines how dreadful it will be for them to hear she has died such an awful death. So much worse to think she died by her own hand. They will feel responsible. In that moment she feels a steely resolve settle on her. 'Shall I make a cup of tea while we wait?'

'One last cuppa? Why not? You're being very decent about it. You can see I have no choice now. No sudden moves, all right?'

'Of course,' agrees Hazel. 'Yes, that's how the cookie crumbles, I suppose.' She switches the Zip back on and waits for it to boil.

Butterby sits down at the table and places the pistol on the table in front of him. 'In case you think of running for it, keep in mind, I can just shoot you here. Bodies are not difficult to get rid of – that's what delivery vans are for.'

Hazel gets down a tin of upstairs biscuits and puts it in front of him.

He takes the lid off and picks out a couple of Tim Tams. 'All the top-notch bikkies in here.'

'Upstairs biscuits,' she confirms. 'Mr Butterby, what I don't understand is, why? You are so well thought of here.'

'And will continue to be once you're taken care of,' he says, biting into his biscuit. 'There are a lot of factors at play that I would not expect a tea lady to understand but, to put it simply, working as a storeman here is nothing short of genius. What a lot of criminals can't seem to grasp is that they need a good cover. The cops could track me for days and not find out what I'm really up to. My gift is that I'm organised. Very, very organised.' He stops as if surprised by another thought. 'And very likeable,' he adds. 'Not many crooks are, you know.'

'But why? Why lead a life of crime? That's what I don't understand.'

'Mrs Bates, you think why, I think why not? The wages here are terrible. In the criminal world I'm what they call an "odd jobs man", basically a free agent who gets paid a handsome fee for contract work. For example, tossing a bottle of petrol into a filthy old bond store returns more than I earn in a year here. So, let's just say we have very different aspirations. How's that tea coming along?'

Hazel gets a teaspoon out of the drawer and quickly slips the spare kitchen key into her pinny pocket. She scalds the small enamel teapot, adds a couple of spoonfuls of tea and fills it with boiling water. She wonders if the teapot is heavy enough to knock him out but decides it might be difficult to get enough momentum and the handle can be slippery. It might just make him angry. She pours his tea and puts the sugar canister on the table. 'So, it was you keeping Natalia Ivanov captive?'

Mr Butterby looks at her for a moment, his expression unreadable, but she suspects he doesn't know about her involvement in Natalia's escape. 'I was glad someone got her out. She didn't do anything to deserve that.' He gestures for her to sit down opposite him and she does as she's told.

'While we're waiting, can you clear something up for me?' she asks.

'What's that?' He glances at his watch and selects another biscuit.

'I heard that Natalia Ivanov was being held for ransom, so it doesn't make any sense that you burnt the building down with her trapped inside.'

Mr Butterby sighs. 'They call it "organised crime" but frankly, it should be called disorganised crime. Left hand doesn't know what the right hand is doing. She was supposed to be locked up in a nearby property but through some miscommunication – nothing to do with me, I might add – the morons put her in the bond store.' He pauses and looks at Hazel. 'What gave me away? What made you search my office?'

Hazel realises that if she reveals that Betty's friend Violet heard him whistling, she could be putting her in danger. 'Just a tea lady's hunch,' she says with a shrug.

Mr Butterby nods. 'Look, Mrs Bates, you're probably the person I would least want to knock off in this building. If you were tempted by the dark side, it might be one thing but you're a goody-two-shoes who cannot be trusted.'

He holds out his cup for more tea and peers into the sugar canister with an expression of distaste. 'You know, something I've never told you is that I much prefer sugar cubes to this loose sugar, which is very unhygienic. People often help themselves and could have licked the teaspoon.' He gives a shudder. 'I don't know why I've never mentioned it until now.'

'I have sugar cubes,' says Hazel. She points towards the cupboard to his right. She gets a nod of approval and, heart thumping, crosses to the cupboard, acutely aware of every movement. On the lower shelf is exactly what she needs. She recalls Irene's instructions on knocking someone unconscious. Short, sharp, hard.

As Mr Butterby leans over to re-examine the biscuit selection, she lifts the rolling pin out of the cupboard. With a quick sideways glance at her target, she pivots on her feet and swings around fast, striking him hard across the back of the head. For a split second nothing happens. He sits frozen in shock, then his head flops forward and he lands face-first in the tin of upstairs biscuits.

Snatching the gun from the table, Hazel flies out the door and locks it from the other side. Heart pounding, legs shaking, she runs down the corridor and bursts out the main doors onto Lisbon Street to be greeted by the glorious sight of Detective Dibble pulling up at the curb. He opens the car door and half steps out. 'You called?'

72

GLORIA ARRIVES TO CONFUSION

Gloria usually enters the factory through the loading dock, contriving to cross paths with Gerry Butterby. He has been constantly on her mind since their embrace in the stock room. Thinking back, she's absolutely certain he wanted to kiss her. She saw it in his eyes. She can still feel the weight of his hands resting on her hips. She keeps imagining the two of them in a passionate embrace in that dark little office in the warehouse and reminds herself to buy some new underwear.

Strangely, the loading dock roller door is closed, with police tape across the entry and several uniformed police standing outside. Perhaps there's been a break-in – it wouldn't be the first time. Gloria walks along the lane and goes through the back door past the kitchen, expecting to run into Hazel, who will know what's going on.

The kitchen is empty, with an unbelievable mess of cups and saucers everywhere, and tea and sugar spilt on the bench. That explains it, the place must have been vandalised overnight. Continuing into the factory, she finds the big sliding doors between the factory and the warehouse, always left open, are now locked with two more police standing guard.

'What's going on?' she asks, approaching them.

'Nothing for you to worry about, miss. Just go about your business,' says one.

Gloria looks from one to the other. 'Where's Mr Butterby?'

'Just go on with your work, miss.' The officer nods in the direction of the girls gathered near the bundy clock, nervously watching the police.

'We need to get into the warehouse, we've got orders—' begins Gloria.

'We've got orders too, miss. This is a crime scene and no one goes in here until the police have finished.'

Gloria gives up and walks over to the girls. 'I don't know what's going on but let's get down to work, we've got a big day.' They all move to their worktables and prepare themselves, glancing curiously at the police from time to time. Gloria goes to her office and rings Edith Stern, but the phone rings out. She stares at the receiver in disbelief. This has never happened before. She tries Mr Levy – no answer.

Long before the morning tea buzzer goes, the strange little woman Gloria often sees having lunch in the laneway with Hazel comes barging through the door with the tea trolley, cups and saucers piled haphazardly on it. She wears slippers and has a cigarette hanging off her lip. Gloria wonders if the world is actually coming to an end.

'Where's Hazel?' Gloria asks, walking over. 'Who are you?'

'Mrs Turnbuckle. Yer seen me before, so don't gimme that.' She crashes the crockery around and slops tea into several cups. 'She's upstairs, talking to the cops. I'm doing her a bloody favour, if yer want to know.'

'Hazel's talking to the police? What's she done?'

'Look, do yer want yer tea or not?'

'Not really, it's not tea time for another hour. What the hell is going on?'

Mrs Turnbuckle taps the side of her nose and grins, her lips peeling back to reveal teeth like a horse. 'You'll find out soon enough. I'll leave this here. Hazel'll come and get it later. Gotta get to me own work now. One bloody thing after another.'

With that she walks off with a trail of smoke drifting behind her, and disappears out the door, leaving Gloria more confused than ever.

73

HAZEL SPILLS THE BEANS

Hazel doesn't recall ever sitting at the company board table before. In the past she has merely hovered around it, serving tea to more important people. Today, Edith Stern serves the tea and Hazel is the centre of attention. Detective Dibble and Detective Inspector MacNee, and a young policewoman taking notes, are present, as well as Mr Karp and Mr Levy. Detective Pierce is conspicuous by his absence but from what Hazel can gather, Detective Inspector MacNee is his superior officer.

MacNee, well-mannered with an air of quiet assurance and a comforting Scots accent, has quickly gained Hazel's trust. She tells the story from the very beginning, explaining how she had seen Natalia in the bond store and found McCracken dead, the discovery of Natalia held captive, being trapped by Mr Sapozhnik and questioned by Mr Borisyuk, the return of Natalia to the circus and the incidental clue that Betty provided about the identity of the kidnapper, which led her to discover Mr Butterby's secret. Everyone listens attentively, and no one asks her for another cup of tea or a different variety of biscuit.

'Mr Butterby is a whistler, particularly of show tunes,' Hazel explains. 'He's the most cheerful person in the building. That's what gave him away.'

Mr Karp shakes his head, pale with shock. 'He had us all fooled. He was a model employee. So organised.'

Mr Levy agrees. 'His paperwork was faultless and timely. He seemed a charming man.'

'We still have a number of loose ends to tie up,' says Detective Inspector MacNee. 'Clearly Mr Frankie Karp has some involvement and we need to interview him urgently.'

Mr Karp nods. 'Mrs Stern is trying to contact him.'

'I've come in on the tail end of this and I'm as shocked as anyone,' says Mr Levy. 'But I do have something else to add to this conspiracy.'

Detective Inspector MacNee gives him a nod. 'We'll be doing more extensive interviews later, but let's hear what you have.'

'I'm sorry to have to say this but Frankie Karp is a gambler.' Mr Levy glances apologetically at Mr Karp. 'He's got himself into debt and then probably more debt, as gamblers do. I think he was offered the opportunity to claw his way out by giving criminals access to this company. He allowed the installation of Mr McCracken, who I can see was not much of a bookkeeper.'

Detective Dibble turns to his senior officer. 'Sir, I have interviewed the victim's wife, Mrs McCracken, and we have the full background on this situation now.'

Mr Levy continues, 'Mr McCracken was drawing cheques to pay fraudulent suppliers, something I would have noticed, and it explains why I was removed from my position. I imagine Frankie was put under pressure to put this in place. I've known him since he was a young man – he's not a bad person, simply misguided.'

'The octopus had his tentacles right inside this building,' muses Hazel.

'I'm not sure what you're referring to,' says Mr Levy, 'but it's a common method of funnelling funds from a legitimate business into one where they can hide dirty money.'

Hazel turns to Detective Inspector MacNee. 'Mr Butterby described himself as an "odd-jobs man" and I gathered he didn't mean home repairs.'

Detective Inspector MacNee nods. 'A gun for hire with a bit of arson and kidnapping on the side.'

'I think that Frankie was sent to collect Natalia from the restaurant but he may not have realised that he was kidnapping her, thinking he was just giving her a lift. It's possible that Frankie himself was also a kidnap victim,' suggests Hazel. 'He disappeared for two weeks and reappeared after five thousand pounds was withdrawn from the company account.'

Mr Levy looks at her in surprise. 'I knew about the bank cheque, of course, but I wasn't aware the two events were connected.'

Detective Inspector MacNee smiles. 'Takes a tea lady to put it all together, it seems.'

Mr Karp puts his head in his hands. 'I'm speechless. All this has been going on right in the building and all I was worried about was next season's orders.' He straightens himself up. 'I assure you, Detective Inspector, I simply had no idea what was going on. None whatsoever. I'm sure when you interview my son, you'll discover he's a victim of circumstance and his own poor decisions. To be perfectly honest, he doesn't have a business mind. I sincerely doubt he's capable of being involved in any complex criminal activity.'

Detective Inspector MacNee nods. 'It's too early to say how this will play out and I'd prefer not to comment until we have interviewed young Mr Karp.' He turns his attention to Hazel. 'And, to put your mind at rest, Mrs Bates, we have enough physical evidence to convict Mr Butterby. We will likely not have enough to pursue our friend Borisyuk at this stage, unless the Ivanovs bring a kidnapping charge against him. In any case, we would not involve you because of the risks to your life. Your identity and testimony will remain with Detective Dibble and myself. Butterby is safely locked up and will be in high-security remand while the investigation takes place – so you have no fears for your safety.'

Detective Dibble grins. 'Mrs Bates seems to know how to look after herself.'

Hazel's almost sorry when the meeting is over and she finds herself back in the downstairs kitchen, marvelling that Irene could have created such a mess in such a short time. Detective Dibble appears in the doorway, giving her a start. 'Sorry, Mrs Bates, your nerves must be on end. I didn't mean to scare you.'

'That's all right, Detective. How can I help?'

He leans in the doorway, tapping one foot as if working out what to say. 'I came to apologise. I underestimated you and the other ladies and, quite frankly, we couldn't have solved this case without you. Butterby covered his tracks so well, he could have gone years without being caught. And he underestimated you too, Mrs Bates. He would never have spilled his guts to you if he thought there was any chance you'd overpower him and get away.'

'Never underestimate a tea lady – we're ready for any eventuality,' says Hazel.

'Lesson learnt. I won't let you down again, Mrs Bates. I promise.'

74

BETTY SHOUTS BUBBLY AT THE HOLLYWOOD

'Evening, Mrs B, T, P, D – the usual?' calls Shirley from the bar.

Betty glances at Hazel, Irene and Merl. 'What about something bubbly to celebrate?'

'Not too bubbly,' says Irene. 'We don't want you firing off on all cylinders.'

Betty ignores her and goes to the bar for a bottle of her favourite Seaview Sparkling Wine and four champagne glasses. She's almost bursting with pride that she, Betty Dewsnap, provided the vital clue that cracked the case. She'd like to shout the whole bar and tell absolutely everyone but Hazel has explained that they have to be careful and never forget the Tsar and his tentacles.

'I don't know what we're celebrating,' complains Merl when Betty brings the bubbly to the table. 'I heard that fellow Butterby has been arrested but DS Pierce, for some unknown reason, has been suspended from duties pending some investigation. There's a lot of jealousy in the police force; not everyone's aware of that. They resent his successes.'

'You may be right, Merl,' says Hazel, accepting a glass. 'If that's the case, I'm sure it will come out in an investigation.'

Irene gives a snort. 'I reckon.'

Betty raises her glass. 'What will we talk about now that all the mysteries of Zig Zag Lane have been solved?'

Irene gives her a sly look. 'There's always yer imaginary illnesses, we haven't heard about them for a bit.'

'At least we won't be subjected to your ridiculous lists,' says Merl.

'I have to correct you there, Merl dear. It was actually something on Betty's list that helped the police crack the case.' Hazel raises her glass. 'So, cheers to Betty!'

Merl raises her glass reluctantly and Betty thinks it's a shame that she will never know the full story.

'To think I fancied that Butterby,' says Irene, shaking her head. 'Dark horse he turned out to be.'

'I would have thought a dark horse would be right up your alley,' says Merl.

'I see what yer saying. Bit out of me league, but.'

'I know what you mean, Irene,' agrees Betty. 'Mr Butterby seemed like the nicest sort, like someone in a film – a romantic hero.'

Merl nods. 'He was quite charming. He even had me fooled.' She takes a sip of bubbly and gets out her knitting. 'Anyway, the police have solved the crime, as I said they would, although I was surprised to hear that Detective Dibble made the arrest. I didn't think he had it in him, quite frankly.'

'Yes,' says Hazel. 'He came through with flying colours.'

Betty lifts her glass in a secret toast to Hazel, and gets a wink in return.

75

CHRISTMAS EVE

Every year Hazel spends Christmas Eve with Betty before taking the early-morning train to Norma's place in the country for Christmas Day with her family. She and Betty like to walk about the city centre and admire the department-store window displays. During the day, chaos reigns with shoppers ransacking the stores for those last-minute gifts and stocking fillers for the kiddies, perhaps a few hair ribbons for the girls and a Dinky toy for the boys. For daddies, there will be the usual pair of socks and some liquorice allsorts. For aunties and nanas, the timeless gifts of lily-of-the-valley talc and some embroidered hankies. But now the shops are closed and harried housewives and mothers are at home wrapping presents. They're putting out beer and fruitcake for Santa and a carrot for Rudolph, and starting preparations for tomorrow's lunch, knowing the household will be woken at dawn and it won't stop all day.

Hazel and Betty have the evening streets almost to themselves. They wander from one department-store window to another, admiring the artistry and the clever details in various displays of Santa's workshop and nativity scenes. They stop outside Cashell's and Betty presses her nose against the window. 'Oh, look at the tiny elves, Hazel, so sweet. Mrs Santa is wearing her slippers under the table. I wonder if they're holy like Irene's – I wouldn't be surprised.'

'They look quite new to me,' says Hazel.

'It's so beautifully lit with the little gas lights they had in the olden days, and that snow around the windows,' continues Betty.

They walk along to David Jones to find the window dressers have broken from tradition and created a startling tableau of mannequins in bright mini-dresses, their limbs twisted in strange contortions, heads thrown back in a frenzied dance with colourful paper streamers threaded through their rigid hands.

'I expect they're on LSD,' says Betty. 'It's all the rage now. Are they Empire frocks?'

'Yes, they are. David Jones placed a big order, so it's a good Christmas for the firm.'

When they've seen all the windows, they cross the road and walk through Hyde Park towards the fountain and the sound of church bells ringing in St Mary's Cathedral. From somewhere in the distance, Hazel hears a choir singing 'Silent Night'. She feels a sense of contentment settle on her and realises that it's a good week or more since she's even thought about Bob.

It's such a beautiful evening, she suggests they sit down on the grass for a few minutes.

Surprisingly, Betty doesn't say anything about the health risks or her piles. In any case, they have their cardigans to sit on. They settle themselves comfortably, looking towards the lights of the city. As young women, she and Betty often sat in this park to eat their lunches and imagine their future lives.

'I've been thinking about the next year and what it might hold,' says Hazel.

'Just the usual, I expect,' says Betty. 'Nothing much changes around here unless there's a murder or kidnapping. We can't expect that sort of excitement every year.'

'When I was in the kitchen with Butterby, I had to consider that that could be the end for me. I never gave up, I was looking for any opportunity to escape, but I had to face the possibility that was it.'

'Did your life flash before your eyes, like they say?'

'I wouldn't say flash exactly, but I did see the faces of people I love. Yours was one of them, of course, and Norma and the boys.' Hazel pauses. 'And I realised there was one big regret in my life.'

'Bob, I suppose?' asks Betty. She turns to Hazel with an earnest expression.

'No, that was taken out of my hands. I've done what I needed to do there.'

Betty raises her hand. 'Oh! I think I know what it is, Hazel!'

'I always thought it was too late for me, but Maude next door told me that what I have is called word blindness. She talked to one of the nuns at the convent who is teaching children a new method, and the nun said she's prepared to teach me.'

'That's very brave, Hazel. But you are the bravest person I know.' Betty succumbs to her emotions and weeps quietly for a minute, an endearing habit that Hazel is used to by now.

When she's recovered, Hazel continues, 'I want to read a story to my grandsons. I want to read the encyclopaedia myself and find out about the Hippocratic oath. I want to pick up the newspaper and read it aloud, the way other people do. I'd like to read the books of Mr Charles Dickens and a bus timetable. I'd like to try and get the Tea Ladies Guild running again—'

'Open to tea ladies of every creed and colour!' adds Betty.

'Exactly, but most of all, I don't want to have to keep this awful secret any more. Reading is a whole world that has been closed to me all my life. It might be impossible to learn now, but I can at least try.'

Betty's arm encircles Hazel's shoulders, hugging her tight. 'Hazel dear, you solved a kidnapping, a murder and arson, and knocked a dangerous criminal out stone-cold with a rolling pin. I'm sure you can do this, and I can help you too.'

'Thank you, Betty.' Hazel looks up into the blackness of the night. The sky is sequinned with stars and the moon is rising over the cityscape. With that momentous discussion behind them, they talk for a while about nothing in particular. When it's time to go, they help each other up off the grass, shake out their cardigans and walk together through the darkness towards home.

ACKNOWLEDGEMENTS

I am so grateful to those people who offered their insights and expertise to help bring this story to the page. Tinny Lenthen, Library Manager at the Sydney Jewish Museum provided valuable background information on the 'rag trade' in 1960s Surry Hills. Candice Fox, crime writer extraordinaire, offered excellent tips on tension and pace. Billie Trinder provided thoughtful notes, ideas and enthusiasm. Jane King, Frances Francis, Christine Winterbotham, Jill Taylor, Julian Canny, Helen Thurloe, Joe Harrison and Diana Qian generously gave their time to read the manuscript and offer valuable feedback – thank you!

Many thanks to Laurence Burgess, a former detective with the NSW Police Force, who had many years working in the Kings Cross/ Surry Hills area and provided his expertise in the area of criminal investigation.

Many thanks as always to the brilliant team from Penguin Random House: Ali Watts, Amanda Martin, Saskia Adams, Bella Arnott-Hoare, Sonja Heijn and Debra Billson, as well as those behind the scenes in marketing and distribution and, most importantly, booksellers everywhere.

BOOK CLUB QUESTIONS

1. *The Tea Ladies* showcases a tight community of strong women pushing against the sensibilities and limitations of the times. In what ways did the actions of Hazel, Betty and Irene surprise you?

2. Did you have a favourite tea lady and why?

3. Is it easy for you to imagine a time in which ladies served tea to employees in large organisations such as Empire Fashionwear?

4. In what ways was life in the 1960s easier, and in what ways was it harder? Do you think life was better back then?

5. This book celebrates the swinging sixties in all its technicolour glory. Other than the fashion, what aspects of the era did you think the author captured well?

6. Did your impression of Hazel change over the course of the story?

7. Do you think Hazel made the right decision about Bob?

8. Who do you imagine playing the roles of the tea ladies in a television series?

9. What other authors writing in this cosy crime genre do you like to read?

10. Have you read any other books by Amanda Hampson, and if so, what aspects of her storytelling do you most enjoy?

AVAILABLE FROM PENGUIN BOOKS

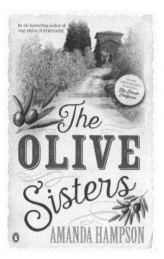
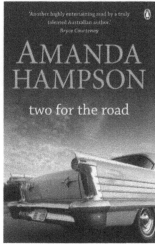
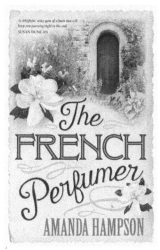

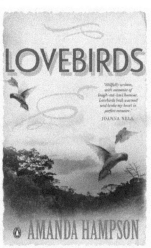

Discover a
new favourite

Visit **penguin.com.au/readmore**